PROSPECT FOR MURDER

ISBN: 978-1-932926-45-3 (hardback edition)
Library of Congress Control Number: 2016940169

Copyright (c) 2016 by Jeanne Burrows-Johnson

Cover Illustration and Design:
Yasamine June (www.yasaminejune.com)

Printed in the United States.

Artemesia Publishing, LLC
9 Mockingbird Hill Rd
Tijeras, New Mexico 87059
info@artemesiapublishing.com
www.apbooks.net

First Edition

PROSPECT FOR MURDER

By

Jeanne Burrows-Johnson

A Natalie Seachrist Mystery

Artemesia Publishing
Albuquerque, New Mexico
www.apbooks.net

For my husband John who has always inspired my work.

...the past is gone, the future is not come,
and the present becomes the past
even while we attempt to define it, and,
like the flash of lightning, at once exists and expires.
Charles Caleb Colton [1780-1832]

CAST OF CHARACTERS

Henry Au	Assistant Archivist, State of Hawai`i Archives
Jade Bishop	Sister of Pearl Wong; co-owner, Makiki Sunset Apartments; widow of Richard Bishop II
Richard K. Bishop III	Stepson of Jade Bishop
Al Cooper	Handyman, Makiki Sunset Apartments
John Dias (JD)	Detective Lieutenant, Honolulu Police Department
Maria Espinoza	Tenant, Makiki Sunset Apartments
Ben Faktorr	Neighbor of Keoni Hewitt
Ariel Harriman	Grandniece of Natalie Seachrist; the victim
Brianna Harriman	Identical twin of Ariel Harriman
Nathan Harriman	Twin brother of Natalie Seachrist; semi-retired psychologist
Keoni Hewitt	Friend of Natalie Seachrist; retired homicide detective
Aidan Jackson	Son of Nathan Harriman's neighbors
Theresa Jenkins (TJ)	Friend and potential roommate of Ariel Harriman
Caroline Johansen	Sister of Lillian Harriman
Lani King	Non-denominational minister
Chú Huā Lee	Amah of Yùyīng Wong; guardian of the Wong sisters
Ashley and Cory Lowell	Tenants, Makiki Sunset Apartments
Miss Una	Feline companion of Natalie Seachrist
Ken'ichi Nakamura	Detective Sergeant, Honolulu Police Department
Dan and Margie O'Hara	Friends of Natalie Seachrist
Natalie Seachrist	Semi-retired journalist; the protagonist.
Evelyn and Jim Souza	Neighbors of Nathan Harriman; retired restaurateurs
Martin Soli	Assistant Coroner, State of Hawai`i
Anna Wilcox	Friend of Natalie Seachrist; manager of Natalie's condo
Hiram Wong	Father of Jade Bishop and Pearl Wong
Pearl Wong	Co-owner and manager of the Makiki Sunset Apartments
Yùyīng Wong	Mother of Jade Bishop and Pearl Wong

PROLOGUE

Those who have compared our life to a dream were right....
We sleeping wake, and waking sleep.
Michel de Montaigne [1533-1592]

Sepia brown images flicker in slow motion, then shift abruptly to full color in real time as I look through the fence of Honolulu's old Makiki Cemetery. Some of the aging headstones lean in to one another, as though in conversation. What secrets they would share if they could! I look up at the luxury, high-rise condominium looming like a night watchman above. My eyes pan across the low-rent apartments and million-dollar houses stretching into Honolulu's foothills and then toward the University of Hawai`i. A breeze rustles the long dry grass at my feet. Black as death, a mynah bird shifts in its perch in the penetrating fragrance of a eucalyptus tree. I blink and brush a veil of dust from my eyes.

The vista shifts. I am suspended above the roof of a four-storey apartment complex. Below, a young woman is sprawled face-down, awkwardly hugging the hood of a vintage car. The heat of the first day of summer shimmers across the polished copper of her long, tangled hair. I observe the scene with the dispassionate interest of a newswoman. A uniformed police officer takes notes while interviewing a small elderly Asian woman. The demanding wail of an approaching ambulance slices the midday air. Everything freezes mid-frame, again subsiding into sepia tones that harmonize with the trail of blood pooled and drying below the girl's out-flung right hand.

I stare as a silver bracelet flashes the sun's rays up at me. My breath catches on the sickening sweetness of a blended scent of plumeria flowers and blood. I exhale and try to resume breathing normally. My heart throbs in rhythm with a metallic ringing in my ears. Slowly my hand reaches for the telephone. My twin brother Nathan is calling to tell me what I already know—that my grandniece will not be graduating from college, will not be participating in this weekend's pā`ina, or anything else on this plane of existence.

CHAPTER 1

Great ability develops and reveals
itself increasingly with every new assignment.
Balthasar Gracián y Morales [1601-1658]

I t came again—my vision from that first day of summer—when I learned my grandniece Ariel had died.
My awareness of the realm of the paranormal began
when I was a small child. Since losing an hour sitting against
a wall of the old Waikīkī Natatorium as a preschooler, the
edge between life awake and vivid dreaming or visioning
has remained blurred. As for most people, the majority of my
dreams and visions are nocturnal and predictably focused on
my personal journey across the world stage. However, some
scenes arrive without the benefit of sleep. Like viewing Ariel's
body in grotesque deathly repose, they depict moments I have
not experienced, or ever contemplated.

Today's newsreel-like scenes swept in while I was taking a
break from research at the Hawai`i State Archives. After tak-
ing early retirement, I am fortunate to supplement my income
with occasional research and writing projects. My current
assignment is on behalf of my friend Keoni Hewitt, a former
homicide detective turned private eye. When he called with
an unexpected request the night before Ariel died, I had no inkling of the complications that were about to overtake my life.

"So what're you doing these days, Natalie?" he began.

"Not a lot, really," I said, petting little Miss Una, my new
feline companion of the tortoise shell variety. "I'm enjoying
my personal leisure after all those years of reporting on other

people's travels, as well as events of actual newsworthiness."

He laughed and said, "Well, if your schedule can handle it, there's some research I'm hoping you'll consider doing for me."

I have always enjoyed listening to Keoni's rich baritone voice. I could picture him savoring the day's sunset from the covered *lānai* of his cottage in Mānoa Valley. Since he has announced he is cutting down on alcohol, he was probably stretched out on his favorite recliner sipping a tall glass of iced tea.

We are both past the half-century mark, with deepening age lines and more gray than blond in our hair. Nevertheless, Keoni still wears his signature wardrobe of crisp walking shorts, leather sandals and classic 1950s aloha shirts with great style. I could almost smell the exotic notes of his aftershave and jumped at the chance to see him again.

"I said I was getting spoiled, not bored. But what's on your agenda?"

"Oh, let's say circa 1905. I'd like you to see if something significant occurred in the last century that would convince my relatives to halt their plans to demolish the old family home in Kaimukī."

I mulled over his proposal for a moment. "I seldom decline an assignment, but I don't see what I can do to halt perceptions of progress in the twenty-first century."

"I'm hoping you might find some social connection or historical event to reinforce my pitch. I'm trying to get my relatives to opt for architectural preservation, rather than this year's interpretation of suburban renewal," he pleaded eloquently. "I could justify it, if something significant has happened there. You know, like royal princesses having tea with my aunts. Or maybe studying with my grandmother, who was a recognized *kumu hula*. Depending on what you learn, you could write one of your colorful articles for the newspaper or *Honolulu Magazine*.

"I'd be happy to pay for your time and any expenses you

incur. You have a flair for sharing an event that makes readers feel like they're experiencing the moment you're describing. Applying that talent to my project could make all the difference in achieving my goal."

I certainly possessed the skills to do the research. But that did not mean that anything I learned would alter his family's desire for a cash sale—unless something truly noteworthy had occurred on the premises to fill them with pride, or allowed them to charge admission to history-hungry visitors. My mind wandered through the possibilities for a couple of moments. I doubted Keoni's family had hosted any gala events attended by royalty and almost laughed at the image of elegant horse-drawn carriages pulling up to what I envisioned was a modest bungalow.

The bottom line was that Keoni was offering to pay me and I was delighted to accept his job. "Well, I'm already familiar with that era and the task seems straightforward. You've got a deal. I'll be happy to spend a several hours nosing around the neighborhood's history during the last ten decades or so."

"That's great," responded Keoni. "I look forward to seeing what you find. Besides, we haven't seen each other for a while and it'll be good to catch up."

I concurred. Before hanging up, I asked a few questions about his family's property and its sequence of owners. I then checked the lock on the front door, closed several windows, and carried Miss Una into the bedroom. After setting her on top of the velour catsack beside my pillow, I went into the bathroom to brush my teeth. Staring into the mirror, I thought about the passing decades of *my* life. While I may chemically enhance my hair, I have never considered plastic surgery. But I would bet my friends with eyeliner tattooing look great in the morning.

With gratitude for many things in my life, I pulled back my bedspread and snuggled down next to Miss Una. It was time for our nightly exploration of the world of classic fiction. Tonight I was finishing a re-read of one of my favorite J. A. Jance novels.

As her heroine turned to kiss her new husband goodnight, I found myself entertaining a warm curiosity about where my relationship with Keoni might be going. I realized I had been a widow for over three decades. Although I date occasionally, there has not been anyone interesting on the horizon recently.

The next day was a Friday. I awoke with a renewed sense of purpose. Everything started normally, with no hint of what was to come. At the launch of every new assignment, I begin by organizing my personal life. As I tidied my home that morning, I contemplated the parameters of the work I was about to undertake. After cleaning out the refrigerator, I shared a lunch of mystery leftovers with my four-legged roommate.

I carried my cup of mint tea and a ginger cookie into the living room and sat in my reclining wingback chair. Grabbing one of the steno pads I always keep at hand, I leisurely began noting the resources I would tap for Keoni's project. Just as I ran out of ideas, I began to feel drowsy and decided to have a nap. I laid my notes and reading glasses on the coffee table and rose to stretch my back and fingers. After clicking on the ceiling fan, I sank onto the welcoming cushions of the old *koa* wood framed *pune`e* my mother had upholstered repeatedly.

I glanced up to find Miss Una regally washing her disproportionately long white whiskers in her favorite daytime roost on the sofa's back. Lying on my side, I slipped my right hand under a pillow and turned my face toward the open patio door. I felt refreshed by the cool breeze off the ocean and quickly slipped from consciousness into the fate-filled vision of Ariel's ghastly and improbable death.

When I awakened to the urgent ringing of the telephone, I knew the call was from my twin Nathan. With shaking hands and a heart rate far above normal, I put the receiver to my ear. After the horrifying confirmation of his granddaughter's death, my life devolved to one of its lowest points.

Between sketchy news reports and the lingering impact of my vision, I was too stunned to do much for a couple of days. I knew there was no need to rush over to Nathan's home on the shoreline of Kāne'ohe, as his friends and neighbors would be supplying him with a world of provisions he would barely touch. We were both in a state of shock and it would not have helped to overwhelm him with my own tears and expressions of grief.

As Nathan had done when my husband died, I served as my sibling's emotional lifeline. Each day I listened with compassion to his emotional outbursts that followed hours of conversations with the police, friends and neighbors. With an unattended death, we could plan elements of Ariel's Life Celebration, but we could not schedule a time for it. More importantly, since we did not know if foul play was involved in her sister's death, we insisted that Ariel's identical twin Brianna remain at her college on the mainland, despite her pleas to return home.

For the benefit of Nathan as well as me, I tried to remain composed. I was glad our conversations were over the phone. At the least, Nathan could not see the empty tissue boxes piled around me, or the state of my personal disarray. Unfortunately, during my own discussions with Honolulu Police Detective John Dias, I broke down and could not conceal my tears. I was grateful the man was compassionate and gentle in asking the questions he needed me to answer.

Aside from calls to Nathan and suppliers of funeral products and services, I spent most of the weekend sitting on my balcony going through photos and other memorabilia. I savored the significance of each item. For decades I was gone for months at a time and therefore did not appear in many of the pictures. But even when I was on assignment out of the country, someone always made sure I knew about our family's celebratory moments. Perhaps that was why Ariel's death was so devastating to me. I had thought life would slow down eventually and I could catch up with everyone's lives. But there would never be an opportunity to fully know the bright young girl whose life had been cut off before she could fully blossom.

Throughout the turmoil, Miss Una remained at my side—

sympathetically studying the pain on my face and periodically mewing apt reminders of mealtimes. To be honest, my primary nutritional sustenance was liquid. I consumed untold pots of tea during daylight hours and several bottles from my small wine collection between sunset and midnight.

On Monday morning, I rose from a third nearly sleepless night. I looked around the condo and knew I could not bear another day within its restrictive walls. I dreaded the likelihood of a continuing stream of disturbing thoughts and uninvited images. Although I had no idea what I would do, I showered quickly, put on a short *mu'umu'u* and fluffed my graying strawberry blonde hair. Knowing the puffiness of my usually bright green eyes would call attention to my sorrow, I applied a bit of makeup.

I doubted my body would tolerate even mild Kona coffee, so I brewed a pot of Earl Grey tea. I was not in the mood to eat but knew I needed some nourishment. There is nothing like a quick granola bar to solve that dilemma. Sipping my heavily sugared tea, I flipped through pages of notes detailing plans for Ariel's memorial. There were a multitude of arrangements to be considered before her body was released by the Medical Examiner's office. Although hard news had not been my specialty, my colleagues had taught me that while an initial autopsy report may not take long, completion of the toxicology tests and reports could not be predicted.

Hurry up and wait seemed to be the directive for our schedule. To accommodate everyone who wanted to help us celebrate Ariel's life, Nathan and I were planning two memorial events. As we considered the participants, we noted the sad fact that there were only four family members—the two of us, Brianna, and Auntie Carrie, our mother's sister. That number dropped to three when we realized that with her advanced Alzheimer's disease, Carrie would not even be aware of Ariel's passing.

The first part of our celebration would be a memorial service at Kailua Beach Park. For this public occasion, we had found a non-denominational minister to officiate and Ariel's former outrigger canoe club had volunteered to scatter her ashes at sea. Our second event would be a sunset gathering of family, friends and classmates from high school and college. Nathan's immediate neighbors (retired restaurateurs) would handle the food and beverages. Beyond refreshments, there were musicians to book, photographs to assemble, floral decor to select, and....It all sounded more like a wedding or birthday party, rather than recognition of the tragic conclusion of a young woman's life.

Despite my own weekend of sorrowful reflection, I could not grasp the breadth of what Nathan was facing. Not only did he love her deeply, but he had been Ariel's primary legal guardian since she and Brianna were orphaned at twelve. And although I was listed as co-guardian on official paperwork, every aspect of the twins' lives had been his responsibility. If there had to be a funeral in our small family, it should have been for Nathan or me.

I finished my tea and thought of the red tape involved in any death. I resolved that once the official minutiae of this sad chapter in my life were concluded, I would make certain my own legal affairs were in order. Picking up my day planner, I leafed through the previous week. As I glanced at my notes on Keoni's research project, I realized this was the ideal alternative to another day of long, empty hours.

Before leaving home, I set out bowls of fresh water and dry food for Miss Una. I then cracked the *lānai* door open to afford her a sniff of the greater world, and positioned the security rod to prevent the entry of any "Breaking & Entering" artists. Without the joy that normally accompanies the launch of new work, I woodenly gathered my laptop, miscellaneous supplies and a handful of my favorite, almost calorie-free snacks. Then I grabbed a banana leaf sunhat from the coat rack and headed out the door.

My journey began with a short, post rush-hour ride on "Da Bus," as our local transit system is sometimes called. It took less than half an hour to travel from my Waikīkī condominium to the business hub of downtown Honolulu. Feeling better, I set aside my resolution to curb calories and stopped for a cup of mellow-fragranced Kona coffee and one of my favorite baked delights from Cookie Corner. Enjoying my snack, I meandered toward the municipal buildings and museums that line King Street.

At another time, it would have been a great day to laze in the sun, but my current assignment demanded spending a few hours indoors. After disposing of my garbage in one of the plentiful cans marked *Mahalo*, I entered the archives. I checked my pockets for my camera, pencils and the maximum three sheets of paper. Then I selected a locker and crammed in my purse. Queuing up to inquire about the availability of several historical materials, I smiled at sight of the sole man on the research assistance team.

"Hey, Natalie. I really liked your last article in the *Honolulu Magazine*," welcomed Henry Au, who stood at the check-in counter. "We got a lot of calls and some new visitors after your reference to our holdings. And that always helps our pleas for funding with the legislature."

"Great. I'm glad to help ensure the infusion of a few extra tax dollars for my favorite research institution!"

Nodding, he inquired, "So, what are you pursuing today?"

I hesitated for a moment. Did I want to mention that death now permeated my personal life? That I was planning my grandniece's funeral? No. Avoidance of these issues was my reason for being here.

"Oh, losing myself in days of yesteryear. I'm hoping a few of these materials are available," I said, handing over request slips for reference books that might touch on the history of Kaimukī and some microfilm from the long-defunct *Pacific Commercial Advertiser Newspaper* to cruise for other potential points of interest.

"Give me a few minutes, and I'll see what I have for you," smiled Henry.

His friendliness beckoned me into old routines and I began wandering the public rooms of the squat old building. With the expectation I felt at the start of a new project, I leafed through numerous finding aids. From there, I would move on to the leather-bound friends waiting to present their varied tales dating from the age of Victorian Island splendor. Due to problems with mold, the books themselves are stored beyond the public's reach. Checking back at the counter, I found that most of the biographical books I sought on leaders of the Territory of Hawai`i had been claimed by other researchers. Other items I had requested from the closed stacks were checked out or in the shop for repair, as well as control of mildew and dust mites.

I took the two reference volumes Henry had found for me and sat down to think about how I would approach this project. As I perused their tables of contents, text and indices, I periodically added notes to my personalized timeline of Hawaiian history. After returning the books, I sat at my work table and considered the notable men and women from politics and commerce who might have graced Keoni's corner of Kaimukī.

With a vague restlessness, I glanced out through the old wood casement windows. Undulating shadows cast by the branches of banyan trees beckoned me to escape my drudgery for a while. Inspired, I returned to my locker and shoved in my laptop. I then grabbed my phone, a can of orange-passion juice and a few nibblies before exiting the building.

After the cool temperature of the archives, the sultry atmosphere of a bright Hawaiian summer day was a welcome change. Munching bites of fragrant, dried pineapple and sweet mochi, I sauntered across the grounds of `Iolani Palace. For a few minutes, I watched as tourist couples in matching aloha shirts and dresses disembarked with joyous laughter from a bus across the street at the Mission Houses Museum. I set my bag on a shaded bench, shook the remains of my snack from the front of my dress and sat down. Pushing back thoughts of Ariel's perplexing and gruesome death, I slipped beyond consciousness to that state beyond normal dreaming.

With the repeated coo of a dove overhead, my eyes opened. I looked around in a daze. Now that I am retired, I do not wear a watch. Often too lazy to pull out my cell phone, I use the lack of a watch as an excuse to chat with bus drivers and strangers on the few occasions I need to keep to a schedule. Noting that the shadow of a nearby garbage can had shifted and lengthened, I realized that more than a few minutes had passed while I was lost in the less-than-pleasant scene in which Ariel had died. I sat up and stretched my neck from side to side, trying to focus my attention outward as I was still immersed in the numbing vision from which I was struggling to emerge.

*　*　*　*　*

I am trapped in the expanding scenes of my home movie of personal horror. This time I face the unfolding story from the front row. Again, I cringe at the sight of the young woman face-down across the hood and windshield of a vintage car I now see is a Ford Mustang coupe. Counter-balancing the car's metallic aquamarine paint, her bright red hair is splayed out across the back of her classic white tennis dress.

Today, I observe a gathering of onlookers casually restrained beyond a sagging perimeter of yellow plastic tape. Ambulance personnel speak quietly, awaiting instructions beside their two trucks. As before, a uniformed police officer interviews a petite, elegantly clad Chinese woman in front of an aging, four-storey building. The tall young man's shiny name badge reads, "Yamato." He scratches his pen across a blue notepad. He then nods, striving to show respect to the elderly woman I somehow know is the manager of these apartments. I now realize there are two cement block buildings in the complex. Surrounded by parking spaces on three sides, they face each other across an unkempt courtyard.

The now familiar sequence of scene processing and incident report writing fades again to sepia and then disappears. A new scenario opens silently in full color. I watch the manager smile as she opens the door of a top floor apartment. Turning, she ushers the now-vibrant girl into an unfurnished unit, with white walls and terracotta colored vinyl floor tiles. They both remove their shoes at the door. Brushing a strand of black hair behind her jade-studded ear, the manager pulls a pen from her pocket and poses with clipboard at the ready while they glance around.

I feel as though I am watching the video of a stranger's first adventure in real estate...not the last moments of my dear Ariel's life. In tandem, the old woman and girl move through a two bedroom, two bath apartment. I notice that the doors, closets, and refrigerator stand open. I smell cleaning solvents and fresh paint. The angled light coming through screened, west-facing windows foretells the heat of the day's end.

The property manager closely examines the beautiful girl in front of her. I know she is evaluating her suitability as a tenant. The girl is polite and respectful in demeanor and speech. The elderly woman nods periodically. She is pleased the girl is a local student on scholarship at the University of Hawai`i. The girl smiles with expectation and says she will be sharing the apartment with a roommate, who will arrive soon. As the image freezes, I smell dead flowers.

*   *   *   *   *

Slowly, this new scene in my vision receded. My mind's eye struggled to withdraw from the jarring pictures now permanently etched in my mind and heart. Hearing the intruding laughter of elementary students on early-release from school, I blinked. I was not surprised to note the traffic on downtown Honolulu's King Street. I was back. From where and by what mechanism, I did not fully understand. The one thing I knew for certain was that the girl, my dear grandniece, was dead.

There was no going back for Ariel. No chance to alter her journey. No opportunity to say farewell to anyone: not to the woman who was to rent her this first taste of social freedom; not to her friends at the University; not to her sister in distant Oregon. Worst of all, there had been no parting words to her grandfather. A man who now sits with memories frozen in time since calling to tell me of the shattering of *his* visions for our family's next generation.

My reverie ended abruptly with the shrill ring of my cell phone. One of the biographical books I had requested was ready for pickup at the archives. Returning to the demands of the day, I tried to set aside my anxiety over the latest revelation about my grandniece's unexpected death. I debated whether to call Nathan to ask what he knew about the friend who was to have rented the apartment with Ariel. But that would mean revealing my visions.

Currently, Ariel's death is an open case. Homicide Detective John Dias has told Nathan that, so far, nothing has ruled it as suspicious, nor has it been declared an accident. While the official autopsy report is not yet available, a preliminary examination of the site of her fall and the balcony of the apartment she was previewing did not reveal any signs of a struggle. But then, there is no explanation of how a healthy young woman with a lot to live for, ended up face down on the hood of a car. And no one has mentioned why a homicide detective is in charge of the case if there is no clear evidence of murder.

I re-entered the archives and retrieved my laptop, then queued up at the counter. In a moment I had one book and two reels of microfilm in hand. With my emotions still submerged in a land of non-enchantment, I focused on the work before me. The vinegar scent of the microfilm helped to keep me in a detached operational mode. For a couple of hours, I numbly went through the motions of examining the social doings of the rich and infamous of Kaimukī during the early twentieth century. Viewed through weddings, births, christenings, anniversaries, divorces and deaths, the details of lives from that era reminded me of the diversity of our Island culture and the blending of more than food at any social gathering.

Looking up at the clock on the wall, I considered whether to initiate analysis of Honolulu's newspapers. Like most cities, our papers have changed names almost as often as their ownership. And although I could read the last decade of recent publications on-line, I would have to go next door to the main library for comprehensive files for the *Honolulu Advertiser* and the *Honolulu Star Bulletin* newspapers.

Uncertain of my next move, I input a few notations in the computer file for Keoni's project. Next I checked the Internet for media updates on Ariel's case. Nothing new had been reported. It was only mid-afternoon, so I decided to take an unscheduled trip into lower Makiki. Within a half hour and a single bus transfer, I was speeding along the road that passed near to what could have been Ariel's home. I leaned against the back of the bench seat, and sank again into that indefinable point between time and space that my brother and I have shared throughout our lives.

CHAPTER 2

There is no pain so great as the memory
of joy in present grief.
Aeschylus [525 BCE-456 BCE]

The bond I share with my brother is strong yet flexible, like multi-strand electrical wire. I do not know if it is because we are twins, but we share a link that periodically reaches through the time-space continuum to surprise and sometimes protect us. When did I realize Nathan and I share this bond? My first awareness was as a toddler, trapped for hours within the confines of my crib.

The scene was framed by well-chewed, vertical bars of white pine grasped between my fingers. Vigorously rattling my cage for attention, I barely noticed the muted daylight peeking in through still-closed drapes. I knew that something was wrong. No one was paying attention to my raucous insistence to be set free for a normal day of pushing the footstool around my family's small apartment.

It might have been the first time I was truly angry. From today's vantage point, I realize I must have been puffing from my prolonged exertion and I can almost feel my beet-red face. Where was everyone? I did not even see the cat who normally scooted between Mom's legs, when she brought me a bottle of oatmeal thinned with milk.

After what seemed a lifetime of watching changing patterns of shadows creep across the floor, a sense of peace reached out to quiet my breathing and still my hands. "It's all right," I heard within my mind, rather than with my ears. "Lie down and go to sleep, because they aren't coming for a while. Mom's sick and Dad went to the store to get something to help her feel better. They'll come for us when they can."

I looked to the right, as though just discovering the pristine crib that stood perpendicular to my own. Peeking between the bars at mattress level, Nathan's deep hazel eyes gazed over at me. He must have heard my gyrations. But he had not uttered a sound or otherwise made his presence known until this moment.

I blinked and stared back at him. "What's wrong with Mom? I hope she doesn't have to go to that man in white with the big, hairy hands and cold necklace that he puts on our chests."

"I don't think so. It was confusing. First they talked about her being cold. Then they said she was too hot. I'm sure she's going to be all right. She just needs Dad to get her something at the store. Since we can't get down to play, we might as well have another nap."

So much for my living up to my role as a big sister! Foreshadowing what became the norm, my younger brother—by nine minutes—demonstrated the serenity he would bring to the ordeals our family faces. And when the resolution of our mother's illness proved Nathan's projection correct, you could say we had experienced our first foray into the land of mysteries.

From that day, Nathan and I communicated without spoken words. Once they became aware of it, the situation bothered our parents. But when our Auntie Carrie pointed out that we were happy and interacted normally with family members and playmates, they accepted our unusual bond. As to other unique behaviors, it soon became clear that Nathan and I had remarkable and different abilities. Nathan has always had prescient awareness, kennings, that allow him to know things in advance of their being revealed on *terra firma*. On the other hand, I experience visions, usually concurrently, or in advance of the occurrence of events.

The few people who have become aware of our "gifts"

sometimes expect us to know what is going to happen in tense situations. And that, for good or ill, has never happened—at least not by our willing it to be so. While I may recognize people or elements within my visions, often I have no understanding of what is unfolding on my mental movie screen until a situation has occurred in real time. That was not the case of my recent vision about Ariel's death. I had immediately recognized the reality of the scene I was shown.

*   *   *   *   *

Pulling my thoughts back to the sights along Wilder Avenue, I decided to get off the bus a few stops early and walk around the neighborhood surrounding what might have become Ariel's home. For a moment, I stood without determination, tracing a crack in the old cement sidewalk with the edge of my sandal. Turning to the right, I moved slowly toward Pensacola Street. I considered whom and what I might see on my investigative journey.

Stalling for time to focus my intention, I paused and inhaled the hint of eucalyptus in the air. I was tempted to forget the purpose of my visit to the neighborhood where I had lived two separate times, and simply stroll through the hilly grounds of Makiki Cemetery, where Nathan and I loved to play. Even as a child, the views from the top were spectacular. As an adult, they remind me of the richness of the land and cultures of Hawai`i.

By habit, I jiggled the cemetery's slightly rusted wrought iron gate. It was locked, but that never stopped Nathan or me when we were kids. Merely looking through the fence at the eroding headstones provided sufficient inspiration for my contemplation of the past. A light breeze rustled the leaves of a nearby breadfruit tree and I remembered another summer's day.

Nathan and I had been walking with Auntie Carrie when we heard a beautiful falsetto voice singing in Hawaiian. It was Lena Machado, who was sometimes billed as the "Songbird of

Hawai`i." Her music was a favorite in our aunt's vast record collection, but it had been many years since I had thought of Lena. I knew she was in this old graveyard that has cradled the remains of Hawaiian, Portuguese and Japanese populations since the late nineteenth century. Considering all the joy she had brought to others, I hoped she enjoyed a good view of our beautiful city lights from her hillside resting place.

Remembering Lena's joyful embrace of life brought me a sense of peace I had not had since Ariel's death. I was not handling the music for Ariel's memorial, but I hoped Nathan would find lyrics and harmonics that would bring a sense of renewal to those of us who had loved her so much. I sighed and glanced up at the assisted living condominium that now towers over the cemetery, before continuing my physical and mental journey up the hill. Even the lower streets of Makiki twist and turn, and sometimes change their names. But being a pedestrian, I was not concerned about the one-way streets. After turning right onto Pensacola, I moved toward its merging with Prospect Street.

It had been awhile since I had been up this way. After moving to my condo in Waikīkī and trading my old Buick Regal for a bus pass, there have been few reasons to pass through the neighborhood of my early childhood. Maybe that was why I had been pleased to learn one of my grandnieces wanted to move into the area for her final year of college. It was like an affirmation that the next generation was preparing to take the helm of our dynastic vessel, although it seemed like only yesterday Ariel and her twin Brianna had been born. I remember being surprised when I received their high school commencement announcements, when it seemed I had just attended their graduation from kindergarten.

Fortified by happy memories, I walked up the hilly sidewalk, thinking about what I would say if the apartment manager was available. I arrived at my destination and halted. In front of me was a low wall of faded, battleship-gray cement block set back from the curb. It was four tiers high along the front of the property and stepped down at the sides of each of the entrances that flanked the open parking lot. General neglect showed in the traces of celery-green paint framed by dead weeds poking up from a thin layer of gravel at the bottom.

The same casual interpretation of xeriscape landscaping covered a two-foot parking strip bordering the street. Like my second vision, I saw two buildings in fading buff white, with door and window trim in chipped charcoal. Island winds keep a layer of dust on almost everything out of doors, but it was clear there had been no attempt to maintain even a semblance of the original colors.

"May I help you, Ma'am?" A man's gruff voice called from across the nearly empty parking lot that showed it had been many years since it had been paved with fresh asphalt.

"Oh. Hello. I... I was taking a walk through the neighborhood, and wondered if I might visit with the manager?" I replied.

Brusquely he said, "I don't see her truck. But that doesn't mean anything. That nephew of hers is always borrowing it." Dressed in cutoff jeans from another decade and a green and white T-shirt from the University of Hawai`i, the tall, leathery *haole* was so tanned he must not have heard the decades of reports on the causes of skin cancer. My eyes glanced over at the large rag mop in an industrial bucket on wheels. With a sharp intake of breath, I recognized what he was doing—attempting to scrub away impressions of what might be my grandniece's blood on the cracked asphalt paving.

I stared with revulsion at his labor and the bucket of soapy reddish brown water. Following my downward stare, the man casually noted, "Guess you heard about the jumper we had last Friday. Don't know why she'd pick a low-rise. There's no accounting for kids these days. HazMat folks've finished, but there's always a bit of a mess to take care of with so many vehicles going in and out. And it's probably going to be months before I'll have my car fully repaired!"

"It was *your* car she landed on?" I asked in a barely audible voice.

Leaning on the mop's handle, the man's black eyes lit up while he moved into high gear. "Yup. A 1969 Ford Mustang Mach 1. Being a Friday, I was finishing up some errands so I would be ready to take my baby down for a car rally at the Ala Moana Shopping Center that night. That coupe's a real mover, with a 428 V8 Cobra jet engine and five-speed manual transmission."

I nodded, trying to fill the gap of my non-interest in this earth-shaking circumstance in his other-wise magnificent life.

"It's a real classic." he continued. "Chrome rally wheels, aquamarine exterior, black leather, high-back bucket seats, electric windows, and air conditioning that beats a lot of today's models. And now I've got to start all over."

With a wave of his hand, he continued. "Miss Wong's the manager. Her unit's at the far end of the building to the left side of the courtyard. It's A101. Actually, it's units A101 and A102, since she renovated a couple of years ago. That was really something. The tenants were looking forward to seeing some real improvements around here—like getting' the exterior painted and the parking lot repaved. But she only took care of herself. Oh, well, that's management most everywhere these days." Then, with a brisk shake of his head, he returned to his own home-improvement project.

Nodding my head, as though in agreement, I looked away from the remains of my grandniece's last day. I followed his directions to a pathway of gray cement pavers ahead on the left. Walking carefully along the hexagonal stepping stones through the neglected courtyard, I realized, with a jolt, that this was the path Ariel would have taken on her final afternoon. From the University, she would have taken the same bus line I had. And she would have walked the same winding blocks to arrive here at these buildings that would become the scene of her last breaths in this life.

How had she learned of the apartment? Did she read an

ad in the *Honolulu Star-Advertiser*? Or maybe *Ka Leo*, the UH newspaper? Perhaps she had found the apartment listed online, or in one of those penny-saving publications that list a variety of housing opportunities, old cars and lost dogs. Of course, someone could have recommended the building personally.

This brought me back to the question of her potential roommate. The police report that the manager of the apartments said Ariel had mentioned a roommate who was going to join her on the tour of the apartment confirmed what I had envisioned. As a leasing agreement had never been completed, the manager had said she had no idea who that roommate was to have been.

Aside from that phantom friend, it did not look like there was much to pursue, investigation wise. Like any other unattended death, the inquiry into Ariel's demise would begin by questioning her immediate family. Brianna was on the mainland, so there were only three of us here. Nathan is a semi-retired psychologist and I knew he had been consulting with a client at the time of Ariel's death. Carrie certainly could not add anything to the inquiries since she was bedridden in her Lanikai home on the southern edge of Kailua. So she was out of the loop both geographically and mentally. As to me, well, I had been home. And as I do not have a car, I could not have gone to Makiki even if I had known of her appointment to see the apartment.

Since Ariel had been living at Nathan's home, he was the best source for learning about her schedule. I was sure the police had already asked him about her closest friends and daily routine. Until I had explored the locale of her death, I would avoid bringing up details of the investigation to Nathan. If I was lucky, the apartment manager would provide facts beyond what my vision had revealed. Then I could avoid asking my brother probing questions that could move his mind in disturbing directions.

Looking around, I considered the layout of the property. In

the courtyard between the buildings, a decrepit volleyball net waved a forlorn greeting in the gentle breeze. At the back was a tall, three-tiered, black granite water fountain topped by a dragon spewing out uneven rivulets of water. At the far end of the rectangle of weeds and grass, I saw three *plumeria* trees, the probable source of the rotting flowers I had smelled in my visions.

I paused to look at the strip of first-floor apartments whose doors stood like soldiers at attention. The glossy, white, wood paneled, double-door entry to Unit A101 looked like something from a property featured in *Architectural Digest*. In place of the flat push button doorbell of the units flanking it, A101 sported a classic brass door knocker with a roaring lion head. Completely out of character with the Colonial theme, a soft tinkling of bronze temple bells floated in the wind. What kind of person would pick this jumble of design features for an otherwise run-down apartment? Abruptly, the right door opened, and a petite Chinese woman peered up at me. While she might be quite old, she had black hair and that beautiful glowing unlined skin of many Asian women—even if they have not spent a life-time wearing rice face powder and broad sunhats to protect their skin from UV rays.

Her voice was surprisingly strong. "You are early. I did not think you could come until after five o'clock."

Obviously she had me confused with someone else.

"The police have just returned the keys. But, since you are here now, we can take a look at the apartment and see if it meets your needs."

Did I want to break the flow of the moment to let her know who I am? Or why I am really here? Not yet. I could always tell her there was a mistake—after I had had a chance to see the place where Ariel met her untimely demise.

Coming out onto the large red doormat, the woman reached into the pocket of her long orange and blue orchid patterned *mu'umu'u* and pulled out a key. She turned to close and lock the doors carefully, then turned back and peered up at me. For a moment, I stared into her eyes, thinking we had met before; but I could not imagine when or where.

Beckoning me to follow her with a hand adorned with diamond rings and jade bracelets, she walked across the courtyard to the center of the second building. A steep, cement stairway with peeling, twisted, wrought iron banisters greeted us. She grabbed the right railing, glanced over her shoulder to make sure I was still behind her, and began climbing.

"As I said on the phone, I am Pearl Wong, co-owner of the Makiki Sunset Apartments. The unit I am now preparing to rent belongs to my sister. I manage both of the buildings now that Jade has moved to an assisted living facility. It is her hips, you see. She cannot get around this property easily, even with her walker or wheelchair."

I nodded, too out of breath to respond vocally. Feeling like I had been climbing the face of a mountain, I was relieved when we arrived at the fourth floor. Miss Wong turned right and walked toward what I knew would be the end unit whose rear overlooked an outer section of the parking lot. Sighing to express her displeasure, her elegantly French manicured fingers tore off a fragment of yellow tape dangling from the doorknob of unit B406.

"After disturbing our lives for several days, you would think the police could tidy up after themselves!" she harrumphed.

"Are you sure it's okay for us go in?" I asked innocently.

"Oh, yes. They said I can return to normal business operation, since there is no evidence of a crime having been committed."

Her words gave me pause. *Had* a crime been committed? Or had the initial view that Ariel had mistakenly fallen over the edge of the balcony been correct? I tried to shut my mind to this entire line of thought, while Miss Wong opened the door.

The irritating sound of squeaking hinges brought my focus back to the moment at hand. With a sense of *déjà-vu* I entered, wondering how much of the scene would parallel my previous visions. It was what I had seen—and slightly more. Following Island custom, we removed our shoes outside the door that was inset with a louvered-window. For a moment I stared at our contrasting shoes: hers, almost child-sized woven straw slippers; mine, sleek, new gel sandals, one of the few popular fashion statements in my working wardrobe.

We entered the unfurnished unit directly into a small rectangular living room, painted in flat, yellowing white. Ahead to the right of a sliding door to the *lānai*, I saw a small dinette area with corner shelving. To the left was the start of a wall of kitchen cabinets. The trim had many coats of harsh white enamel paint, with some areas scraped down to the original wood in more than one place. Around a half-wall of glass-doored shelves, I knew I would find a vintage apartment kitchen with chipped black and yellow tiled counters, a stained enameled sink and the apartment-sized refrigerator and stove.

Calling for my attention, Miss Wong said, "Here, to the left of the front door are the two bedrooms, the first with an attached bathroom." I glanced into the first bedroom and joined her in the small suite that was comprised of a bedroom, closet and three-piece bathroom. The bedroom walls bore the torn remains of old posters. A couple of metal hangers with dry-cleaner paper inserts dangled from the bent rod in the closet. Rust stains pulled my eyes to the bottoms of the sink and shower stall.

"This configuration is standard for buildings of this type and age. Generous in size, compared to what is being built today. I am sure your granddaughter will be comfortable here. It is very safe and many of the tenants are also students."

Startled at the word *granddaughter*, I mumbled something indistinct. We walked back into the living room. I looked across the terracotta stick-and-place tiles to the slider door I knew led out to the small balcony from which I was told Ariel had dropped a mere four floors to her death. I glanced at my companion. She brushed a strand of hair behind her ear, pulled a pen from her pocket and raised the clipboard I remembered from my last vision.

We moved into the kitchen where cupboard doors, a small pantry closet and the refrigerator stood open. The sharp smells of ammonia and bleach from recent cleaning contrasted with the pungent aromas of the foods of many cultures stored through the decades. I opened a couple of drawers to confirm my feigned interest. I looked around the rooms made light and airy by aluminum-framed jalousie windows, most of which were discolored with age and pitted by salt air. Some, screened and west-facing, offered warmth that again hinted of the heat to come at day's end.

Like most of the visions I experience, there was little or no dialogue. However, in this unfolding reality, I was responsible for the silence. As I followed her descriptions, Miss Wong stood quietly, waiting politely for me to express my approval of the unit. Clearly, with the barest indication of my positive response, she would declare my supposed granddaughter to be an ideal tenant for this gem of an alternative to on-campus housing.

Reluctantly, I moved in the direction of the slider. Although I was at the apartment complex where Ariel had died, I had hoped to avoid any site that might reveal specific details about her death. Fortunately, I was saved from this second potentially gruesome scene when the electronic strains of Beethoven's *Moonlight Sonata* broke the silence. I turned immediately toward Miss Wong, who was answering her cell phone with focused attention.

Holding the phone against her chest, she said, "I have to take this call. You know how it is with an older sister—always wanting to burrow into your business to ensure everything is all right."

She then pulled several pieces of paper from her clipboard and handed them to me. "We may have discussed merely evaluating the apartment's potential today, but things are moving faster than I had originally expected. It will be just a couple of days before we have finished painting the apartment and the new ad comes out in the paper. So please take this rental application and lease forms and call me if you decide you wish to rent the apartment."

"Certainly. And thank you for accommodating me today," I replied, folding the papers and placing them in my shoulder bag.

Miss Wong then nodded to me with a slight bow and turned to address her demanding sibling. Almost in a daze, I put on my shoes, descended the stairs and walked back across the courtyard. With each step I took, it felt like someone was watching me with interest. As I left the nearly empty parking lot, I noticed an embossed metal sign I had not seen on my arrival. It said, *Makiki Sunset Apartments*. Below, looped over rusted hooks, a faded red add-on announced, *VACANCY*.

Had it not been for a minor incident on the world stage, Apartment B406 would no longer be available. And I would not be contemplating the implications of a sign that swayed in a breeze that had intensified as I approached it. As my feet directed themselves down the winding sidewalk, I pondered the few facts I knew about Ariel's death. I also thought about Miss Wong's observations on the role of an older sister.

CHAPTER 3

I'm not afraid of storms, for I am learning to sail my ship.
Louisa May Alcott [1832-1888]

I knew there was nothing I could have done to save my grandniece from death. My first vision was after the fact, too late for me to do anything about what I had seen. It was really presumptuous to think that I, or anyone, could have prevented what had happened.

Perhaps, however, I could do something to resolve the issue of *how* Ariel had died. I dislike the term "closure," but our family's current experience of death has opened a ragged hole that feels like it could have been caused by a roadside bomb, waiting impersonally to catch the next passerby.

After visiting the apartment she was thinking of renting, I questioned how Ariel could have fallen accidently. I also rejected the idea of her committing suicide. As to "murder," the final item on the checklist of causes of death...it was too painful to say aloud. What on earth could this personable young girl have done to anger someone so much that they wanted to see her dead?

Emerging from the morass of my inner dialogue, I arrived at the bus stop at the bottom of the hill. There was no bus in sight, so I pulled out my cell phone. I should have checked in with Nathan, but hesitated to do so. Although we had spoken frequently during the last few days, I knew he was incapable of prolonged conversation. Besides, what did I have to say at the moment? I had perused the grounds and the apartment at the complex where Ariel had died, but had not seen anything extraordinary. There was nothing I could have told him that would answer any of his questions, or bring him any measure of peace.

I was saved from my dilemma by the arrival of the bus that would take me to Ala Moana Shopping Center. Once there, I could transfer to a bus to take me home, or I could stop for a quick dinner at the Food Court. Since Ariel's death, I was not in the mood for anything approaching fine dining. But as I have told Nathan, food is a necessity of life, regardless of one's circumstances. Thank goodness I live in an age of ready-to-heat meals and home delivery.

Within an hour I was home, Chinese takeout in hand. Although I am used to living alone—except for Miss Una—I opened the door to my twentieth-floor condo with dread. It was as if I, rather than Nathan, was the one entering the silent shell of a home. I tossed off my shoes in the entryway and went into the living room. I then propped my laptop against the sofa and dropped my handbag on the coffee table.

Next, I checked each room to ensure everything was as I had left it. As I opened the *lānai* door, the welcome scent of ocean air rushed in. It almost masked the lingering odor of melting of plastic and rattan transformed into cindered shavings from a fire in the condo above me. I looked at the clock on the cable box below my new flat screen television and saw it was time for the evening news.

After setting my dinner on the kitchen counter, I checked my voicemail. The majority of calls were solicitations from neighbor island resorts. There were also messages of condolence from well-meaning callers expressing sorrow for my loss. But because Ariel had a different surname, few people outside of family and close friends knew the girl's death was connected to me. After a couple days, even casual acquaintances had learned of Ariel's death. The last voice message eliminated a need to explain my situation to Keoni.

"Hi, Natalie. It's Keoni. I was speaking to one of my buddies at the Medical Examiner's office, and was sorry to learn of your niece's death. I'm thinking that... maybe we should put off my project until things have settled down for you."

There was a short pause, and then he continued. "But don't hesitate to call me if there's anything I can do to help you and your family. I guess with the Hotel Street knifing of those two sailors and the auto accident in the cane fields, it'll be a few days before you get the preliminary autopsy report."

With the unfolding of my personal tragedy, I had lost track of basic news coverage. I had completely forgotten there was a massive presence of the U.S. Navy in town. This was because it was the start of RIMPAC, the biennial, multinational, maritime exercise scheduled to play out in Hawaiian waters over the next couple of weeks. Since I had not opened my snail mail in days, I did not know if I had received any invitations to social functions related to the event.

Normally I look forward to such opportunities as a means for reconnecting with men and women I knew during my five years as the wife of a naval officer. My husband Bill had been a lieutenant in the U.S. Navy. We had only been married a few years when he died of encephalitis while on an overseas tour. Most of my friends from that phase of my life have retired from military service. However, with several working for the Federal government and a few with kids in the Navy, the event is a great excuse for many to visit the Islands.

That reminded me that my friend Margie O'Hara and her husband Dan (who had served with Bill) would be arriving in Honolulu shortly. I added them to my list of people I needed to contact about Ariel's death. Most could be notified with a generic email. However, I needed to call the O'Haras personally since they would expect to see me at a couple of events related to RIMPAC.

I monitored the audio of the evening TV news program while setting out a plate and wine glass. Then I opened the boxes of Chinese take-out containing enough food for several days of meals. At the tantalizing scent of non-tinned food, Miss Una finally arrived from hideaways unknown to remind me it was dinner time for both of us. "Well there you are. What do you feel like tonight?" I then selected a pork casserole from an array of delectables for felines and finished assembling both of our dinners.

I contemplated calling Nathan to nag him about eating. Instead, I decided to wait until later. With the arrival of sunset, he was probably surrounded by friends or neighbors equally concerned with his well-being. Besides, I was really hungry for the first time in days. I guess there was something to be said for putting in a day of meaningful labor.

I placed my dinner tray on the coffee table and sat down on the couch. Sipping a glass of Storybook Mountain Zinfandel, I channel surfed to see if there was any follow-up coverage of Ariel's case. There was none, which meant that officialdom had no new findings to report. With my mind already swimming with conflicting theories about the case, my emotional responses to even everyday events and fluffy entertainment pieces were nearly out of control so I turned off the television.

The instant silence was almost as unbearable as the mayhem being reported that night from overseas. As I clicked on a cable station that played light classical music, I was joined by Miss Una. I was happy to have her company until I recognized her intentions. Responding quickly to her apparent interest in comparing the qualities of our meals, I said, "No, you do *not* want this. The spices would have both of us up all night if you ate even a few morsels."

She looked at me with eyes that betrayed an inherent distrust of my analysis, but quickly recognized there would be no recall of my judicial ruling. I barely tasted my first glass of wine and ate so slowly that the Sichuan pepper steak and vegetable *lo mein* had become cold and rather coagulated before I had consumed my meal. After pouring a second glass of wine, I picked up Miss Una for our ritual viewing of dwindling twilight from my small *lānai*. The lingering streaks of color in the sky and the twinkling lights of boats visible in my slice of a view of Waikīkī Bay brought momentary peace to my jumbled state of mind.

I knew it was getting late and that I could not delay in calling Nathan much longer. Once I finished my wine, I went inside to make the call I was dreading. But first I turned the television back on and pulled a chair around for Miss Una to commune with the evening's featured felines on Animal Planet. Then I cleared my tray and cleaned the kitchen, focusing my thoughts on the conversation to come. Picking up the phone, I pressed number one on speed dial. The ring tone chimed four times before I heard the familiar click to begin Ariel's voice-mail recording.

"Hi, this is the home of Ariel and Nathan. We're not in right now, but if you'll leave us your message, we'll return your call as soon as we can."

Because Nathan had answered the phone each time I had called since Ariel's death, I had not had to face this final reminder of her vivacious personality. Like friends who have lost their husbands, I doubted that Nathan would be changing that outgoing message any time soon.

It was not surprising that my dinner break brought neither a sense of sustenance nor a focus to my wandering thoughts. I meandered around for a few minutes before returning the living room. Glancing at the television, I saw that golden retrievers were now being offered for those preferring dogs as their animal companions. Sitting on the couch, I was quickly joined by Miss Una who desired her usual post-prandial petting. For a while, it was easy to lose myself in the soothing comfort of her velvet-like fur and the rhythmic sound of her deep purring. Typical of cats, I was permitted only a brief time for active disruption of her coat. Soon she returned to her perch above me to straighten the direction of her fur and renew its gloss with a vigorous washing with her tongue.

Like it or not, it was time I tidied some of the mess that was beginning to surround me. I began by sorting the pile of mail that had accumulated over the last several days. Only a few items required any action. I paid a couple of bills on-line and jotted a few notes in my calendar. After tossing unwanted fliers and solicitations in the recycle bin, I held the ivory envelope that I knew was an invitation to a post-RIMPAC event.

I might miss seeing Margie and Dan, but doubted I would be in any condition to attend. I knew they would understand the uncertainty of my schedule. At least we had gotten together during the preceding exercises, when their son's ship had been part of the exercises. I dashed off a preliminary email to them, as well as a few other friends I needed to inform about Ariel's death.

Next, I glanced through assorted papers related to Ariel's upcoming memorial. Fortunately, it was too late to call potential service providers. Relieved about what I did not have to do, I sorted my notes from my day of research. I was glad that everything dealing with Keoni's project had already been entered into computer files. That left my findings at the Makiki Sunset Apartments.

Opening a new document file, I input my impressions of what I had seen and experienced. Little of investigative value had emerged from my afternoon of sleuthing. As I did this, I considered excuses I could invent for another trip to the apartment complex, although I was concerned about Miss Wong's initially mistaking me for someone else. If that woman had arrived after my departure, Miss Wong would question my identity...and the real purpose of my visit to her apartments.

As I thought about my options, I closed my laptop and turned to cleaning out my purse: coffee receipt; requests for Archival materials yet to be submitted; and the lease form for apartment B406. Hmm. Miss Wong had not seemed interested in my name. So, with my cell phone set to block both my name and number, I could call her and act like everything was in order—per her initial assumption that I had been at the apartments to consider leasing a unit. If things got awkward, I would merely hang up.

I opened my binder to a clean sheet of lined paper and spread out the six pages of the lease agreement. Looking the document over, it seemed like an awful lot of red tape for such a lackluster dwelling. I guess you get all kinds of applicants in her business. It was probably harder to rid oneself of an undesirable tenant than to attract a new one.

One thing was clear—I would need to provide the truth of my identity for her to consider me as a renter. Then there was the issue of my supposed *granddaughter*. Obviously it would be too awkward to lasso a student as a fake relative. If I were going to pursue leasing the apartment, it had to be in my own persona.

Okay. I would be myself. I wanted to rent the apartment. Why? I came home to the depressing smell of the fire above me. And as I thought about my trip down memory lane in the neighborhood in which I had lived, I was inspired to temporarily vacate my condo while the repairs were completed upstairs.

Would Miss Wong accept such an arrangement? I felt sure that if I offered an exorbitant fee, the matter of a short-term lease should become a non-issue. All I had to do was keep my story simple. Resolved, I picked up my cell phone. The phone rang a couple of times and I thought I had been transferred to voicemail and prepared to leave a short message.

"Hi, Miss Wong. This is Natalie Seachrist. I dropped in this afternoon and looked at apartment B406." Following a click, the phone was answered.

"Good evening Mrs. Seachrist. This is Miss Wong. I was finishing my dinner when the phone rang."

"I just finished mine a few minutes ago and wanted to call before you placed your ad in the morning."

"That's fine. Most evenings I let the machine pick up, but I can hear messages being recorded if I am in the room. That's the nice thing about vintage answering systems."

"Yes, they make it convenient when you're savoring that last delicious bite of Szechuan pepper steak or your Thanksgiving turkey!"

"Ah, you like Chinese food," Miss Wong observed.

"Oh, yes. When I was a little girl, my brother, mother and I lived in an apartment not far from yours. And our favorite weekly treat was when our Auntie brought home *mushu* pork to wrap in Chinese pancakes," I said with genuine fondness. "That's why I was so pleased when my, *granddaughter* expressed interest in living in my old Makiki neighborhood."

"Oh, yes. This is a good location for University students," agreed Miss Wong.

"Indeed. Unfortunately, my granddaughter has decided to take a room on campus, for that *complete college experience*. But I have decided *I* am interested in renting the apartment. There's been a fire in the condo above me, and the smell is intense. It's going to be a while before insurance issues are resolved and the remodeling is completed. I don't think I can stand the stench any longer and the construction noise would be disruptive to my writing."

Rushing on to keep her interest, I said, "This afternoon was so peaceful. As I walked through your lovely neighborhood, I remembered playing with my brother along its streets."

"I see," commented Miss Wong, with warmth in her voice. "How long a lease would you wish to have?"

"I'm not sure how long the renovations in the upstairs condo will take. But I need to be in lower Makiki and Mānoa throughout the summer. I'm volunteering at the learning center on Wilder Avenue, and doing some research at the University for an historical writing project. So it makes sense for me to live there, close to everything—for at least the rest of the summer."

"Normally, I lease the units for a year. Occasionally, for six months during the winter tourist season...at a higher rent."

"I can appreciate you're doing so. But would you consider a three-month rental at a high season vacation rate?" I asked.

"Well, all of the other units are rented at this time...and it is true that my best opportunity for obtaining a full year's lease is in the fall. Yes, I believe we can come to an agreement for the next three months, Mrs. Seachrist."

After revealing Miss Una's existence, we came to terms that were financially beneficial to her—or should I say to her sister. I agreed to send her the signed release form to check my background and credit, the completed lease, and my check for all three months, plus a security and cleaning deposit. She said it would not take long to complete preparations and I should be able to move into the unit within a couple of days.

I was so lucky that the woman for whom I had been mistaken had not shown up or called! I would be spending a lot of money to pay for the ability to investigate the premises at my convenience and depending on the Medical Examiner's report, it might prove to be a total waste. However, I could not think of another way to help my brother learn the truth about his granddaughter's death.

At that moment, Miss Una swiped a paw across the top of my head. "Yes, I know. This is the only home you've known in your short life, and now I'm going to disrupt our entire living arrangement. But we'll be together, and you'll have all your usual toys and treats. So now I'd better start preparing for this great adventure."

I could not conduct business of any kind until the next morning. And I certainly did not want to discuss my plans with Nathan—at least not until the details had been ironed out. That left returning Keoni's call. I checked my day-planner for his number and dialed his home. He must have been sitting on top of the phone because he answered up on the first ring.

"Hewitt here," Keoni answered.

"Well, hi. Natalie here," I responded.

"Oh, Natalie, I'm so sorry about your niece."

"Thank you for your concern. Actually, she's my grand-niece, the granddaughter of my twin Nathan. He's raised Ariel and her twin Brianna since their parents died when the girls were twelve."

"Oh, yeah. Nathan. Is his surname Harriman? He's a psychologist? Or a social worker? I think I worked with him on a couple of cases dealing with families receiving government assistance. They were being victimized because of drug deals gone wrong in their building. His assistance was key in obtaining the services of a Vietnamese-speaking counselor."

"Yes, that's Nathan. His PhD was in psychology. He worked as a social worker for the State until officially retiring a couple of years ago. He still sees a few clients in his home office. Not only is he a great counselor, but he's got one of the best data bases for local, mainland, and even international resources in physical and mental health."

"How is he handling all this? I've seen a lot in my career in law enforcement, but I can't imagine anything worse than losing a child."

"It's been rough. He's holding up...largely due to his training and the support of family and friends. Of course, with my Auntie Carrie having Alzheimer's, our family really consists of just me and Ariel's twin Brianna."

"Well, please call me if I can do anything, anything at all. Except for a missing person case I'm wrapping up, there's nothing on my calendar right now."

Looking down at the lease for apartment B406, I made a quick decision. "Uh, there might be something you could help me with," I began.

"Like I said, *anything*. My chariot and I are at your beckoning."

"It's funny you should put it that way. I'm actually looking for someone to help me move a few of my belongings."

"Sure. How much do you need to move? And when? I've got a new Ford F150 truck with an extended cab, so we should be able to handle most anything you need to haul."

"Well, I need to move some boxes and a few pieces of furniture, my cat and myself. It'll probably be at the end of the week."

"No problem. I've got a few movers' blankets and bungee cords for tying everything down, so we should be fine. Are you still living in Waikīkī? You may need to make arrangements with the management to schedule the freight elevator."

"Yes, I'm still in the Waikīkī condo. Good point about the elevator, I'll touch base with my manager tomorrow."

"Gee, with Ariel's death, this must be a really awkward time for you to be moving."

I debated about how much I wanted to tell Keoni. I knew that as a retired policeman, it was unlikely he would appreciate my plans for playing detective. However, regardless of whether I disclosed my overall intentions, it would be difficult to hide *where* I was going.

"Mmm, to tell the truth, the condo upstairs had a fire last month, and it's going to be awhile before the place is fully restored. So I'm thinking it might be best to move out for the duration of the renovations. Since I'm going to be volunteering at a learning and literacy center for teens and young adults on Wilder Avenue, I've decided to rent an apartment in the building where Ariel was thinking of living."

"What? Are you serious? You're going to move into the place where your grandniece just died?"

"It may sound odd, but its location is convenient for everything I'm doing this summer. Nathan and I actually lived in the area when we were little kids. You see, our dad was in the Navy and we moved around a bit. Our Auntie Carrie had an apartment on Wilder Avenue, so when he was stationed in Japan a couple of times, our Mom packed our suitcases and we came to enjoy a bit of sun and surf."

"Uh, whatever you say. I'm happy to help, but I don't understand why you'd want to be anywhere *near* that place."

I kept the rest of our conversation to a minimum, saying I would call him when the details were finalized. Now all I had to do was start packing the household items I might need for the next several weeks.

CHAPTER 4

Before beginning, plan carefully.
Marcus Tulius Cicero [106 BCE-43 BCE]

Somehow my choice to walk in Ariel's footsteps felt right. I did not know what I might learn, but it would certainly be more than if I did nothing at all. At the least, I should be able to place what the authorities told Nathan and me within a broad context. It could not bring Ariel back to us, but perhaps those of us left behind would find a modicum of peace in knowing *how* her death had occurred.

To pursue my grand scheme, I needed to be ready to move on a moment's notification. My method of beginning every project with a clean home and concise to-do list has proven to be my personal and professional recipe for success. Having prepped my home for the launch of Keoni's job, I was already ahead in my preparations for my temporary relocation. Tonight, there was little I needed to do in the housework department, so I drifted from room to room, considering the few things I would move to the apartment in Makiki.

As I conducted this mundane chore, my thoughts floated freely...my creative mind suggesting situations in which Ariel died at the hands of evildoers who used the innocuous appearing apartments as headquarters for nefarious enterprises. Perhaps they were white slavers who had met their match in an unwilling Ariel Harriman. Or, while the apartment complex seemed a playhouse for innocents, she might have interrupted a transaction by manufacturers of a new blend of potent narcotics. Worst of all, maybe she interacted with international terrorists planning a deadly attack on the port of Honolulu. Such scenarios might sound like crackpot thinking, but since 9/11, any of them could be at the root of an unexplained death. I was certainly glad I was not part of a law enforcement agency in our new world of global disorder.

My decision to move into the apartment was not motivated by any doubt about the Honolulu Police Department's ability to investigate the death of a young college co-ed. In fact, my confidence in them was reinforced when I realized Detective John Dias, the lead investigator on Ariel's case, had been Keoni's last partner in HPD's Criminal Investigation Division.

Remembering comments Keoni had made at his retirement party, I knew Dias was one of the best trained first responders in today's age of cops and robbers. Between the skills of such detectives and the new thirteen-million-dollar crime lab, the Honolulu Police Department has an excellent record for crime solving. The fact that Dias was assigned to Ariel's case, showed the Department was taking her *unattended* death seriously. Also, with Keoni's reference to the ME's Office, I knew he still had access to official information that might prove useful.

Gruesome as it was, I pictured the police examining the scene of the death...and their launch of an investigation of Ariel's life and her few family members. That made me glad I had known Keoni for several years. For although we were not deeply involved in each other's lives, I knew he would attest to my credibility. More importantly, he would be able to vouch for Nathan in a professional capacity, since my brother had helped him on a couple of cases. In fact there should be several officials who could confirm Ariel's grandfather was a straight-arrow man and unlikely person of interest.

When you ruled out our family, the pool of characters at the apartments where Ariel had died was the most likely source of persons of interest. There was also her circle of intimate friends. I doubted any of them was involved in her death, but they would know the details of her life as a student. They might also be aware of issues that could have been a reason for her death—if it had resulted from foul play. But so far, none of them had provided any useful leads, notably the identity of the mysterious young woman who was to have been her roommate.

Befuddled by my fanciful suppositions and the overlapping of tasks I was facing, I decided to take a break. Setting my duster down on the Italian inlaid teacart in the dining room, I went into the kitchen for a long sip of O`ahu's crisp artesian water. Then I collapsed in my wingback recliner for a brief respite from my evening's chores and negative thinking.

I looked across the room filled with art and keepsakes from both my personal and professional lives. Posters from exotic locales spoke of the freedom I had enjoyed in my decades as a journalist. Stacks of family photo albums and scrapbooks were poignant reminders of our family's rich but often distant activities. Beside them sat project workbooks, some with details for the beach-side memorial service and life celebration Nathan and I were planning.

Seeing me seated and unoccupied, Miss Una determined her presence was required. With a mew of joy, she jumped onto my lap. For a while, I satisfied us both by stroking her rabbit-like fur. The momentary break was exactly what I needed to clear my mind. After a while, I set the cat gently on the floor and got up to turn on some of my favorite Island music. I felt re-energized immediately, as I enjoyed pieces ranging from the golden operatic voice of Emma Veary, to the slack key guitar classics of Gabby Pahinui.

For a couple of minutes, I limbered up my body and mind with a few creative dance moves. With a sense of purpose, I picked up my pen and opened the notebook dedicated to my forthcoming adventures in sleuthing. Nodding to the changing rhythms of music, I noted what I needed to accomplish in the next couple of days. Under the heading, "Move to Makiki," I listed everyone I needed to inform about my short-term move.

I was again grateful for Mother's little lessons on listing.

If I had had my way as a child, my life would have relied on a whim, if not a prayer. But even as a youngster, my mother had instilled the usefulness of organization in me—and Nathan for that matter. Her views had certainly proven useful in both our lives. Meeting my deadlines as a writer, and sometimes commentator, was often achieved by her little one, two, three method of organizing each day. Of course there were times when natural disasters and warfare interfered in my scheduled leisure reporting, but those interruptions to life normal were rare.

The next category of my evening's ruminations was more complicated. Who did I need to *avoid* telling about my plans? At the top of this list was my brother. I knew it was going to be difficult to keep from blurting out my activities to him. I just hoped I did not have a dream that inadvertently reached across the universe to him.

Then there was Brianna. Even if she meant to keep silent, she could easily slip and reveal everything to her grandpa Nathan. And if she knew of my plans, she might feel it was her duty to tell Nathan simply as a means of protecting me from myself. Worse yet, I was sure she would be homeward bound in a heartbeat. And that really would upset Nathan, since we did not know *what* or *who* had caused Ariel's death.

And what about the people connected to my condo. First there were my neighbors, Louise on my right and the Dorsons on the left. Then there was my close friend Anna Wilcox, who worked as the resident manager. Since I knew she was enjoying dinner and mahjong with area property managers that night, there was no reason to rush to call her. Sometimes, when one of the ladies of the mahjong gang is tied up, I am lucky to sit in for an evening. Oh, well, another thing I would not be able to do until I moved back home.

I decided that I would check in with Anna the next evening, after completing another round of research at the archives or library. That would give me the entire day to think about which details of my plan I wanted to share with her. I knew

I would ask her to keep an eye on the condo and take in my mail. I also thought I would have her housekeeper Rhoda tidy up after I moved. As to the rest, I was leaning toward a minimalist approach. I sighed. This was only the planning stage and I was already tired from thinking about the move.

Next I noted the furnishings, kitchen equipment and supplies I would need. The double-sized bed and dresser from my guest room and a side chair from my *koa* dining set would nearly fill the apartment's "master" bedroom. The apartment's dining area was too small for the *koa* dining table and while my parents' old Formica breakfast set might fit the space, it was not very attractive. The simplest solution was my glass topped wrought iron patio set.

My biggest concern was the living room. I did not require much for myself, but what about potential entertaining? On moving day I would need to accommodate Keoni. That meant I should take my reclining wingback. The *koa pūne'e* was a given. Its simple frame and loose cushions would seat three people if I had guests. And although the matching *koa* tables were too heavy, I could use a rattan coffee table and matching stacked tables from the guest room to fill in the setting. Add a couple of lamps and my furnishing of B406 at the Makiki Sunset Apartments was complete.

Other than food and supplies, what else could I need? Hopefully not a gun. Now there was an unsettling image. I had never before thought of entering Keoni's world of detection, and here I was contemplating a worst case scenario requiring fire power. The topic of guns had first come up when my husband Bill had expressed concern for my safety the first time he went to sea. I had kidded him somewhat seriously that the last thing we would want was Nervous-Nelly me sitting up in bed with a drawn weapon if his ship returned to port unexpectedly at three in the morning.

Pen behind my ear, duster in one hand and notebook in the other, I continued working my way through the condo, sprucing up the belongings I would take and jotting down a variety of notes. For a while Miss Una followed me around acting as though we were playing a new game. Eventually she gave up and headed out of the kitchen and toward the bedroom. I turned my thoughts to her needs. The most important thing in moving a cat, or any pet, is demonstrating that life as usual will continue. This meant her food, water, bedding, and treats needed to remain consistent. The one thing I would not be able to maintain was our weekly visit to Anna's condo for Miss Una to play with her mother.

Returning to the living room, I began shuffling the photo albums and started to replace them in the bookcase. Soon our family would have to move forward, making new memories. At the moment, it was good to pause and examine where we were and where we had been. I looked down at the cover of the last album. On it was a formal portrait of my father in his naval uniform centered between my Mother and Auntie Carrie who each wore a long white muʻumuʻu.

Forgetting about the work at hand, I sat down on the palm-patterned cushions of the pūneʻe. With or without a cat on my lap, this simple piece of furniture has proven to be my place of retreat in many moments of crisis. It had been one of my mother's favorite purchases for the home she and my dad had built after his retirement.

The photos I had been looking through recently showed how much my parents had enjoyed being together. They had been apart so often during his working years that when his naval career ended, they became virtually inseparable. After building their dream home on the windward shore of Oʻahu, Lillian and Jeffrey Harriman spent nearly every waking moment wandering the island they loved, in search of unique furnishings. What a shame that the sunset phase of their lives had lasted so few years.

The passing of my parents from the stage of their blissful retirement was as surreal as if a Hollywood writer were scripting a classic operetta set in the Islands. While returning from a child's first birthday lūʻau in a thick fog, they had died together in an accident just down the road from their beloved home. Their unexpected deaths came at a time when I was on assignment in South America and could not be reached immediately. As usual, Nathan met the needs of our family and friends. When I finally arrived in Hawai`i a week after our parents' memorial service, I found it difficult to travel the road on which they had crashed. For several days, I sacked out on the *pūne`e*, while Nathan and his wife Sandy tiptoed around me, trying to bring order to the chaos that always accompanies death.

This line of thought may have been what triggered my meandering through lower Makiki, where Nathan and I had had such fun as little kids. Looking back, I realized we had seldom been a secure nuclear family. Both sets of our grandparents died before Nathan and I were born, so Nathan and I had only our parents and each other to rely on—except for our dynamic Auntie Carrie, who was a strong presence in our lives. Twice while our father was overseas with the Navy, we had been fortunate to live with her in her small Makiki apartment.

The first time was when we were toddlers. With sandcastles to build and wonderful taste treats, we barely noticed when our mother departed on multiple vacations with our father. Later, following our dad's shore duty in California, we returned to stay with our fun-loving auntie while our mother remained with our dad throughout his deployment to Japan.

Carrie was a teacher at Punahou School, where our parents enrolled us for first grade. We even found our bus trips to and from school with her wonderful, since they allowed us to prolong our daily adventures with her. With our family at the center of her life, Auntie Carrie determined that even mundane activities should be celebratory events. Her mirthful personality shone in everything she did. Whether she was cleaning house, baking delicious sugar-sprinkled *malasadas* or dragging us out on Saturday shopping trips to restock the pantry, she practically tap danced while singing popular refrains from radio and television shows. I have always thought how delightful it was that she got to showcase her spirit through the occasional bit parts she played in many of the movies filmed in Hawai`i. I guess that was where I got my first taste of the art of language.

In our generation, I had been widowed early in life, and Nathan and Sandy had only had one child, a son named Jon. When my husband Bill died, I was in my late twenties. For several months, Nathan's family was my safe haven as I stumbled through the necessities of life in a daze. Then, almost overnight, I left the cocoon of their love when I received a contract with an international travel publication. It was an ideal answer to my prolonged contemplation of what I should do with the rest of my life.

Except for my prolonged absences on assignment, our family life was somewhat *normal* for a couple of decades following the deaths of my parents. The cycle of untimely deaths began again with the deaths of Nathan's son Jon and his wife Patricia. When their twins were twelve, they had taken an anniversary vacation to the same Paris hotel in which the couple had honeymooned twenty years earlier. A few hours after checking in, a rapidly-moving fire engulfed their floor and they died of smoke inhalation.

Nathan and Sandy had had no time to grieve before assuming the role of surrogate parents for the girls. Although they were not very old, the toll of being parents to a pair of lively tweenies impacted both of their lives. With the demands of the girls' after-school activities, Sandy left her job in banking. And although Nathan remained committed to his work, he seemed to back away from a full investment in every case that came through his office.

As the girls entered their junior year in high school, Nathan and Sandy began making plans to embark on the kind of sunset years our parents had enjoyed. Unfortunately, their dreams were never realized. Within a few months, Sandy died of complications during an emergency appendectomy. Overnight, Nathan became the sole guardian of the twins. With the unexpected death of his beloved Sandy, he seemed to freeze emotionally, except for his devotion to the girls.

It has only been a few years since Sandy passed. Nathan and I are cautious in expressing our affection for one another. We still love each other intensely, and as always, it takes few words for us to communicate deeply. But there has been a gulf between us since he mistakenly thought I withheld experiencing a vision about Sandy's surgery. I am glad that we came to a harmonious resolution of the issue, with him accepting the fact that I never had such a vision. Nevertheless, he remains uneasy about the visions I do have and questions me about my perceptions of their relevance to our family.

Since my official retirement, we have established an amicable means for addressing potentially contentious issues. Having been absent from most of our family's day-to-day activities, I have learned to accept the decisions he makes without my input. When I do offer suggestions, Nathan knows they come from an attempt to play honest broker within the framework of my world view. In terms of mental health, lately I have wondered if I am the one with frozen emotions. Perhaps the shock of Ariel's death has reawakened the grief I never fully resolved following my husband's sudden death nearly three decades ago.

The one person in our family who never had a mental health issue until recently was our Auntie Carrie. After Sandy died, she assumed the role of our family's maternal figure. From speech contests to science fairs, she has been available for art projects, late-night study, and performance rehearsals. No other teen had a more vocal advocate in the audience. And for every special event, our auntie could be counted on to arrive with food and intricate *leis* in hand.

One spring, the twins' windward outrigger canoe team was practicing for a major event to be held on the island of Maui, where none of us would be able to attend. At the end of the practice, Carrie arrived with platters of Hawaiian food for all the paddlers, their coaches and parents. While they ate, she strummed an `ukulele and serenaded them with a song she had written to encourage their efforts. Even if her home had not been around the corner in Lanikai , I know she would have managed to arrive with the full array of foods from a lū`au feast.

That was why everyone has been especially saddened that Auntie Carrie is nearing the end of her life. Although she is our mother's younger sister, she is in her late eighties and has reached the point of Alzheimer's where she no longer recognizes anyone for more than a few minutes. Nathan and I visit her about once a week and she always remarks that she is glad to meet new people. I am glad she has a wonderful team of caregivers who are adjusted to being her *new* friends during each of their shifts. It's not much of a silver lining to the storm clouds under which our family is living, but I am glad she cannot grasp what has happened to Ariel.

Knowing that our dear auntie could pass at any time, our goal has been to see that her days are filled with the words and music she has loved since her youth. During their last Christmas break, Ariel and Brianna recorded some of her favorite poetry and short stories, plus selections from Broadway musicals. With Carrie's quaint cottage being close to the beach, it is important to keep her calm and within locked doors at all times. Quite often, these recordings have proven to be the perfect means for keeping her entertained when caregivers Marilyn, Jordan or Kimo are busy elsewhere in the house.

Inserting my copy of one of their CDs into my sound system, I enjoyed listening to the girls' alternating voices reading from Shakespeare's sonnets. The similarity between the girls has always amazed me. It is more than their features, voices, and dimensions. Their sophisticated expressions of style, *joie de vivre*, and parallel focus on balancing personal and public living have always made them seem more mature than other people of their generation.

As I looked up at the shelves that held so many memories, I thought about the last time we had all attended the *Wind-*

ward Ho'olaule'a—Windward Community College's annual festival and fundraiser featuring Hawaiian music, arts, and food. Without pulling out the album, I could picture the girls presenting their creations to the judge in a lei-making contest. Positioned at opposite ends of a large work space on sheets of plywood atop saw horses, they had designed identical *leis* of maile twisted with white orchid and pink tuberose strands. With their quality workmanship also being parallel, they had shared the first prize of dinner for four at the popular restaurant Haleiwa Joe's at Ha`ikū Gardens.

Until this, their junior year in college, the girls were seldom separated for more than a few hours. When they chose institutions of higher learning, it was not surprising that both of the twins decided to begin at Windward Community college. At the time, I was commuting twice a week to teach a couple of courses in creative writing at WCC. It was the closest we had ever been, physically or emotionally. I cherished every moment we had together during that time and was delighted whenever they joined me for a *teriyaki* sandwich or plate lunch of chicken *adobo*. Life did not get much better than sitting on the stepped slopes of the hillside campus below the Ko`olau Mountains with the girls.

Too quickly, their years at WCC flew by. During this time, their scholastic and leisure interests began to diverge. Perhaps because of their grandfather's career, they were both innately interested in the welfare of others. However, while Brianna decided to follow her grandfather into a career in psychology, Ariel opted to pursue a career in nursing.

As I looked to the future, I could not imagine events at the college engendering the pleasure they once had. Sighing, I brushed off the coffee table and thought about what had come next for the girls. Surprisingly, for their upper division coursework, the twins had chosen to separate for the first time in their lives. They felt that one of them should remain in the Islands to be with their Grandpa Nathan and Auntie Carrie, while the other explored life elsewhere.

Each girl applied to several programs on the mainland and then they helped each other evaluate their opportunities. Eventually Brianna chose a path to allow her to complete both her bachelor's and master's degrees in psychology at Portland State University in Oregon. Ariel chose to attend the University of Hawai`i for her bachelor's in nursing. She had hoped to unify her interests with a master's in teaching English as a second language so she could help children in war-torn countries realize their full potential. It pained me to think about what she might have achieved if she had not died so early.

We were only halfway through the year, and I doubted that Auntie Carrie would outlive Ariel by very long. Unwelcome as that thought is, we have all accepted the fact that Carrie is at the end of her life. In contrast, I did not see how we would ever make sense of Ariel's passing. And I do not mean the usual trite application of the word *closure*. Despite all of Nathan's professional training, he has always agreed there is never *closure*. That seems especially true in the death of a girl who had barely begun her life as an adult.

Depressed by my musings and memorializing, I clicked on the nightly news. With the buzz of the broadcaster's deep voice, I returned briefly to my listing of work to be completed prior to moving to Makiki.

CHAPTER 5

The best thing you can do is the right thing;
the next best thing you can do is the wrong thing;
the worst thing you can do is nothing.
Theodore Roosevelt [1858-1919]

I felt guilty about lying to Miss Wong regarding my reasons for renting the apartment. But since the cause of Ariel's death has not been pronounced officially, I have wanted to avoid tipping off anyone who might have had a hand in it.

Arriving at a compromise between my natural honesty and the need to learn the realities of the Makiki Sunset Apartments, I was ready to move into unit B406. All I had to do is substitute *granddaughter* for *grandniece* and pretend she was still alive. By mixing verity with exaggeration, it was not difficult to maintain my rationale for wanting to rent the apartment. And thus I slid smoothly into the role of a new tenant who had paid an exorbitant fee for the ease of a three-month lease.

On Tuesday morning, I prepared the paperwork to mail to Miss Wong, gathered my usual work tools, and headed into town. After dropping the heavy envelope off at the old Post Office, I sauntered back to the archives for another peek at things historical. Not knowing what I might learn after I was living in the apartment, I chose to avoid pursuing topics that might prove unnecessary. Once I had specific names and dates, I could access a variety of resources. Since I lacked that data, I decided to focus my day on a general review of Honolulu's growth—work that would be useful to both my study of Makiki as well as that of Kaimukī.

I began by going through a plethora of maps available in hardcopy, microfilm and microfiche files. The chemical smells of the old film were often worse than aging newsprint and ink, but the results were much faster. While Henry processed a second round of map requests, I let my fingers do some fast tracking through several finding aids to refresh my memory of materials that might prove useful to both prongs of my inquiries.

Next I moved on to a general analysis of the growth of Makiki. After that, I perused newspaper articles addressing the late nineteenth-century expansion of Honolulu's eastside suburbs. The development of Kaimukī contained many surprising elements. During the early years, the area featured cattle and ostrich grazing. Later, efforts to provide potable water and easy transportation slowed the migration of city folks to the countryside.

I found it especially interesting that many of the area's bungalows had been built from mail-order kits from the mainland. Who would have thought that pre-fabrication homebuilding techniques were so old? One of the differences between construction at that time and now is that the quality of the materials used a hundred years ago has been proven to be substantially better. Except for the effects of salt air and termites, many items used in the construction of those homes a century ago are in better condition than those installed within the last couple of decades. Oh, for the days when wood was solid and the glass for lighting fixtures was thick enough to withstand being dropped!

For years, I have been as amazed at the lack of truth in product descriptions as I am in the statements of politicians. I remember once having Thanksgiving dinner aboard a beautiful Chinese barge that offered fine dining plus boutique shopping to delight a multitude of appetites. While waiting to be seated, our bevy of young military wives was encouraged to window shop the security-gated stores on the lower level. The shops displayed varied Asian arts and crafts, each with a slightly different emphasis, perhaps so you would not recognize the possibility that all these recreations of "Oriental" classics came from the same child-labor driven factory. As we turned back to mount the stairs for our long-anticipated holiday celebration, a sign caught my eye. Poised on a high shelf filled with delicate blooming bonsai trees I encountered the words, "Genuine synthetic jade."

After ruminating on the decaying quality of modern materials and processes of fabrication, I decided it was time to check back with Henry. Unfortunately, he informed me that the maps I was most interested in would not be available until the following week. Nevertheless, my trip was not wasted; I had new directions for on-line research. Besides, the break would allow me to return whole-heartedly to the packing that had to be done.

Knowing I needed to consume the leftovers that had accumulated at the back of the refrigerator, I bypassed the Food Court to catch a quick bus transfer home mid-afternoon. After a snack, I made another round of calls to well-wishers with whom Nathan was too stressed to converse. Then I turned to finalizing arrangements for my departure from Waikīkī. Since Anna already knew about Ariel's death, I was saved from having to go through another painful recitation of the vague circumstances in which the girl died. All I needed was a logical explanation for why I was leaving my home and uprooting my cat to land on the death scene of my dear brother's granddaughter.

Anna answered her door with her eyes glued to a sheaf of papers and her mind focused on the person speaking to her. I was sorry she appeared to be having a stressful day, but it was unlikely that she would grill me closely about my motivation for the temporary relocation. With a nod and a smile, she waved me through to her living room and disappeared into her office. From behind the door I heard the end of her conversation.

"I'm positive I told you the board of directors will have to make that decision, and they won't be meeting again until next month. Yes, I understand your concerns, and will make sure your issue is on the agenda."

After a moment of silence, she popped back into the room to find me looking out the sliding door to the *lānai*. "I can't decide whether it's going to rain or not, and since I'm going out for dinner, I decided I'd err on the side of caution and close everything," she explained.

"I know what you mean. Every time I leave home, I wonder whether it's better or worse for Miss Una to have fresh air, or take the chance that a face full of driving rain would dissuade her from wanting to sit outdoors with me."

"So, how about a glass of a bright Australian Chard and a nibble of a new pâté with pistachios I've found?"

I am always delighted to sample a new wine and nodded happily. Since Anna is the human companion of Miss Una's mother Mitzy, I indulged in a few snippets of recent feline frolicking while she prepared our afternoon repast. As we settled on her Danish modern ivory leather sectional, I began to feel the stress of the day slipping away. The ritual of wine tasting was in itself refreshing. It also delayed addressing the underlying reason for my visit.

After wiping my lips with an intricately embroidered napkin, I petted Mitzy for a few moments. Like it or not, it was time to launch into setting the stage for my upcoming debut as a detective. I sighed and pulled at the edge of my napkin.

"I know life must be difficult for you right now," my friend said, trying to ease my obvious distress.

"With everything that's going on, Anna, I'm simply trying to make it through one hour at a time. I try to prioritize the things on my to-do list for each day, and then work through them sequentially."

She nodded encouragement, without trying to interfere with my train of thought.

"I can't begin to say how sorry I am for your loss, and Nathan's."

"I know that Anna. You're one of the few people who understands first-hand what it's like to lose a child." We seldom discussed it, but tragedy had been her companion for many years. Both her son and husband had died in a diving accident in Tahiti during what was to be a vacation to celebrate her son's high school graduation.

"I've...I've decided to do something that almost no one else knows about," I said quietly. I then rushed forward with a verbal stream of consciousness about my intentions—but not about my visions, which had never come up in our normal conversations about the idiosyncrasies of life. She nodded supportively but did not interrupt my ramblings.

Finally, I ran out of steam and stopped. Anna stared directly at me. She blinked once and said, "Oh, my dear. I can't imagine what you've been going through to arrive at *this* solution."

"Well, it's not really a solution. It's simply a means for opening a window into what might have happened to Ariel."

"Mmm. What have the police said? About the cause of Ariel's death?"

"Nothing. That's the issue. Her death is an open case. There's nothing definitive—not even an autopsy report. You know, it was only a four-storey drop onto a vintage Mustang. I thought a car like that would have softened her landing. But when one of the investigating officers at the scene asked the Medical Examiner about the short fall, all he said was that whether a person lives or dies depends on *how* they land, not *how far* they fall."

I continued explaining myself. "Oh, Anna. It was such a terrible way to die, no matter how short the fall. There were cuts and abrasions, and broken bones, and blood...a lot of blood, running down from her body, across the hood of the car and pooling on the ground. And her neck was twisted and broken horribly."

I shuddered at the reawakened image from my vision. It

was the first I had spoken these words aloud, and I choked on my next attempt to speak. For a while, I could not control the torrent of tears that nearly gave me the hiccups. Anna left the room and returned with tissues and a cool damp cloth. Kneeling before me like I was her injured child, she reached up to wipe my face. Then she stroked my arms until my sobs subsided.

We stayed like that for a while. When she sensed my returning calm, she went to the kitchen and returned with a glass of water, which she handed to me silently.

"I'm sorry, Anna. I thought I was handling everything so well, calmly doing what needs to be done, one logical thing at a time."

"Yes, my dear, but that's often how death is experienced. You're so busy doing what must be done that you can't take it all in—at least not emotionally. The grieving process is different for each of us. I know that Nathan has the background to describe the process. But that isn't the same as living through it. He's had *your* support. But *who* have *you* had? You really haven't had anyone except Miss Una."

"And what a Godsend she's been. It's like she knows. She actually put out her paw and touched my face when I was crying one night."

"That's why they're called our 'animal companions.' It's amazing, what they sense and how they can ease our pain, in the midst of our sorrow."

I nodded and wiped my face with the handkerchief I always keep in my pocket.

"And what about Miss Una, if you're going to be hauling yourself up to Makiki for who knows how long? You know she's welcome to join Mitzy and me, but I hate to separate you from her now that you've truly bonded."

"Oh, no. I appreciate your offer, but I wouldn't just leave her here. You're so right. I couldn't bear to be apart from her. Except for Nathan, and Brianna, and a few friends like you, she *is* all I have. No, I'm packing her right along with my parents' sofa, my favorite chair and several bottles of wine."

She chuckled and said, "Well, it sounds like you'll have the essentials for life at hand. How are you arranging to do all this?"

"I've recently heard from a friend who asked me to do some research for him prior to Ariel's death. He's a retired cop turned private detective. Anyway, he's going to help me move whatever I'll need to the apartment."

"An ex-cop you say? Perfect. I'll bet he loves the idea of you going up there, all alone, except for your valiant feline protector."

"Well, I've promised to keep in touch with him at all times. You might know of him. It's Keoni Hewitt. He used to be partnered with John Dias. The two of them worked a case you must have heard about. It was all over the papers for weeks after they broke up that white slavery ring that was shipping would-be actresses to Japan?"

"Yes. I do remember the case. Who wouldn't, with a state legislator's daughter missing for two months? And in the end, it was a corporate lawyer who'd started the scheme as a way to up his finder's fees! So, when is *your* gambit taking place?"

"That's the catch. I'm not sure. It could be any day. I called you initially because Keoni thinks I'd better reserve the freight elevator for the move. The problem with setting a firm schedule is that while I've mailed the paperwork and my deposit to the manager of the apartment, she needs a few days to complete the cleaning and painting. That leaves me dangling until she gives me the green light."

"Well, you picked a good week to be doing this. There's only a tentative hold on the freight elevator for this Saturday at two. Other than that, there's nothing until next week."

I put the tissues I had used in my pocket and handed Anna the mascara-stained cloth.

"Sorry about the eye makeup. You'll probably be washing this for a month before it'll be clean."

She laughed lightly. "An easy chore, compared to what's on

your plate, honey. All I ask is that you add me to your list of check-ins, and I'll rest easier. You and I go back quite a while and I know there's no way of talking you out of something to which you're committed."

We moved toward the door, agreeing that she would hold my junk mail and call before forwarding anything that seemed important. I then handed her the checklist I had prepared for her housekeeper and some cash to cover miscellaneous expenses. We hugged goodbye and I left feeling better prepared for what was to come.

I entered the elevator thinking about the deep friendship Anna and I have developed over the years. Several times when my scheduled assignments on travel in exotic locales had turned into covering hard news events, I had her watch over my affairs. Like in late August of 1988. At the time, I was between cruises in the Mediterranean Sea and decided I would play tourist for a couple of days in the Israeli seaport of Haifa.

As a travel writer, I knew it was important to be cautious in the Middle East—even before today's proliferation of suicide bombings. I thought that I would be safe if I stayed away from public transportation and outdoor cafés. It was a Saturday. The Jewish Sabbath until sundown, when the city came alive with couples and families out for an evening of refreshment and entertainment. The weather was hot and muggy, and I decided I needed to go shopping for lingerie and sundresses.

After cruising through a couple of elegant stores at the downtown Nordau Street Mall, I stopped for dinner. At a crowded Arabic restaurant, I enjoyed a delicious dinner of grilled lamb and a pilaf of lentils and rice with blackened onions. I remember completing my savory meal with a dessert of saffron *labneh* with dried apricots poached in orange juice.

I was so tired by that point that I forgot about any further shopping and returned to my hotel. Just as I was about to turn in for the night at about nine, I heard an explosion. I knew better than to go back out on the street and remained in my room. After turning on the television, I called the local affiliate of the media giant for whom I sometimes presented. Since there had been no major assaults or other challenging events recently, the staff was at a minimum and they were glad to have me help cover the story the following morning.

The crime scene had been examined and much of the initial clean up completed by the time I arrived on the scene. With only twenty-five injuries from shrapnel and flying glass, members of the media were allowed closer access than if someone had died. Looking around, I counted my blessings for a filling dinner that may have saved my life.

Although information was slim at the time, I eventually learned the event was instigated by four young Bedouin Arabs who were citizens of Israel. Their attack consisted of lobbing an army grenade into the crowded mall in front of a toy store and coffee shop. I wondered if any of them had any regret for the young girl who had lost a leg while shopping with her family.

With everything that has happened since 9/11, I am truly glad to be retired from active journalism. After my meeting with Anna, I returned to my condo, feeling drained emotionally. I walked into the kitchen and looked at the blinking light that indicated I had voicemail. Before facing any more crises, I decided to have supper. I resolved the final refrigerator cleanout and my need for sustenance by pouring the contents of several storage containers into a base of tomato and thyme soup. The refrigerator was now the cleanest it had been in months and my latest interpretation of gourmet cooking would provide several quick meals.

Satisfied with a sample teaspoonful, I ladled some of the soup into a bowl and poured a glass of Alexander Valley Merlot. After tossing Miss Una a few treats, I returned to the blinking light that continued to demand my attention. Knowing I was incapable of even a cursory conversation at the moment, I was grateful that none of the calls required an immediate reply. If we had spoken, I knew Nathan would have "sussed" me out as the Brits say. I did not want burden him with my visions *or* my plans for exploring the apartments where Ariel had died.

The rest of my evening was unremarkable, except for a couple of dishes I broke during a round of late night packing. One of the highlights of the evening was playing with Miss Una as I turned down the bedspread. After she settled on the baby blanket I had substituted for the catsack I had packed, we enjoyed a short session of bedtime reading. Since Ariel's death, I could not face murder mysteries, so I had turned to poetry and song books in search of material that might be appropriate for her memorial service.

While slipping off to dreamland, I offered up a silent prayer that I would not have any troubling visions that night. I did not. What I did experience was a pleasant dream of my parents.

*   *   *   *   *

I entered dreamland viewing an early morning sky rich with the promise of another day of pleasure for my parents. They were enjoying their first cup of coffee on the back lānai of their waterfront home in Kāneʻohe. I could hear the cooing of doves calling to one another while partaking of the water in the volcanic stone fountain my mother always kept flowing. The scent of her carefully tended rose bushes was as real as being in the garden that is now Nathan's.

I watched as they drove to the Koa Pancake House for a shared Portuguese sausage omellete and stack of buttermilk pancakes topped with citrus compote. Next, my parents embarked on what I knew was one of their early Sunday morning jaunts around the island of Oʻahu. Luxuriating in their companionship, I joined silently in their favorite weekend pastime of yard sale shopping for small treasures for their beautiful, almost Asian styled home they'd built to celebrate their love for each other. Sans ads or maps, they often wandered for an entire day. They always returned with more than one item they declared to be "exactly what we were seeking."

In my dream that night I watched them drive through miles of changing Island scenery. Eventually, I saw them standing over a card table in a carport beside an old wood frame plantation cottage on the North Shore. They were chatting with a Senior Chinese woman in a cheongsam *the color of dark emperor jade. She offered an array of small mirrors, bookmarks with calligraphy, and albums with images from the early part of the twentieth century.*

Surprisingly, my Mother was speaking what I somehow knew was the Yue *dialect of Chinese. I understood they were discussing Singapore and Shànghǎi before the Second World War. While I knew my parents had met overseas and took periodic vacations in Asia, I did not know either of them spoke any Asian language.*

As I stood unnoticed in the midst of this chance meeting of unknown yet kindred spirits, all of my senses were awakened: I heard the rustle of the woman's silk dress and the click of her gold and jade bracelets; the purple velvet covered scrapbooks felt soft beneath my fingertips; I smelled the paper of old newspaper clippings from a remote era and locale; my eyes absorbed the love emanating from precious family photos now turned a rich brown.

*   *   *   *   *

Abruptly, my secret window to the Realm Beyond closed, like so many of my dreams and visions have ended. Perhaps my parents had dropped in to add their blessing to my forthcoming inquiries into a culture with which they were surprisingly familiar. At peace at last, I fell into a dreamless state of rejuvenating sleep.

The next morning I awoke with an undefined sense of urgency. I quickly finished assembling the clothing, toiletries and kitchen kitsch I would need in the foreseeable future. There was not much else to do until "launch day" had been designated. I checked in with a few key people, and moved on to the main event on today's agenda, a trip to a combination grocery and drug store for everything I might need during my stay in Makiki.

I am truly grateful for the modern convenience of obtaining meat, wine, baked goods, fruits and veggies plus cleaning supplies in a single store. My appreciation of the ease with which Americans live their daily lives was reinforced during visits to Iron Curtain countries, where I watched women dragging themselves between half-filled shops after a long day of work, hoping to find even the bare essentials of life.

A couple of hours later, I watched the conveyor belt move toward the cashier, and realized I would need a taxi to get all my purchases home. Thank goodness my condominium provides carts and dollies for major uploading of supplies and furnishings. They would certainly come in handy on moving day. Despite this array of paraphernalia, the thought of even a short-term move made me ache. I vowed to allow time to soak in my condo's pool and spa that night.

After returning from my whirlwind of shopping, I faced the minor inconvenience of rain water deposited by Mother Nature at my back door. Of course, it was preferable to a message that might be left by a neglected feline. While organizing my purchases and settling in for the night, I was gratified to find the phone message I was awaiting from Miss Wong. Quickly, I called her to confirm that I would be delighted to "start" moving in a few items the following morning. Thank goodness both Keoni and Anna were able to accommodate this spur of-the-moment sign from the heavens that I might be doing something right. By the time I was through prepping for the day to come, I gave up on my idea of a prolonged soak in the spa, and fell to sleep after a quick shower.

CHAPTER 6

I hear there are people who actually enjoy moving.
Jan Neruda [1834-1891]

Given my cover story, it was logical to move only a few possessions to the Makiki Sunset Apartments. Keoni arrived at my condo on Thursday at about seven-thirty a.m., the earliest I could reserve the freight elevator. We began by loading the few large pieces of furniture I was taking. Next we wedged in the boxes I had packed with clothing and kitchen miscellany. Within a couple of hours, it was time for Miss Una and me to join Keoni in the cab of his sleek black Ford F-150 pickup.

"You're sure you didn't forget anything that's vital—like the cat's food, toys or litter box?" queried Keoni.

"Yes. Meeting her needs was at the top of my list when I planned all of this. There's no way I could have left her behind, and I don't want to ruin all of her daily routine. I even have some new treats and toys to lessen the effects of uprooting her from the only home she's known since leaving her mother."

Despite my projection of her continued grand lifestyle, Miss Una crouched unhappily in the pet purse on my lap. She loudly voiced her concerns all the way from Waikīkī to Makiki.

We pulled into the apartment complex about 10:00 a.m., with Keoni's truck packed to capacity. The handyman I had met during my brief reconnoitering was trimming shrubs along the edge of the low wall at the front of the parking lot. I introduced myself as the new tenant of B406 and Keoni as my friend. In turn, the man introduced himself as Al Cooper and showed us general parking for guests, deliveries and re-pairmen, plus the single parking stall assigned to my apart-ment. Somehow I managed to control my revulsion to the site of Ariel's death and silently thanked heaven I would never be parking a car there.

Affirming his vital role in the local operation, Al declared, "I handle most anything that needs doing around here day-to-day. Of course, no one can do everything alone, so sometimes I call in reinforcements from the utilities or a palm-trimming company."

That seemed a strange remark to make, but it got me to thinking about the lengthening list of people who might have been on the property the day Ariel died.

All of a sudden, Miss Una, who had been left in the truck, announced her presence with increasing volume.

"I sure hope your roommate isn't going to be that noisy all the time," grumbled Al.

"Oh, you'll hardly know she's here. She's normally very quiet, and being an inside kitty, she won't be in your way."

He rolled his eyes and returned to his chores with a "Humph."

Staring at the bed of the truck, Keoni and I contemplated which items to carry on our first trek up to the apartment. Bringing the basics of life had included furniture, a small tele-vision, clothing, dishes, cooking pots and utensils—plus spices and one bottle each of Aloha Gold soy sauce and San Antonio Marsala. With those last items and some take-out delicacies, I was confident I could handle almost anything in the culinary department.

I hoisted a travel bag over my shoulder, and set Miss Una's carrying case and other essentials into her new litter box. Walking in rhythm to her protests, I carefully traversed the stone pathway on the right of the volleyball court. Keoni fol-lowed with a dining chair stacked with boxes.

After I parked the cat and her accoutrements in the "mas-ter" bathroom, I found him sorting the boxes he had brought up, one of which was not mine. Approaching me with a large plastic refrigerator container, he said, "Since I didn't know how much shopping you would be able to do in the next few days, I brought you some left-over shrimp curry and a bag of Caesar salad with dressing on the side."

"My goodness, aren't you thoughtful." I crooned and gave him a quick hug, before refrigerating his kind gift.

We then spent a couple of hours hauling and arranging furniture, and setting boxes in their assigned rooms. After untangling hangers and clothing, I declared "mission accomplished" and we took a break.

"I know you don't drink alcohol on a regular basis anymore, but does this count as a special, if not festive, occasion?" I asked.

"I guess it might," Keoni replied. "What do you have to tempt me with?"

"Well, you might prefer a beer after all this manual labor, but what about sharing a bottle of Jacob's Creek 2003 Grenache Shiraz, with a loaf of fresh sourdough bread and some Havarti cheese?"

"That sounds good! You don't have to twist my arm over that menu."

"If you'll release Miss Una from jail, I'll pull our snack together."

He nodded, and moved off toward the uncanny silence that reverberated volumes from the "master suite." The apartment might be small, but being an older building, it had enough space within the rooms that I would not feel claustrophobic.

Keoni re-entered the living room with Miss Una nestled in his arms and settled on the reclining leather wing back chair. They both looked satisfied with the arrangement.

"I see you have a new friend," I observed, bringing in a tray with our refreshments.

"Hey, what's not to love about your rescuer?" He retorted, focused on stroking her cheeks and throat which elicited a steady sound of purring.

I poured a large glass of wine and set it down with a plate of cheese and bread on the table at his side. As if on cue, Miss Una sprang onto the back of the chair, and openly contemplated her chances for pilfering one of the delectables below her. I zipped open a fresh sack of green cat treats and rattled it. She sprang down immediately and pranced in front of me until I tossed a few across the floor.

"This wine is a great pairing with the Havarti. Its body and degree of sweetness are perfect and, not overpowering like a cabernet would be," Keoni said with a satisfied smile.

I returned his smile and nodded. Clearly, he knew more about wine than I would have thought.

We were silent for a few moments, enjoying our wine and watching Miss Una's antics as she crept up on an open cabinet at the entrance to the kitchen as if it held a monster. Eventually, our conversation turned to the purpose at hand.

"I still don't like your striving to become Hawai`i's Jessica Fletcher," Keoni began.

"It's only for a short while—until the toxicology report comes back to the Medical Examiner's Office," I replied huffily. I knew he was looking out for me, but I did not enjoy feeling like a schoolgirl in front of the principal's desk.

"I don't mean to add to your anxiety, but I spoke to my old buddy Marty at the ME's Office. He said that although there's no unusual bruising on Ariel's body, they found a tear in the lobe of her left ear that could be an indication of foul play in her death. And if *that's* the case, here you are, ensconced on the premises of a murder scene."

"I know, I know. That's precisely why I'm here. It's been several days since she died. Even I am aware that the likelihood of solving a major crime decreases with every passing day."

"It's a little too late to change your plans now. You've already moved in. But it would be good for you to keep a low profile. And remember your promise to call me every day. Why don't you put my cell number on speed dial whenever you're prowling around the property?"

"Yes, yes, and yes. I appreciate everything you're doing to help and I promise to stay in close touch with you."

Shaking his head about the entire situation, Keoni helped me clear our dishes. I walked him down to the parking lot and he hugged me tightly before getting into his truck. He backed up carefully before pulling out slowly into the street. As the truck moved away, I saw his blue eyes looking at me intently from his rear view mirror.

I turned to the row of aluminum mailboxes and tried the key for the box assigned to me. It opened easily, as if newly oiled. At the back, I saw one label with my name printed on it and another that probably offered the forwarding info for the tenant who had moved out. I made a mental note to try to check on the time of mail pickup and delivery, to know when I might get a look at the information about the apartment's prior resident. Turning around, I almost walked into a tall blond woman with a small red-headed boy in her arms.

"I'm sorry. I didn't hear you behind me," I said apologetically.

"Oh, it's not your fault; I was wrestling with Cory here. He's always wanting to run around freely, but I don't want to take a chance on his running into traffic."

The young boy being discussed had turned his head into his mother's shoulder.

I laughed. "Well, I think the matter is solved. He looks content in your arms."

"Quite the brave boy when there's only me to tussle with," she said, ruffling his hair.

"Is that a slight Southern accent I hear in your voice?"

"Yep. The hills of North Carolina. Pardon me for not introducing myself. I'm Ashley Lowell. My husband is on a destroyer stationed at Pearl Harbor. While he's gone on a cruise, I thought Cory and I would hang around and enjoy Hawai'i's sun and beaches."

"Good choice. I did the same when my husband was a Navy

lieutenant a few decades ago."

"My, that's been a long stay. Or did ya'all come back to the Islands to retire?"

"Not exactly. Bill died on that Westpac, and I've lived in Hawai`i off and on since then." I reached out my hand. "I'm Natalie Seachrist. I'm the new tenant of B406."

"I'm so sorry about your husband."

Clearly, she did not know what to say. With her being the wife of a man embarking on a cruise that could last for months, I wanted to avoid building on any fears she might have.

"It was a fluke, the authorities said. He may've reacted to an inoculation or it simply may not have worked." Moving the conversation in another direction, I asked, "So what apartment are you two in?"

"Oh, I was lucky. The manager, Pearl Wong, has a nephew, Richard Bishop. He's the son of Pearl's sister Jade. He'd just finished painting A104, so I got the ground floor unit I wanted for Cory to be able play outside. I was thrilled it was all updated. I guess Richard wasn't too happy about being put out of his home, but that's how it works around here—he just moves from apartment to apartment, whenever one needs sprucing up."

I congratulated Ashley on her good fortune in housing and before saying goodbye, we laughingly anticipated meeting in the laundry room—if not over the volleyball net.

After the excitement of the move, I enjoyed some quiet time arranging the closet and making my bed. Before beginning to organize the kitchen, I savored a bit of the leftover salad and curry Keoni had given me. With a glass of Sterling Pinot Grigio in hand, I placed my nightly call to Nathan. I was glad I had managed to bite my lip before telling him where I was and, more importantly, what I was planning to do.

For a while Miss Una continued to prowl through the apartment, sniffing each of her belongings to feel assured that the basics for her survival were in place. Once we settled down, I quickly fell asleep and experienced no memorable dreams or visions. I actually slept until the early morning call of resident doves alerted me that Friday had arrived. Taking my first cup of coffee out to the *lānai*, I attempted to quell the discomfort the view stirred within me. Especially unsettling was the thought of ever sitting on the balcony.

Glancing over the rail produced a catch in my breathing and rising nausea in my throat. It brought me close to feeling like I did on my first ocean voyage, when I had been hired to write promo copy for a cruise line. After a few trials and errors with over-the-counter meds, and stern pep talks to convince myself of the benefits of experiencing this aspect of the tourist industry, I had been okay. But since then, I have never willingly boarded a boat of any kind.

Despite my feelings about where I was standing, I enjoyed having the early morning light shine on my face and hearing the coo of doves. I tried not to think about what such a morning would have meant to Ariel. Would she have maintained her morning routine of a long run or tennis match prior to attending classes at the University? Or, would she have slipped into a ritual like mine—allowing a sip of fragrant tea or coffee to beckon her forth to the day at hand? Sadly, I would never know.

Turning to practical matters, I spent that day and the weekend settling in. After Richard Bishop's thorough cleaning and painting, I knew there could not be much evidence left from Ariel's brief interaction with the property. In fact, everything was so pristine that I barely wiped anything off before installing my belongings. Despite his dour countenance and numerous mumbled complaints, the pudgy man must be very dedicated to his occasional work.

Interspersed with organizing my temporary home, were tours of the amenities of the complex. I also conducted online research from my laptop, since the building was wired for Wi-Fi plus satellite television reception. I was grateful that Keoni's project provided breaks from the quasi-reality of living in the apartment that should have been Ariel's. Between my real-time research for him and exaggerated schedule of volunteer work, I would have plenty of excuses for coming and going at various times. And *that* would allow me to learn the rhythms of activity at the apartments.

I might never feel at peace in unit B406, but I had given myself an assignment, and I would be damned before I would fail in it. Once the apartment was ship-shape, I began my private investigation of the complex by playing the role of a new tenant surveying the prospects of her abode. With regard to the premises themselves, except for the normal wear one would expect on older buildings, I did not see or hear anything that seemed out of place.

As I explored the property and its resident personalities, I mentally noted the flow of activity throughout each day. In those first appraisals of life at the Makiki Sunset Apartments, I learned that I am not the only occupant with an erratic schedule. But like me, everyone I have encountered seems to have logical-sounding reasons for their exits and entrances.

First on my list of occupants was Al Cooper, whom I had met twice. He seemed efficient, if not friendly. As the part-time handyman, he is found at various places at all times of day and night. Since his vintage Mustang was the site of my grandniece's unplanned landing, Al was forced to obtain a rent-a-wreck vehicle until he can rebuild his favorite toy. Most of the time, I encounter him near his rental car, or Miss Wong's truck, when he needs pick up a large quantity of building materials or supplies.

My next person of interest is Pearl Wong. But until I got a chance to know her better, there was little for me to record in the file I have opened regarding her. Being the owner of one building (and the manager of the one owned by her sister Jade Bishop), Miss Wong has a multitude of reasons to pop up whenever and wherever she wants. Surprisingly, she does not seem to go out a lot—at least not on her own. Occasionally, I see her sitting regally in the passenger's seat of Al's car. More often her nephew Richard Bishop is playing chauffer in either

her truck or a classic black Mercedes Benz I have seen on the property.

Although nothing has been said, I am guessing the car belongs to Jade. Other than her possible link to the car, I know very little about her. I have never seen Jade and, unless I ask, no one mentions her. She is an invalid who seems to depend on close interaction with Pearl and Richard...at least when her caregivers are unavailable. But since she has not been at the apartments for several months, I do not see how she could have been involved with Ariel's death.

The second person who remains a mystery is Jade's son Richard. So far I have not been able to determine where he fits into the operational hierarchy. I have been told that the only activity he performs with regularity is taking his mother to medical appointments and Miss Wong to legal and financial meetings. From what I have observed, he is as happy in his role of chauffer as he is about shifting apartments constantly. Glaring at anyone who looks his way and muttering to himself most of the time, he is a man who is ill at ease with his world.

As to the overall vibe, the only note of discord I have found at the complex is the toxic relationship between Richard and Al. One day I saw the two men tussling in a closet in Building B's laundry room. It sounded as though they were arguing over some old tool box. With Al being the resident handyman, I would have thought anything having to do with tools or equipment would be his concern. However, I regularly see Richard coming and going from the many nooks and crannies of the aging complex with a jangling tool kit in his hand. Whatever the source of Al's displeasure with Richard, I doubt that it has anything to do with tools.

Another point of contention is Pearl Wong's classic, but not valuable green Chevy Silverado pickup. On more than one occasion I have seen the two men jockeying for right of usage. One night, I stepped out onto the *lānai* to investigate a noise coming from behind the apartment and overheard Al scolding Richard. Unseen, I watched as Al pulled a ring of keys from

Richard's hand. Nearly screaming, he said, "You have no business going out on the road. You may be fooling your aunt and mother, but you can't put one over on me. You're not getting these keys back until I'm sure you're straight and sober."

I had no idea what Al was talking about, but the relationship between these men-who-would-be-boys was not healthy. One thing was certainly clear: Richard can never satisfy Al, who calls him "kid," even though they are both beyond forty-five. Most of their disagreements remind me of children arguing over a toy they are supposed to share—especially when I have watched them shouting about who is in charge of an errand on behalf of Pearl.

Another question I have concerns Richard's origins. He does not look Chinese, so I have wondered whether he is related to Jade biologically. Perhaps he was adopted or is the product of a previous marriage of Jade's deceased husband. As to the focus of his life, it does not seem related to the apartments. Although he is past the usual age of schooling, the only time I have heard him speak about his life, he was rambling on about the culinary classes that he is taking at Kapi`olani Community College.

It was nearly noon on Monday when I finished my musings and note-making. After heating a saucer of milk for Miss Una, I sat down at the table in front of the slider to savor a final cup of coffee. As I rinsed our dishes, the phone rang. It was Miss Wong checking to see that her newest tenant was satisfied and settling in.

"Perhaps you would like to come for tea some afternoon?" she queried.

"That would be lovely. As I told you, I lived in this area when I was a young child, and I'd love to visit with you about its history," I responded, trying to open our dialogue wider than she might have intended.

"I would be delighted to tell you all about our family's life here."

How grand! I had picked the right *entrée* for learning what

I could about the apartments and their inhabitants. "Let me know when you'd like me to come."

"Well, I know you are busy with your research and volunteering, but late afternoons are usually good for me. By three-thirty, my sister Jade is resting and my work for the apartments is generally finished."

I pretended to check my calendar. "Mmhm. Well, I'm free tomorrow afternoon and Wednesday," I said, letting my voice trail off.

"Since I must attend the wedding of a friend's daughter on Wednesday, may I ask if tomorrow is too soon for you," Miss Wong politely inquired.

"Not at all. I'm looking forward to getting to know you and your lovely apartments much better."

"Very well, shall we say four o'clock?"

I agreed and hung up the phone with a near pirouette. I could not have asked for a better opening to my study of the apartment complex. I only had a day until our "tea party," so I decided to do a bit of research on both of my projects at the Hawai`i State Public Library next to the archives. With the library being the main repository of daily newspapers in the twentieth century, I figured I could squeeze in review of articles about the Makiki and Kaimukī neighborhoods—after checking on some unusual topographic maps Henry had told me would be available for viewing at the archives.

Once I had more information on the current owners of the apartments, I could check the tax rolls for information on the history of the property. With correct name spellings and, if I am lucky, a few dates, running checks on the Wong and Bishop families should be fairly easy. I was curious to find out if this Bishop family was related to the illustrious Bishops who sprinkle the history of the Kingdom of Hawai`i.

After a brief bus ride, I entered the archives and looked at maps Henry had pulled for me showing Honolulu as it changed through the twentieth century. I then went next door to the main branch of the Hawai`i State Library and spent several hours scanning reels of microfilm of the *Star Bulletin* and *Honolulu Advertiser*. With textual descriptions of both Makiki and Kaimukī fortified by the maps I had seen, I considered the buildings that had been erected, modified and demolished to accommodate the outward migration of Honolulu's populace. I was disappointed that I did not learn anything new or surprising about lower Makiki: Wilder Avenue had been widened; water, gas and sewer lines had been augmented; and thousands of individuals and families had moved in and out of the area.

Between admitted escapism and serious research, I passed the afternoon without any emotional stress. For the first time, I returned to my temporary home feeling almost like this was my normal life—without concerns for the present, or fears for the future. Miss Una and I finished one of the last frozen dinners I had brought from the condo, and I actually went out on the *lānai* without too much discomfort for my second glass of wine. Our early supper was followed by an immediate turn-down of the bed.

CHAPTER 7

If you tell the truth you don't have to remember anything.
Mark Twain [Samuel L. Clemens, 1835-1910]

Tuesday morning, I decided to stay home and do a little more reconnoitering. After breakfast and a perusal of hardcopy and online newspapers, I put Miss Una's harness on her and attached her lead.

"All right, Sweetheart. Be a good girl. We're going for a stroll across the top deck of our palace, but that's all."

Since day one, Miss Una has sat in front of the long louvered windows to the right of the front door every morning. Unfortunately, the view is not that great and I thought she might like to see what lay beyond her senses. She seemed to be the only animal companion on the fourth floor, so I doubted there would be any intoxicating scents to tempt her into mutiny during our short sojourn.

After locking the door and pocketing the key, I gestured toward the right. "Lead on McGruff, but don't get too close to the railing."

We walked down the row of apartments toward the back of the property. Although I saw no one, I felt as if someone was watching the progress of our little walk. Unlike most of Honolulu's low-rise apartment houses, the stairs were located in the center of the building, rather than at the end. Approaching the staircase, Miss Una decided she had had enough regimental marching and sat down to peer at the tangled grass and weeds below us.

"Uh, that might seem inviting, but we're not going down

there." She stared at me like I had taken a mouse from her. I joined her on the top step and we sat looking out across the property. I did not know what was on the cat's mind, but I wondered about what would have attracted Ariel's attention. The vibe of the tenants at this apartment complex is young and lively. I could see that Ariel would have enjoyed the overall atmosphere. Maybe she would have ended up dating one of the other students—or one of the young servicemen I have watched playing volleyball. I sighed. There was no point in continuing that line of speculation.

After a few minutes of musing about what would never come to pass, the dampness of the morning's dew crept up from the concrete to give my hips a reminder that swimming or vigorous walking needed to be resumed in my daily routine. Miss Una seemed to agree it was time for action. Without the flutter of bird wings, or even a creeping gecko to greet, she stood up and yowled to announce it was time to get the show back on the road.

Turning around, we bypassed Number B406 and continued on to the small cubicle with its decorative arched cutout at the end of the open space. Like guests in a low-end hotel, tenants were tempted with an ice dispenser (empty) and an old 7Up slider soda machine that stood ready to serve one's beverage needs. Although there were a couple of benches, we had already had our breather, and I thought we should get home so I could prepare for tea time with Miss Wong.

"Well, that's all there is to this storey," I joked to my faithful feline, who seemed inordinately interested in the cutout in the back wall. Pulling gently on her lead, I encouraged Miss Una to leave the empty space and we returned to the apartment. After setting her free, I settled down on the sofa to review my notes on the Makiki neighborhood. The next couple of hours passed without any highlights. Hearing my stomach growl, I realized it was time for lunch. I pulled out the final bowl of my catch-all soup and the last of Keoni's curry. After carefully rinsing the curry sauce from some chicken pieces, I sprinkled them on a plate for Miss Una. Nathan might have grimaced, but I then poured the soup into the curry and heated it in the microwave. I looked over at my darling kitty who seemed quite satisfied with her fare. As I savored the results of my new dish, I determined that curry would become my secret ingredient for brightening any soup I might concoct in the future.

Feeling fortified nutritionally, but uncertain about my meeting with Miss Wong, I decided a short rest was required. Although I usually nap on my sofa, I felt Miss Una and I would rest better in the bedroom of this strange environment. Pulling her catsack next to me, I invited her to curl up for a short summer's nap and we both fell asleep quickly.

I awoke refreshed but alone, as my animal companion had moved elsewhere. Although I had showered in the morning, I washed my face before applying makeup and stood at the closet debating what to wear. Being a mature woman, I felt I should choose something reflective of the rich experiences I have enjoyed as a travel and leisure journalist. One of my better dresses, new patent leather sandals and the Egyptian gold *cartouche* pendant I had already set on top of the dresser should fit the bill for my slightly exaggerated cover story.

Today's tea party was merely a door opener. However, I knew I needed to impress Miss Wong sufficiently to be allowed entry to her inner circle. Perhaps my age alone made her feel as though she had something in common with me. Regardless of what had motivated her to invite me to her home, it was an opportunity to learn what I could about everyone and everything connected to the Makiki Sunset Apartments.

Despite my professional background (and knowledge gained in oral history courses), I was as nervous. It was almost as if I were auditioning to play MC for a travelogue or interviewing for syndication of a column. While an interviewer can try to steer their subject toward or away from topics that might arise, there is no guarantee such efforts will succeed. The only thing I could do was go with the flow. I needed to insure that Miss Wong felt I was interested in whatever she chooses to share with her new tenant, while remaining poised to spring on anything pertinent to Ariel's death.

I left the apartment with sufficient time to check the mail and saunter slowly along the courtyard to arrive promptly at Pearl's door. I was pleased there was a garbage can positioned near the mail boxes to facilitate swift dispatch of undesired junk mail. Today I found a letter addressed to Danielle Roberts in unit B406 who, presumably the previous tenant. This would make a good opening line of conversation about the complex. Had she been a student? Had she lived here very long? Did she have friends who are still tenants here? How far should I push my inquiries and how pertinent would the answers prove to be?

Walking back into the courtyard, I saw a number of young men and women assembling for what looked like a major event. While assorted people pulled lawn chairs from the barbecue area, the volleyball net was being tightened by two guys whose physiques looked like they should be on an Olympic team of some kind. One woman was giving a practice overhand serve, just as Richard Bishop passed the far side of the net. When the ball bounced off his shoulder and out toward me, I bent to pick it up.

"What do you all think you're doing? It's one thing to play volleyball, but those chairs are supposed to be around the tables in the barbecue area," he said with displeasure.

"Ah, come on Richard. Some buddies from our old ship are dropping in. This is the only time we can get together before we put out to sea," moaned a short blonde guy with a dash of freckles across his sunburned nose.

"Yeah, man. Chill out. We'll put everything back. In fact, we're going to be using these chairs in the barbecue area ourselves, aren't we, Vic?" chimed in a tall African American guy I knew to be another tenant.

At that moment, Al came around the corner from the parking lot to the left of Building A. He was carrying a couple of large sacks of groceries and did not look too pleased to see people standing on the path to his apartment.

Without any attempt at politeness, he scowled at Richard and barked, "Hey, what's going on? Are you bothering your aunt's tenants again, Richard? You know what happened the last time you did that."

Richard sent an equally venomous look in Al's direction. Then he turned and stomped off as firmly as one can on uneven grass. I tossed the ball to the girl who had served it, and Al continued on to his door. I watched for a moment as everyone returned to setting up for what looked like a great time for anyone spry enough to play the game or at least enjoy a barbecue.

I would have stayed for the fun and to catch a few names and apartment numbers, but I had my own date with destiny. Despite the delay, I arrived at Pearl Wong's at precisely four o'clock. I checked my elegant Princess Kai`ulani *mu'umu'u* and sandals for any signs of dirt or grass. I was glad to note I was still in pristine condition to play the role of a lady of distinguished background.

Miss Wong opened the doors to her apartment widely. "Come right in, my dear."

She smiled and beckoned me inside, giving no indication that she had observed the altercation in the courtyard. She then indicated a two-tiered stand for me to add my shoes to her considerable collection. "Please be seated wherever you wish, Mrs. Seachrist," said Miss Wong as she closed the doors behind her. She must have included double-paned windows in her remodel because none of the outside noise carried into her living room.

"Please call me Natalie. You know that joke about a bride feeling like her mother-in-law when called by her surname. Bill was actually orphaned as a young boy, but I've always felt that name belonged to *her*."

Gesturing toward a sectional sofa covered in apricot-colored silk, Pearl said she would return in a moment with our refreshments. Nervous about maintaining my cover as a woman of substance, I sat down somewhat stiffly, feeling as if I were in a modeling class for adolescent girls. I faced a large, round coffee table featuring music boxes, crystal paper weights and jade eggs. The entire living and dining space was beautifully appointed with medium-toned rosewood chairs, tables, and a buffet with china cabinet filled with porcelain, silver and jade. Money was clearly not a problem in this household.

Miss Wong returned shortly with a large silver tray with tea service, covered platter, tea cups and dishes in bone china. As she slid the tray onto the already crowded table, I reached forward with the envelope I had been holding.

"Before I forget," I began, "Here's a letter I found in my mail box. It's addressed to Danielle Rogers at unit B406."

"Thank you for bringing it to me. She was a student who completed her master's program this spring. To save errors in postal re-routing, I have been collecting her mail and packages as they arrive. Periodically, I send everything to her."

I quickly absorbed the fact that the prior tenant could not have had anything to do with Ariel's death. "I'm sure Danielle appreciates your doing that. It really simplifies life. I'm having my condo manager do the same thing for me."

She set the letter on the table to her left and passed me a plate, fork and napkin. "Perhaps you would care to pour?" Miss Wong asked, turning the tea tray toward me.

At the moment I was focused on playing detective. Fortunately, I have poured tea in many settings and hoped to look like the world-savvy matron I had dressed to be.

I carefully followed teatime protocol, asking whether she liked sugar, cream, and/or lemon. I was delighted when she said she liked her tea with nothing added to it. After a few opening pleasantries, we settled with napkins and plates of delicious *hors d'oeuvres* balanced on our laps and our cups ready to be raised to our lips politely.

"I am so pleased you could join me today. Although I am happy the Makiki Sunset Apartments is home to many young people, I enjoy sharing a cup of tea with someone of your age and background occasionally. How fortunate for me that circumstances have brought you our way.

"The pleasure is mine, Pearl. I look forward to enjoying a cooler summer than I would have had in Waikīkī. And as I told you, it's so convenient for my volunteering at the educational center down on Wilder."

"Yes. That's what you said when we first visited about the apartment." She paused and set down her teacup. "I realize that by now you may have heard that we had an unfortunate occurrence here before you moved in. I want to assure you that nothing like that has ever happened before, and I'm sure it never would again."

I had not expected her to say anything about Ariel's death. But being a logical and honest business person, she probably felt it was better to say something herself than allow idle gossip to worry a new resident.

"Well, yes. I did hear something. I believe a young woman died in the parking lot?" I queried.

"That is correct. One of our young sailors found her lying on our handyman's car. We are not certain of the circumstances surrounding the girl's demise, but the police are looking into the matter."

"That must have been difficult for...everyone here."

"Indeed. I shall be glad when the mystery of her death is solved, as will my insurance company. More importantly, I can only imagine what her family must be going through. I met her for just a few minutes, but I could tell she was a very positive young woman with a bright future."

I controlled my desire to reveal the truth of being related to the deceased and the reality of why I had come to Makiki. But to do so would have completely undermined my ability to observe the surroundings where Ariel died without alerting anyone to what I was doing. Even if I could not imagine Pearl Wong being involved in Ariel's death, there was no way of knowing who might have been. And since I could not prolong our discussion of the circumstances surrounding my grandniece's death without revealing myself, I simply nodded like the uninvolved bystander I was pretending to be.

"As you might guess, we have seen many things through our decades at these apartments."

"I can only imagine."

"When we are young, it seems that all of life is ahead of us. As the years progress, we don't realize that time has caught up with us and the road ahead is shorter than that behind us. Sometimes when we look back, it is difficult to see how the turns in our journey have brought us to where we are."

"You're so right, Pearl. I may be younger than you, but I can't believe some of what life has brought me." I was tempted to add, "and taken from me."

"Earlier, you expressed interest in learning about the history of our home here in Makiki. The story of these apartments—and even the necklaces my sister Jade and I wear—actually begins in China. You see, it is the parting gifts of our Chinese mother and Hawaiian father that have allowed us to have the living we enjoy." She rubbed the large, silver-edged necklace on her chest as though it were a touchstone for conjuring the presence of the woman she clearly missed.

I nodded enthusiastically. "I assure you I'm truly interested in all of your history...here."

"Then I will start at the beginning. The bounty which has allowed us to have these apartments started with our father, Hiram Wong. He met our mother, Yùyīng Sūn, in Shànghǎi between the two world wars. It was love at first sight. She was the petite, pale and delicate Asian flower, and he the tall, dark and exotic stranger from *Tan Heong Shan* or Sandalwood Mountain, as Hawai`i was known."

She paused for a moment, as though envisioning their meeting. She then poured another round of oolong tea and passed a plate of the best almond cookies I had ever eaten.

"As you may know, the ties between Hawai`i and China are long-standing. Even before the nineteenth century, Hawai`i was a supply point in the fur trade between the American

Northwest and China. The Islands were also the source of sandalwood, which Chinese artisans used extensively in the early Nineteenth Century. You might remember the sandalwood fans offered to guests at high tea at the Moana Hotel in Waikīkī."

"I do recall them. As a little girl, it was thrilling to wear your best *mu`umu`u* and sit on the old fashioned veranda inhaling the scent of your fan while waiting for your server to bring the tea cart to mix your individual blend of teas."

She nodded, her eyes sparkling at my remembered joy.

"Hawai`i was considered to be full of opportunity for enterprising Chinese. Many people do not realize that the Chinese were marginally involved in the start of the Hawaiian sugar industry. Of course, it was the arrival of steam power in the mid-1800s that brought the mass of plantation workers from Canton, now the Guǎngdōng province of China. Once their contracts ended, many returned to China. Others, like our paternal grandfather, stayed and married local women, thereby increasing the cultural mixture of Hawai`i."

I was surprised by the complexity of the history linking Hawai`i and China. "I have many Chinese friends here in the Islands, but I didn't know about all the business connections."

"Oh, yes. The commercial ties between Hawai`i and China were, and are, quite considerable. I do hope you do not mind this bit of cultural history?" she questioned.

It was true that I wanted to get to issues pertinent to today—particularly the death of my grandniece. But I replied quickly to keep her talking, "Oh, no. I have a minor in history and as a journalist I've travelled extensively in Asia."

I took a quick sip of tea and continued my response to her. "Following Deng Xiaoping's reforms of 1978, the U.S. Consulate in Shànghǎi reopened in 1980. I was part of a tour that visited Shànghǎi. It was a last minute add-on to my trip to Hong Kong to begin my career in journalism. It was only a couple of days, but I remember parts of it vividly. I especially enjoyed walking along the waterfront area of the Bund. While time for shopping was limited, we enjoyed listening to the old-timers who had jump-started the renewal of the classic Jazz Bar at the Fairmont Peace Hotel. After that, I went on to Hong Kong, where I was to meet my husband, whose ship was to make a port call. Unfortunately, my Asian sojourn was cut short by his unexpected death."

"Oh, my...I am sorry to learn of your loss. It must still pain you to think of it."

Not wanting her to think too much about my personal tale, I rushed to move her back into her own story telling. "Thank you. It was a long time ago. Despite the outcome of my trip, I recall the excitement of my visits to both cities. Although I was supervised by the government's guides at every step in Shànghǎi, I was delighted to have made the trip. It was fortunate my passport didn't show travel to any country in conflict with China, and that I didn't have to disclose that my husband was a naval officer. During the Cold-War, either of those circumstances could have meant China would have refused to issue me a visa."

Pearl nodded. "Yes, there have been many periods of darkness in the land of our birth."

I hurried to finish the details of that first trip to Asia so we could return to her story. "In contrast to Shànghǎi, I had complete freedom in Hong Kong, which was still under the control of the British. Like any tourist, I could go everywhere and see anything I desired. It was a wonderful experience: the junks floating in Victoria Harbor; the bustling movement of people and the mixture of their languages; the rich fragrance of garlic, ginger and dark soy sauce floating through the marketplaces. My favorite shopping was with the purveyors of jade and gems hidden in ornately-gated shops."

Miss Wong smiled at the recitation of my own vibrant memories. "Yes, Hong Kong is a delight for travelers of every taste. And I am glad that you saw at least a part of Shànghǎi which is where my elder sister Jade and I were born."

I nodded silently, to keep from interrupting her memories.

"I should tell you that what I know of life in Shànghǎi in the nineteen twenties and early thirties is drawn from the stories told by our *amah*, Chú Huā Lee. You see, she raised our mother before caring for Jade and me. Telling the history of China and our family was her way of keeping our parents in our lives."

"I know how important that is," I said, thinking of Ariel and Brianna losing their parents when they were young. Nathan and I had also brought stories from our family history into daily conversations with the twins.

As Pearl moved into the lecturing mode of a teacher, I realized I was hearing the story of her coming to America with her sister Jade. Glancing at the buffet, I saw a picture I knew was of the Wong sisters as young women. Aside from the difference in their height, they looked very similar. Immediately, I knew why Pearl had looked familiar to me the first time we met. Her sister Jade—the mother of Richard Bishop—had been my first-grade teacher at Punahou School!

It was during our stressful second, long-term, visit with Auntie Carrie. Prior to that time, Nathan and I had been inseparable. Even our year in kindergarten had been a shared experience. But when we arrived at Punahou, our parents were informed that in keeping with the latest sociological studies, it would be best for us to be placed in separate classrooms for first grade.

I doubted that our auntie thought very highly of that analysis, but as a single woman and recent hire, she was in no position to rock the school's administration. Nathan did not seem as negatively impacted as me. In fact, I do not think he remembers the name of his teacher that year. But I have had no trouble remembering Jade Wong—primarily because she made a tremendous effort to make me feel comfortable in her classroom. In spite of her kind attention, it was the unhappiest school year of my youth.

The reason I had not made the connection immediately was that Jade would have been single at the time, and would have been formally addressed as "Miss Wong." I loved to collect rocks as a child—everything from the ones I picked up on the ground to gifts I received from those who knew of my fledgling hobby. But the stone I prized above all others was jade. I would have to check my jewelry box at the condo, but I was fairly certain that I still had a small piece of pale green jade Miss Wong had given me at the end of the school year.

She probably thought I was thrilled to be advanced to the second grade. In truth, that was a minor issue for me. I was truly happy because I knew that I would soon be rejoining my mother and father. And, I was fervently hoping that in another school I might be allowed in the same classroom as Nathan.

Biting down on a brittle piece of almond, my attention sharply returned to Pearl's recitation of her family history. It was all the more interesting now that I recalled whispers among classmates and their parents about the mysterious Wong Sisters. I might not have understood what was unique about these women, but Jade Wong was a childhood heroine and anything mysterious about her or Pearl must have been very special.

Hoping to get her tale back on track, I inquired, "Did your father enjoy his sojourn to China?"

A faint smile softened the lines in Pearl's face as her thoughts focused on an unseen distance...

CHAPTER 8

Everything must have its roots,
and the tendrils work quietly underground.
The Tao Te Ching [circa 500 BCE]

As I think about my origins, I realize that I think of myself as being more Chinese than Hawaiian. Perhaps this is understandable since I spent my earliest years in China and am three-quarters Chinese. Also, while Jade and I spent our formidable years in Honolulu, outside of school our home life was conducted under the tutelage of our *amah*, in the style and language of our mother.

"When I consider the journey of my father to meet my mother, it is the life of an American immigrant in reverse. Throughout his own childhood, our father was inspired by the stories he had heard from his father's cronies in Honolulu's Chinatown. For, like many other immigrants, our father's father was a member of a financial and social support group referred to as *huay* or *gōngsī* in Chinese, and *hui* in Hawaiian. Coming from his home province of Guǎngdōng, these men were bonded together by their common cultural history, the *Yue* dialect of Chinese, and often, by membership in the same family.

"Our father was an only child. As a young man, finding success in business was very important to him. When Hiram decided to journey to *Zhōngguó*—or the Central Kingdom, as our mother's homeland was known traditionally, he turned to the members of his father's *hui* for advice and support.

"I am not familiar with his initial days in China, after he

worked his way to Shànghǎi aboard a freighter. But I do know that his father's friends had entrusted him with funds to invest on their behalf. These men knew that to honor his family, Hiram would be prudent in his use of their money."

She paused and again touched her necklace. It was a *yin* symbol of pearlescent white jade framed in silver. We quietly sipped our tea. I looked down at the traditional Asian teacup without a handle. It was old and valuable, with detailed paintings of flowers and vertical Chinese calligraphy in gold. Obviously, financial gain would not be a motive for a member of the Wong family to kill anyone.

Pearl set her cup down gently before continuing. "Although it is an antique, and therefore not accurate in dimensions or current labels, the map hanging above the sofa showcases the major cities of China. Like Hiram's family, our maternal Grandfather came from the Guǎngdōng Province. His name was Sūn Shǔguāng. He was a distant relative of the famous Nationalist and first president of the Republic of China, Sūn Yìxiān, better known in the West as Dr. Sūn Yat-Sen.

"While our Chinese grandfather's family controlled much agricultural land in the countryside, they also had commercial enterprises in the provincial capital of Guangzhou. Being approximately one hundred miles from the coast, it was a far different city than Shànghǎi. And although it had once been the most influential metropolis in the region, Guangzhou had been eclipsed by the thriving port of Shànghǎi long before World War I. Not only did Shànghǎi benefit from commercial contacts throughout the seaports of the world, but it was then the most industrialized city in China.

"By the time our father Hiram met our mother Yùyīng, Grandfather Sūn had become a business visionary and spread his investments to both Shànghǎi and Hong Kong. In his daily operations, he relied greatly on his daughter. This was because he was a widower without sons.

You see, the boy the family had picked to marry Yùyīng had died of dengue fever during the same epidemic that killed our grandmother. Alone and in sorrow, our Grandfather left his home in Guangzho to personally oversee his business interests on the coast.

"To accomplish all that he desired, he needed someone on whom he could trust to deal with European and American clients. Being a gracious woman of good family, with language and cultural training provided by Western missionaries, our mother was a great business asset. When she was not closing deals, Yùyīng went to the horse races, attended high tea in elegant hotels and danced in nightclubs patronized by the powerful international set. While the treaty-port city had an indigenous population measured in millions, a mere sixty thousand, largely Westerners, controlled the city's commercial and social life. With her bobbed hair and lipstick, plus fluency in English and French, Yùyīng was the quintessential modern young woman in the city that was often called the "Paris of the East."

"One Sunday at the Shànghǎi Race Club, Yùyīng bet just enough to blend in with the ever-growing crowd of lovers of equine sport. In a sea of disappointed onlookers, she and my father seemed to be the only ones jubilant at the end of a *tierce* or trifecta race. With the large number of horses entered in the race, their bets on the first three winners paid out at odds of 300 to one. Walking with Hiram to the payout window, she commented that her only regret was that she had wagered so little.

"I remember how popular horse racing was in Hong Kong, although I felt too ignorant to place any kind of a bet," I remarked.

Miss Wong nodded and shifted in her chair. "They congratulated each other on their good luck and parted, saying they looked forward to seeing one another the following week. Life can be so surprising. Later that night, at a dinner club owned by one of Yùyīng's cousins, they saw each other again—across a crowded room, as the song goes. When they met at the race club the next week, neither they nor the horses they chose made as good a showing. Nevertheless, they enjoyed watching all of the day's events together.

"Weeks passed and Hiram and Yùyīng established a regular luncheon date following the races. They also saw each other periodically at the ever-popular polo matches, art and music events, as well as nightclubs like Ciro's and elegant hotels like the Cathay. Even before their professional spheres of work merged, their circles of friends intermingled and their friendship had grown into love. Romance is certainly the key in many people's lives, don't you think?"

I agreed heartily, warming at the thought of my own short, romance-filled marriage and that of my parents which has surely outlasted their lives on earth.

"Our *amah* often said that Father referred to Yùyīng as the most delicate of flowers. Perhaps because her name translated as *Jade Flower*, every Friday he brought her a single blossom of exquisite color and flawless detail: rare exotic orchids from the South of China; camellias of pure red and enrapturing fragrance; roses with deepening wine in their centers—all reminders of the home of his Hawaiian relatives in upcountry Maui.

"As Grandfather Sūn aged, he became even more reliant on his daughter for negotiations with the Westerners who wanted to buy the beauty embodied in China's incomparable silks, jewelry and antique furnishings. While he focused on the flow of goods and currencies, she concentrated on the people who could facilitate the greatest profit. With all the connections she had made, she was able to convince our Grandfather to diversify even further.

"Through introductions facilitated by both his father's *hui* and Yùyīng, our father was invited to a meeting of our grandfather's growing consortium of Chinese and European dealers of art and antiques. The group included Jews who had fled the Russian Revolution. While many were no longer customers for the high-end goods of the Pearl of the Orient Trading Company Limited, they often had attributes that made them important contacts. Several were jewelers or artisans whose masterpieces appealed to the elite of the growing global economy.

Hiram's bi-culturalism fit well with the economic climate emerging in the world. With finesse and cultural sensitivity, he proved himself invaluable in negotiating complicated multi-nation transactions. Soon he fell into partnership with Sūn Shǔguāng and, the rest, we may acknowledge, became history, as the young man from the new world joined the land of his Chinese ancestors."

Again Pearl Wong's story was put on pause. We sipped our tea and daintily ate our cookies like polite ladies of any era. I wondered how I could steer her tale toward the here and now. But recognizing that this was merely the opening of our relationship, I decided to accept the pace of the exotic tale she was sharing.

"Within a few years, our father had amassed considerable wealth and proven his respect for Chinese culture. Consequently, our aging grandfather granted permission for our parents to marry without the customary rituals of proposal and betrothal. The marriage of these lovers in 1925 was a sign of the Shànghǎi modernity in which they lived. Yùyīng may have been disappointed that she had no female relatives to prepare for her wedding. But there was joy in the young bride's heart for not having to follow the tradition of abandoning her own family for that of her groom, since Hiram had no close relatives in China.

Their wedding was a blending of their worlds. Our mother rode to the missionary church ceremony in a silk-draped sedan chair carried by four of their warehousemen. To clear the way through the crowded streets, she was preceded by one escort holding a ritual umbrella and another playing a gong. While she wore a traditional Chinese red silk dress, shoes, and veil, Hiram waited at the altar attired in a charcoal morning coat and pinstriped pants. Unusual for their day, they exchanged vows they had written in both Chinese and English before an audience of her family and their mutual friends. At the ten-course feast celebrating the joining of *yin* and *yang*, Grandfather Sūn gifted the couple with the family compound near the French Concession. He then announced he was immediately returning to his ancestral lands to be with his remaining brother in the latter days of his life."

Periodically I nodded or mumbled "Mmhm," to let Pearl know I was following her story. I *was* fascinated, but feeling the pressure of time at my back.

"Yùyīng and Hiram had decided to delay taking a honeymoon trip until there was an opportunity to visit Hawai`i. After partying with their friends, they returned home to find that the family's servants had followed traditional customs in preparing for the arrival of the newly-weds. In the wee hours of the morning, our parents found the new spring bed in their candle-lit sleeping chamber strewn with red dates, lotus seeds, and pomegranates—all classic Chinese symbols of fertility.

"The marriage of our parents began in a golden age that seemed without end. Despite the turmoil of building a new nation, the Great World War that had ended before the onset of the nineteen twenties was believed to herald an end to all wars. As the Roaring Twenties heated up, the vibrant economy seemed to benefit people of every class and background, especially women, traditionally repressed in much of the world. Flappers, in short hair and skirts, openly used tobacco and liquor, and wildly gyrated in song and dance—proclaiming a freedom for women previously unknown. Even demure women like our mother could enjoy exciting professional, as well as personal, lives."

The diminutive woman then looked directly in my eyes. "I trust you don't mind this old woman's wandering memories and dreams."

While I did want her to bring her story into the present, I was thrilled to learn anything I could about the family that owns the apartment complex. "Oh, no. Being a writer, I've collected stories my whole life. And what is more romantic than a story of both Hawai`i *and* China."

She smiled. "I have some of our mother's belongings in the china cabinet. For many years we did not know we had them. But one day my sister Jade and I discovered some old crates in our attic. Among expected household items, we discovered that Chú Huā had carefully wrapped Yùyīng's silver cigarette holder, an art deco jeweled garter and a beaded headdress. Sometimes, when I feel the absence of our parents, it has been comforting to picture her using them during an exciting night out in the Shànghǎi of the Roaring Twenties.

"Of course, I do not mean to infer that our parents merely lived lives of privilege and pleasure. Our Grandfather Sūn had trusted our parents to run the family's day-to-day business and they did not disappoint him. The Pearl of the Orient soon grew to be known in Hawai`i and across the Pacific to the West Coast of America, as well as in the capitals of Europe that hungered for our unique wares. Beyond the usual carpets, chinaware and rosewood furnishings, the firm offered vintage carvings made of cinnabar from the land of the Mongols in the north and ivory from the southern islands. For their most discerning clients, they also offered an assortment of exquisite jewelry finely crafted in the finest pearls, jade and diamonds."

Perhaps feeling the pulsating excitement of her parents' romantic lives, Miss Wong looked into the distance. Uncertain of her direction, I sat quietly to avoid interrupting her reminiscing.

"Modernization for China was a mixture of progress and challenges. Foreign control of the land through continuance of "unequal" international treaties was still abhorred by Chinese at every economic level. And yet our people had eagerly accepted the paved streets, running water and contemporary plumbing brought by the Westerners. Our own family's burgeoning wealth allowed them to have almost anything they desired. Soon the traditional compound of our home was modernized to afford a quality of life that matched that of the foreign "land renters."

"Around all of this, the changing tides of the young nation swirled. As I have mentioned, there are many links between Hawai'i and China. Dr. Sūn Yat-Sen had attended Honolulu's Iolani and Punahou Schools as a youth. After travelling the world as a young man, he returned to China and joined with other Asian anti-imperialists. From a base of power in Guǎngdōng, he rose with many others overturn the Qing Dynasty in 1912. He then co-founded the Chinese Nationalist Party, the Guómíndǎng, which was once known in the West as the KMT. He then helped establish the democratic Republic of China and became known as the father of the modern Chinese nation."

I nodded my awareness of this part of the Chinese historical timeline.

"Dr. Sūn died in 1925. Leadership of the Guómíndǎng then passed to Generalissimo Jiǎng Jièshí, or Chiang Kai-Shek as you may know him. He soon married a sister of Dr. Sūn's widow."

"How interesting. As a child, I remember the Soong sisters touring America to plea for support of the Republic of China."

Pearl Wong nodded and continued her story. "While uninvolved politically, our father supported Jiǎng's efforts to unify our country under a modern system of government equal to the burgeoning commercial landscape. Of course, business was not the only focus of our parents' lives. Our *amah* often told stories of our father showing our mother off to the moguls of politics as well as commerce. In elegant dining rooms they partook of rice wine or champagne in the thinnest of jade bowls and plates of the smallest and most tantalizing oysters from the waters off Shànghǎi. Afterward, they danced for hours to the pulsating rhythms of the hybrid form of Shànghǎi jazz that raged in places like the Yangtze River Hotel Dance Hall.

"Within a year of their marriage, my elder sister was born. To Father she represented the dawning of a new age. As plum blossoms were one of our mother's favorite flowers, they named their daughter *Méilingyù,* meaning Plum Jade Dawn of the Universe. She was the crowning jewel of this vibrant family in the expanding twentieth century with the delicate skin of our mother and the dancing eyes of our father.

"Our parents then spent most evenings with their treasured daughter and their Sundays shifted from the racetrack to the Nanking Theater, where they watched silent movies from across the globe. One of my favorite pieces of art is the promotional poster in the dining room of one of our father's cherished Chinese movies, *Lustrous Pearls.* It was a slightly risqué romance of 1927, accented with Art Nouveau title cards featuring drawings of semi-nudes. Like the plot of an action film today, clever strategies and daring feats over land and sea highlighted strong women, who save two glorious pearls and a weak hero," she chuckled.

"It's all so exciting, like a mental movie," I said honestly. I only wished there was no need to leave the land of make believe.

"That is how it seems to me—a movie far removed from Jade and me."

Changing tone, she said, "The next part of our story is complex, as familial and global circumstances collided to prevent our parents from living out their lives in China."

Finally, it looked like this tale might be moving closer to the here and now.

"Not all aspects to life in Shànghǎi during the late 1920s were glamorous. Not even the elite could ignore the Green Gang and other criminals who ran opium, heroin, cocaine and salt in and out of China through the city's port. Accordingly, my parents' lifestyle came at a price, as their home was modified with high walls and manned gates. Worst of all, they were always accompanied by bodyguards to protect them from thieves and kidnappers seeking young women to put into prostitution and children for the slave labor market."

I shook my head at the thought of such turbulence in any child's life.

"From the ease and comfort of today, there is no way I can fully describe the growing turmoil in the land of my birth. My few words are a gross oversimplification of the complex political, social and economic issues involved in the high stake chess game in which Jiǎng Jièshí tried to unite the country. When the Generalissimo embarked on his Great Northern Expedition in 1926, our parents avidly followed the National Revolutionary Army's efforts to eradicate warlords backed by the encroaching Japanese Army.

"This was but one aspect of the confusing milieu. Sadly, in 1927, the same year as the release of *Lustrous Pearls*, our city became the springboard for the Generalissimo's purge of communists from the Nationalist Party and all of the government. Known as the Massacre of Shànghǎi, the war between these factions continued until 1949 when the government of the Republic of China was forced to retreat fully to the island of Taiwan.

"As I have said, Generalissimo Jiǎng Jièshí faced many challenges in the years before then. Making the most of his preoccupation with warlords, communists and other internal problems, the Japanese Imperial Army successfully spread their sphere of influence forcing the Nationalist Army to withdraw from Jǐnán in the Shāndōng Province in 1928.

"Fascinating," I responded. "I have never understood how a small country like Japan gained so much control of China and other Asian countries."

"It is amazing. The following year, our family's pathway changed forever. Shortly before the disastrous Stock Market Crash of October 1929, I arrived. With an eye toward the movie celebrating modern womanhood (and the myths of pearls born of moonlight and dragon's breath), I was named *Míngyuèzhū*, or Bright Moon Pearl. Sadly, the birth was long and difficult and Yùyīng's physicians said she must not bear more children. Although Hiram would have loved to have a son to carry his name, he loved our mother too much to endanger her life.

"Celebrating his two priceless daughters, our father commissioned an exquisite piece of jewelry for our mother. The unique design was conceived by a member of the famous Lee family of jade carvers who worked for prominent Hung Chong and Company. The eternal *taijitu* symbol of the balancing of *yin* and *yang* reflects the Shànghǎi deco style. I wear the *yin* half, which represents the moon. It is made of carved white jade framed in silver and features a circle of gold. Jade wears the *yang* half, representing the sun. It is carved in black jade trimmed with gold and features a circle of silver.

"The last tangible reminder of our father's love for the women in his life is the painting you see at the head of the dining table. In the center, our mother is seated on an antique hand-carved dragon's chair in beautiful mahogany. Although Mother sits in front of the entwined bodies of the dragons at the back, you can see pearls in their mouths on the armrests. I am held in her arms while Jade stands regally at her knee as a toddler. At Yùyīng's throat, you can see the beautiful *yin-yang* necklace united in its full beauty, highlighted by the rich blue silk of her traditional *cheongsam* dress. Separate or joined, these necklaces are our greatest treasures—reminders of the deep roots from which we sprang.

"All too soon after this painting was hung in our family's dining room, the lives of everyone in our family and indeed most of the world changed. What many younger Americans forget, is that the Great Depression extended to every corner of the world. Regardless of ethnicity, economic status or age, the life of ease enjoyed by so many in the Roaring Twenties was gone almost overnight."

As Miss Wong continued her tale, I could imagine the impact that decreased wealth had had on her family.

"Within a short span of time, the effects of the Depression, coupled with the efforts to unite a country plagued with antiquated institutions and anarchy helped sink the Chinese Republic's prospects. Living conditions in Shànghǎi worsened for people at every economic level. For us, that meant a shrinking of our world, as building by building and room by room, the need for space in our compound diminished. With less demand for entertaining, the number of people who surrounded us in our daily living decreased as well.

"As the economy contracted, even the presence of our father lessened. Although there was little commerce, he had to work longer hours to close the shops and warehouses of our family's business. Most days, he left home before dawn and seldom returned until we were asleep. Sometimes we heard sounds in the night as he brought home the most precious goods to be tucked into storage or had unmentioned meetings with people of various backgrounds and languages.

"Perhaps unsurprising for those with small children, the misfortune of our family provided unique opportunities for Jade and me. When the adults were too busy to notice our absence, we spent hours in fantasy play among the growing number of boxes and piles of furnishings. There was even a wedding sedan chair that graced an inner courtyard by our favorite fountain—until Jade fell while swinging from one of its long carrying poles.

"Throughout all the change and turmoil, the one constant was Chú Huā Lee. Adding to her care of us, she had to meet the needs of our mother, who now oversaw the maintenance of our home. With few of the rooms remaining in use, our only other staff members were a housekeeper, an old gardener and a pair of young guardsmen who assisted wherever they were needed.

"Mealtimes most reflected the changing economic climate. Unless our father was at home, the entire household ate together in the kitchen. Our dinners usually consisted of a single bowl of rice topped with limp vegetables and small amounts of fowl or pork past its prime. Even when Father was at home, the menu remained simple, but our dinners became festive with his stories of the city and questions of how each of us had passed the day..."

CHAPTER 9

Few people have the imagination for reality.
Johann Wolfgang von Goethe [1749-1832]

To nudge our conversation toward things closer in time and geography, I asked, "How much longer did they live in China?"

"It seems like a lifetime, but it was only a few years. For the Chinese Republic, the effects of the Great Depression went far beyond financial concerns. Coupled with failed efforts to unite a country plagued with antiquated institutions, the economic circumstances helped sink the Chinese Republic's prospects for survival.

"Despite the decline, our family still had considerable wealth. Therefore, our parents had to remain even more vigilant about our security. To avoid attracting attention from the growing hordes of thieves, our Mother put her prized jewels in cases for safekeeping and our parents seldom entertained. While retaining security personnel, Father reduced our domestic staff. Soon the outer buildings in our compound became dark and silent as we seldom ventured into them."

At that moment, our conversation was stopped by Beethoven's *Moonlight Sonata*.

Miss Wong said, "I am so sorry. Let me see if this is an urgent call. Yes?" she answered.

There was silence for a moment, during which I finished one of the chocolate iced petit fours and sipped my tea. When Pearl raised her index finger to indicate she would be more than a moment, I got up and walked toward the dining area. Looking through the glass doors, I realized that the china cabinet was filled with thousands of dollars in precious antiques and furnishings.

"Very well. I will be there shortly." Miss Wong rose and turned toward me. "I regret interrupting our visit, but my sister's caregiver has encountered a family emergency and must leave unexpectedly. My nephew Richard is helping with the catering of an event at Kapi`olani Community College this afternoon, and there is no one but me to take Jade to physical therapy."

"I completely understand. It's fortunate you live close enough to be able to help her," I commented.

"Yes, indeed. She is making great progress since having a stroke last year. She may never walk unaided again, but we are hoping that soon she will be able to personally handle her activities of daily living."

Miss Wong then put her cell phone into its case and picked up her purse. "May I look forward to entertaining you with something stronger than tea next time? Perhaps on Thursday evening or Saturday afternoon?"

"That sounds lovely," I replied. "I thought I had plans for Thursday, but that's changed. It will be fine to reschedule our visit for then. But after that, I would love to entertain *you*."

"Very well. Shall we say Thursday at five?"

"Yes. I look forward to seeing you then and hearing more of your family's story." I answered truthfully, moving toward the entryway to put on my sandals.

Walking back to my temporary home, I felt caught between two worlds. Still immersed in the fragrance of ginger flowers and almond cookies, I had to consciously pull my mind from the Roaring Twenties in Shànghǎi to the many questions I had about this complex, and its residents and visitors. I considered everything I had to accomplish in the next couple of days. In the morning, I had an initial meet-and-greet for the learning center where I would be volunteering. Although I had only obligated myself for a single weekly session, I planned to use my volunteerism as an excuse for wandering in and out of the apartments at any hour.

Once I was free the next afternoon, I would start preparing for cocktails with Pearl. Some of the research could be executed on-line, but other information was only available at the state archives or public library. I might not be able to redirect Pearl's waltz through the decades, but if the opportunity arose, I needed to ask intelligent questions about the property and neighborhood—if not about her family and staff.

Being a new tenant, it was logical for me to research garbage and recycling schedules. I could also call FedEx and UPS about their pickup and delivery routes and times without tipping my hand. And I could conduct Internet searches focused on the address of the complex. Since many government agencies have digitalized their records, I might be able to track the Wong family's real estate transactions including the Makiki Sunset Apartments.

At both the Hawai`i State Archives and Library I would be able to check on a variety of publications. Although only a few may have fully digitalized morgues of past issues, I could check hardcopy of archived newspapers and magazines and even the newsletters of some organizations. All that was required was time and effort.

Moving across the courtyard, I again felt that someone was watching me. The only person I had seen staring at me openly was Richard Bishop. But he did not seem dangerous, just weird. At the moment, I had no apprehension of imminent danger. Maybe my discomfort was simply the fishbowl effect of walking through a volleyball court flanked by two buildings whose open doors and windows could shield anyone who was peering out.

Most of the individuals I have encountered at the complex are like me, walking purposefully from one point to another, apparent residents or their guests. Generally, people nodded and said "Hello." But unless you met someone while getting your mail, doing laundry, or barbecuing, there was not much impetus for engaging someone in prolonged dialogue.

After dragging myself up the unyielding concrete flights of stairs, I entered B406 ready to declare the day complete. I kicked off my shoes and dropped my keys beside my purse on the coffee table. Moving on to the bedroom, I pulled off my go-to-meeting frock and slipped on a favorite shorty *mu'umu'u* from the Hilo Hattie collection. As usual the classic style and print brought a smile to my face. It reminded me of entertainer Clarissa Haili, who had changed her name to Hilo Hattie. She was often compared to Sophie Tucker, with lively audience interaction and jokes that elicited an enthusiastic response from both locals and tourists.

Re-entering the living room, I expected to find Miss Una perched on the back of the sofa or recliner. However, there was no evidence of a feline presence. It was not a good sign when Miss Una fails to meet me on my return from any outing. Continuing toward the dining room and kitchen, I found the object of my quest. Miss Una was sitting on top of the table as regally as a kitten can. She completely ignored me, and continued to look intently out the slider.

"What? No greeting? No demand for a treat or a little supper?"

Finally, her tail thumped the table once and she looked over her shoulder at me.

"You know you're not supposed to be up there. You have a perfectly good kitty perch beside the door."

Silence and a hard stare were all I got in reply. After a pause, she gracefully jumped down and crossed the room to sit in front of her empty dry food bowl. Despite her reproachful look, I glanced out the small window over the sink. I realized that without the interference of the balcony, I would look directly down into the parking lot. From my current vantage point, Al Cooper's slot seemed a bit far to the right for Ariel to have landed on it from this apartment's balcony. I shivered at the image I envisioned, for the precise point from which she fell did not matter in the general scheme of her death.

After feeding Miss Una, I poured a glass of wine and went out onto the *lānai*. So far, I had avoided standing at the railing. But now I walked right up to it and peered straight down. It was clear that where Ariel had landed was definitely to the *right* of the apartment's balcony—*not* directly below it.

With growing apprehension, I thought about what that could mean. Glancing above the immediate scene into the hills, I watched the gathering of dark nimbus storm clouds. I hoped my living room at home would not get too wet if the wind shifted and rain inched in through the tiny gap I had left open. While I could check voicemail messages from anywhere, I realized I would need to go home periodically to check on things—or, ask Anna to monitor my home for me.

After tea with Pearl, I was not really hungry, but knew I would not last the night without eating something solid. The issue was resolved by popping some sweet and sour shrimp and a vegetable stir fry from my favorite deli into the micro-wave to defrost slowly. One day soon I should consider using the gourmet stainless cookware I had received as a wedding gift. Through the years, I never managed to learn how to pre-pare even the simplest dishes I enjoyed in the countries I vis-ited.

I walked into the living room, reflecting on my examina-tion of the balcony. Sitting on the sofa, I turned on my laptop and opened my file on the Makiki Sunset Apartments to note the angle of Unit B406's *lānai* in comparison to handyman Al's parking space.

In my first visit to Pearl Wong's home, I had not learned anything that seemed pertinent to Ariel's death. At any other time, I would have enjoyed the slow stroll through the ear-ly twentieth century. The absence of hard data was an acute pain in both my mind and heart, since it meant I was unable to perform any fact checking. It would be two days before I had another chance to glean anything concrete from her. If only I could determine a strategy for visiting the tenants in every apartment. That however, seemed like wishful thinking.

Hearing the microwave bell ding, I knew it was nearly time to eat. A couple of minutes later, I was considering checking in with Keoni when my phone rang.

"I was just thinking of calling you." I said looking at caller ID.

"Well, great minds and all that," Keoni responded. "How did your day go? Anything special come up when you met with the apartment manager?"

I caught him up on the minor details I had learned during my tea party and relayed my observation about the balcony's position in relation to the space where Ariel had landed.

"That's interesting, because a lot of suicides are almost ritualistic about executing—forgive the verb—their deaths. They leave notes explaining how their lives have become un-bearable. Sometimes, they thoroughly clean their homes and even the site where they're going to do the deed. Depending on their chosen method of self-destruction, they may decide to kill themselves in the nude. In such cases, they can be ob-sessive in folding their clothes and neatly aligning their shoes and accessories, as though they're about to put them back on.

"If Ariel had jumped off the apartment's balcony of her own volition, it probably would have been from somewhere in the middle, not skewed to one side," he continued. "By the way, I don't have any details for you, but Nathan and you will probably be getting a call from the ME's Office sometime soon. I ran into my friend Marty tonight. The one I told you is an assistant coroner. I was having a final meeting with a client at the Beach Bar at the Moana Hotel, when he walked in for a drink with his wife."

I gulped. "Did he reveal anything about Ariel's death?"

"We weren't speaking privately and he can't divulge any-thing that isn't public knowledge. He just announced that the initial autopsy report had been written up, although the com-prehensive toxicology report usually takes a few weeks. With you, as well as her grandfather, being listed as her next of kin,

I know *you'll* be included in the reporting process."

Keoni paused for a moment. "Listen Natalie, I want you to know I'm not withholding any information from you. But I don't want you to get your hopes up about receiving immediate answers to your questions and concerns. With all the testing that comes into play in deaths that aren't attended by a physician, it's probably going to be a couple more weeks before the comprehensive report is finished."

"Mmhm," was all the reply I could muster.

"That's why you've got to be patient and continue to be vigilant about your safety. You should know that if a clear determination of suicide had been made, you'd have received a call saying, 'we regret to inform you that Ariel may have been responsible for her own death.' And if they had found indications of foul play, detectives would have shown up at the apartment for a full-blown investigation. And if it ever comes to *that*, they're going to want to know why *you* are on the premises!"

"I know that, Keoni. And I've been thinking about what I'd say, if it reaches that point. You know I'm going back to Miss Wong's for cocktails. After that I may know a few more specifics about this place and its cast of characters."

"Okay. But keep in touch with me every day. And if you find the smallest reason to be suspicious of anyone, or are nervous about anything, call me immediately. I'm never that far away and I'll have you and Miss Una out of there in a flash."

That was what concerned me. I knew Keoni would do his utmost to safeguard me, but I wanted the freedom to be able to explore the answers to my questions for myself, as well as for Nathan. Nevertheless, I assured Keoni of my continuing adherence to his rules, and we signed off for the night. Next, I checked the voicemail for my land line at the condo and was happy there was nothing that required a response until the next morning.

I set the microwave for one last round of cooking. Two minutes later, I was sitting down with my plate on my lap to watch the evening news while I ate. There was no further information on Ariel's case. Despite the lack of news, I decided to call Nathan. If nothing else, we could compare notes on our preparations for Ariel's memorial service. My primary responsibility was selecting photos to be enlarged, framed and captioned for a display of the key moments in her life. So far, all I had done was bookmark the ones I intended to use.

By discussing this aspect of the memorial, I could push aside the issue of my true location and focus. In order to limit the direction of our discussion, it was best for me to control when and how we spoke. Otherwise, voices or background noise might give away the fact that I was not in my condo.

"Hi, Natalie. You timed your call perfectly. I was video conferencing with Bri."

"How is she doing Nathan?" I responded.

"She's regretting taking summer classes and is so upset that she can barely keep her mind on her end-of-term assignments. She's decided to cancel an additional class she was going to take this summer."

"I think it's good she's had school to occupy her mind—especially since we're not sure when the memorial will be. I...I have a feeling we'll be getting a preliminary call from the ME's office soon."

I did not want to mention that Keoni had tipped me off about the forthcoming call regarding the autopsy. Any further conversation about the topic might have aroused his curiosity about why I was in close touch with Keoni, since he is a retired homicide detective.

Like most of our nightly chats, the pauses between our sentences were pregnant, with undeclared and to-be-continued issues. I got through the call with my emotions intact, but I had barely refrained from revealing what I was doing in Maki-ki. That is the beauty of a telephone; unless you are speaking with the authorities or a computer geek, no one knows your location.

After turning down the bed, I went into the bathroom for

my nightly "beauty" routine. When I came out, Miss Una was waiting for our usual reading session, during which I slipped off to dreamland. After a short while, I awoke short of breath and feeling weighted in my extremities. I glanced around. No cat. That was not unusual since she had taken to nocturnal guard duty at the slider. I sank back on the pillows and tried to recapture the flow of sleep. But it was not to be. Gradually, my breathing slowed and I felt my body becoming lighter.

* * * * *

My vision has returned. The scene is brighter than before. I am exiting a bus on Wilder Avenue. I look left and right, then down at a note scribbled on a white, lined, three-by-five inch card. I look closely. The writing is not mine.

I stare at the hands in front of me. No rings. There is a Hopi silver bracelet on my right wrist. The face of a stainless steel Seiko diving watch on my left is turned to the inside of my wrist to keep it from being smashed. How do I know this? Ariel always wore her watch this way so she did not have to remove it if she had an opportunity for unexpected tennis sets.

Okay. This is a new phenomenon. In this vision, I am not me. I am Ariel. It has been hard enough having visions throughout my life, but now I am personally experiencing the action as one of the people involved in it. The scene around me fades from full color in real time to dull-toned images that reveal themselves in cadenced slow-motion. I am literally of two minds, observing myself thinking and behaving as Ariel.

I float along the sidewalks, looking around as the newcomer to the neighborhood that Ariel will be. I consider the bus routes I'll take to school, for grocery shopping, and to meet friends or Aunt Natalie in Waikīkī. Suddenly, my slow-motion progress up the winding street snaps.

Now in real time and full color, I look at the front of the Maki-ki Sunset Apartments as though for the first time. A sign below the name of the complex announces "Vacancy" in large letters. I walk into the nearest entry to the parking lot. It's nearly empty.

There are two buildings separated by a large patch of scraggly grass. Mid-way, an old volleyball net announces there may be fun-loving residents waiting for a new player. Toward the back, a fierce dragon breathes out a stream of water from the top of a tall, three-tiered, rectangular black granite water fountain.

A fancy door stands out from others on the building to the left. A brass-edged sign with black lettering announces this is the manager's office. Hanging off the bottom is a smaller sign in stenciled aluminum that says Open. *I approach the door and knock.*

A small Asian woman in a long orange and blue mu`umu`u comes out onto the tiny cement slab in front of the apartment. She welcomes me for a scheduled preview of an apartment. Introductions are simple: she's Miss Wong; I'm Ariel Harriman. Reaching back through the doorway, the woman pulls a ring of keys and clipboard from a table just inside the entrance. We walk across the courtyard, chatting about my upcoming year at UH and the many perks I'll enjoy as a tenant in this excellent property.

We arrive at a steep set of stairs at the center of the second building. Miss Wong grabs the railing and begins climbing. She glances over her shoulder occasionally to ensure I'm with her. By the time we reach the top floor, I've learned about the many amenities that come with the apartment: In addition to the volleyball court, there's a patio along the back of the two buildings with hibachis for grilling. Each building has a laundry facility on the ground floor; and, on the top floors there are soda and ice machines.

Miss Wong escorts me to unit B406. We face a door flanked by a narrow strip of louver windows. She inserts a worn brass key in the lock. Although the apartment is about to be painted and cleaned, we take off our shoes before entering. We're standing in a large living room. Along the left wall are three doors. The first is to the master suite, with a bedroom and attached bathroom. Next is a slightly smaller bedroom, followed by a guest bathroom.

Ahead are narrow pillars framing an arched entry to the kitchen and dining area. On each side are cabinets with leaded-glass doors and open shelving above. I can already picture displaying my collectibles. To the right is a space for a dining table, in front of a slider leading to the lānai. To the left is a small kitchen with lots of storage and counters with way cool old black and white tiles.

I look down at my watch and wonder when my friend TJ will arrive. We're both signing the lease, but as the primary tenant, I get to enjoy the master suite. *I try not to laugh. The bedroom's closet is the size of Grandpa Nathan's broom closet. Although the bathroom has a vintage pedestal sink and convenient tub-shower combination, it needs a thorough scrubbing. It's too bad that Auntie Carrie is no longer capable of conversation. I'll have to ask Aunt Natalie about removing rust stains.*

Classic music interrupts Miss Wong's launch into the benefits of the investment she's made to provide her tenants with Wi-Fi and cable connections. She looks at me with a blank stare while she listens to the voice coming through her cell phone. She hangs up and says she has to take care of a family matter.

Yes, I like the unit. Yes, I can finish exploring the complex by myself. Of course, I'll close and lock the door on my way out. Yes, I'll meet her at her apartment when I am through looking over the property. And I'll call my friend TJ to find out when she'll arrive.

Miss Wong departs. I walk through the living, dining and kitchen areas, picturing how I'll arrange the few pieces of furniture that we'll need. I'm only going to be here for a year and since I'll be travelling through Europe after completing a class this summer, I don't need to bother with much more than a bed before the fall. As TJ's only a sophomore, she may decide to get another roommate when I leave after graduation next year.

The refrigerator and cupboard doors are open. The shelf-lining paper looks clean enough, but smells like a combination Korean barbecue restaurant and pizzeria—sure signs there's a healthy—or maybe not-so-healthy—student population on site.

The sliding door to the lānai *is cracked open. I walk out onto the balcony and look down at the parking lot. Although neither TJ nor I have cars, the space will come in handy when our friends come for a volleyball game or barbecue.*

I pull out my smart phone. I text TJ. Twice. No reply.

I walk back through the small apartment and put on my shoes at the front door. I look over the walkway railing and down into the volley ball court. Yeah, that could be a cool way to end a day. No sign of Miss Wong. She must have returned to her apartment.

I call TJ. No response. She calls me back, out of breath. She's sorry she got held up. Her English prof called her in after her exam. Sooo sorry. She'll try to call again before she and her boyfriend Sean board their flight to Hilo. I can fill her in on the apartment later. If I like it, I should sign the lease and offer a deposit. We joke about the lingerie shopping we did in hopes that Sean's ready to pop the big question during their weekend getaway.

Well, I guess I'm on my own. It's awfully hot and I'm thirsty. I might as well get a soda from the refreshment alcove that's next door. That's what it's here for—aside from generating some extra income for Miss Wong. I turn and walk the few steps to the open archway. There's a slight movement to my side and I see the back of a man in a work shirt crouched down beside the soda machine that's pulled out slightly from the wall. He's staring intently at a metal box in front of him. I hope he'll be through fixing the machine in a minute.

Despite the open space, it smells like a sweaty men's locker room. I walk toward the back wall's arched cutout and look down at the parking lot. Turning around, I see the repair man is still working. I guess I won't be able to get a drink. I walk toward the doorway. Suddenly, my vision is blocked. My breath catches and I hear the abrupt cry of a mynah bird.

CHAPTER 10

Put yourself on view. This brings your talents to light.
Balthasar Gracián y Morales [1601-1658]

riel definitely did *not* fall off the *lānai*. Like you said, even if she had wanted to commit suicide, she would *not* have landed where she did—if she went straight over the railing of the balcony of apartment B406. She had to have fallen from that little alcove with the ice and soda machines. I *know* that's where she fell from. While she was waiting for her friend TJ to show up. Pearl Wong had to follow up on a phone call, like she did with me the day I came to look the place over." I paused, if only to catch my breath.

"Hold on, Natalie. What are you saying? It goes way beyond what we discussed last night. How do you know all this? Did something happen after we spoke?" I could tell Keoni was trying to constrain his impatience with the disjointed information I was imparting and the tone of desperation in my voice.

I tried to calm my inner self. Maybe I should not have called him. We did not know each other all that well and I needed to weigh how much of myself to reveal. How much did I want to tell him about my unique ability to ken the shape of a situation before all of the concrete facts are visible to the rest of the world.

"I just know. You have to believe me when I say *I really know something.*"

"I'm not *dis*believing you. But let's pull back and start over."

He paused, more for my benefit than his. "All right, Natalie. It's now seven-thirty a.m., and I'm having my first cup of coffee. Since I finished my last scheduled case last night, I slept in this morning. So, how about you? Have you had your coffee yet? Or anything else?"

"No, I haven't had any coffee, or anything else for that matter. I just wanted to tell you what I've...what I've surmised."

My mind and pulse were racing. What next? I really should not have called him until I had sorted out my last vision and arrived at some plausible reason for my assertions.

"Natalie, are you still there?"

"Uh, yeah. I'm thinking you're right. I need to go make a cup of coffee and think all this through."

"You still haven't told me what *all this* is. You know, I'm suddenly remembering something about your brother Nathan. You know what they called him, in his department and mine? Nate the Gate. It was like he could enter some gateway to the minds of some of the worst offenders. That didn't always bode well for the system. Sometimes he came up with scenarios that allowed the bad guys to get off with a visit to a cushy facility for reconditioning their thought processes, rather than the sentence in the slammer we thought their actions deserved."

Silence. I had nothing to say. I knew what Keoni was talking about. Both Nathan's uncanny ability to nose out the truth, and his desire for fairness to all concerned, have brought consternation to both his family and colleagues through the years.

"You're twins, right?"

"Mmhm." He could find that much out on his own.

"So, uh, do you two have that twin bond I've read about? That ability to communicate with each other on a different wave length than the rest of us?"

Another pregnant pause. I was not sure if I liked where this one-sided conversation was going, but it sure saved me from having to fully explain myself.

"I'll take the silence to be a 'yes.' And what about everything you've been telling me this morning? You said nothing happened during the night, and you've barely started your day."

"Mmm. Well, I didn't say *nothing* happened last night."

"Okay. So *something* happened that gave you all this information."

"Sort of." I was squirming at the thought of having to explain my visions. It had been a long time since I had told anyone about my unusual viewing of life's unfolding moments. Until recently, I could always share my concerns about my visions with Nathan. And nothing had occurred since my return to the Islands that required me to reveal myself to anyone else.

"Look, I'm here for you, Natalie. I've told you that. There's not much I haven't seen, heard of or read about that's going to shock me. Am I right, it's one of those *kenning* things the Irish talk about?"

I was impressed. He knew the word *kenning*. Maybe this time, revealing myself was going to be a lot easier than it had been earlier in my life.

"I guess you've caught me. Yeah, it's that 'kenning thing.' I've had visions since Nathan and I were kids. Most of them have to do with him or others in our family. Every once in a while, it's something else, but not often."

"So, you had a vision about Ariel's death last night?"

"Yes. And it's not the only one I've had."

That was it. The dam burst, and I could not stop myself. I told him about all three of the visions I had experienced, each with increasing detail—especially the last one, in which I literally experienced the review of apartment B406 *as* Ariel. It had revealed the initials, 'TJ,' of the friend who was to be her roommate and confirmed that I was right about Ariel *not* falling off the apartment's balcony in some crazed suicide.

Although I was sure it was a lot for him to absorb, he did not interrupt with words of doubt, and even made reassuring sounds of support in all the right places.

"You've really been through the ringer. No wonder you wanted to move into that apartment. And you've been bottling all this up, without sharing with anyone. You're smoother than most of the undercover cops I've worked with."

From that point, we tried to steer the conversation back into the calmer waters of "normalcy" in our relationship. Except for the minor detail that we would never be able to go back to the polite banter that two people can enter into when they only know each other casually. We finished our call by agreeing he would come over for a round of "housewarming" cocktails and *pūpūs* that afternoon.

I put down the phone in a slight daze. I felt more grounded than I did most times after a vision, but there was still that gap between what I envisioned and the concrete world around me. Hearing Keoni's support and his acceptance of my "gift" had definitely helped my self-esteem and confidence that I was not crazy.

While the vision provided confirmation of my analysis of the physical space from which Ariel fell, it was only a start. I needed to know the autopsy results. Thank goodness I would now be able to share both my real-time analysis and vision-driven speculations with someone like Keoni who would bring decades of professional experience to the examination table!

It was nearing two weeks since Ariel's death. I could not sit on my hands waiting for the call from the ME's office to come through. It would have been logical to discuss Ariel's friends with Nathan—especially the mysterious "TJ" whom I had never heard mentioned. Beyond that general level of inquiry, it was almost time to engage Nathan in a serious contemplation of several key questions. *Why did Ariel die? Had someone intended to harm Ariel?* If so, *Who might have taken action to harm her?*

Despite my immersion in the world of detection, it was my first day in the volunteer tutoring program so I could not pursue my personal inquiries immediately. In addition to being a cause I care about deeply, my volunteering was part of my cover while living in Makiki. Gladly, no one at the apartments needed to know that I would not actually be tutoring until the second summer session. That left me plenty of time for my real job of sleuthing.

"Sorry, Miss Una, it's another day on your own," I apologized while checking her food and water. Getting ready was a cinch, since I did not have to impress anyone with my sense of style today. I looked at the stove's clock and was glad I did not have far to go for the morning's briefing.

In spite of my late start, I arrived on time for the opening salvo of volunteer recruit training. Having been fortunate in my own education, I looked forward to being a one-on-one tutor for young adults who had missed their chance to graduate with their high school class, or were foreign students preparing to enter classes in the fall.

Since I have tutored in literacy and college prep programs before, there was nothing stressful in my readying myself for this round. However, every organization has its standards and teaching materials, and I wanted to perform at my best, despite my personal tragedy. I had resisted the opportunity to participate in both summer sessions, knowing I needed to be available for anything that might come up with regard to Ariel's case. Nevertheless, I was glad to set aside my nagging doubts about my darling grandniece and concentrate on other people's challenges for a couple of hours. By morning's end, we had heard an opening lecture, received our initial assignments, and had a half-hour of team building.

Fortified with orange passion-juice, tuna cone *sushi*, and miniature shrimp egg rolls, I was ready to face my real work of the day. I debated whether to pursue fresh topics at the archives or continue going through latter-day newspapers at the library. After completing my journey downtown, I opted for the peace and quiet afforded by the archives.

After stowing my personal belongings in a locker, I pulled out a chair at one of the old library tables and set up my laptop to review my files of sparse notes. I had gleaned the names of a few residents during my days at the apartment. But my list of potential questions was longer than the list of people with whom I might familiarize myself.

With trepidation, I opened my file on Ariel's death. The first major question was still *Why? Why* did Ariel die? In my own mind at least, there were many reasons why her death could not have been a suicide. First, she was approaching the final year of her bachelor's degree and was anticipating a fabulous month of travel with her sister and friends. In addition, the girl was not into drugs, had a great relationship with her former boyfriend from high school, did not gamble, and had a good source of income from the trust fund set up by her parents.

Being an amateur athlete, she was in great physical condition and should have been able to handle most situations that might have endangered her. So, how had she come to take a fall from the low-rise building in the first place? One resulting in her death? I knew it was not a question of the *height* from which Ariel fell, but rather the *way* in which she had landed that had proven fatal. After repeating these facts for the umpteenth time, I remained unable to see a clear direction for my inquiries. Unless the Medical Examiner found some unexpected pathology in the autopsy, her death seemed linked to the apartments and the people inhabiting it on that particular day.

But at the moment I had so little data there was not much point in dwelling on the *whys* or *hows* of her death. Turning to the file I had on the Makiki Sunset Apartments, I looked at the single page of facts and issues I had noted. In the middle was a question regarding shifts in ownership of the property and buildings. With leasehold lands in Hawai`i, ownership of a building and its land can be two separate issues. But how relevant would such minutia be?

Since I was not in the right place for checking land transactions, I next opened my file on the apartment complex's cast of characters. Where should I focus my attention? Should it be the few people I could identify at this point? Beyond the handful of tenants I have met, and Al Cooper, there is the family that owns and manages the apartments.

While I did not think either of the elderly Wong sisters

had a direct hand in Ariel's death, I was intrigued by the setup at the complex. This was a family of obvious wealth. Yet they chose to live in a small apartment complex in an area of Honolulu that also features high-end condos and, moving uphill, streets with exclusive homes.

Even when the economy is slow, the land is worth a lot of money. With all the art and other valuables I had seen in Pearl's home, it did not appear there was any need for either of the women to live on the premises of such a mediocre property. In fact, why was Pearl continuing to work at all? Why not move in with her sister and hire a real estate management company? Or let nephew Richard and handyman Al duke it out until they arrived at a peaceful compromise in handling the women's property?

I recalled that Pearl had remarked that everything about their lives in Makiki had begun with the *gifts of her mother—* or *both* of her parents? If the comment about the gifting was true, it was logical to look into her parents' lives. I could do a cursory search here in the archives, and later pursue anything I learned at cocktails with Pearl. And if I had complete names, I could follow up with an on-line search of Federal immigration records.

After reviewing the few notes I had entered after the tea party, I roughed out a family tree. At the top was the sisters' father, Hiram Wong. If he had been successful in China, he would have returned to Hawai'i a prosperous man. Beside him I placed the girls' mother, Yùyīng. Married to a U.S. citizen, she still would have been an immigrant. With two growing daughters and a husband who may have entered a new career, would she have continued working outside the home?

The answer to that question might determine whether I would find any mention of her in the archive's commercial records. Many Chinese women were successful entrepreneurs with or without a husband as a partner. If Yùyīng had chosen to remain out of the workforce, she might appear in the ample society pages of newspapers of the early and mid-twentieth century—most of which would be next door at the library.

While I was at the archives, I wanted to check the finding aids that might pinpoint where I could obtain data on the couple. In terms of a timeline, Pearl's recitation of her parents' early marriage had not moved beyond the Roaring Twenties. I figured they had to have come to Hawai`i sometime between the Depression and the onset of World War Two. But even when I allowed for variations in the spelling of their names, the archives failed to reveal references to either Hiram or Yùyīng. That brought an end to that line of research, and it was getting a bit late to hop next door.

That is the beauty of having multiple research projects. When you hit a stumbling block with one, you can turn to the next topic under consideration. I suppose that is also how the police conduct their investigations; when they cannot pursue one line of inquiry with a witness, they move on to one that might reveal some pertinent facts. Unless I stretched my list to include Al and Richard, I had no witnesses to interview other than Pearl. If I was lucky, I might have further information on the Wong family and their tenants by the next night. Therefore, I decided to shift directions and examine issues pertinent to my work for Keoni.

Families can be fickle. There was no telling what might prove impressive to his relatives...impressive enough to forego selling, much less demolishing, their home. Many of the historic bungalows have already given way to McMansions across the island of O`ahu. I truly appreciated Keoni's desire to honor his past, but so far I had found his forebears unremarkable.

I decided to move on to considering two other threads of research during the last century. The first was general Island history. The second focused on special events in Kaimukī. What I learned in this double-pronged effort would provide a backdrop for the family's genealogy.

After checking my notes, I followed Henry's suggestions like a recipe card. There were almost too many private and public collections of historical material dealing with the Hawaiian Kingdom and the U.S. Territory of Hawai`i. Newspaper columns carrying detailed accounts of social history tended to highlight the arts and non-profit fundraising events.

Even coverage of the cycles of life was limited to those who were wealthy or notorious enough to warrant ink and newsprint. Neither category of newsmakers seemed relevant to my project. Many of the roots of Keoni's family lay in the laboring classes of Portugal and England. The Hawaiian side of his family was of the commoner class.

During a water break I thought about how quickly I was able to delve into a project that did not arouse any emotional involvement. The sheer escapism had propelled me through the unending announcements of births, marriages, deaths and high teas—not to mention the oceanic arrivals and departures of the rich and infamous. I had also found interesting items in the reports of the Portuguese social club in which his family had been active in the nineteenth century. But there was little to change the thinking of his twenty-first century relatives.

Next I examined the neighborhood surrounding the family home. The hot and dry climate of Kaimukī featured thorny *kiawe* trees and rocky red soil in contrast to the classic picture of tropical Hawai`i. Until paved roads were put in, it was hardly an inviting scene for picnicking ladies in long lacy dresses... or men needing to commute into the city for work. Another necessity was a reliable source of water. That problem was solved with the building of a reservoir to meet the demands of neighborhood stores, churches and schools, as well as homes. The outward migration from the city was also encouraged in unusual ways, including a cash award of fifty dollars for each child born in the area.

Once there was easy transit for both carriages and cars, middle-class families began moving out to Kaimukī. The Hewitt family bungalow was built in one of the first large subdivisions of *high class* homes beyond Honolulu proper. I already knew there was no need to research ownership of the house or the land on which it sat. Throughout the last hundred years, one or another of Keoni's relatives had owned the property. His grandmother had been the last long-term resident. Her grandfather had built the home...or rather he had hired Lewers and Cooke to build it for him.

I began my consideration of the house by reviewing the photos and slim amount of information Keoni had given me. Next I examined old newspaper advertisements for the prefabricated kits that had been the basis for building the bungalow. I soon confirmed that neither the land nor the house was remarkable. Clearly, it would be the people who had wandered in and out through the years who might have made the property worth saving. That meant I was looking for people and circumstances sufficiently noteworthy to appear in recorded history.

I tried to think of distinctive features and events that had taken place on the east side of O`ahu in my next round of research. Despite my limited knowledge of Hawaiian history, I did not think that the Hewitt house was located on Pu`u o Kaimukī. This had been the site of the lookout post of King Kamehameha I, who remained diligent about potential threats from off-island. Nonetheless, I cruised through articles from *The Daily Hawaiian Herald* and predecessors of modern newspapers. I found no pertinent mention of Telegraph Hill, as it had become known by the end of the nineteenth century.

Hitting a dead end with that line of inquiry, I turned to articles about the finely attired notables of Hawaiian society. But the gala events at which they were featured were located in the center of town. I found little coverage of popular newsmakers trekking out to the hinterlands—except for special occasions in their summer homes in the cool valley of Nu`uanu, and later, around Kailua beach on the windward side of the island.

I discussed my research strategy with Henry during one of my stops at the front desk to rotate microfilm and books.

"I think you're right, Natalie. The key to your search will be people, rather than everyday life or commerce in the neighborhood. And you'll want to remember that people are driven by the same issues a detective follows in a murder investigation—motive, means and opportunity."

My eyes must have bulged in response to that quip, because he stared intently at my face for a moment before shrugging.

"You know? Like, *why* would someone of prominence go out to Kaimukī in those days? It had to be an occasion of importance for them to bother going there—and for the media to cover the event. It would be logical to assume the occasion was a one-time occurrence. But it could have been a repetitious activity that was deemed newsworthy."

I nodded to cover my surprise at his comparison to things murderous—and to keep him articulating issues I should be considering.

"I don't know if it will help in your project, but there's one event that was pertinent to the movement away from town. You might not have realized its importance since it wasn't prominent in either advertisements or contemporary analysis of the migration. You remember the horrific Chinatown fire of 1900? Well, it forced a lot of people to start looking outside the city for places to live. In turn, that helped the developers of Kaimukī increase sales of both property and homes."

"Thanks for pointing that out. You're right about my missing that issue during my cruise through the papers."

"Don't fault yourself. That's where PhD dissertations come in handy—finding someone else who has already explored the topic. But if you lack the basic facts, you won't know the right search terms to employ in either hardcopy or electronic research."

Henry continued to offer subjects for me to consider. "I think you'll want to consider the question of *how* the high and mighty got out there. There were still a lot of horse-drawn vehicles at the turn of the century, but only a few automobiles. When you consider that the extension of the streetcar line from Kapahulu to Koko Head Avenue wasn't completed until

1903, you realize that only people with individual transportation could consider moving to the area prior to that time."

"Henry, where would I be without your thumbnail sketches of days long gone?"

"You know my specialty is the Hawaiian language, but there are many days when I don't get an opportunity to delve into that category of my knowledge at all."

"I am aware of your specialization. But there has been more than one occasion, when your general knowledge has saved me from making a fool of myself in my reporting."

"Well, I appreciate your caring enough to ask in-depth questions. I just wish we had more conscientious writers and reporters."

I laughed, "Well, I guess we've had enough of this week's meeting of the Honolulu Mutual Admiration Society. But please let me know if you can remember anything else of significance on the early 1900s chronometer."

"Hmm. The only other event I connect with Kaimukī at that time would be the 1910 passing of Haley's Comet. The best viewing was at the observatory of the old College of Hawai`i up on Ocean View Drive. There were people from every walk of life and every social and economic stratum enjoying *that* event."

Again, in my judgment there was little likelihood that a convergence of Keoni's relatives and the viewing of the comet would appear on the same historical page. Even if they had been part of a front page story, I doubted that the passing of a comet would influence the family to keep their home.

Oh, well. Another day for researching both of my projects would arrive soon enough. I could no longer delay in calling Nathan. The wounds from which we were both suffering were still raw and unlikely to improve in the near future. But if we were to learn the *how* and *why* of Ariel's death, some tough questions had to be examined. Unfortunately, I was the designated inquisitor for that day.

CHAPTER 11

...at my back I always hear Time's winged chariot
hurrying near.
Andrew Marvell [1621-1678]

Walking to the bus stop, I thought of the evening ahead. Maybe Keoni and I should expand the cocktail hour to include a round of volleyball. Or, a couple of steaks barbecued on the hibachis out back, to justify our personal tour of the grounds. Since there was no convenient grocery store on my way home from downtown, I gave Keoni a quick call. He answered on the second ring.

"Hi. It's Natalie. I see you *are* readily available."

He laughed in that warm baritone voice and I found myself thinking of his strength of both body and spirit. It was a nice departure from my preoccupation with death's unpleasantries.

"I told you I'd wrapped up that last case on my calendar. With our getting together later today, I decided I'd tend to the neglected home fires of my own abode for a few hours. What's up?"

"I was thinking that since you're my *dear friend*, maybe we should expand our plans to include dinner, so you can join me in a comprehensive tour of the grounds of my new home."

"Sounds good to me. Is there anything I can bring?" he queried.

"I think I can handle the bread and wine department. My rice steamer's always at the ready. I've also got the makings for a salad. There's no grocery on my bus route home and I was wondering if you could bring some meat for the famous hibachis out back."

"No problem. I'll also bring supplies for making a good hot fire, assuming the grills are usable. I hope you have a frying pan as a backup?"

"Yes. You could be right about the gap between the promises of the amenities and the reality. The ice machine in my building has a fading sign that reads, "Soon to be replenished.""

He snorted at the image. "Well, it looks like we've got the menu covered. What time do you want me to arrive?"

"Umm. That's a good question. I really need to have a serious conversation with Nathan and broach the issue of Natalie's friends—especially the previously unknown TJ. Why don't we say around seven?"

We were signing off when my bus pulled up. Since it was before rush hour, I was able to get a seat in the back where I had the peace I needed to prepare for my conversation with Nathan. It was clear that neither of us wanted to burden the other with the pain we were experiencing. Each of us was barely squeezing through the *have-tos* of each passing day. In my case, I have the added burden of avoiding telling him I am playing detective at the scene of Ariel's death.

Despite the depth of my somber thoughts (or maybe because of them), I arrived at the bus stop nearest the apartment in a short period of time. Walking up the hill, I again glanced into the cemetery. Nathan and I had decided Ariel would not want to be in such a place. She loved wandering in nature, especially near or in the waters off the windward side of the island. Therefore, we had decided to scatter her ashes at sea. By the time I spoke with him, Nathan should have called the Kailua paddling club in which she and Brianna had been members during their high school years. We were hoping the club would help with the ocean-side memorial service.

I arrived at my temporary home to find Miss Una again poised to spring into action from the dinette table. I walked over and tried to discipline her. She graced me with a brief look and returned to an intent consideration of the panorama of the parking lot below her and the streets of homes stretching *mauka*, into the hillside. I opened the door fully to let in the island breezes.

"We've had this conversation several times now. You never do this at home, our real home, that is. What's so important that you have to get up on the table?"

I glanced out hoping to find something relevant Ariel's death, but I did not see anything of note. The only person I saw was Richard, who did not appear to be doing anything threatening. Since he was grumbling as he removed a large brown paper bag from Pearl's truck, he must have been running an errand for one or both of the Wong sisters.

I turned and walked into the bathroom with thoughts of the upcoming evening. Twenty minutes later, I re-entered the living room, renewed from a shower, fresh clothes, repaired hair and makeup, and a splash of sweet *pīkake* perfume. I hoped Keoni was not allergic to floral scents.

After checking voicemail for both my cell and condo phones, I sent a couple of emails to free my schedule for the foreseeable future. Finally, after delaying as long as possible, I positioned a pad of lined paper before me and pushed number one on speed dial. No pickup.

"Hi, Nathan. It's Natalie. Are you home? I thought you'd be there. I should remember this is voicemail, not an answering machine, so you aren't hearing me. Call me whenever you get this message."

I had turned to prepping for dinner with Keoni, when my phone rang.

"I saw it was you on caller ID, Natalie. But I was on the phone with HPD Lieutenant John Dias and didn't want to interrupt his train of thought. He called to tell me the initial autopsy has been completed. Because of my professional background, we've been invited to meet with Dr. Martin Soli. He's an assistant coroner I've dealt with in the past. After that, the Lieutenant would like to go over some aspects of Ariel's case."

This was the call we had been waiting for, but it still made me ill. I choked back a wave of nausea working its way to my throat. With a death by falling, I was glad that today's investigative procedures did not require us to make a visual identification of Ariel's body. Since I was not up to a prolonged conversation, I refrained from mentioning that I knew who Dr. Soli was.

In a hoarse voice, I simply replied, "I see...when will this take place?"

"He was trying to be accommodating, since I would need to call you. However, he asked if tomorrow was possible."

"My schedule's pretty free tomorrow, Nathan. When were you thinking of going?"

"I set a tentative appointment for eleven in the morning, so we'd have time to connect after the morning rush."

For a moment I panicked. I needed to forestall his offering to pick me up, since I did not want him coming to Makiki. "Eleven's fine. But you won't need to get me. I'm...I'm doing some work for Keoni Hewitt. Do you remember him? He's a retired HPD detective. He's actually John Dias's former partner. He and I are...having coffee early in the morning, and I can have him drive me out to the medical examiner's office. By the way, he's also a friend of Dr. Soli's."

"I think I do remember Keoni, and it would be good if he can take you, Natalie. That way I can keep an early morning appointment with Evelyn and Jim Souza to finish planning the food for Ariel's Life Celebration.

"Okay, Nathan. The ME's office is still out on Iwilei Road, right?"

"Yes. With Keoni being a former cop, I'm sure he knows the way."

"All too well, I'm sure." We were silent for a moment. Then I terminated our conversation, saying I needed to take an incoming call. I had meant to ask him about Ariel's friend TJ, but since we were meeting in the morning, I would ask him then.

At the moment, I needed to finalize everything for my evening with Keoni. Not knowing how things might progress, I checked to be sure I had two bottles of chilled wine. Next, I brought out sourdough rolls and butter. Then I layered fresh spinach from a friend's garden with Maui onions and baby yellow tomatoes in a large salad bowl.

I polished the table and set out a runner, wine glasses, dishes and flatware. Then I added the butter dish to the bottle of reduced-sodium soy sauce and salt and pepper grinders that were always on a lazy-Susan on the table. I would not start the rice until we were ready to cook the meat.

What was next? Miss Una's dinner. Looking at the empty cat perch by the back door, I realized she had left for parts unknown a while earlier, even though it was time for her to eat. I took out one of her favorite delicacies and banged a fork against the can to announce her meal was served. No response. No rubbing of soft fur along my hem line; no applauding meow for my choice of entrée. Where was she? I walked past her usual spots for relaxation and glanced into the guest bedroom. Not a hair in sight. Turning into my bedroom, I found no evidence of her.

I was starting to get concerned. Could she have gotten out? The security rod was still in the *lānai* door and the window screens seemed tightly secured. I peeked in the shower and under my bed. What was left? Seeing the door to the closet slightly open, I pulled the door toward me and glanced in. No sign of her up on the shelf; no tail dangling over my shoes. In the back was my square straw laundry hamper. Sure enough, from the back right corner a mottled black, brown and gray paw stretched out, beckoning to me.

I pulled the hamper forward. "You scared me. One minute you're up where you're not supposed to be, and the next, you've disappeared. What are you doing now? I know I need to do laundry, but you're never taken such an interest in domesticity before."

She rose slowly and stretched, emphasizing her disinterest in clarifying her actions. "Go on, your dinner's waiting.

And you'd better be a good girl tonight. Keoni's coming and I can't be worrying about what *you're* up to."

Bending down to re-position the hamper, I noticed a patch of the wall that seemed to pop out from the surrounding surfaces. The entire unit had been cleaned and painted before I moved in, but a two-foot square of the wall seemed raised and marred beyond the usual wear and tear you would expect in an old apartment building. But when I knocked on it, I found the wall solid, with no hollow sound to indicate anyone had hidden the family jewels or anything else within it.

While I was closing the closet, I heard a knock at the front door. I shook my hair into place, smoothed my hot pink silk Chinese tunic and went out to the living room. Glancing toward the kitchen, I was pleased Miss Una was busily nibbling her supper.

I opened the door widely to greet my first official company. "*E komo mai*. I don't know how refreshed you'll feel after going up and down the stairs to cook our dinner, but I promise a couple of cooling drinks and later, some macadamia nuts covered in succulent dark chocolate."

Keoni dropped a blue carryall bag inside the door. Turning back, he gave me a quick peck on the cheek and handed me a plastic grocery bag. Clearly appraising my casual elegance— at least that was the look I desired—he said, "Who needs dinner with a promise of such a dessert? Not knowing the size of the hibachis, I settled on a couple of thick boneless rib-eyes."

I inhaled his Cool Water cologne and hoped he liked the *pīkake* fragrance I had dabbed strategically. "Perfect. I'm making great strides in the detecting department. I recently found the broiler pan for the oven, so I'll season the meat and let it rest while we have a drink."

"Great." Turning back to his bag at the door, he said, "I didn't want to put you to too much trouble making cocktails, so unless you've mixed margaritas or some other decadent drink special, I thought I'd contribute a jar of my home-brewed cinnamon sun tea."

"Thanks." I said as we moved toward the kitchen. "I've been meaning to stock some soda and beer, but I haven't gotten around to it. Aside from iced tea, what are your non-alcoholic favorites?"

"I pretty much stick with iced tea. I love the way a few local restaurants still put a strip of pineapple core in it. I'm not a big soda drinker—too many when I was a kid. But I do enjoy a glass of root beer occasionally—with or without a scoop of vanilla ice cream."

I filled a tall glass with ice for him. He poured his drink and passed me the jar.

"Why don't you sit down in the living room and I'll join you in a minute." He settled into the recliner, while I seasoned the meat and set it aside. I didn't want to spoil our dinner with a heavy *pūpū*, but after pouring myself a glass of Pinot Grigio, I picked up two small bowls of Maui potato chips and put everything on a tray.

"So what's on tonight's agenda," questioned Keoni.

"Well, Miss Una might like it to include laundry, but I thought we'd saunter around the grounds going to and from the hibachis. That way it'll look like there's a plausible reason for my giving you the grand tour."

"That's logical. Too bad we can't bring out the notepads and measuring tapes. But you're fortunate to have the benefit of my keen investigator's memory."

We laughed and toasted the evening's forthcoming adventure. Assuming drinking alcohol on the grounds of the apartment was permitted I grabbed a tray for our drinks and the meat and clicked on the rice steamer. Keoni picked up his sack and opened the door. We chatted about the balmy weather while walking down the stairs and to the back of the property. We set everything down on a picnic table near the hibachis and Keoni began unloading his tools.

I was relieved to see how organized he was. "Great. You brought a steel brush, pair of tongs and *kiawe* twigs. Barbecue is definitely a category of supplies I forgot about when packing for this move."

Keoni shook his head. "The means for executing good barbecue is something a true man of the Islands is seldom without—plus a supply of beer and a macho vehicle."

"Well, you certainly have the latter," I remarked, sipping my wine.

"I will confess to the vehicle with pride. These days, certainly while the sun is overhead, it's more often tea for me than beer, but I sure enjoy the brews I *do* drink," he said.

He then began pulling the grill apart and building a fire with a small pile of the wood twigs.

Even on a small task like this, his well-defined musculature and skillful hands were inviting. "You've dropped a few pounds. Giving up a few bottles of beer must be doing you some good."

"That's one benefit. The big motivator was realizing what drinking has done to some of my buddies over the years. When JD, John Dias, nearly died after a perp high on drugs and booze nearly separated his head from his neck, I decided there was a lot to be said for sobriety, on and off the job."

"I think we're both at that point in life where some tough choices have to be made. With all the walking up and down the stairs here, my hip is sending SOS messages that I need to get back to some regular laps in the pool. But that'll have to wait until I get home."

"Give me a call any time you want a ride to Ala Moana Beach Park. I used to enjoy a quick dip there before going on night shift. Now about this grill. Is there a hose somewhere to give it a quick scrub?" he asked.

I spoke softly, not knowing if there might be someone behind me. "Good idea, on a couple of fronts. It gives us an excuse for that tour we were talking about."

We looked around, and since there was no hose bib nearby, we walked over to Building B's laundry room. Despite the fresh breeze blowing through the open door and windows, the smell of soap, bleach and fabric softener left no doubt about where we were. No one was in the room at the moment, but one of the washers was chugging away and two of the dryers were vigorously spinning.

Like every apartment in the complex, the laundry facility was long and narrow. With windows on three sides and overhead fluorescent lighting, we had no trouble seeing the layout of the space. Keoni dropped the grill in the sink, and began opening the drawers to the left and the cabinet below. Finding a bottle of liquid dish washing soap, he smiled and said, "This should do the job. I think we'll let it soak for a bit while we take a look around."

On that note, we turned to three large double-doored closets on the right side of the room, across from the laundry equipment. The first looked recently vacated and the second was filled with floor-cleaning equipment and supplies. Behind the door of the third, we were greeted with what seemed to be a catchall for items accumulated over the last several decades. There were shelves with worn dish towels, sheets and tablecloths, dusty picnic hampers and tangled strands of Christmas lights. At the back were assorted pieces of outdoor furniture, battered suitcases and two chest-high stacks of cardboard boxes that were sloppily closed.

I struggled to reach one of the boxes at the top. "I can't seem to open this flap," I said, disappointed to have to ask for help.

"I'll get it. Just stand at the closet door with one of those towels? In case anyone comes in."

"Okay," I replied, scooping up a couple of stained red and white linen towels that had clearly known a better era.

While I watched the laundry room for activity, Keoni systematically, but rapidly, took inventory of the boxes. After several minutes, it was clear he had found nothing relevant.

"Some of the walls seem worn, but they're all constructed of uniform cement block. There's no telling what this space might have been used for in the past, but I don't see anything that relates to our investigation."

We walked out of the closet and looked at two single doors at the back of the opposite wall. Opening the first, we found a long narrow space without shelving that appeared to be another miscellaneous junk storage room. We each pawed through a stack of wooden boxes clearly dating to an earlier age in Dole Pineapple's packaging. Moving on, we found the second door locked.

"I guess that's it for this area. I'll try to find out what's behind door five when I get around to doing some laundry, which needs to be sooner than later for several reasons." I said.

We returned to the sink, where Keoni rinsed off the grill and wiped it with one of the towels I had appropriated.

"If worse comes to worst, and we really need to get in there, I have a little tool to lighten the task. But based on what we've seen so far, it's probably more of the owner's junk. Unless you find it wide open, just leave it alone until something suspicious materializes around here."

"OK. If there is something related to Ariel's death on these premises, we don't know what it is or where it might be located. There's no attic access in my apartment, there are no storage units for the tenants, and we've found nothing here. Cement block walls aren't easy to open up, but they're easier than a cement slab floor. And from what I've seen, I doubt that I'll be prying up any sagging floor boards. Except for the bamboo in Pearl Wong's renovated apartment, I doubt there's any wood flooring or paneling in the entire complex."

"Good. I don't want to worry about you doing any breaking and entering any time soon."

"I assure you that's not on my to-do list. Although I've met a few of the tenants, I haven't seen or heard anything noteworthy. I don't know enough yet to recognize a clue if I found one."

Keoni shook his head and patted my shoulder while we laughed heartily at that reality. I felt myself begin to blush and turned to walk back to the barbecue area. The fire in the hibachi looked fairly hot, so Keoni re-assembled the grill, seemingly unaware of my momentary discomfort.

"Natalie, it looks like we forgot one thing. Since the steaks are thick, why don't we pop them on the grill and go back to the apartment for a platter to put them on when they're cooked. And while we're up there, let's take a quick look at that refreshment alcove you've been telling me about."

We then positioned the steaks, gathered up Keoni's barbecue supplies, and began walking back toward Building B. We were no longer alone in the courtyard. Proudly sporting U.S. Navy ball caps, a pair of young guys I had seen before were engaged in a fearsome one-on-one volleyball challenge. Not wanting to interrupt, I simply waved and Keoni nodded as we continued on to the stairs.

Keoni dropped his bag inside the apartment's door. Knowing our meat might be getting overcooked, we hurried next door for a quick look at the alcove with the drink machine and empty ice dispenser.

"I haven't seen a soda machine like this since I was a kid," commented Keoni.

"And the ice dispenser isn't much newer. I'm lucky the washers and dryers are new enough to handle lingerie," I said.

Keoni gave me a wide grin in response to that comment. After glancing around at the barren space, he walked down to the cutout in the back wall that overlooked the parking space where Ariel had fallen to her death. After a couple of minutes, he turned and walked back toward me.

"Like the rest of the complex, this space looks worn but pristine—evidence-wise. But that doesn't mean that a closer examination with luminol wouldn't reveal something. And you're right about the angle from here to the parking space where Ariel landed. But until the ME comes up with something solid, I don't think HPD will be sending out a team of CS investigators."

CHAPTER 12

I not only use all the brains I have, but all I can borrow.
Woodrow Wilson [1856-1924]

Don't judge my barbecuing ability by tonight's steaks. After our little errands, they may be cooked far beyond medium." Keoni said while we paused at apartment B406's door.

"With the number of items on tonight's schedule, I think we should count our blessings if they're not charcoal," I replied, smiling.

I dashed inside and returned to hand Keoni a clean platter. As he ran downstairs to get the steaks, I went inside to uncork the wine. When he arrived a few minutes later, I had tossed the salad with my favorite Caesar dressing, spooned the rice into a serving bowl and sliced fresh sour dough bread. As he set the platter on the table, we looked at the crispy exterior of our *entrée*. We laughed as he pointed out that we would *not* be having medium-rare steaks that evening.

While he went to wash his hands, I prepared a special treat for Miss Una. Although she is usually satisfied with her organic designer canned cat food, I knew the aroma of steak would draw her like iron filings to a magnet, so I opened a pouch of tuna fillet. She certainly is spoiled. I seldom eat that well myself. As I had hoped, the scent of quality fish caught her attention and she made a bee-line to her plate as we approached the table for our own delectable meal.

Keoni politely pulled out my chair and I mentally observed there was something to be said for men of a certain age. He then poured us each a glass of Black Box Cabernet Sauvignon and lifted his glass for a toast. "Here's to friendship in pursuit of truth."

"Indeed," I responded and lit the spice scented candle I had brought from home. "And what about truth in friendship?"

"Amen to that," he said, again lifting his glass. "That's one quality I've found lacking in a lot of relationships—whatever their basis."

We smiled in mutual recognition of the depth of those words and began passing dishes of food.

"Mmm. Regardless of the degree of doneness, this is great meat," I said truthfully.

"Kūka`iau Ranch. The healthiest cattle in the country. Their secret is the air, water, and grassland of the Big Island. No grain feed for that herd."

"I'll remember that next Christmas when I need a prime rib roast." The reality of the purpose for our evening hit me: Never again would Ariel join a family holiday celebration—at least not physically.

I quietly sipped my wine and we continued eating. I doubted that Keoni had noticed the change in atmosphere, but I resolved to halt any negativity on my part and make the most of the occasion. It was what Ariel would have insisted upon, aspiring match-maker that she had been. I could almost hear her mirthful laughter and see her teasing eyes in the darkening room.

The weather was delightful that night and I was glad I had opened the slider fully. And aside from the parking lot, the view was beautiful, with passing clouds sweeping across the sky at twilight. Although we had known each other casually for several years, Keoni and I seemed to be moving closer on several levels. Without the encumbrance of superficial words, a rich unspoken dialogue was taking place between us. Smiling as our eyes met over the candle, I felt certain that in other circumstances, our evening would have proceeded quite differently.

"How about a little of that dessert I promised you? Not too filling, but definitely decadent?"

"I seldom say 'No' to a beautiful woman, and I'm certainly not going to start now," Keoni responded.

I could feel my face flushing again and covered my unexpected pleasure by picking up a couple of dishes. Although the evening was balmy, I was not prepared to spend a prolonged amount of time on the balcony. I suggested Keoni finish his wine in the living room while I got our dessert. Ever the polite gentleman, he carried an armful of dishes over to the sink before moving back to the wingback chair. Entering the living room a couple of minutes later, I saw Miss Una had arrived to claim his lap.

"I see you've about finished your wine. Can I tempt you with a little peach brandy? I promise it's a great compliment to the dark chocolate-covered macadamia nuts."

"Only a sip. A glass and a half of wine is already over my usual quota."

I set down my tray on the coffee table and poured a finger of brandy into a small snifter. Passing him the glass, I returned to the table and placed one piece of candy on a dessert plate.

"I may have said just a sip of brandy, but are you going to limit my intake of candy, too?" asked Keoni.

"Well, I don't want you to totally blow your diet," I teased.

"Natalie, with the chips, steak, and bread, I think that's already a non-issue tonight. However, I doubt you've been eating wildly lately, so let's enjoy ourselves without any guilt."

I took in that remark in more than one way before handing him the plate of chocolates.

"Now, don't get too carried away. You have to help me eat a few of these."

"Oh, I assure you I will." I was thinking it would give me an excuse to get up and move over to him periodically.

For a few moments we concentrated on savoring the great blend of flavors.

"Mmm. Maybe one more sip of brandy," Keoni requested.

I was only too happy to oblige him, but I did not want to be responsible for him breaking his vow to cut back on alcohol.

I left the bottle on the small table beside him and reached above him to pet Miss Una, who was now seated on the chair back. She looked at my hand like it was an affront to feline tidiness, and immediately set about licking her fur back into place.

"You seem to have made a friend for life," I commented while reaching for another piece of candy.

"I hope I've made two" he said smiling at me as Miss Una staked her claim by pawing Keoni's shoulder.

"*We're* already supposed to be friends, but I don't know if Miss Una will be willing to share," I chuckled, returning to the sofa to look at them both over my glass of brandy.

Somehow, I managed not to blush at this bit of *repartee*, but I definitely felt my spirits lift. "I have a few notes I thought I'd review with you, in preparation for my next meeting with Pearl Wong."

"Good idea. Read away." Settling in, Keoni steadied the cat and slid the chair back into a three-quarter recline.

Munching my last macadamia nut, I opened a spiral note-book and shared a summary of what I had learned during my short residency at the Makiki Sunset Apartments. First I went through the schedules of mail and shipping deliveries. I had found that all of them were completed by noon, unless there was a special delivery of some kind. Next, I provided an over-view of the tenants I had met on my walkabouts and recapped the little I knew about the Wong sisters. Finally, I turned to their extended family.

"Jade's son is Richard. With the name *Bishop*, Richard's fa-ther could have been a high profile lawyer, minister or busi-nessman—or a major landholder—like other bearers of the eighteenth-century missionary name."

Keoni quickly quipped, "Or an insignificant and wholly-unrelated person."

"That's true. As to the familial dynamics, I've never seen

anything warm and fuzzy between Richard and his aunt Pearl. And I think I've told you that he doesn't look like either of the Wong sisters, so I doubt the man is biologically related to Jade. But if I learn his father's full name tomorrow evening, I can prowl through newspaper announcements of engagements and weddings to see if he was married to someone before Jade."

Keoni nodded. "That's a good strategy. I doubt that searching the Web for 'Richard Bishop' would yield much by itself. But with his father's middle name—let alone verifying who his mother is, or was—you might trace him through birth records."

"You're right. And even if he isn't related to the Wong family, there might be adoption records or other information that is relevant."

I paused to think about the members of the Wong family I had met. "Well, except for the unknown details of their wealth, that takes care of the family that owns the apartments. I'm still wondering if there might be anything unusual about the complex itself? I guess I can run a quick check of title records to see if anything odd pops up."

"It may be the cop in me, but I think it's more important to check for media accounts of crimes that may have occurred here or any that involved the complex's residents. There's also the civil side of the law. You might look into whether there have been any lawsuits brought against the current or previous owners."

I busily wrote notes on the issues Keoni had raised. "I think I should have called you before starting this project."

"You see what materializes when you're forthright about things?"

"Well, I couldn't be sure how things would develop between us."

"You mean by trusting me enough to give me the full story?" Keoni asked.

"Well, it would have meant divulging details of my life that

I'm seldom prepared to share with anyone."

"Natalie, we've known each other for quite a few years. And we've been friends for more than four. In that time you should have realized you could be straight with me."

"I'm sorry...Few people understand how it is with my "gift." I thought your work with the law would have made you suspicious of anything you can't see and measure."

"Where have you been the last twenty years? Haven't you noticed all the reports on government agencies working with psychics on a daily basis? Sure there are nuts and quacks out there, but I've seldom known a cop who's going to say 'no' to any kind of help, especially if it's offered free of charge."

I sighed and looked into his eyes. "I'm not a psychic. Not anything like that. I just have dreams and visions sometimes."

He laughed and replied, "From my perspective, it looks like these visions of yours can be damned on-target. I'm open to hearing more about them, any time you'd like to share. Right now I'm contemplating how we might confirm some of what you've seen. Even if the information doesn't seem concrete, it could be your *interpretation* that needs deeper examination. For now, let's consider the elements of your next round of research."

I nodded, trying to keep the tension I felt from showing in my face.

"Is there anyone else you've run into who's worthy of a little attention from some of my 'official' connections?"

"In terms of the management, there's *one* non-family member we could look into. Al Cooper, the owner of the Mustang, on which Ariel...you know. Since he seems settled in his position of resident handyman, I doubt that he's a newcomer to Honolulu. But if he's not a known criminal, I don't know how easy it would be to check on him."

"Mmm. His surname's pretty common, which could be a problem without a middle name or initial. But I think I know someone who can get a line on him through his vehicle registration. And *I* can look into whether he's repaying a loan on the Mustang."

"Of course. I remember his talking about that man-toy of his the first time I came here. He said he was getting ready for some kind of auto event at the Ala Moana Shopping Center scheduled for the night Ariel died. He must belong to a classic car club. If it's big enough to hold events at a shopping center, I can check the newspapers for contact persons."

"Good thinking. But before you get carried away and buy one of those vintage babies, why don't you let me run that end of things past a few of my buddies who are noted for collecting more than guns. Also, I know you haven't been here very long, but have you seen or heard about any patterns of activity relating to Fridays? Like regular pharmacy or grocery deliveries being made to the same tenant? Maybe a delivery person being overly interested in some aspect of life in the complex or making repeated visits to someone unrelated to their job?"

"I've looked into everything I can, Keoni. Except for the mail, UPS and FedEx, the only other consistent interaction with a service provider is the Department of Environmental Services—That's garbage and recycling to the layman. They come on Tuesdays and Thursdays. Unfortunately, I haven't found anything that occurs on a regular basis on Fridays... the day Ariel died. Aside from the small number of delivery people, there are the tenants to consider. The only thing I can tell you about them is that their movements are erratic. Like you'd expect, students and military personnel come and go at all hours.

"As to the military guys and gals who live here, their schedules fall into three categories. Those stationed here on O`ahu are usually on pretty rigid timetables, with pre-dawn departures and late afternoon returns. The second group is virtually invisible, because those people are deployed and therefore gone from here for months at a time. Our third group comes from the Navy...personnel stationed on ships that remain pier-side most of the time, but pull in and out of the harbor sporadically. Of course, there are the buddies who visit with no discernible pattern.

"I haven't seen any other recognizable patterns of movement. I've even checked to see if anyone—military or civilian—has moved in or out since Ariel's death. No one has left. A couple of people, like me, have moved in."

"It must be the magnetism of that great volleyball court. Or maybe the exotic allure of the dragon fountain."

"Now just a minute. Outside of the stash of valuable antiques and furnishings in Pearl Wong's apartment, that fountain is one of the best features in this place."

I scratched a few more lines in my notebook. Miss Una then decided it was time for a change in venue. Jumping down from her perch above Keoni, she cocked her head at us and sidled up to the slider, like she does in the condo.

"I guess the honeymoon is over," observed Keoni. "It looks like your roommate is getting bored."

"Some girls just don't know a good thing when it's right in front of them," I said, standing up. "Thanks for helping me brain storm. I think I've got several ideas for making the most of my upcoming cocktail hour with Pearl Wong. Let's take a break. May I offer you something else to drink, maybe some iced tea?"

As Keoni stood at the door, the cat rubbed seductively around his ankles. "Sure," he replied to me, bending down to Miss Una. "So, you think you need to go out? Do you promise to be a good girl?"

She batted her amber eyes, reeling in her conquest. Keoni obliged and picked her up.

"I've got her securely in my arms, she won't be jumping anywhere," he assured me.

I juggled our glasses into one hand and opened the door. Keoni stepped out. Without any urging, Miss Una sprang up to Keoni's right shoulder and wrapped her tail around his neck.

"Thanks for the tea," he said, reaching for the glass I offered.

With Keoni by my side, I felt secure on the balcony for the

first time. It felt so normal, standing close together, appreciating the lights of the distant hillside homes and beauty of the starlit sky overhead.

"Are there any *pīkake* vines around here?" Keoni asked breathing in deeply.

"I cannot tell a lie. It's my perfume.'

"Hmm. Combined with the scent of the brandy and the *plumeria* trees, it's quite an aromatic summer's eve."

Enjoying his presence as well as the night air, we stood there a while looking at clouds that periodically swept across to mask the twinkling stars peeking out above the foothills. Momentarily I felt both peaceful and anticipatory. But when Al Cooper's rent-a-wreck pulled into his parking slot, I plummeted back into reality.

Getting out of the car, he banged his door shut and shouted words that carried up to us in the clear night air. "Bitch, bitch, bitch. That's all that old woman does. How about *my* feelings? Not a moment to myself since that little dyke ruined everything by dying on my car. Think they're real funny, those lipstick lezzies. All dolled up and shakin' their booty at normal guys. It's disgusting, that's what it is. And what's a guy supposed to do? A woman like that doesn't deserve the life God gave her."

Stunned, I looked up at Keoni who shook his head, indicating we should remain still and silent. Cooper then opened the rear passenger's door and brought out a couple of paper bags. After bumping that door closed with his hip, he turned and walked into the courtyard, trumpeting "Depraved. That's what they are, depraved."

After a moment, my dinner companion steadied Miss Una's hindquarters with his right hand, and put his left arm snuggly around my waist. I was too choked up to speak as we re-entered the apartment. He then released his comforting hold on me and dropped the cat onto her perch by the door.

Unable to process what I had just overheard, I cleaned the kitchen like an automaton. I began by rinsing the glasses and setting them on the counter. I then opened a lower cupboard door and pulled out the garbage can. After scraping and rinsing our dinner plates, I stacked them in the dishwasher. Eventually there was nothing more to be done. I sighed and tried to sweep away the mist clouding my eyes.

Throughout my pantomime, Keoni had stood behind me in silent support. Slowly, he turned me to him and lifted my chin with a crooked forefinger. Before he could speak, I erupted.

"I don't understand anything we just heard, Keoni. He sounded more like Richard Bishop. I get that his precious car was ruined, but clearly he doesn't care that a person has died. And what did he say about Ariel? And what did he mean, when he called her a 'dyke?' Not that I would have loved her any less if she had been gay, but *what* could have given him the idea that she was a lesbian?"

"I don't know, Natalie. From the pictures I've seen, it wasn't her hair, clothes or jewelry. I don't know what else a person would notice about someone when seeing them for the first time.

"Well, if they actually met, I can't imagine any kind of conversation they could have had that would lead him to such a conclusion. And why would a potential tenant being gay matter to a handyman. Do you think that a complex like this has never had a gay person living or visiting here before?"

I nodded my head in agreement. Keoni then poured some water into one of the brandy snifters, took me gently by the hand and escorted me into the living room. Setting the glass down on the coffee table, he pulled me onto the sofa. Sitting beside me, he handed me the glass and nodded for me to take a sip.

"Natalie. I know you're upset. I agree with your response. But let's carefully review what we've overheard.

"One, Al, the ever-present handyman, is extremely angry. Two, he thinks Ariel was gay. Three, from his tone and vocabulary, it's a safe bet he hates gays. Although it may seem unlikely he would have consciously ruined his precious Mustang,

I can easily count on one hand the number of perps who have worked against their best interests in the crimes they commit. One thing's clear, that man's venomous words make him a person of interest."

I drank some water and tried to slow my breathing. "Speaking of evidence, I haven't had a chance to mention that tomorrow is the day Nathan and I are meeting with officialdom. Shortly before you arrived, he called to tell me we're going to see both Marty Soli and your old partner Lieutenant Dias at the ME's office late tomorrow morning. I didn't mean to delay in telling you. But we got so busy with dinner and the tour and all that it slipped my mind."

Keoni nodded. "I knew you'd be hearing from the ME's Office. I wonder what the initial findings are? And what JD's has been looking into?"

I disliked imposing on his schedule too much, but wanted his support in getting through the appointments. "Do you have anything planned for tomorrow?" I asked quietly.

"No, Natalie. As I told you, I just finished the only job I had on the books." He paused for a moment. "Would you like me to go with you to see Marty and JD?"

Relieved, I answered immediately. "Yes, very much! With everything he's facing, I haven't told Nathan about...my little project here. It would be beneficial to have you at the appointments, since you know both the assistant coroner and the detective who's in charge of Ariel's case. Even with Nathan's professional background, I know he'd appreciate your experience in dealing with whatever might come up."

"You know I'm glad to help. What time shall I pick you up?"

"Nathan's set up an appointment for eleven to meet with Marty. Why don't you pick me up at about ten fifteen?"

"Fine. Now if you think you're okay for the night, I'd probably better hit the road."

I nodded and rose to walk him to the door. Keoni stepped into his sandals and turned to look at me deeply. We moved closer together and he reached forward to pull me toward him. He gave me a prolonged hug and brushed my hair from my face. Bending his head he gently placed his lips on mine. After kissing me tenderly, he stepped back and squeezed my hands firmly before picking up his bag and opening the door to leave. I closed the door behind him and leaned against it. At any other time...

A tragi-comedy. That was what my life felt like: weeping one moment; becoming flighty like a teenage girl on her first date the next; delving into exotic Asian history, while examining the preservation of a humble abode in suburbia. All of this bound together by the entangling threads of Ariel's horrific death!

CHAPTER 13

Love is not in our choice but in our fate.
John Dryden [1631-1700]

S avoring that kiss, I walked through the apartment, tidying sofa cushions and straightening things that were already in their right places—doing anything to avoid going to bed alone. Well, not quite alone. Miss Una was there to assure me I was loved. The night air was refreshing with both a slight breeze and hint of flowers, so I left the back door open a crack, hoping there would be no "second-storey men" poised to climb over the balcony.

I then turned off most of the lights and went into the bathroom to prepare for bed. Slipping on a plain cotton nightgown, I thought about upgrading my lingerie wardrobe. Tonight had marked the beginning of a major shift in my relationship with Keoni. I felt awakened on every plane and was looking forward to seeing him the next morning, even if it was for the unwelcome trip to the Coroner's Office.

I wondered how Ariel would feel about being the impetus for my developing a romantic relationship with Keoni. Knowing her ironic sense of humor—sometimes bordering on the macabre—she would probably find it appropriate, if not downright complimentary to her passing. I tried to muster a smile at that thought, but the death of anyone Ariel's age causes a thinking person to examine their own life seriously.

I might have predicted that I would dream deeply after a good meal, wine and stimulating companionship. I had not thought about my husband, Bill Seachrist, for a while. But with our friends arriving for activities related to RIMPAC and my conversation with Pearl Wong, my memories of the unrealized holiday we were to have had in Hong Kong had been reawakened.

I have heard that in the relaxed state between waking and sleeping, we can be receptive to the thoughts of those who have passed from this plane. As I fell asleep contemplating my short marriage, I may have inadvertently opened a pathway to the other side of the *veil*, as some call it. As always, it seemed strange that I had *not* had a vision of my husband's impending death, no inkling that our pier-side kiss would be the last time I would see him.

*   *   *   *   *

I dreamt my way through the night, alternating between re-experiencing and analyzing that life-altering period. Throughout our five years together, we were full of the promise of youth, especially in the romantic moments of that final cool February morning before my tall, dark and handsome warrior departed on what was to have been a six-month voyage.

Bill and I had just moved to the Island of O'ahu. We had leased a small one-bedroom condo in Waikīkī, envisioning honeymoon-style living during the few months of the year we would both be there. He was a lieutenant in the U.S. Navy; assigned as a communications officer aboard a tender—a repair ship sent abroad to replace the bits and pieces that were in disrepair or had gone missing from other vessels.

It is the early a.m. when we have our last intimate good-bye, bouncing over a briefcase, two suitcases and a duffle bag, to land once again in our bed's tangled sheets. Were it not for that last early morning delight, I might not have paid much attention to any of his baggage. It was not like this was his first tour at sea in our marriage. But thinking in the present as I experienced the past, I realize how strange it is that with all the changes in military uniforms and other paraphernalia, the lowly duffle bag has seen little modification.

Too soon, it is time for Bill to catch a ride to Pearl Harbor. He and shipmate Dan O'Hara were going in to stow their belongings and get organized for the ship's departure on a cruise across the western Pacific Ocean. As he kisses me, we confirm that I will arrive at the harbor at a tolerable hour in his beloved 1977 MG B roadster with a V8 engine—MG being Morris Garages to the true aficionado.

In my dream, I continue to luxuriate in the bed so recently warmed by our love. I am excited to contemplate my own career opportunities. With a major in journalism and a minor in history, my compound BA will allow me to have it all—long before the term "yuppie" is popularized. I savor the thought of my upcoming launch into journalism through a series of articles for a new travelogue magazine being marketed to military families.

As I dream, I remember my younger self contemplating flying over the seas my husband's ship floats upon. Following a slow saunter across the Pacific, his ship is due to arrive in Hong Kong for a unique cultural exchange. There, the lucky few wives and girlfriends who can afford the time and money will greet their men pier-side, as water taxis bring them in from the ship lying at anchor in the outer harbor.

At the agreed time, I walk to the bottom of the gangway of Bill's ship. He walks jauntily down to greet me and we walk along the pier toward the back of the ship, where there are less people to view our farewell. Even though I know I am revisiting a time in my distant past, our last moments seem very real...with his breath on my neck and his hand firmly holding my waist.

The noise of heavy equipment fills the air as civilian and U.S. Navy personnel load the supplies needed for the next several months. The smells of fresh maritime paint, aging metal, and brackish water again fill my nostrils. Bill is so vibrant, so handsome, even in his khaki work uniform. He looks down at me with a small smile. "See you in Hong Kong, darling. Don't miss me too much. This is the start of our great adventure."

He steps in front of me and turns. Pressing the small of my back into his hips, he gives me one last passionate kiss. Then he is gone, moving up the gangway, already concentrating on the duties of the day ahead of him. He turns and we wave before moving on to what we each need to do. Even in sleep, I feel myself nod and my throat tighten. Again I pull the light cashmere sweater I am wearing tighter as I walk toward the car. I struggle to open my left hand which has been grasping the car keys so tightly that I have lost circulation. Seated behind the wheel, I open my bag for a tissue to wipe my eyes and nose.

Peacefully I lie in my bed dreaming of that past time of sorrow. I remember many things. After the togetherness Bill and I enjoyed during his previous shore duty, I had dreaded facing mealtimes alone during this cruise.

Standing by myself I watch another family say their farewells. Even at a distance, I can tell the man is a senior officer. His wife wears a nondescript coatdress that seems better suited to San Francisco than Honolulu. I speculate that the strand of pearls at her throat is cultured and that she has a pair of white gloves in her undoubtedly shipshape handbag.

To her left, two small children stand with upright posture. The girl wears a classic blue and white sailor dress, frilly white ankle socks in black patent leather Mary Janes, and a round straw hat. Next to her, a small boy stands at attention in another interpretation of a naval uniform. As though triggered by a bosun's pipe, the woman shakes hands with the officer, now facing her in regimental stance. Stepping to the left, he then exchanges a salute with the girl.

I watch the man proceed with his troop inspection. I remember wondering if he even notices the wavering hand of the little boy who is obviously new to this bit of familial pomp and circumstance. Finally, the man fiddles with the boy's backpack and straightens his hat. After delivering another formal salute to his family, he pivots sharply on his heel and moves up the brow without a backward look. Within a few minutes I pull out of my parking space and join the line of cars exiting the naval base.

Moving between dream and remembrance, I smile at the pleasure I feel at joining Dan O'Hara's wife Margie at Coco's

Coffee House for breakfast. We are meeting to plan how we will cope with being "grass widows," something Army wives were called in the nineteenth century when their husbands were sent on patrol into the American West. I watch as the two of us devour a breakfast of fluffy Belgian waffles with strawberries, crispy bacon and Kona coffee—something even national restaurant chains offer in the Islands. To work off the calories we have consumed, we enjoy a day of power shopping, as we prepare for our upcoming trip abroad. By the time I return to the Waikīkī condo, I am not hungry for dinner and fall asleep quickly.

After the first few days of withdrawal from Bill, life resumes. My mind's eye watches the "me" of yesterday research places I will visit on the initial part of my journey. I also spend time shaping the sparsely furnished apartment into a cozy home... or at least a luxurious hotel suite into which Bill and I will drop between sojourns near and far.

In addition to finalizing my travel itinerary, I am preparing to welcome my twin Nathan and his family to Honolulu. Having completed a PhD in clinical psychology, he has just accepted a job with the State of Hawai`i. I am glad his family will not have to worry about housing in the perennially high-priced local real estate market, since he and I inherited our parents' home in Kāne`ohe. Given Bill's short-term assignments, I doubt we will be in any place long enough to put down roots, so I have told Nathan and his Sandy to enjoy the house for as long as they wish.

Time flies quickly in my nocturnal reminiscing. Soon it is the day of my departure on what was to have been the most joyous trip of a lifetime. I flash through images of our group of women enjoying typical tourist attractions in Australia and New Zealand. Then, as the rest of the party moves on to Hong Kong, I take a side trip to Shànghǎi.

Although the People's Republic of China has not been opened to the West officially, Vice Premier Dèng Xiǎo Ping has instituted policies to modernize his country's economy and pro-

mote tourism. Since journalists are still restricted in their access to the country, I join a small number of visitors sampling tourist offerings in Shànghăi. From the airport to the hotel and every shop, market and restaurant, the moments of our short trip are orchestrated and supervised by our Chinese "minders." Nevertheless, I happily soak up the local culture, knowing it will provide background material for my article on the pleasures of vacationing in the British Crown Colony of Hong Kong.

I arrive in Hong Kong a week ahead of the expected arrival of Bill's ship despite of my stopover in Shànghăi. The raging Cold War necessitates keeping the times of U.S. naval ship departures and arrivals secret. The few days of independent adventures do not bother the women who await their husbands and lovers. If nothing else, the silks, fragrances, and jewelry they purchase will enhance the exotic tone of their romantic reunions.

Following a delay in my flight, I arrive at my hotel later than expected. And when I find there has been a mix up on the sea view room I booked, I switch hotels. Due to the late hour, I do not notify the rest of my travel group. The next morning I embark on a day of sightseeing in Kowloon to get a head start on the research I need to do. Later, I will appreciate the time I have taken to prepare an annotated list of pictures for the publication's photographer to shoot to accompany my pithy text.

At day's end I return to my hotel tired but thrilled at the progress of my first professional assignment. Rather than calling Margie to arrange an adventurous night out, I soak for a long time in a hot bubble bath and enjoy a bottle of wine and a sandwich in my room. I finish the evening by savoring the dazzling view of the city's harbor lights while sipping the last of my wine.

Sighing, I recall the pleasant dream I enjoy that night, watching my parents putter in the garden they nurtured at their home in Kāne`ohe. How appropriate, I thought at the time. Here I am in Hong Kong, ready to rejoin the love of my life, and Mom and Dad have dropped in to add the blessing of their love to my experience of a romantic land of enchantment.

After a light breakfast of fresh oolong tea, oranges and an English muffin the next morning, I call the hotel where the other women were staying. Even within my dream, I hear the voice of the desk clerk become tense at the utterance of my name.

"Mrs. Seachrist? You are Mrs. William Seachrist?"

"Yes, I am."

"I see. The other ladies in your party have been looking for you. Let me look for the message they have left for you."

"All right." I could not imagine what could be so important that anyone was looking for me.

"Ah, yes. Mrs. Seachrist, I have been asked to inquire as to which hotel you have moved."

I answer him and dictate a carefree message for Margie.

Watching the next scenes from the perspective of my twenty-first century self, I again hear the tinny ring of the hotel room phone. I pick up the receiver. The gentle voice of a woman speaks. "Mrs. Seachrist, a Lieutenant Commander Beal has asked permission to come up to your room. Is that satisfactory with you?"

In my dream, I feel my right hand freeze on the telephone handset as my left clenches the cord. I have never remembered much else about that call, or the outgoing ones I will place soon after. Almost immediately, I hear a polite but firm knock.

I open the door to a petite woman in full dress uniform. Lt. Commander Karen Beal introduces herself and I verify that I am Mrs. William Seachrist. At some point in our conversation, the impact of her title of Naval Casualty Assistance Calls Officer dawns on me.

She is calm, dignified and soothing. She reveals the reason for her presence in short and concise sentences. Bill's ship experienced mechanical problems and had to stop at a port in Africa whose name I do not know...Equipment and personnel were taken aboard...Someone had been ill, but the ship's medical staff did not recognize the man had encephalitis... a surprisingly short incubation period...Everything happened so fast... All that could be done was done...No one realized the serious-

ness of the situation until it was too late. The United States Navy and everyone aboard my husband's ship are so sorry for my loss.

In my dream, I complete travel plans and pack, grateful for the officer's companionship and assistance. After the bellman removes my luggage, I gather my jacket and purse and have a final look around the elegantly-appointed room where I was to have rendezvoused with Bill. My impression of the last minutes of what was to be our ultimate holiday has remained imbedded in my senses throughout the decades: Again, I smell the scent of rare orchids sitting on the bedside table. I listen to the jolting ping of the elevator's bell at each floor as we descend to the opulent lobby. I touch again the rich leather of the Mercedes Benz taxi we take to the airport. Even in my sleep, it all combines to make me feel nauseous.

My mind fast-forwards through the trip back to Honolulu. I am disconnected from the scene emotionally. I watch as my young self sits stoically in the Waikīkī condo to which my husband will never return. Nathan and Sandy gently help me finalize the plans for Bill's memorial. Despite everyone's good intentions, there is nowhere I can be alone in the small space. The arrivals of elegant Island floral arrangements are unending. The fragrance is overpowering.

Bill was an orphan raised in foster care. He has said that if anything happens to him, he wants to be cremated and buried at sea. With his shipmates still on cruise, there are few people in the small chapel at Pearl Harbor. Aside from the chaplain and an officer representing the Navy, the only mourners are Nathan, Sandy, their baby Jon, and me. Saddened, I watch my slim figure sit in a daze during the brief memorial that overflows with a background of droning canned funeral music. On my behalf, Nathan accepts a tri-cornered, glass-faced oak box with a flag that had flown over the U.S.S. Arizona Memorial. He then presents the simple wooden box with Bill's cremains to the solemn Lieutenant Commander who will facilitate their burial at sea with full military honors.

Scenes from the following week pass rapidly through my

mind. There are so many calls I have to make, so many forms I must fill out. When the pain of it all overcomes me, I sleep on the sofa by day and night. When I am able, I methodically clean closets and cupboards. Slowly I box Bill's belongings for donation to a men's shelter. I am being logical, I tell myself. But in my heart, I know I am emotionally frozen. Aside from our king sized bed, the one thing I cannot face is the medicine cabinet, where the lingering aroma of Bill's aftershave permeates the cabinets. Tears fall onto my cheeks as I watch young Natalie line up her toothbrush and makeup on the counter.

Soon the luggage that departed with Bill only a few weeks earlier arrives at the door of our condo. It is the duffle bag that is most upsetting. Everything is so neatly folded. One piece lies on top of the next, with nothing gaping over the edge. Each layer reveals the attention to detail with which Bill had lived every day of his short life.

That bag will remain at the back of the bedroom closet in the condo that becomes a shrine to a sparkling lifestyle that will never be experienced. I never live in the condo fully after my return from Hong Kong. I merely store the remains of my last days and nights with Bill. Then one afternoon when I have gone shopping with Sandy, Nathan removes the last of my husband's belongings, saying they will be waiting for me when I am ready for them.

With mixed feelings, I watch myself type up the notes of my first assignment as a journalist. Despite the deep grief that will accompany me for a couple of years, the result will be a lively article that woos the reader into contemplating a journey to the exciting port of Hong Kong.

* * * * *

I awoke from my dreams of Bill warmly remembering what I loved about him. He had been the perfect companion for the short-lived marriage of my youth. It has been a long time since I felt committed to him, but I never thought of remarrying.

Part of the reason for my continuing single status was

my hectic schedule. I bought my current two-bedroom condo in the mid-1980s. But being an international journalist
meant that I did not reside there regularly. Living overseas for
months or even a year at a time, made it difficult to maintain
a long-distance relationship with even a special person. Eventually I realized that most men of my generation wanted their
significant other to commit to a full-time relationship. My career precluded that.

There was also the issue of my independence. To be honest, I have appreciated being on my own most of the time. Even
with the love and companionship provided by my brother and
his family, I liked my life as a transient writer. In fact, assignments in the leisure industry provided a wonderful means for
interacting with family and friends who enjoyed journeying
to exotic locales to share in my adventures. Luckily, none of
my loved ones were ever endangered by the few times when
circumstances on the news front forced me to shift into emergency coverage of events during my travels around the world.

In short, between my love of work and desire to maintain
my free lifestyle, I had only one long-term boyfriend after Bill's
death. But despite Gary's waiting patiently for me to settle
down, after nine years it became too much for him. And even
though I had felt committed to our relationship, the breakup
was not upsetting to me.

After so many years on the road, I am settled and enjoying life in Honolulu. But recently, I have felt restless on the
romantic front. That's why my dinner with Keoni was fruitful
in more than one way. Professionally, we are a balanced team.
Personally, I really enjoy his companionship. Beyond that, he
is good looking, has a resonant voice, and a keen mind. Our
goodnight kiss was definitely a sensual promise. I am looking
forward to pursuing our relationship, despite the sorrow that
has brought us closer. The next trip to the condo, or round of
shopping, will have to include a recharge of lingerie and perfume.

CHAPTER 14

The beginning of wisdom is found in doubting...
Pierre Abelard [1079-1142]

When I finally emerged from my night of dreaming, it was later than I had intended to awaken. I rushed to start a pot of coffee and laid out a portion of Miss Una's morning favorite, canned duck.

"Thanks for letting me sleep in for once," I told her, sneaking in a few pets while she daintily picked through morsels of her breakfast. "Unfortunately, you chose the wrong day to be so generous."

While the coffee brewed, I hurried to complete a few chores before leaving for the Medical Examiner's office. As usual, the mundane housework settled my nerves and focused my thinking. I poured some almond milk and agave syrup into my coffee and sat down to reflect on the rollercoaster ride of emotions I was feeling after my evening with Keoni.

My elation over my developing relationship with Keoni was severely undercut by the devastation I felt from listening to Al Cooper's revelations about *his* feelings toward Ariel! Did his words point toward sinister action? Maybe I was approaching resolution of the question of *what*, or perhaps *who*, had caused her demise.

Like the first days following her death, I was not hungry, but knew I needed to have my wits about me if I was to absorb what the coroner and police had to tell us about Ariel's case. What a shame that my meals did not come packaged neatly in a small pouch or can. With my nervousness, the most I could swallow was a breakfast bar. But since I did not know what lay ahead, I dropped a couple of my apple and nut interpretations of military Meals-Ready-to-Eat into my handbag.

Shortly after I had showered and dressed, Keoni called.

"Good morning, Natalie. I hope you slept well." he said.

"Beautifully, thank you. How was your trip home?" I asked him.

"It seemed like it took longer to get down the stairs and to my truck than it did to drive home to Mānoa."

"I've noticed the stairs have that effect myself," I laughed.

"Are you ready for today?" asked Keoni on a more serious note.

"As much as can be expected. It's a complicated issue. I have to go if I want to learn what happened to Ariel. But I don't know if I'm prepared for what I'm going to be told."

It was not a conversation either of us wanted to prolong. After confirming his arrival time, we said goodbye. I combed my hair and added a few items of jewelry before checking that I had locked the patio door and left enough food for Miss Una. Picking up my handbag, I looked around the living room of the apartment Ariel had never had the opportunity to enjoy. Even with my furnishings, it felt bereft of life, like the first time I had seen it.

In a thoughtful mood, I walked down to the parking lot that was nearly empty at this mid-morning time. I had a couple of minutes until Keoni was due so I looked in my mailbox, in case the carrier had been early. No, there was nothing addressed to me, or even "occupant."

Keoni pulled up right on time. Before he could get out to open the passenger's door, I popped the latch and hopped into the cab.

"My, it's certainly more spacious without piles of boxes and a cat," I observed.

"It's even roomier if I fold down the back seat," he noted, with a sidelong glance at me.

Not knowing what lay ahead today, I had foregone trying

to look svelte and lovely. Instead I had opted for a loose shorty *mu'umu'u* and my comfortable red gel sandals. I was now re-thinking that choice.

"I won't insult you by asking how you're feeling," said Keoni. "I'm here to support you and Nathan in any way I can, without interfering with the official proceedings. If you need me to help clarify something that Marty or JD are telling you, or asking of you, just give me a sign."

"Keoni, I'm grateful for your help and friendship...on lots of levels," I replied.

He took his right hand off the steering wheel for a moment and gently squeezed my knee. Was this a neutral gesture of reassurance, or something more? No verbal response came to mind. Except to confirm the protocol to be followed, we did not converse much on the trip to the ME's office.

Timely as always, Nathan was waiting for us by the building's entrance. The men shook hands and Nathan and I hugged. I tried not to stare, but my graying twin looked unkempt in his rumpled aloha shirt and shorts. Slumped like he was, he looked shorter than his Viking height of six foot two inches. It had been only a couple of weeks since Ariel's death, but he looked like he had been on a starvation diet. What could I say? The main reason I kept stoking my inner fires was my cat's need to eat on a regular schedule.

Keoni sized up the situation and took charge. He opened the door and moved us toward the reception counter. Recognizing him, the clerk addressed him by name and greeted all of us warmly. The man invited us to be seated and asked if any of us would like coffee or water. Both Keoni and I declined any beverage. With a healthy dose of cream and sugar, coffee appeared to be the perfect means for enlivening my brother.

I reflected on my relationship with Nathan while we sat listening to the click of the clerk's keyboard and occasional phone calls. Keoni had been right about Nathan's uncanny ability to see into the heart of many matters. In our family, he sometimes provided solutions to problems before we had a chance to introduce the topic to him.

How does he do this? Beyond his personal gift of kenning, I sometimes learn he has shared a dream of mine. Throughout my career as a travel reporter and sometimes travelogue presenter my dreams have been filled with idyllic scenes from a mountain-top Shangri-La or the deck of an elegant cruise ship sailing on undulating ocean waves. In contrast, until his retirement, Nathan's work in family services has produced dreams filled with intense images I would prefer not to have seen. I think this explains why he has withdrawn from me in many ways.

Throughout his career in social work, he demonstrated an uncanny ability to know when to separate members of a family in distress. This prompted his bosses to load his in-box with cases that demanded the wisdom and patience of Solomon. Sometimes when he has faced the worst of scenarios, a short ethereal video might would slip across the night skies and into my unconscious mind. But while sharing a dream with his big sister might serve as the perfect catalyst for determining an appropriate path to judicial prudence, the resulting stress I experienced was overwhelming.

Looking around the reception area of the coroner's office, I suddenly wondered if Nathan had been partaking of my recent dreams—let alone the visions I had had about Ariel. I hoped not. But if he had seen some of what I had in my visions, it would explain his current appearance and demeanor. Shortly, I was relieved of my disquieting thoughts by the appearance of a man of medium height and build who introduced himself as Dr. Martin Soli.

"I'm sorry to be late" he said gently, offering his hand to each of us. "Please follow me," the whitish-blond man said, gesturing down a long hallway. Beyond the lobby, the lighting was dim and the air reminiscent of a hospital. Except for the squishing sound our hard soled shoes made on the green rubber flooring, we walked in silence. After passing several security glass fronted doors, we halted in front of a solid wood door without signage. As he waved us in, Dr. Soli's white lab coat opened and revealed an aloha shirt with reverse printing of blue Hawaiian quilt squares. The pattern matched the red shirt Ariel and Brianna had given Nathan last Christmas.

We entered a clean but cluttered office and arranged ourselves on standard government chairs of thinly upholstered metal tubing. The doctor sat down behind a massive metal desk that looked like it had been in service since World War II. He then deftly shifted two stacks of file folders to the top of a refrigerator crammed in the middle of a row of cabinets behind him. We stared at the single remaining file in the center of the desk.

"Natalie, Nathan, I'm so sorry to be seeing you under these circumstances. Although this is an official meeting, please call me Marty."

He looked at Keoni and then my brother. "I think we've actually met before, Nathan. It happened during the case of a Marine corporal who'd gone over the edge and murdered his wife after learning she'd taken a lover while he was overseas."

Hearing his name, my brother came out of his reverie. "Yes, I remember that case. We'd had difficulty in placing all three of the children in a single foster home. I was grateful for your tip about that new shelter for multiple siblings."

Marty nodded and turned to open the door of the refrigerator. "May I offer any of you some water?" I was glad there were no odd sights or smells when he opened the hotel-sized appliance and answered "yes" for all of us. As he passed out the well-chilled bottles, I noted a box of tissues at the ready. The man was not new to making these personal reports and must have dealt with a variety of responses through the years.

Keoni and I opened the bottles we were handed and took generous sips. My brother held his in his lap. The air was heavy with the dread we all felt: Nathan and me for the gruesome details we would have to receive about Ariel's death; Marty for having to impart such news; and Keoni for having to help each of us steer our way through the proceedings.

Clearing his throat, Marty said, "This is a summary of my initial findings in Ariel's case." He opened the file and leaned forward to extend it to Nathan. Nathan demurred and Marty passed the papers to me.

Taking them from his hand, I looked down at a multi-paged form with enumerated block-printed sections. Keoni slid his arm along the back of my chair, without obtrusively moving into my space. I set the file down, pulled my reading glasses from their case and unconsciously rubbed them on my dress. Then I set them on the edge of my nose, far enough from my eyes to blink away the tears that were already forming.

My hands shook while I tried to analyze the formulaic pages before me. I returned to the beginning. Only fragments of the words registered in my conscious mind. Seeing Ariel reduced to this brief description was enormously painful.

The victim is wearing a white sleeveless tennis dress and one Nike sports shoe on the left foot...Undergarments include a white sports bra, white cotton underpants and white tennis socks with the signature green "H" denoting the University of Hawai'i...thejewelry included: one carved silver pierced loop earring with floral design, 1-inch diameter, in right ear; one half-inch wide stainless steel Seiko watch on left wrist.

I turned the pages slowly, aware that Keoni was reading the text along with me. With his knowledge and experience, it was not the hollow verse of a coroner's report that he was seeing. Beyond his professional response, he was my friend. I knew he was feeling the edge of the trauma being inflicted on my brother and me.

The report clarified that in addition to what she was wearing on her body, her second shoe and a silver bracelet had been collected as separate evidence. The report unfolded in standard forensic style without further preamble. The neutral tone of the language employed did not lessen its impact on me.

The body is that of a twenty-two-year-old, well-developed, well-nourished Caucasian American woman. The woman was pronounced dead at 16:25 with closed eyes, no heart sounds, no pulse and no spontaneous respirations. Height, sixty-seven inches...Weight, one hundred eighteen pounds...red hair, apparently naturally bleached by the sun...Freckles across cheeks, nose and chest...Fingernails, short, manicured with a clear polish...The patient has no surgical scars....

I shuddered slightly. Keoni patted my shoulder. My mind wandered for a moment. I was reminded that Ariel and Brianna were identical twins. The obvious differences are few. Since Brianna lives in the Northwest and is seldom in the sun, her hair is darker and she has fewer freckles. I looked up for a moment to see that Nathan continued to show no expression; he simply looked down at the water bottle in his lap. Except for the hum of the air conditioner, the room remained silent as I continued reading this document that felt as if it were written about someone I had never met.

Cause of death is asphyxiation due to spinal shock caused by severe trauma at the fifth cervical vertebra...The fatal injuries are consistent with a fall from a four-storey building... trauma to the head...Bruising on the sternum probably caused by the victim bouncing from the top of one vehicle onto the hood of the same vehicle...hyoid bone broken...Right femoral head fractured at the acetabulum of the hip bone...Fragments of foreign material in the epidural abrasions and contusions across the body... Fragments within the knuckle lacerations of the right hand are consistent with paint from both the building from which she fell and the auto on which she landed...The preliminary toxicology screen indicates no alcohol, prescription or illicit drugs in the deceased's blood or urine; comprehensive toxicological analysis to follow.

I understood most of the medical terminology, but no matter what words had been used, one thing was clear: Ariel had fractured her neck when she landed on Al Cooper's car. She would have been a quadriplegic even if she had survived the short fall. She would have been confined to a wheelchair, requiring professional healthcare supervision around the clock for the rest of her life. Something I doubted she could have endured for very long.

I sighed and looked up into Marty's pale blue eyes to let him know I had read all that I could. Keoni again squeezed my shoulder as we both looked over at Nathan, who exhibited no curiosity about the final pronouncements on Ariel's life.

What should I say? I inhaled deeply and then stated the obvious. "Nathan and I appreciate your taking the time to meet with us personally, Marty. It's clear from this report that your office has been thorough in its analysis."

Marty responded softly, his look encompassing all of us. "We've given Ariel's case our fullest attention. I only wish we could provide you with answers to the question of *how* Ariel's death occurred. But I know you're meeting with Lieutenant Dias shortly, and he'll be able to put some of our findings into a larger context."

Rising, Marty walked to a lockable steel cabinet beside a refrigerator positioned behind his desk. "If you're up to it, I'd like to go through the belongings that Ariel had with her."

He opened the door and reached up to a shelf for a large, brown envelope, and looked questioningly at my twin. Nathan again gestured toward me and Marty handed it to me. I looked at the label and noted Ariel's full name and a case number. I gingerly opened the envelope. The first thing I pulled out was Ariel's cocoa-colored, calfskin fanny pack, ideal for her active life of study and sports.

Setting it on the desk, I tipped the envelope until a small folding comb, a beeswax lip balm, and her watch tumbled out. It was a stainless steel Seiko diving watch Nathan had presented her upon graduation from high school. He had given Brianna a similar one, not out of laziness or an obsession about providing matchy-matchy accessories to the twins. Being sportswomen, he knew that they would appreciate the practicality and multiple features. Ariel had liked the simplicity of glancing down at her wrist, palm turned toward her, to view the classic positioning of the arrow-like hands presented in black by day and glowing green at night.

No one would ever wear this watch again. Its band had dings in several places and was broken at one side of the clasp. Most depressing was the watch's broken crystal, its dented casing, and its hands that were frozen at 16:30. Clearly, the ME had had no trouble in determining the time of her death.

I knew there would be no keys. For transportation, she took the bus most of the time, precluding the need for car keys. She did not need a house key since Nathan's home was unlocked by pressing the palm across a pad that read one's print. He might be an old-fashioned guy in many ways, but not when it came to the security of his home or his adored grand-daughters.

The next items to come out of the envelope were a few coins and a small wad of folded money: a single dollar, two twenties, and the hundred dollar bill Nathan insisted the girls carry for an emergency tow if they drove their parents' classic Chevy Malibu. I sighed, and we looked at each other, remembering when they had needed both of their stashes to get the car out of hock after the vehicle was towed when they neglected to feed a downtown parking meter.

I tipped the envelope further and Ariel's barrel bracelet rolled out onto the desk, in surprisingly pristine condition. It was a Navajo design in sterling silver, with blackening to emphasize the interwoven squash blossom design. Brianna had one too. They were expensive mementos the girls had bought when their outrigger canoe team participated in a paddling event in Arizona. Sliding out last was a delicate dangling loop earring that matched the bracelet. I shook the envelope, expecting its mate to appear. Nothing else came out. I bent back the flap, opened the envelope widely, and peered into its interior. There was one last item. It was not her earring.

I reached in and pulled out a folded piece of paper. Even before I opened it, I recognized the security pattern of a check. It was number 1635—depressingly close numerically to the official time cited for Ariel's death. Like the hundred dollar bills, Nathan had always encouraged the girls to have at least one check with them at all times, for unexpected expenses. This time, it was probably for a planned purchase, since Ariel might have needed to leave a deposit with Miss Wong, if she chose to move ahead with the lease.

For a couple of minutes we all sat quietly, if not calmly. I looked at the earring on the table before me, then at Nathan's bowed head. As I raised my eyes, I found Keoni staring at me intently. It did not take any kenning to know he was thinking exactly what I was—*Why is there a single earring?* Ariel was not into grunge, multiple body piercings or exotic displays of jewelry.

In fact, she seldom wore dangling earrings because they might get in the way during a spur-of-the-moment tennis match. She had wanted to be on the UH tennis team. Although she was a keen player, tournaments would have interfered with her studies and volunteering in a program for elementary students at risk.

"Uh, Marty," I began. "I don't see the second earring. It wasn't Ariel's style to wear just one, was it Nathan?"

Nathan shook his head to the contrary.

Marty responded, carefully. "We only found this one, in her right ear. I'm sorry to have to broach a painful topic. However, I need to ask you about the solitary earring because there are no rigid standards in today's style norms, especially among the young."

Marty and Keoni passed looks. "So you're confirming there should have been two earrings?"

Nathan and I both nodded.

"As you may have noticed in the report, her left ear lobe was torn, so we couldn't be sure that it had been pierced like her right one was."

At that point, there was a knock on the door.

"Come in," invited Marty.

In the doorway stood a short, stocky man with pocked face and salt and pepper hair.

"I hope I'm not too early," the man began."

"No, you're right on time, John." Marty replied. He then looked at us. "I have another case I have to check on now, but I'll walk with you to the conference room."

Accordingly, we stood and Marty carefully replaced Ariel's belongings in the brown envelope and handed it to the man I knew must be HPD Detective John Dias.

Marty conducted introductions while we moved out of his office and down the hallway. Facing an open doorway, he paused. "I'm sorry to have to leave you. The Lieutenant has a copy of my report. And since I'll be in the building, you can call me if you need further clarification."

He continued down the hall and the rest of us entered the spacious room that featured a large table and chairs, obviously intended for meetings larger than ours. At the head of the room were a drop down projection screen, a flat-screen television with video connections, chalk board, white board, podium with mike, and a larger-than-life human skeleton. In short, there were all the essentials for a day-long presentation on the mechanisms of death and dying. I wondered how many of the features we would be utilizing.

The Lieutenant waved us toward the chairs at the head of the table, explaining, "Sergeant Ken`ichi Nakamura will join us momentarily with a presentation of his findings at the Makiki Sunset Apartments. I think you know him, Keoni, he'd just passed the sergeant's exam when you retired."

"Mmm, yes I do. Wasn't he the martial arts champion the department brought in to enhance cadet training?"

"That's right. Until he fractured his shoulder on a major drug bust, he was a leading contender in Japan's Kendo competitions. Before that, you would have been amazed to watch him whip his *shinai* through the air.

"What's a *shinai*?" interjected Nathan, fully awake.

CHAPTER 15

...By doubting we come to the question...
Pierre Abelard [1079-1142]

The Lieutenant continued his explanation. "A *shinai* is a split bamboo sword. Once used as a practice sword, it's now a distinct martial arts weapon. During his recovery, Ken`ichi started studying computer simulation software and cybercrime. That's become his specialty. But unless he's involved in a case calling for that skill set, we still pair up on a daily basis."

I looked to my left and right, at the men who were *my* compadres for the day. We settled into our seats, and John Dias said, "It seems empty to say, but I'm truly sorry for your loss. It's especially tragic when it's a young person with their whole life ahead of them."

Although he remained subdued, Nathan finally spoke, revealing more about himself than I had expected. "Natalie and I really appreciate what you're all doing. I agree it's difficult to find the right words for something this horrible. I saw a lot of sad situations in my work, but nothing could have prepared me for this. It's been two weeks and I still expect Ariel to come dashing in at dinner time."

Lieutenant Dias nodded and sat down across from Nathan, Keoni and me. He laid the envelope with Ariel's belongings on the table in front of him and his briefcase on the chair to his left. Snapping its latches open, he brought out a steno notepad, a small blue case notebook and a copy of the Coroner's report. Looking over the report, he said, "First of all, since there were no signs of a struggle, or a suicide note, the case remains officially listed as an 'unattended death.' Knowing this, do either of you have any questions about the Coroner's findings?"

Nathan looked at me and I shook my head. "No, it was quite thorough—especially since there were no indications of pre-mortem wounds."

"Mmhm," concurred the Lieutenant. He looked at Keoni before continuing. "I know you've gone through Marty's initial findings. Although you've seen Ariel's personal belongings, I thought we might walk through everything one more time."

With care, he emptied the envelope and arranged everything in a straight line. "These items appear entirely normal for a young girl to have. But is there anything that stands out as unusual?"

The first item was Ariel's watch. The damage to it showed that something violent had occurred. But the source of its rumination appeared to be the result of Ariel's impact with the car.

Nathan looked at me but remained silent, obviously expecting me to respond for both of us. "In our meeting with Marty, we confirmed there should have been a second earring," I replied.

Keoni's former partner stared at me silently for a moment and then opened the small notebook to his left. "I see that aside from her right shoe being found on the ground, and this bracelet on the antenna, nothing else of hers was found on the Mustang or the area surrounding the event."

"How can her bracelet look so perfect?" asked Nathan, pointing.

"That's a valid point, but it can be explained. When she... fell...it must have tumbled off her wrist and slipped down the antenna. It blended in so well with the polished chrome of the vehicle's details, that we almost missed seeing it. It is amazing that the bracelet remained untouched in all the...commotion. I must say, except for the hood, car was nearly spotless."

For the first time, Keoni spoke up. "I think that's due to the fact that the owner had just finished detailing the vehicle for a car show that was to be held that evening at Ala Moana Shopping Center."

We watched while John Dias paged through his small report notebook. "Yes, I see that was mentioned repeatedly by Mr. Cooper. He seems quite fond of that car, and is really upset that it hasn't been returned to him."

I could not contain myself for an appropriate opening to broach the topic of Al. "There are a lot of things that appear to bother Al Cooper. You wouldn't believe what Keoni and I heard him say last night."

Keoni gave my shoulder a squeeze. Both the Lieutenant and Nathan stared at me.

"I guess there's no better time to tell you what's been transpiring. We'd had dinner and were standing on the *lānai* when Al pulled into his parking place."

"What do you mean? How could you have been standing anywhere *near* his parking place?" Nathan blurted out. "What on earth have you been up to, Natalie?"

That answered the question of whether Nathan had any knowledge of my sleuthing. But it did not reveal whether he had been tuning in to other aspects of my dreams or visions.

I looked at Keoni, whose blank face made it clear this revelation was strictly in my ball court. "You know that volunteering I'm doing on Wilder Avenue this summer?"

Nathan nodded expectantly.

"The other day, when I was doing some research for Keoni at the archives, I realized how much travel time I was going to spend on the bus...And...well...I thought that I could save some energy and maybe do a little...um...looking around, if I rented a unit at the Makiki Sunset Apartments for the summer."

John Dias let Nathan do the questioning, but continued to look at me intently.

"You mean to say that you are *living* at the apartments where Ariel *died*?" said Nathan with an escalating pitch to his voice.

Fudging a bit on the details, I continued. "Uh, yes. I was in the area and when I passed the apartment complex, I saw there was a vacancy sign. And then, when I visited with the manager, Pearl Wong, she seemed to think I was someone else...who was looking for an apartment for her granddaughter...and...things just developed after that conversation."

Nathan ran his fingers through his hair and shook his head.

I started to choke. Keoni squeezed my shoulder and slid a box of tissues to me that I had not noticed was sitting on the conference table.

The lieutenant decided it was time to move forward with his official inquiries. Clearing his throat, he politely asked, "You are currently living at the Makiki Sunset Apartments?"

"Yes. Keoni helped me move to where Ariel died on Thursday."

John Dias then gave Keoni a questioning look. I quickly said, "It wasn't Keoni's fault. He didn't want me to do it, but I'd already signed a short-term lease and paid for three months."

"Oh I'm sure it wasn't Keoni's fault, Natalie," said Nathan with a rising tone. "But what on earth gave you the lame-brained idea to move yourself into the place that caused Ariel's death? We don't even know if it was an accident...or... if she was murdered."

Keoni responded. "I couldn't have stopped her from doing what she'd already set in motion. But I cautioned her about her safety and we speak several times a day. Yesterday I had a chance to tour the complex—something I could not have done if Natalie wasn't a tenant. Like you've said JD, this is an open case with no clear indication of the cause of the girl's death."

I jumped back into the conversation. "You need to hear what Al Cooper said last night. He didn't even know Ariel, but he hated her. For some reason I can't fathom, he thinks she was a lesbian and that she didn't deserve to live on God's good earth. He even quoted what sounded like a Bible verse as he was slamming the door of his rental car and marching off last night."

Lieutenant Dias rapidly wrote a couple of lines on his notepad before saying, "Mmm. So, I take it you're living in an apartment on an upper floor—if Cooper wasn't aware you two were listening to him."

"Yes. I, um, ended up renting apartment B406."

"Did you say unit B406? The apartment Ariel was looking at?" asked the detective.

"Yes, Lieutenant. That's the apartment Miss Wong took me to see. She had to remove scraps of police tape to open the door."

"At this point, Natalie, let's dispense with formalities. Please call me John, and I'll call you Miss Marple."

I smiled wanly.

The detective looked across at Keoni and me, and then at Nathan. "Well, Nathan, I guess you and I are both learning a lot today."

Nathan grimaced and shook his head again.

Keoni then offered his concern about the violence that Al had evidenced in both his words and demeanor. "I was thinking of calling a couple of guys I know who have vintage cars and might be involved in the car events Cooper participates in."

"That's a good idea, Keoni. I'll appreciate the names and numbers of any contacts you find," said the Lieutenant, confirming his role as the person of authority in the investigation.

At that moment the door opened, and a tall, thin Japanese man with black hair pulled back in a ponytail entered the room with a briefcase in one hand and a laptop in the other.

"Sorry to be late, I was editing some footage for today." He set everything at the head of the table, and came around to shake hands with each of us. After introducing himself as Detective Sergeant Ken`ichi Nakamura, he nodded to Keoni and shook hands with Nathan and me. He then began connecting his computer to the room's video equipment.

"We have some new information to work with, Ken`ichi. It seems Natalie has signed up to be our on-site eyes and ears," said John Dias.

Completing preparations for his presentation, the Sergeant mumbled "Mmhm" indifferently.

"Yes, she's actually living in unit B406 at the Makiki Sunset Apartments," continued the Lieutenant.

"Oh?" replied the Sergeant, clicking on a screen filled with the HPD logo. "Ooh. I see," he said, now looking up at all of us. "Well...I've brought a video of the grounds, the two buildings in the complex and the apartment itself, but maybe it's irrelevant."

"Not everyone has seen the place," noted his boss. "I think Nathan might appreciate being able to reference what the rest of us are talking about."

Sergeant Nakamura looked at each of us with a rather blank look on his face.

"Like I said, Ken`ichi, Natalie's moved into the apartment her grandniece was considering renting. And Keoni, the valiant knight in shining armor that he is, has given the site a wee glance or two," clarified John Dias. "So if you're ready, why don't you take us through the property."

"Mmhm," was the Sergeant's only response.

I could not see Keoni's face, but his neck looked crimson. I had a feeling he would soon be doing some explaining to his friends at HPD.

The Sergeant then repositioned the podium to the side of the large drop-down screen, placed a few notes on it, turned on a laser pointer, and began his presentation.

"First of all, I obtained blueprints of the complex from Miss Pearl Wong, owner and manager of the apartments where the deceased died. There have been few alterations to the site through the years—aside from her modification of two units she has combined for her personal use. As you will note, the layout is fairly typical for this type of building. I won't bother repeating dimensions since they are on the drawings and most of you are familiar with the site.

"The complex is comprised of two four-storey cement-block buildings facing onto a courtyard. The property is edged with parking on three sides. The back of the property is bordered by several lemon and *plumeria* trees. There is a barbecue area near the tree line; there are two large, standing hibachis flanking one wooden picnic table with attached benches on its two long sides. In addition, there are four white plastic tables. We counted ten white stackable plastic chairs, but I'm told volleyball players and residents frequently borrow them, so the number is subject to fluctuation."

Within a few minutes, I had trouble focusing on the details of his methodical reporting. I wondered if a boost in sugar level would help my concentration. Pulling out my stash of snacks from my bag, I set them on the table for everyone to help themselves. Munching an energy bar and sipping the remains of my water bottle, I managed to survive the detailed description of the complex's amenities. I knew that if Pearl Wong had been present, she would have beamed with pride of ownership.

At last, the Sergeant concluded his presentation. "Nathan, from what was said earlier, I believe you're the one person who hasn't seen the grounds. Is there anything I haven't covered...that you have questions about?"

Nathan took a deep breath and let it out slowly. "I realize this is only an overview, but are you going to show us where the car was, the one that Ariel...landed on?"

"Uh, no. I have some video of the property that I'm going to present next. But let me assure you there will be nothing... mmm...too graphic. Most of this recording was made after the first responders and crime scene techs had left."

Setting up for his next segment, I noticed Sergeant Nakamura look at both his boss and Keoni. No one spoke, but I had a feeling that was only because Nathan and I were present. I was not sure whether I wanted to be a fly on the wall after we left or not. Nathan now knew about my residency in the infamous apartment. However, I did not think he should face the scene so soon after the unfolding forensic story and was grateful that Keoni would be taking me back to the apartment. Whatever Keoni did after we parted was up to him...and maybe Lieutenant John Dias.

Soon the Sergeant's tour of the Makiki Sunset Apartments resumed—this time in living color. His video opened at the front of the complex. It focused on the mail boxes and parking spaces for disabled persons, as well as delivery and moving companies. The videographer then drew his audience into the courtyard, up the stairs of Building B (on the right), and along the walkway to the front of apartment B406. After a brief tour of the apartment, scenes shot from the *lānai* were shown, but fortunately that segment had been edited so that little was shown of the parking space onto which Ariel had fallen.

Finally, the audience was taken on a tour of the perimeter of the property. We began by moving to the left, around the corner of Building A, to view its assigned parking spaces and a couple of trees at the back. Next we moved around the right corner of Building B to the parking assigned to its tenants. The space where Al Cooper's Mustang had been parked was the fourth from the corner of the building.

Clearly, part of the video had been shot before the HazMat people arrived, so we had to look at the blacktop darkened with any number of substances...many of which I simply did not want to think about, let alone identify. This was where Ariel had breathed her last breath. I was glad the scene was brief.

Ken`ichi Nakamura cleared his throat, while clicking off the image of the site where Ariel had died. "I think this provides you with sufficient information for now," he said.

John Dias then took up the mantle of dealing with the bereaved family of the deceased. With a polite "thank you" to his sergeant, he again opened the floor for discussion.

Nathan roused himself to ask quietly, "So, she fell from...the balcony of the apartment she was planning to rent?"

"Well, um...with her hitting the car twice, the angle of her fall is not clear, and there is no physical evidence above to indicate the exact point of her drop."

"I, I think that she actually fell from the refreshment alcove next to the apartment." There. It was said. I did not know how I was going to explain why I thought so, but I was hoping the detectives would not press me for proof.

"That's an interesting idea, Natalie. Is there something specific that leads you to think that's what happened?" questioned the Lieutenant.

"Mmm...," I began.

"She's right about the possibility of the girl falling from the refreshment alcove, John," offered Sergeant Nakamura. "Initially we didn't pay much attention to the idea. But when we didn't find any obvious evidence on the *lanai*, we did look at the alcove briefly. We've been waiting for the findings of the autopsy and the forensic examination of the Mustang before pursuing a couple of theories we've been considering."

John resumed the lead. "That brings us back to the car—and the single earring. As you were coming in, Ken`ichi, we were discussing the fact that Ariel was found wearing a single earring, and the fact that she should have been wearing a second one. Of course, it's possible it was lost in the impact with the car. Clearly we have to give that car another going over.

"Also, the owner of that Mustang...the handyman Al Cooper...has made some...extreme remarks about the deceased. I want you to get started on a background check as soon as we're through here. Also, Keoni will be contacting us after he calls a couple of his buddies who may be involved in the car club that was exhibiting at Ala Moana Center that night."

Turning to me, he pushed his inquiries. "So Natalie, while you've been at the apartment, have you learned anything else that can help us in our investigation?"

I looked at Keoni, who again patted my shoulder. "Well, most of all, I've been getting to know Pearl Wong, the manager. I expressed an interest in the history of the apartments and during teatime she started sharing her family's story—beginning in Shànghǎi in the 1920s."

"Now that's really beginning at the beginning," chortled

the Lieutenant.

"I'm seeing her again tonight, for cocktails. I plan on steering the conversation to the present to learn more about life at the apartment complex. But having specialized in oral history in school—and doing more than a few celebrity interviews—I know I can't grill her with direct questions," I volunteered.

"Well, it'll be interesting to hear what you learn tonight. What about the place in general, what have you discovered so far?" asked John.

All eyes in the room turned on me.

"Pearl Wong and her sister, Jade Bishop, each own one of the two buildings. Jade owns the one I'm in. She's had a stroke and now lives in a nearby assisted-living condo. Her son, or maybe he's her stepson, Richard Bishop, lives on the property. He's belligerent and creepy. But aside from staring at me a couple of times, the only thing objectionable about him is his constant battling with Al Cooper.

"So far I haven't met many of the tenants personally. There's Ashley Lowell, a young Navy wife, and her little boy Cory. Mrs. Espinoza, an older Portuguese woman, has lived at the apartments for many years. Both of these women seem to do their errands in the morning and by afternoon they're back in their apartments, probably for nap time."

I paused to take a sip of water. "Beyond that, the tenants are largely UH students and young soldiers and sailors—pretty much around Ariel's age. Several of the military guys are semi-permanently absent; they just rent a budget apartment to stow their gear while they're overseas. There's no swimming pool to hang around and the various groups don't seem to interact much, except in games of volley ball. When outside, they're usually coming or going from their cars, getting the mail, or barbecuing. Keoni can tell you about what he saw when we toured the grounds."

"Thanks for that thorough report, Natalie! I can see that working in journalism trained you well for on-site research," responded John. "Without witnesses, unexplained trauma to

Ariel's body, or forensic evidence at the scene, we were at a standstill. So I know your input will prove invaluable.

"Make sure you keep in close touch with Keoni, who, I *know* will be sharing his perspective with us. It's okay for you to continue observing daily life at the apartments and conversing with Pearl Wong. But don't, I repeat, don't do any further investigating on your own.

"I'll personally review the preliminary CSI reports. Kenichi, I'd like you to have the car's exterior and interior re-processed as soon as you leave here. Evidentiary wise, the sites we examined at the complex were clean, with no scuff marks indicating a struggle. However, depending on our review of everything, we may need to go back for a second CSI round."

After we said goodbye to Sergeant Nakamura, Nathan reached into his pocket. "I didn't know what might be useful, but here are some of Ariel's recent records." He reached forward with an envelope. "There are a few bank statements, a print out of outbound and incoming emails, her schedule from last month through next month, and a copy of the bill for her smart phone account, which just arrived. I didn't have a chance to go through it, but you'll be able to see her... last calls, John."

John and Keoni looked at each other. John then turned to Nathan. "Did she usually have her phone with her? There was so little in her fanny pack. We thought that she was either planning to hop the bus back to campus to pick up the rest of any other belongings she'd have had with her on a normal day...or...she didn't want contact with anyone."

Although he did not say it aloud, I knew there had been speculation that Ariel might have jumped on purpose. Surely he must realize how stupid that idea was. Especially on the first bright day of summer, with her life was in perfect order. How could it make sense for a young girl to have gone to look at an apartment that was to bring her independence as an adult and instead of leasing the apartment, she chose to kill herself? It was probably a good thing that no one in the room had dared to put this suggestion on the table for open discussion.

Calming myself, I answered as though unaware of the unspoken current in the room. "You're right. There's no phone. I can assure you she was never without her phone."

I could not deal with the tension any longer. There was no way I could avoid revealing my visions. I looked at Keoni, who gave me a small nod. With little preamble, I began. In total silence and with few changes in facial expression, Nathan and the Lieutenant listened to my descriptions of the three visions I had had regarding Ariel. Especially the detailed one I had experienced *as* Ariel. After I finished, John Dias looked at Keoni for a long moment.

Nathan eventually commented. With sardonic humor he said, "You can't imagine how much fun it was as kids to be on the playground when she'd conk out during one of her trips to the other side."

"Well," said the lieutenant, turning to me, "Now I understand your decision to move to that apartment." Beginning anew, he turned to Nathan. "Did you and Ariel talk about what she had scheduled that day? Did you see anything unusual on her calendar?"

"I knew she was going to look at an apartment. When I looked over her calendar in preparation for today, everything looked normal. On the printout I brought, you'll see that aside from her classes, she'd circled "3 pm" and wrote "APT" and "TJ" in capped letters. At the time, I thought "TJ" was an abbreviation for the apartment or maybe a realtor."

"Given the name of the apartments and their manager, it's unlikely that the letters "TJ" have anything to do with either. From Natalie's vision, they appear to belong to someone who was going to become her roommate. We'll check her phone bill and track the numbers listed. Did she use a computer contact data base...did she have a separate hardcopy address book?"

"She and Brianna are strictly electronic. Once I asked Ariel what she'd do if she lost all the information stored on her computer. She said that wouldn't be a problem, that she and her twin provided backup storage for each other."

Looking up from the papers he had been sorting, John Dias said, "That makes two items that are missing from her belongings. I don't think our CSI team would have overlooked a cell phone. Ariel's phone bill will provide her carrier and number, but thank you for bringing it. It'll give us a jump start. Maybe you could describe the phone—color, manufacturer, style, features...." He then opened his notepad to a new page and passed it to Nathan.

"Of course," answered Nathan, quickly jotting down the requested information.

"Well, I think that's all we can cover today. We'll be reporting back to you once we've been able to process these latest leads," John concluded.

We all shook hands before exiting the room and Keoni again served as doorman when we left the building. After shaking hands with Keoni, Nathan hugged me closely and cautioned me again about keeping safe. Keoni then took me by the elbow gently and escorted me to his truck. Opening the door, he helped me into the cab and folded the edge of my dress inside.

After getting into the truck, he glanced at me before turning his full attention to backing out of the parking space and moving onto the roadway. We did not speak on the return trip until he pulled into the apartment's parking lot. He smoothly put the gear shift in park and turned toward me fully.

Staring into my eyes, he quietly said, "I think it's good that you brought up your visions. It put all of your observations in perspective for JD, and like I said, the police have dealt with gifts like yours before. You haven't had another vision have you?"

"No."

"Do you want me to come up for a while?"

Shaking my head, I patted his hand. "I think I need to be alone for a while." I stepped down out of the truck with a sigh and turned toward the apartment I was beginning to loathe.

CHAPTER 16

...he who never made a mistake never made a discovery.
Samuel Smiles [1812-1904]

When I walked into the Makiki apartment, I felt physically and emotionally drained. Simultaneously, I was mentally stimulated by having examined the facts surrounding my grandniece's death with medical and law enforcement professionals. They had confirmed my suspicions, although they had not answered all of my questions, or those of my twin Nathan.

I was grateful for having had Keoni's presence throughout the stressful ordeal. His experience as a former homicide detective, combined with his concern for my brother and me, made his silent support invaluable. That had been especially true when I was confessing my recent activities—and visions. I was glad none of the men had ridiculed me or discounted my input. In fact, they seemed to recognize that by surreptitiously renting the apartment, I was positioned to observe daily routines at the complex. Therefore, I was determined to be thorough in reporting anything I might learn in the future.

The day had been a fine example of optimal information gathering. While neither Nathan nor I had been grilled by the officials with whom we met, their carefully drawn questions had encouraged our fullest participation in the investigative process. In addition, since Nathan and I had substantiated our whereabouts at the time of Ariel's death, there was no question of our having been involved. More importantly, with Keoni to verify our authenticity, I hoped we had proven our value as sources of background information that would help the authorities.

Tonight would be my second opportunity to meet Pearl Wong in my role as a new tenant for whom she felt an affinity. Despite my sense of urgency, in the long run it hardly mattered whether I could direct our conversation to issues relevant to the here and now. The key to unlocking anything she might (consciously or unconsciously) know about Ariel's death lay in developing a good relationship. That meant expressing interest in *whatever* Pearl had to say.

In truth, I had enjoyed the story of her family's roots in China, even if it did not seem relevant to learning how my grandniece had died. But if the answer to the riddle of her death lay with the family that owned the apartment complex, it was not a waste of time to learn *how* they had ended up here...or the nature of their complex relationships.

After reviewing the issues I wanted to explore that evening, I was pumped intellectually and poised to ask Pearl several questions. Unfortunately, as a journalist who sometimes conducted oral history interviews, I was again reminded of the discrepancy between my need for succinct answers and the methodology by which I would gain the most information from my interviewee. This was especially true since Pearl did not know she was being interviewed—much less by someone related to the death that had just occurred on her property.

Having completed my preparation for my evening of congenial research, I answered the gourmand demands of a yowling Miss Una. Next I assembled a plate of leftover salad, focaccia bread, and papaya-orange juice from the refrigerator for my own late lunch. While nibbling my solitary meal, I thought about my dinner with Keoni. I found it hard to believe it had been less than twenty-four hours since we were prowling around the grounds of the apartment and sharing an intimate evening of mixed metaphors and tentative feelings. Not only were his skills as a detective proving vital to my current inquiries, but our acquaintanceship of several years was moving toward something far more personal.

While today's meetings had been satisfying on some levels, several issues remained to be resolved. At the forefront of my mind was the statement that Ariel's case was still classified as an "unattended death," sometimes used as police-speak for suicide. But regardless of the category of her death, my grand-niece's second earring remained missing. This seemed like a vital clue to me. She never would have left home with only one earring. And, unlike me, she had not needed to remove an earring to make a phone call—which is the only reason I can see for having pierced ears.

Where *could* that earring *be*? And, in addition to the earring, where was her smart phone? It was good that Lieutenant Dias was ordering a second examination of the Mustang on which Ariel had fallen. However, I doubted that the techs had been remiss in investigating a straight-forward scene like a single vehicle parked at a small apartment complex. That meant someone or something was responsible for the disappearance of at least two of Ariel's possessions.

The two missing items brought me to the primary question: If someone had purposefully removed them from the scene, was that person involved in her deadly fall onto handyman Al's car? If that was the case, what was their motivation? Perhaps the lack of obvious marks of "pre-mortem trauma" meant that a weapon had not been involved—other than my growing suspicion that a pair of hands had been set in action by a malevolent mindset. And while first degree murder may not be the right label for the crime that resulted in my grand-niece's death, dead is dead. I had come here to learn the truth of the circumstances surrounding her death and that was what I was going to do.

This was all the analysis I could cope with prior to playing dress-up and make-believe that evening. I had a couple of hours before I needed to get ready for cocktails with Pearl, and even though I was tired, I was too agitated to sit around the apartment.

What could I accomplish in two hours? Before anything else, I should phone Margie and Dan O`Hara. I needed to let them know I would not be attending tonight's cocktail party for some of the RIMPAC Naval exercise organizers and their friends. I hated to disappoint the O`Haras. I had delayed in calling them until the last minute in case I could go. As it was, I had neither the time nor the inclination to go to a celebratory party attended by military, political, and business powerhouses. My call to Margie's cell phone immediately went to voice mail, so I was not able to set up contingency plans for seeing them while they were in Honolulu.

Now what? I could go online and work on the research that had brought Keoni into the forefront of my schedule on the night before Ariel's demise. Or I could recolor my nails, or... No, the logical thing would be to do a load of laundry. I quickly assembled a basket of delicates and went to the kitchen for laundry soap and some quarters from my emergency cash box. In a few minutes, I was ready for today's interpretation of R & R. As I held the door open with my foot to pick up the laundry basket, I saw a flash of fur fly past my ankles. Good Lord, no!

"Get back here," I cried dropping my laundry basket and closing the door. Rushing down the walkway, I caught sight of Miss Una's tail joining the rest of her body in a dash for freedom down the stairs. Considering the shortness of her legs, it was amazing to see how fast that half-grown cat could fly when motivated.

Running to catch up with her, I changed verbal tactics. "Oh, Una, sweet Miss Una. Natalie has a treat for you." I was already out of breath, but determined to sound calm and soothing. "Wouldn't you like to have a little dried chicken? Mmm, it's awfully nice..."

As I rushed around the last turn in the stairway, I glimpsed Miss Una charging toward the back of the property. It was clear I would not be able to match her speed, and there were any number of places she could hide. I slowed my pace to catch my breath and looked around the courtyard. Even from a distance, I could see the door to the laundry room in my building was closed. That was one less place to consider as a feline hideaway.

Glancing across at Building A's ground floor apartments, I noticed a couple of open doors. As they had screens, I did not think she would be able to get into them. If she had dashed inside, their occupants would be clamoring. I crossed the courtyard and began walking along the pathway between the left side of the volleyball net and Building A. I looked toward the picnic area and the tree line at the back of the property, but saw no sign of a retreating tail. As I approached the end of the walkway, I debated the choices that might appeal to my four-legged roommate.

At that moment, I noticed the last screen door jiggling ever so slightly. Too bad it was the entrance to Al Cooper's apartment. I had seen him pulling out of the parking lot when Keoni and I drove in a short while ago. Not knowing Al's intentions, I did not want to confront him with either my cat or my suspicions. Quietly, I approached the door hesitantly, looking around to see if anyone was watching me.

I knew I should not go any farther. In fact, if I were a cop, I would be prohibited from doing anything at all. But I am not an officer of the law or the courts. I am merely a tenant looking for her cat. *"The screen was open, sir."* I could say to a police officer. *"I thought I saw her tail sweeping from view around the edge of the door."* Hmm, what next? *"The screen was already open, I thought if I peeked in, I could call her and she'd come running back to me."*

Accordingly, I called out, "Miss Una, are you in there?" Again I looked around and upward to the walkways and higher apartments. There was no sign of humans or their animal companions. I did not want to leave any indication that I had been there, so I reached into my pocket for the hanky I always keep handy. It had been one of my mother's the last gifts to me. It had served me well in many situations over the years—

although never on what an unkind official might label an exercise in Breaking and Entering.

Regardless of what I might learn from another afternoon of detecting, I would eventually have to let Keoni in on my activities. At least the door was open. I would not be charged with breaking into the property. Of course, a charge of "illegal entry" remained a possibility. I could honestly say I was hoping to prevent Miss Una from bothering Al Cooper—since he had expressed concern initially about her being a nuisance. After one last glance around me, I gingerly pulled the screen's handle outward and looked into the living room. No sign of Miss Una, but there was no telling where she might have run to find cover.

To latch or not to latch, that was the question of the moment. If I left the screen door open, I could say that was how I had found it; but if I left it open, the cat might sneak out again and resume her flight around the complex. One thing was certain: I could not afford for this adventure to last much longer. And if I did not find Miss Una soon, I would be late to cocktails with Pearl, and that would not do at all. Of course, the primary question of the moment was how long it would be until Al returned. The single positive aspect of my current situation was that I had seen the man depart in Pearl Wong's truck. That probably meant he was off doing her errands, which could take a long time. Or not.

Hmm. My reason for being here is Miss Una. If I did not find her, I would have lost the excuse for my presence. And if Al returned to find her in his apartment, I could not predict what he would surmise by her presence. It certainly would not be good. Considering his temper, there was no telling what he might do to her, or me. After a few seconds, I made my decision. I softly pulled the screen to the door jam, without latching it.

I decided that I would take a quick look around while I was inside the apartment. From what friends in law enforcement have said—and from what I have seen on detective shows—

the first thing to do is get a general sense of the layout. Therefore, I began by walking through the living room. It was the mirror image of my own. The unit was sparsely furnished and neat, though a bit dusty. Maybe Al should trade places with Pearl's nephew Richard Bishop in the rotation of apartments. This one did not look like it had seen the lick of a paint brush in the years Al had lived here.

Since the doors to each room stood open, there would be no short-cuts in my hunt for little Miss Una. First I checked the guest bathroom and finding it empty, closed the door. If I did that with every space, there was no way she could sneak behind me—but I would have to remember to re-open the rooms before leaving. My memory is never very good when I get rattled, so I was grateful Al had been consistent in leaving every door open. Next, I walked into the guest bedroom and pulled the door almost closed. No sign of her under the bed, and fortunately, there was nothing but a couple of suitcases and an old overcoat hanging in the closet.

I pulled the door to that bedroom closed behind me and walked back into the living room. After checking under the couch, I walked through to the kitchen that smelled of burnt toast. With no open cupboards, my search in that space was quickly completed. Returning to the living room, I tiptoed up to the front door and looked out. There was no sign of anyone in the courtyard or across on Building B's walkways. That was a very good thing, as Martha Stewart famously says.

I was glad that the apartments are small. Only the master bedroom remained to be checked. I walked into the room, again pulling the door close to the jam, but not closing it completely. As usual, I was not wearing my watch, so even with Al's bedside clock radio, I could not be sure how long I had been in his apartment. I moved into the adjoining bathroom that smelled of cheap cologne and toothpaste. Brushing the shower curtain aside, I quickly determined there was no cat. Creeping back into the bedroom, I carefully bent down and lifted the bedspread that, conveniently for a cat, dragged on the floor. Again, there were no obstructions and the clear view verified that my little darling was not there.

Straightening up, I looked across the room. There was a well-used oak dresser, but all the drawers were closed. There were nightstands that matched the dresser, but they were too close to the wall for Miss Una to have hidden behind. That left the desk and closet. The chair at the desk was positioned awkwardly, leaving a bit of space in the kneehole at the center. I walked softly up to it and wiggled the chair a bit. Looking down, I verified there were only four chair legs in that space.

Glancing across the top of the desk, I found a large and worn Bible lying open. Leaning over, I saw that a brass bookmark highlighted a passage in Romans, Chapter One, Verses Twenty-six and Twenty-seven. Underscored were the words, "for even their women did change the natural use into that which is against nature." Beside the Bible was a lined notepad. In one column were citations from the Old Testament and printed in bold block letters in a second column were the words *evil women*, *vile affections*, *lasciviousness* and *depravity*. I cringed as I read a final, single sentence that said it all, "So, that was why she had to die!"

Obviously, Al had been doing his homework. But it appeared superficial. I am not that great on biblical chapter and verse. However, the major themes had been covered in my courses in history and classic literature and it looked like a key point was missing from Al's research. Clearly, the man had overlooked St. Paul's declaration that homosexuality was not a behavior chosen to offend God, but a *punishment thrust by God* upon sinners who practiced idolatry. Setting that issue aside, Al had found biblical support for his belief that Ariel had not deserved to live. The overriding question remained whether Al had *acted* upon his judgment of her. Of course, I was still trying to figure out why he had concluded she was gay in the first place.

While my mind tried to absorb all this, the phone on the desk rang loudly and I jumped close to the ceiling fan that was rotating at a slow speed. At least I had the presence of mind to clamp my hand across my mouth to stifle the scream that was about to emerge from my throat. Although my discovery made me wonder if there might be any evidence lying around Al's apartment—like an earring and a cell phone—I knew I had to get out of the place quickly.

My reason for being on the premises was Miss Una, and there was only one other place to check. I approached the closet softly and pulled the door knob toward me. Sure enough, in the back right-hand corner, draped over the recently polished toe of a black Johnston and Murphy dress shoe, was the extended paw of Miss Una. Without absorbing its possible significance, on the wall above her body, I noticed a rough rectangular patch—*just like as it is in my closet.*

"Gotcha," I declared. Carefully closing the closet door to keep her contained, I walked back through the apartment and opened every door I had previously closed. Returning to the closet, I pulled the door toward me and reached down to pick up the culprit who had launched this leap into the land of Agatha Christie. Unfortunately, she was not where I had left her. While my eyes were adjusting to the dimness of the closet, Miss Una shot out like a heat-seeking missile. I flew after her into the living room, in time to see her bolt out the screen door into the bright sunlight.

Since she was on the loose again, I decided to take the time to check whether I had left Al's apartment as I had found it. After a quick glance, I determined I was in the clear—at least if I could get back out the door without anyone noticing my departure. If someone saw me, there was no point in pretending I had been visiting with Al, because someone might mention it the next time they saw him. I needed to remain as invisible and silent as possible.

Pressing my nose to the screen, I looked across the courtyard and up at Building B. Luckily, I did not see anyone. Taking a breath, I pushed the door outward, and gave a quick look to the left and the right before slipping out of Al's apartment.

Again using Mother's hanky, I re-positioned the screen.

Safely back in public territory, I looked around for a hint of where Miss Una might have disappeared. At the back of the property I heard someone giggling.

"I'm going to open my eyes in a minute, so you'd better have hidden really, really well...."

With that lovely drawl, it was clear to whom that voice belonged. Ashley Lowell. She must be playing a game with her son Cory. Thank goodness I had been lucky and we had not bumped into each other as I was entering Al Cooper's apartment.

Sure enough, below the fragrant *plumeria* trees, I saw a whirlwind of fallen flowers beside a large wheelbarrow that was turned on its side.

"One, two, three, here I come," Ashley called out.

I watched their play for a moment while scanning the horizon for another small character, equally fleet of foot. I figured I should at least greet Ashley, while continuing my search of the grounds.

"Hi, Ashley," I called out. "I see you're looking for someone too. Maybe you could help me find Miss Una when you and Cory are through with your game.

Suddenly a small figure in shorts and suspenders, but no shirt, peeked out at me. "You mean the kitty? That's Miss Una, right?"

I laughed and squatted down to his level. "Yes, Cory. Miss Una's my kitten. She's a lot smaller than you and she ran away today and I'm worried."

"I'm sorry your kitty is gone, Miss Natalie," said Cory throwing himself into my arms.

Ashley had her hand over her mouth, to cover a laugh that was clearly dying to escape. I stood up and after swinging Cory around, carried him to his mother.

"You look pretty comfortable with Cory on your hip. Am I right that you've had a couple of children of your own, Natalie?"

We moved toward the picnic tables. "No, Ashley. That wasn't in the cards for me. But I've had plenty of practice with my brother's son and granddaughters."

"Uh, that's right. Your husband passed when you were pretty young."

"Yes. We were in our twenties and had only been married five years. I must confess I almost married a handsome stranger I met on assignment in the Middle East many years later."

"So what happened, if you don't mind my being personal?" Ashley queried.

"Not at all. Gary and I dated for several years, but I kept getting overseas assignments and he wanted to settle down. He was a great guy, but I just couldn't give up my work."

Cory started squirming, and I knew I needed to hurry things up.

On cue, Ashley said, "Cory and I would be delighted to help you look for Miss Una, Natalie. What does she look like?"

"Well, she has the usual whiskers and a very long tail for a kitten her size. She has a white patch across her nose and down the side of her face and splotches of brown, and gray and black all over her fur. That's why she has the name Miss Una; *Una* is Hawaiian for tortoise and she is a tortoise shell kitty. Do you think that will help you tell her from all the other kitties we see running around, Cory?"

Cory looked rather serious as he stared up at me. "Oh, yes Miss Natalie, I'm sure I'll know her. Come here, Miss Una," he called out, looking around.

"If you really have time to help me, maybe we'd better spread out."

Ashley nodded. "I'll take the trees, in case she scooted past us."

"And I'll go look under the cars," volunteered Cory.

I looked at Ashley. Before she could express her concern, I said, "Uh, Cory, why don't we all stay together in the courtyard. You can look in the flower beds. Everything is so overgrown, if she's hiding, you might get her to come out to play hide and seek with you."

Ashley smiled appreciatively at me, and turned to scan the ground under the trees. "She's pretty small, right? Do you think she could have climbed into the trees?"

"No, I don't think she could climb any of these old trees. She's still a kitten, so she isn't very big. And since we live in a condo, I keep her claws closely trimmed."

"With the chain link fence at the back, she wouldn't have gotten very far going this way," offered Ashley.

Intent upon his task, Cory prowled around in the dead flower beds. "Come here, kitty, kitty. Would you like to play? I have a ball," said Cory with his most enticing voice. It was probably the same tone his mother used to lure him from something he was not supposed to be doing.

Reaching into his right front pocket, he brought out a small red ball that looked like the companion to a set of jacks. Wondering if kids still played the game, I watched him throw the ball back and forth between his hands.

"Are you watching, Miss Una?" The boy tossed the ball toward the front of the property. It did not have much thrust, but after landing a short way from him, it continued rolling. When it reached the back edge of the fountain, I saw a brown fur-ball fly out of the weeds.

"Well done, Cory," I exclaimed and went running after the cat. Calling back over my shoulder I said, "Thank you both for helping, I'd better catch her while I can."

"Good luck," answered Ashley.

Knowing she was being pursued, Miss Una flew past the ball that had come to a boring stop. Hanging a left at the volleyball net, she continued on to the stepping stones along Building B.

"Oh, please don't go out in the parking lot," I pleaded.

As though she understood the implications of imminent danger to her person, Miss Una dashed to the stairway. With barely a pause to look back at me, she began running up the stairs.

Watching her ascend to what was hopefully a safer environment, I slowed down. While climbing the stairs myself, I became aware of the toll the day was taking on my body, if not my mind. Reaching the top floor, I looked to the right toward apartment B406. There she was, sitting at the door, daintily washing her whiskers, as though she had just awakened from a nap in the sunshine.

I opened the door, and Miss Una regally entered. While she moved calmly toward her food and water, I spoke my mind.

"I don't know whether to scold you or hug you. I certainly did not appreciate the forced exercise, but without your shenanigans, I would never have learned what I did."

Looking at the clock on the stove, I realized I had only a short amount of time to prepare for my date with Pearl Wong. If we were not having cocktails, I would definitely have had a glass of wine. As it was, I settled for a tall glass of ice water. Then, after checking Miss Una's refreshments, I disappeared into the bathroom for a hasty redo of me.

CHAPTER 17

Every new beginning comes from
some other beginning's end.
Lucius Annaeus Seneca [4 BCE-65 CE]

I began walking back downstairs at fifteen minutes before five p.m. Unlike an hour previously, there was now
a lot of activity in the courtyard. I found Ashley and
Cory, as well as several other residents, sitting on worn white
patio chairs set along the perimeter of the grass. Evidently
they were the cheering section for an Army vs. Navy challenge
taking place in the volleyball court.

I had seen most of the young sportsmen around the property before. With the ball caps of two Navy ships and an Army
unit, it looked like they were having a friendly semi-final
competition in preparation for the annual TGIF celebration
tournament I had heard about. Since Ariel's death had also
occurred on a Friday, I wondered if any of them had been in
the courtyard that day.

I still had a few minutes so I continued on to my mailbox.
As I had expected, there was nothing personal. I have hoped
that if someone else's mail lands in mine by mistake, I will
be able add to my growing list of residents. Although there
was nothing addressed to me by name, I grabbed a fistful of
items addressed to "Occupant." In addition to the usual cou-
pons, there was a flier promoting a sunset dinner cruise in the
waters off Waikīkī.

As I tossed the junk mail in a nearby recycle bin, I thought
about the other ways I could identify and connect with the

people who lived here. If only this were a condo. Then I would be able to volunteer to serve on the Board of Directors or some committee and receive a complete list of every owner and tenant, as well as anyone providing services to the complex.

Walking up the left side row of pavers to Miss Wong's, I saluted the young men with U.S. Naval Academy ball caps, to show my support for the blue and gold. They grinned and turned back to the battle before them. Approaching Pearl Wong's apartment, I saw that the door was open. Fanning her face with the evening paper, she was taking a peek at the sporting event of the day.

"Sometimes it makes me feel youthful, watching the young people enjoying life out on their own," she commented, gesturing for me to enter.

"I *so* agree with you," I replied, thinking of Ariel. There was no one who had savored life more than she did. I managed to keep a smile on my face, like I did not have a care in the world.

"It seems like most of the tenants are either students or are in the military," I observed.

"You are correct. We're well-located for both categories. Come in from the heat, Natalie. I have simplified tonight and asked my favorite caterer to provide a few items for our cocktail hour. Although it is traditional to have *yum cha*, tea tasting, with *dim sum*, I felt we would forego that and enjoy some Western libation." Gesturing to her dining table filled with an assortment of Chinese delicacies, she asked, "You did say you like Chinese food?"

The fragrance alone reminded me I had not had much lunch. "Oh, yes. It looks heavenly. You shouldn't have gone to this much trouble," I said.

Pearl passed me a plate and waved her hand toward the food. "Well, it isn't often that I get a chance to visit with a woman over the age of fifty with a professional background like yours and an interest in history. It has been a delight to meet you. And knowing you will not be with us very long, I want to make the most of your company."

"The pleasure is mine. I'm also pleased whenever I meet someone with whom I can discuss history—especially the intersection of Hawai`i and China. My Bachelor's degree was a double major in history and journalism, from Lewis and Clark College in Portland, Oregon."

"That is an excellent school. Several of my Priory classmates graduated from there. Please, come and try a few of these samples of *dim sum*. As you may know, this specialty originated in my mother's home province of Guǎngdōng. My favorites are the *char siu bao*, buns stuffed with barbecue pork and *ha gao*, shrimp dumplings. Since I do not know your taste in drinks, I offer you a choice between champagne and margaritas."

"Miss Wong, you've presented me with a difficult decision."

"I believe we have gotten past the formal phase of our acquaintanceship. As I said before, please call me Pearl."

"I am honored to do so. And, please call me Natalie."

"Very good. Regarding our beverage selection, may I suggest we begin with the pitcher of margaritas. Later we can move on to the bottle I have chilling in the ice bucket. I think there's something special about sparkling wine, especially at week's end, or during a trying time."

"I concur, Pearl. Although I also adore margaritas."

"I hope you will like my special recipe. It is iced, but not blended. Will that be with or without salt," asked Pearl.

"Without, please. And I'm pleased there's no blender in sight. It's rather like a martini. Like James Bond, I believe that to merit the name, it should be stirred and never shaken."

We laughed and while she poured me a drink, I followed her instructions and filled my plate with some of the eye-catching delights set before me. We then moved to the living room where we sat as before, with Pearl again on a beautifully upholstered rosewood wingback chair and me on the sofa.

"And where did *you* attend college?" I asked, thinking this topic might keep us in the mid-twentieth century.

"Like Jade, I attended the University of Hawai`i. Her degree was in education, mine was in English, with a few business courses added for good measure. This was in spite of fact that in my day, women were not encouraged to enter into careers in commerce. That is, unless it was their family's business, which usually meant a career in retail sales. But even if it was through the stories of our *amah*, I had my mother as a role model of a woman who had broken with the tradition of a stay-at-home-mother.

"Jade was embarking on her teaching career as I entered the University. It was logical for me to care for our small home when I was not studying. As life rolled on, this remained our pattern. Jade had her teaching career. After college, I continued to maintain our home and supervised our daily business concerns. Through the years, some of the financial opportunities we had (such as our investments in real estate) were linked to the offspring of the original members of our father's *hui*."

"It sounds like the two of you achieved a balance that's worked well for you throughout the years." I declared.

My hostess laughed in response. "Yes, it has been ideal in many respects. Of course, Jade has always led the way, being the elder sister. And before her hand was at the helm, there was our *amah*, who behaved more like our grandmother than a family servant."

Pausing, Pearl gestured with her own empty glass toward the table of drinks and goodies. We rose and refilled our glasses and plates before settling again for another chapter of her tale. Tonight I hoped to learn of the Wong sisters coming to America, and eventually to these apartments.

"This *char siu bao*, is delicious, I wish I knew how to make barbecue pork like the filling in this bun, Pearl. It is so gracious of you to welcome me to your beautiful home. I feel as though I'm in a villa on a hill overlooking Hong Kong."

Looking across the room, my hostess glowed with pride. "You are most complimentary. I must again say that I am so grateful to my parents for this wonderful life I live." She paused momentarily. "And it was our father who was the consummate host. Regardless of the occasion or menu, he entertained family and friends with stories of his travels or his home in far-off Hawai`i in a way that made the listener feel they were sharing the experience with him.

Glancing at the painting of her mother, sister and herself in the dining room, she continued. "It was truly amazing that no matter what the narrative was, our Father managed to insert us into the story he was telling. And at the end of each tale, he shared his vision of a future glowing with opportunities for his own *lustrous pearls*.

"I was still a toddler when our personal world crashed around us fully. You see, our mother died trying to bring a son into the world. With no relatives in the city, our father and Chú Huā arranged a quiet funeral for Yùyīng and the son who never took a breath."

I nearly choked on a rice cracker with duck pâté. I almost thought I had misunderstood her, as she spoke calmly of the deaths and the desolation that overwhelmed her family.

"I do not know if she had formally become a Christian, but because she had lived among her missionary teachers for so long, they insisted she be buried in their cemetery. I remember holding hands with Jade as we stood beside our father. His face was awash with streaming tears. It was the only time we saw him ravaged by sorrow.

"For our sakes, Father controlled his grief and bravely set about organizing our daily lives. Although his business was a fraction of what it had been, he had appointments beyond the walls of our personal world. Sometimes late in the night, we would hear the outer gate open and our father whisper greetings to unseen guests. As always, we heard a mixture of many languages, with an increasing prevalence of English. Later, we often found new objects for playtime when we ventured out to buildings that had become storerooms for the downsized Pearl of the Orient Trading Company."

As I finished eating a shrimp dumpling, I thought of the joy

Nathan and I had felt when our father brought us toys from the countries he had visited overseas. "I can imagine how fun that must have been for the two of you...to have your own private playground...even in a time of war," I said.

"You are right, Natalie. As little children, we were not aware of the wrenching turmoil in the larger world. In 1930, while Europe moved toward war, China's civil war intensified. Warlords, who had fought in alliance with the Guómíndǎng government of China during the Northern Expedition, turned and began fighting Jiǎng Jièshí's central government. Almost simultaneously, the communists rose in retaliation for the General's purging them from government.

"Making the most of these struggles, the Japanese gave aid to the warlords while flexing their own military strength. In September of 1931, they fabricated what is called the Mukden Incident in English. By staging the bombing of a section of railway line to seem like an attack on their Army in Guǎngdōng, the Japanese had designed a nearly plausible excuse for their invasion of Manchuria, which they renamed Manchukuo and held from 1932 to 1945.

"Many Americans do not realize that warfare in the Pacific began long before December 7, 1941. Despite cries of non-observance of international treaties and pacts, appeals to the United States, the League of Nations, and the world in general, nothing was done to halt Japanese aggression in my homeland."

"I remember holding debates in history seminars about which country should have attempted to halt which aggressor in the march toward the Second World War," I interjected.

My story teller nodded. "What happened was tragic. While much of the larger turmoil could not have been prevented, many of the individual incidents could have been contained, if there had been a strong international body to intervene. Sadly, despite the hopes of President Woodrow Wilson, and most of the world, the League of Nations had no authority or power.

"For us, the escalating chaos soon brought the end to our

family life in China. Overnight, the world arrived on our doorstep. After months of fighting the Chinese Army elsewhere, the Japanese Air Force attacked Shànghǎi on January 28, 1932. Claiming a need to protect Japanese residents in the Hongkou district, the Japanese seized the northern part of the city and declared martial law. In response to the rioting mobs of looters and murderers, American, British, and French troops put bayonets on their rifles and prepared to defend their peoples."

"I've seen footage from newsreels shown in movie houses at the time," I recalled. "Even though the scenes were from another era and country, the horrific scenes made even the most callous person view war in a personal way—especially as you watched little children crying and clutching the hands of whatever adults were near to them."

"Indeed. And although few people were killed, the Shànghǎi Incident was reported around the world, complete with such terrible photos that our Hawaiian cousins were terrified for our safety and feared that they would never get to meet us. A bomb did land near our compound, but we were unaware of how close death had come. Despite the terrifying noise, our father, *amah* and servants remained outwardly calm and assured us we would be safe.

"Seemingly overnight, our father decided that Jade and I would leave China on the 1932 premier winter world cruise of the *RMS Empress of Britain*. While I was in college, I chanced upon some mementos from the voyage in our attic. There were menus and announcements of special events, and a ticket for some items put in storage for the crossing. It was all so interesting that I did some research and wrote a paper about my memories.

"I learned that the *Empress* was owned by the Canadian Pacific Trading Company. The royal mail ship was the largest and fastest luxury cruise ship England had ever produced. She was 760 feet long and weighed over 42,000 tons. Passage for the full 128-day cruise cost up to $16,000. Given the increases in monetary value, you can imagine what it cost our father to send Chú Huā, Jade and me to Hawai`i.

"The cruise was nearly thirty thousand miles and included stops in eighty-one countries. By the time the ship had arrived in Asia, she had passed through the Suez Canal and visited the Indian subcontinent, Java and Bali. Because of the fighting, the Empress could not make a port call in Shànghǎi. We had to be taken from our home in the cover of night to escape to the British colony of Hong Kong where we boarded the ship. I often wonder what bribes our father paid in order to get us to that distant pier."

"Being a time of war, I'm sure it was a sizable sum," I said.

She nodded. "We did not understand the implications of the journey, nor the reality that we would never again see the face of our father. We only knew that we were very tired. Our feet were so sore by the time we arrived at the ship that we paid little attention to what was happening around us. After our father secured our belongings in our stateroom, he left us playing with two new Parisian dolls that had miraculously appeared. Long after we had outgrown playing with them, those dolls remained on our beds as reminders of our father's love."

Sipping our drinks, I was sure we were both immersed in the warmth of remembered gifts from childhood.

"At some point Father gestured for Chú Huā to join him in the hallway. After a while, he returned to the stateroom and knelt to hug us. For the last time, he called us his *Zhū lián bì hé*, his perfect strand of jade and pearl gems. Everything was so exciting that we did not notice the moment of his departure. For some time, our *amah* kept us busy, putting our clothing and toys away. By the time we realized Father was gone, she was preparing us to go on deck to watch the ship's festive departure. There were flags flying and streamers floating on the air, and a band. Best of all, when we pulled away from the pier, the ship's whistle sounded to announce we were departing."

"There certainly is a lot of excitement that accompanies the arrival and departure of cruise ships," I recalled from my own experiences.

"Yes. Anticipation and exhilaration are apt descriptors of the entire cruise. For the short expanse of their lives aboard the *Empress*, guests and even staff lived as though there was no Depression."

Pearl's eyes grew misty. "You should have seen the *Empress*, Natalie. In her coat of shiny white paint, the huge ship rode the waves like a queen majestically in her carriage. Her interiors were a layering of classic design styles, crowned with the hard-edged glamour of art deco. The Mayfair Lounge was especially grand, with silver accented walnut paneling. The vaulted ceiling had amber glass and strange signs I later learned were the twelve signs of the zodiac. And, the Greek columns were ideal for two little girls to zigzag around.

"We were only allowed to peek into the beautiful gymnasium filled with exercise devices. But we enjoyed watching the adults play shuffleboard and table tennis. And Chú Huā had trouble getting us out of the swimming pool that replaced a cargo hatch when the ship moved into warm waters."

"It's almost like you were preparing for life in Hawai`i."

"I think you are right. Even the friendliness of the staff helped prepare us for the warm personalities of the people we would meet in the Islands. We especially liked Captain R. G. Latta, who was like a dashing uncle in a handsome uniform. It seemed like there was always an assistant at his side, ready to reveal pockets containing troves of candy that served to calm the fears of any child who might cry aboard their wonderful ship."

I laughed, thinking of the few times I had needed to pacify Ariel or Brianna.

Pearl continued sharing the sojourn that had brought her to Hawai`i.

"And the food and beverages? We barely asked for anything before it would appear with a flourish. Being little children, we usually ate in our stateroom. One evening, however, we joined Chú Huā in the dining room. We were amazed by the huge portions of roast beef. Our favorite delight was the praline ice cream. I do not believe I have ever had a dessert to equal it."

"Well tonight, this mango pudding is high on my list of unbelievable desserts," I said grinning.

She answered with a smile as she finished a coconut ball. "In every respect, we were treated splendidly aboard the ship and at every port of call the ship made. Not knowing the difference between a royal personage and someone merely rich or famous, the locals who conducted the overland tours were attentive to our every desire. Although we were young, we enjoyed the five-day trip to Běijīng and ten-day cruise around Japan very much. Jade could read a bit of English and with a bit of prompting from Chú Huā, she proudly told me what the Shore Excursion Programs promised. Amazingly, Jade still has one of those programs, as well as an invitation card for a cocktail hour that Chú Huā did not have time to accept."

"I know how that is. Sometimes, when I was on a tour, I simply couldn't attend all the scheduled functions." Despite the fact that I should be clamoring for her to bring us into present day living at the Makiki Sunset Apartments, I was delighted to be relieved of my burdens for one evening.

"We played our way through the five-day crossing of the Pacific, giving little thought to what our new lives would be like. Finally, we arrived in Honolulu on March the twelfth. *Boat Day* was another festive day with thousands of streamers and confetti, dancers of *hula* and young boys diving into the water for coins. It was the first time I heard the Royal Hawaiian Band and I loved their uniforms as well as their music. It may sound silly today, but you cannot imagine the impact of a fantasia of *mu'u'mu'us* and the pervading scent of fresh *leis* in the air had on us.

"It was also a very special time for the denizens of the city who gathered at the harbor to welcome the newcomers and their money which was needed to strengthen the local economy. We were warmly greeted not by strangers, but by many of our cousins who came to welcome us. Some lived in Honolulu, but several had come from Maui for the adventure of meeting their new-found family members. On that first day of our new life, our Hawaiian family fawned over us and showered us with special gifts. Soon we were choked with beautiful *leis* crowding up to our chins and our hands were full of toys and pillows with Hawaiian appliqué quilt squares.

"Before we left the harbor to enter our life in this Pacific paradise, we observed an unusual event. Although Chú Huā Lee was considered a servant in China, evidently she was more highly regarded here. As we waited with our family for our luggage to be unloaded, we looked toward the Aloha Tower. There we saw our *amah* being formally greeted by two men we later learned were political leaders in the Territory of Hawai`i—one of whom would become governor within a couple of years of our arrival. As she nodded slightly to them, they formally tipped their hats to her. Next, she shook the hand of each man. Then, reaching into what we had thought was simply a needlework bag, she brought out a small box tied in string and one large envelope which she handed to them.

"None of this meant much to us at the time. Later, when we were going through some files, we found a torn airmail envelope addressed to our father in China from the Territory of Hawai`i. The scrap was very soiled and its postmark was smudged and torn, but we could read the first three numbers of its date...195. It was the only indication that our father may have survived the war. But the mysteries of what the correspondence was and why it was found in our home were never answered."

Finishing my last piece of *dim sum*, I asked, "You never saw him after leaving China?"

"No. It is the great sorrow and mystery of our lives."

Rising, Pearl walked to the dining table and poured two glasses of Avinyo Brut Cava. I did not see the vintage, but it was clearly not a wine I would have another opportunity to taste in the near future.

After we toasted the evening, she continued. "It might have

been expected that we would live with someone in our father's family. But our father was an only child and we did not have first cousins with whom we could bond as siblings. Perhaps for this reason, our father decided that we should remain in the care of our *amah*. Therefore, we moved into a small bungalow in central Honolulu, where we lived at home while attending St. Andrew's Priory School for Girls.

"So, there we were, or are, in Hawai`i. The years have passed so quickly...Initially our life in the Islands was uneventful and easy. Through our youth, we lived in our home with Chú Huā, who would call out to us jointly, *Come here my zhū yù, my pearl and jade*. Our weekdays were filled with school and homework. On weekends, we went to Waikīkī and often swam at the Natatorium. During summer holidays, we sometimes visited our father's family on Maui.

"But it was not all bliss. Jade and I soon realized that the war we had escaped had spread its arms to ensnare everyone in our lives. We may not have understood the specifics of what was happening, but we knew our father was in a terrible spot. Snippets of news periodically arrived to jolt our personal awareness of the growing global hostilities. We watched with sadness as the countries that had once bought our family's goods were gobbled up by the Axis Powers.

"And with considerable sorrow, we learned that the magical ship that had brought us to Hawai`i was sunk by German aircraft and submarines in 1940. Once I heard Chú Huā discussing the sad state of the Jewish ghetto in the Hongkou district of Shànghǎi with our family lawyer. She questioned the safety of the men who had created much of the beautiful jewelry sold by our family business.

"The details of their conversation were disturbing, even to a young girl like me. Euphemistically called 'The Restricted Sector for Stateless Refugees,' the Jewish ghetto was supervised by the occupying Japanese Army. Their behavior was influenced, if not determined by, the Nazis' hatred of the Jewish people. Clearly the authorities felt no remorse for the overcrowding, poor sanitation, and lack of food in the ghetto. Much later I learned that it was only the in-pouring of international support that kept the number of wartime deaths of Shànghǎi Jews to about two thousand."

"Such facts are difficult for adults, let alone children, to absorb."

"Yes, that is true. We did not understand the fullness of the war's atrocities until we were adults. Of course, war arrived on our doorstep in a personal way on December seventh of Nineteen Hundred and Forty-one. The schools were closed until February, and even our *amah* helped with nursing those who were wounded on the day of the attack on Pearl Harbor."

There was nothing I could say in response to that, so I merely shook my head. At that moment, my cell phone rang. I smiled apologetically, and reached into my handbag. I saw that the caller was Margie O'Hara. Abruptly, I decided that this was the ideal moment for me to conclude my evening with Pearl.

I answered quickly, "Margie, it's so good to hear from you, but I need to call you back shortly."

I hung up and looked over at Pearl, who was politely staring into her glass. "I'm so sorry Pearl. This is a dear friend who is visiting Honolulu for only a couple of days, and I need to finalize plans to see her. But I hate to end our wonderful evening. You can't imagine how much I have appreciated the opportunity to simply rest for one evening...and of course, to get to know you better."

"Think nothing of it my dear. I know the strain involved with any move."

"I look forward to another, recent chapter when I have you to my home, soon."

"Indeed, Natalie. I too shall look forward to it. Enjoy seeing your friend and once you have gotten settled in, we will plan something."

She walked me to the door, and I departed feeling relaxed and at ease. Unfortunately, the sensation did not last long. Walking toward the staircase, I again felt the eyes and thoughts of someone focused on me, and I did not think they were well meaning.

CHAPTER 18

By seeking we may come upon the truth.
Pierre Abelard [1079-1142]

Even though it was early evening when I left Pearl Wong's, I felt as though I had lived a week in the last twenty-four hours. Our cocktail hour had been another *non*-event where the mystery of Ariel's death was concerned. I knew I should call Keoni to confess my afternoon of playing detective. But despite the logic, I could not face relaying all the details without a good night's rest.

I hoped that Miss Una was as exhausted as I was and would permit me to crash. After walking out of my shoes at the front door, I went immediately into the bedroom. There I found my darling roommate curled up in her catsack with only a pair of black tufted ears showing. She moved slightly and poked one eye out to confirm I was present and accounted for. Of course, that reminded me that to fail to check on her food supply would be a major misstep. Turning around with a sigh, I dragged myself into the kitchen. I poured a glass of water for myself, filled her water bowl, and placed a dollop of wet food on a plate beside her dry food.

That completed my chores for the evening...Except for calling Margie to delay confirming plans to meet with her and Dan. I then realized I had not checked my messages all day. By the time I had written notes of the calls I needed to return, I was slightly more awake. But not enough to remain upright for very long. After a quick glance at the slider's security rod, I returned to the "master suite" about which Pearl was so proud. After a quick wash of face and teeth, I pulled on a cotton nightie and crawled in beside Miss Una. After today's multiple adventures, I was too drained for my ritual of night-time reading. I think I fell asleep immediately after laying my head on the pillow. Best of all, I passed the night without any memorable dreams.

When I awoke, I was suffering from a headache. I knew it had been brought on by the emotional highs and lows of the previous couple of days. Coffee or tea? Which would be more soothing? I knew better than to take an analgesic on an empty stomach, so I opted for a cup of yogurt, half a bagel and a large cup of tea laced with almond milk and cinnamon. After that, I had a water chaser with a couple of OTC pain pills. Then it was back to a darkened bedroom with an icepack for half an hour. This little routine has worked for years, allowing me to avoid the short-term prescriptions some of my friends have taken.

In less than an hour, I returned to a state of near-normalcy. Showered and dressed, I sat down at the dinette table and listened to voicemail messages from both my condo and cell phones. I was glad that after the volume of the day before, this morning's crop were few and inconsequential. Looking over my notes, I focused on the few that required immediate attention.

The first call I made was to Anna. After ascertaining that I was safe, she listed the mail she was considering forwarding to me. To simplify life for both of us, I gave her a blanket authorization to send any mail she thought was important and hold the rest until I came for a visit...or returned home permanently. My next concern was Nathan. I was glad I was able to respond to his questions about food and entertainment for the memorial quickly. Thankfully, he was silent about my temporary abode. Finally, there was a call from Margie.

"Hey, Natalie. It's Margie. Sorry we're playing phone tag, but I know you have a lot to keep you busy. Dan and I want you to know that while we miss seeing you, we're enjoying our time at the Halekulani Hotel. I don't think I mentioned that our son Ronny has made Lieutenant Commander. Since he's single, there's no reason to delay the promotion ceremony and he's asked to have it here. So tomorrow, we'll be taking a little break from the sand and surf to head over to the Naval Station to watch the big event.

"Well, I guess that's all our news. Give us a call when you can. I know you've said there's nothing we can do to help at the moment, but please let us know if that changes. We're still hoping to see you before we return home, but you know we'll be on the next plane to Honolulu whenever you and Nathan are able to hold the memorial for Ariel."

I was disappointed to have to pass on the RIMPAC gatherings and Ron's promotion, but I knew Margie and Dan understood my predicament. It was one thing to put on a nice dress and chat with Pearl Wong about a time and place I never knew. It would be another to try and pretend my life was sublime… or worse, to have to share the details of my current reality.

After researching photo printing businesses, I prepared to reorganize my never ending to-do lists. After sitting down in the recliner with a fresh cup of tea, several notebooks and a pen, I spent a while scribbling furiously. As I set my writing materials aside, I looked across the room. Noting the laundry basket sitting by the front door, it took little thought to determine my next course of action.

Planned or not, laundry day had arrived. Deciding to make the most of the trek down to the laundry room, I added another load to my basket. Oh, the joy of having a washer and dryer in your house. I walked back into the bedroom and gathered the catsack and my bed linens.

Making sure Miss Una was on in her cat perch by the back door, I quickly slipped out the front, down the stairs, and along the paving stones to the laundry room. The set-up was pretty good, except for the challenge of carrying baskets up and down stairs. Surprisingly, there were even benches, padded metal chairs, and rolling carts with racks on which to hang clothes.

Reading the signs, I saw that I had sufficient coins for the two thirty-five-minute wash cycles I was doing, but not enough for the drying. Once the washers were noisily gyrating, I went back up to the apartment for more change and my notepad.

When I returned to the laundry room, I found I was not alone. Mrs. Espinoza was already approaching the conclusion of a mega wash day. As I watched, she deftly moved three loads of laundry from washers into a rolling cart already sporting several dresses neatly displayed on hangers.

"Good morning, my dear," she said with a bob of her tight curls and her usual open smile.

"Why, hello Mrs. Espinoza. It looks like you've got this down to a science."

"Hardly. I imagine it would be easier to do just a couple of loads at a time, but I'm too lazy to bother with laundry more than every two weeks."

I then checked the time on my two loads. Turning back to Mrs. Espinoza, I remarked, "I wouldn't call that lazy, simply a good use of your time and energy. If I could afford it, I'd be tempted to hire someone to do my laundry. But if you do that you've not only spent a lot of money, but possibly more time than doing it yourself."

We completed our tasks with mutual laughter and moved toward a bench at the front of the room. I looked over and saw she had brought out some complicated needle work.

"That's beautiful. May I ask what you're making?"

"Oh, nothing fancy. It's a new petite pointe seat cover for the vanity in my bedroom. I'll give it to my granddaughter eventually. She loves lavender roses."

"She's a lucky girl. I'm sure she'll treasure it. The colors of the flowers are so rich."

"Yes, they are. I've tried to match my memories of the roses I grew along the fence of our home on Kauai."

"Oh, I didn't know you'd lived on Kauai. Somehow I thought you and Mr. Espinoza had always lived on the North Shore."

She shook her head. "A lot of people think that, what with

the Sugar Plantation Village Museum out there. But as plantations closed across the state, older workers were retired and if the younger ones were lucky, they moved on to another plantation."

"If I may ask, Mrs. Espinoza, how long have you lived here?"

"Well, my dear, my husband and I arrived here shortly after he retired from the Kauai Plantation back in the 1990s. You see, the kids had already moved here for school and work. After my Benny's retirement, there was nothing to keep us on Kauai. Most of our friends had already left. And with five kids, we'd never been able to save the money to buy a home there."

"I know what you mean about the price of real estate. I'm lucky I bought my condo when I found the real estate market had cooled while I was on a nine-month stint overseas."

"How lucky you were. After the husband of my friend Leana Kamaka died, she had come to Oʻahu where she worked for the Wong sisters for several years. She thought we'd like this bit of green in the middle of the city. She was right. We enjoyed living here from the very beginning. Unfortunately, my Benny lived only three years after we signed our first lease.

"It was his lungs. All that chaff blowing in the wind all those years. He'd always had breathing problems. He was what used to be called a "blue baby" at birth. He wasn't very strong as a boy. But although he couldn't do a lot of heavy work, there was one job he could perform on the plantation. You see, many of the plantation workers who'd come from Portugal were animal handlers. That's what Benny's dad had been—until machinery replaced the livestock. So when he was a young man, my Benny followed in his father's footsteps.

"You must really miss him, Mrs. Espinoza."

"Now don't you feel bad for me. My Benny and I had many good years together. And this little apartment is exactly what I need to keep my independence. I'm much luckier than Jade Bishop, despite all her money. There she is, stuck in that big cold building. Surrounded by only the people she hires to do for her. I have friends here. And there are all the young people coming and going—not to mention my grandchildren and a great grandchild—to keep me feeling young."

Being a new tenant, I could easily slip in questions about the apartments. "You seem to know everyone here pretty well," I said, hoping to widen the conversation.

"Oh, yes. My Leana died several years ago, but there's Pearl Wong, and her nephew. I guess the proper word would be 'step-nephew,' since Richard is not Jade's son by birth. Anyway, Richard has been here since the beginning. And then there are the Mitchells; they're in A303. Bob was a sergeant in the Army until he retired. For several years, he stayed on at Fort Shafter as a cook. His Emma was a nurse, until her hands got bad with arthritis. They've talked about moving to Arizona, or anywhere that's drier, but they love it here and it would be very hard on them to make such a long distance move now that they're older. Maybe if one of them passes, the other will want to go to their daughter's. But for now they're content."

I nodded, encouraging more detail.

"The apartments have changed through the years. Most of the tenants are now students or boys and girls starting their careers in military service. I love watching them play volleyball. It's almost as much fun as the baseball games we had on the plantation. Quite a show and it's right outside my window."

"I've only met a couple of the tenants so far. Do you know Ashley Lowell and her boy Cory? She seems quite lovely."

"Oh she is. She's a southern girl, from one of the Carolinas. We met when she came by to drop off my phone bill that was delivered to her mailbox by mistake. After that, she started bringing me her delicious spoon bread and we've exchanged bean dish recipes. Sometimes I bake cookies for them."

I nodded again and moved on to my real target. "What about Al, the handyman. How long has he been here?"

"My Al? It seems like he's been here forever, but I think it's only been six years. He got injured while working for the government overseas. Then, I guess he floated around until he ended up in Hawai`i. He's such a dear. I don't know what I'd do without him."

Not wanting to interrupt her flow, I mumbled "Mmhm."

"He might not seem the type, but he's always doing something for me—watering my plants, taking me to the store, and to church. Why you'd think that boy didn't have anything else to do," she concluded with a laugh.

"How nice that you go to church together," I said, wondering how I could politely ask about the tenets of their religion.

"Oh, yes. Being Portuguese, I was raised Catholic, you know. But when I fell in love with my Benny—who'd been divorced—we couldn't get married in the Church. I had my personal faith and never really missed the Church itself. But after Benny died, I started going to a little Christian chapel that's not far from here. If you're looking for a church, Al and I would be glad to take you. The music is quite nice. They have a young couple who play the ʻukulele and sing the old songs. It's very uplifting."

"I'm sure it is. I...I have my own... faith...and do my praying at home."

Mrs. Espinoza nodded. "Like I used to. Well, if you change your mind, let me know."

At that point, bells rang on several driers and Mrs. Espinoza got up to put her laundry in a rolling basket. My washer dinged at about the same time, so our carts passed as I put my washing into the driers she had vacated. I strolled over to ask if I could help her fold her towels.

"Thank you for offering, my dear. But I'll be through in a minute. It's good for my hands. I make an effort to put the exercises Emma taught me into most everything I do. It keeps my fingers limber."

"It's so nice to have someone to visit with while doing the laundry. Back in my condo, I do a load at a time by myself. But this is so fast. You can do everything at once."

"That's so true. I just realized, you must be that writer Pearl spoke of. She said you're here for the summer—while some work is being done in your home."

"Actually, the work is being done on the condo upstairs from me. There was a fire, and, well, the smell is still rather strong. Since I'm doing some volunteering at the learning center down on Wilder, it seemed perfect to stay here for a couple of months. Almost a vacation..."

"You're in B406, aren't you, my dear?"

"Yes, I am."

"Well, I don't want to say anything that will be upsetting to you," she said, biting her lip. "But before you moved in, there was an unfortunate, accident...up there."

"Oh?" was all the response I could manage.

"Yes, a young girl was looking at the apartment. Something happened and she fell down into the parking lot. It was a terrible tragedy."

I swallowed. "I see."

"It was upsetting for everyone here. Especially, my Al—I call him that because he's like a son. It was his car she fell on, you see. And being the handyman...he had to handle...well, tidying things up."

"Yes, I can imagine," I said trying to control the visceral response I was feeling. "It must have really affected him."

"You have no idea. He's such a dear. He'd brought in my groceries and we were having a cup of coffee and some fresh malasadas when it happened."

I gulped. "He was with you at the time?"

"Oh, yes. We'd come back from the big Foodland store on Beretania. I'd put on a fresh pot of coffee to brew while I put the groceries away. We sat down to talk about our minister's Sunday sermon. We hadn't been sitting there more than ten minutes when we heard a scream from the parking lot. One of the boys stationed at Pearl Harbor was calling the police by the time we went out.

"It was terrible. Something I never thought I'd see again. After leaving the plantation, that is. I mean, every once in a while there'd be some kind of accident in the fields with the equipment. But this, this was worse. She was so young. I may not be a practicing Catholic anymore, but I can tell you I said a Hail Mary for that poor *wahine*."

At least there was someone who had cared enough to say a prayer and send kind thoughts to my grandniece on her passing.

"It really seemed to upset Al. He's been after me for Bible verses ever since then. I don't quite understand the connection, but he's been asking me about passages in Leviticus and other parts of the Old Testament. You know. Those rules about righteous living. They may have made sense to someone sometime, but I'm not sure what some of them mean."

I was stunned by what I had heard. There was little I could say in response, so I merely said "Oh" and nodded. This certainly explained the verse Al had marked. And his comments did indicate that he is a homophobe, albeit a confused one. But it would have been difficult for him to juggle Mrs. Espinoza's groceries while dashing up the stairs to kill Ariel, and not have the woman notice something was amiss.

By this time, my companion had finished folding her clothes and was preparing to depart. "I can't begin to tell you how much I appreciate our visit, Mrs. Espinoza. Since my laundry is still in the dryer, why don't you let me carry your basket to your apartment?"

"Why, thank you Natalie, that's most kind of you."

I left Mrs. Espinoza's doorstep thinking about what I had to do—immediately pull the plug on consideration of Al Cooper as a person of interest in Ariel's death. Obviously, he had no prior knowledge of her and had not met her while in the company of Mrs. Espinoza. No. If someone on the property was responsible for her death, either he or she knew Ariel from somewhere else, or there was a one-time interaction between them that resulted in her death.

Since my washing was not yet dry, I sat back down and pulled out my cell phone. My first call was to Nathan. When he did not answer, I left a message alerting him that it did not appear that our single lead was a perpetrator of foul play in

Ariel's death. If I was right, it seemed unlikely that the Coroner's office would delay in releasing Ariel's body. That meant we would soon be able to finalize arrangements for her memorial and life celebration.

Next, I tried to reach Keoni. All I got was voicemail for both his home and cell lines. Rather than delay notifying him about my latest findings, I left a message at his cell number.

"Keoni, this is Natalie. I hope you haven't invested much time in pursuing Al Cooper's car buddies. I've just learned there's no way he was involved with Ariel's death. Call me for details, but it boils down to his being a knight in shining armor for a neighbor at the very moment Ariel fell to her death."

Finally, I called the cell phone number of Detective John Dias. He answered immediately. After I walked him through everything Mrs. Espinoza had told me, he informed me that he had completed his own investigation of Al Cooper.

"The man seems to have a spotless record. In fact, he was injured while working as a private contractor for the Defense Department. Looks like he has a reputation for being a by-the-book kind of guy. He may be a jerk about social issues, but he proved himself when he stopped a run-away vehicle from hitting a group of Guamanian school children.

"With his straight-arrow convictions, it's doubtful he'd be involved in anything criminal—especially a murder. With what you've just told me, I can't see any reason for putting either Al Cooper or Mrs. Espinoza under the microscope."

"I agree, John."

"I appreciate every piece of information you've brought me. I think it's time we need get a team out for a re-canvassing of the complex and the neighborhood surrounding it. Maybe that'll help us locate Ariel's missing belongings. Someone could have found her earring and phone and didn't realize they had anything to do with the death at the apartments."

He said he would notify Marty Soli about our conversation and we terminated our call. The day was half over by the time I had completed my updates on Al Cooper's alibi. It was too late to consider going downtown. Undecided about my next course of action, I finished putting away my laundry. Next I consolidated my to-do lists. Knowing I was likely to have visitors around the time of the memorial, I jotted down the groceries and supplies I should get. Next came more planning for Ariel's memorial. I made my final selections of photos and other memorabilia for the gathering at Nathan's home. Some of the pictures were in poor condition and would need to be scanned for enlargement and framing. After a brief look at yellow page listings, I found a downtown photo and frame shop that performed photo enhancement.

Turning back to my foray into the land of detecting, I considered the tally of my accomplishments to date. It could be summed up by a single, large cipher! We still had no idea of what event or person might have been responsible for Ariel's death. Fortunately, John Dias was continuing to pursue the two items of missing evidence—her earring and smart phone. I also knew that the methodical analysis of her calendar and contact data base being performed by other investigators could yield something of significance.

Where did this leave me? After drawing another blank in my latest visit with Pearl Wong, I did not have a clue of what to investigate about these apartments. That might be reassuring to Keoni, John Dias, and especially Nathan, but I was not pleased. To calm my discontent, I turned to the Internet for a couple of hours.

In looking up crimes that had occurred at the complex, I found references to a couple of auto thefts and a burglary ten years earlier. Obviously none of those cases had any bearing on Ariel's incident, so I turned to Keoni's project. To explore the development of Kaimukī further, I examined the local telephone directory for companies I knew began in the early twentieth century. Their web pages often offered *About Us* pages that discussed their roots and noteworthy events in their past. Much of what I discovered was interesting and might prove useful in future writing projects, but had no bearing on the Hewitt family.

Without a firm direction for either project, I returned to cruising through the morgues of past issues that a few publications have digitized and offer on-line. As a journalist, I am grateful to pay a subscription for access to these materials. I wish more readers realized that with so many newspapers opting for electronic publishing, we're all going to have to get used to paying for the privilege of getting news in this convenient format.

For the most part, the newspaper articles and advertisements read like any from today: stand-alone pieces covering single events and promotions. However, after a while I realized there were several pieces focusing on the elementary school named for Queen Lili`u`okalani, the last monarch of the Kingdom of Hawai`i. I learned that despite being frail, she had personally dedicated the school and helped lay its cornerstone. She had even attended its opening in 1912. Of greatest interest to me was the fact that each of these events had involved interaction with area residents eager to glimpse their former queen in the latter years of her life.

Although I knew Keoni was joking when he had first mentioned royalty in conjunction with his family, I had found a royal connection to his neighborhood! And while I did not see how this tidbit of Kaimukī history could help preserve his family home, one cannot predict what a day at the archives might reveal. Therefore, after dropping by the photo shop in the morning, I would visit Henry at the archives to learn more about the revered Queen and the school that was named for her.

Armed with new information, I would then go to the library to scan additional publications for references to the Queen making public appearances in the area. And while I was doing that, I could look for a birth announcement for Richard Bishop. It was not much, but at least I felt I now had a firm sense of direction for both my professional and personal research.

CHAPTER 19

Would you tell me, please, which way
I ought to go from here?
Lewis Carroll [1832-1898]

I took a short lunch break and thought about how to make the most of what was left of the day. Having lost my inspiration for on-line research, I considered the fragmented state of my hardcopy notes on Ariel's death. After consolidating them and transferring the results to my electronic files, I realized there was one vital line of inquiry I had neglected—Ariel's potential roommate TJ.

So far, all I knew was that the girls had known each other well enough to consider sharing an apartment. But I had never heard her name mentioned by Ariel and Nathan had said he had no idea who she was.

Since he knew about my sleuthing, there was no longer any reason for me to put off involving him. I was lucky to catch him between errands so we could go over Ariel's data base.

"Natalie, I'm glad you called back. I was over at the mall getting some photos printed that I found on Ariel's camera. They're beautiful shots of windward O`ahu beaches, including a few from around here. I don't mean to horn in on your assembling memorabilia for the life celebration, but I thought that making a montage of Ariel's own photographic work would be a nice addition to your display."

I could tell he was about to break down again. "That's a wonderful idea Nathan. You got *my* message, right? About Al Cooper having an airtight alibi?"

"Yes, I don't know how to express my thoughts about that issue. I wouldn't want the wrong person accused, but now we're back where we were at the beginning...with no obvious means for resolving how Ariel died."

"You're right. Except for looking more deeply into the apartment manager's family, I haven't a clue about what else *I* can do to help solve the mystery of her death."

"Well, you know I don't like you being on the premises of where she died. There are still two pieces of evidence missing and no plausible explanation of how she fell, but we know she would never have committed suicide. That leaves some bizarre accident...or murder. And if she was murdered, you could be in danger."

"I know that. I'm being very careful. You know there's no way my archival investigations, or use of the Internet or telephone will arouse anyone's attention. Besides, whoever might have been responsible for her death may not be here at the apartments."

There was no reason to set Nathan's alarm to a higher setting than it was already, so I did not reveal that I feel I am being watched whenever I walk through the grounds of the complex. Flipping to the notebook page I had headed "TJ," I plunged ahead and asked him to check Ariel's computer contact data base for surnames beginning with "J." I then asked him to check for anyone with a first name beginning with "T," knowing that the "T" or the compound "TJ" could be a nickname wholly unrelated to her legal name.

"Give me a moment to get to her bedroom. I'm in the kitchen, but I left her computer on when I was uploading some of those pictures I found."

While he got organized, we chatted about the photos I was assembling. Shortly, I heard the clacking of a keyboard, and then he gave me a list of five surnames under the heading of "J" and another three names under the heading of "T" that showed no surname."

"Could you check one more thing? I haven't heard back

from John Dias and I'd like to know the numbers of her last couple of outgoing calls."

"Sure. Ariel's cell phone bill's right here. As I told the Lieutenant, I didn't get a chance to look it over before giving him a copy. The last number Ariel dialed shows up several times."

I quickly wrote the number down. *That's it, Nathan,* I wanted to say. *That has to be* TJ. *I can already see that the number is not one you gave me from Ariel's database.*

This would make sense if the girl was a new friend and Ariel had not yet entered her information into her computer data base. The number might be in the database of the missing phone, which might be a better record of Ariel's current contacts.

"That's great, Nathan. I'll follow up on these numbers and let you know what I learn."

"All right. That sounds safe enough—if the numbers aren't for the local telephone exchange for Makiki. But I thought John Dias said his department would be looking into that."

"We don't know if he's had a chance to go through the records you gave him. And, after looking at the first three numbers in the entries you just gave me, it doesn't look like they're from this area of the city." I did not mention that if a number was for a cell phone, it would not be based on the person's neighborhood and there would be no way of knowing where they actually lived. "If they're associated with someone at the complex, don't you think Ariel would have simply gone to the person's apartment."

"Well...I guess so," agreed Nathan.

We signed off and I sat quietly for a moment, deciding how to proceed. I had already circled the number I was certain was TJ's. Sadly, there was a good chance that she did not know Ariel was dead. Like a lot of students she may not pay attention to media reports. Regardless of that possibility, if she was a new acquaintance, she might not have contact information for Ariel's other friends—or our family. Not knowing what kind of reaction I might get to the news of Ariel's passing, I decided to take a break and clear my mind before making the call. After drinking a tall glass of water and eating a couple of mints, I dialed the last number Ariel ever called. The phone was answered immediately.

"Uh, hi. Is this TJ?" I asked.

"Yes, it is," she replied tentatively.

"You're Ariel Harriman's friend, right?

"Yes, I am. I'm Theresa Jenkins. I've been trying to get her since I returned from a vacation to Hilo, but I haven't been able to reach her."

Oh, dear. This was the part of the conversation I dreaded, being the one to tell her Ariel was dead. And so I did, as gently as I could.

After a moment, she responded in a shocked voice. "You say you're her aunt?"

"Actually, I'm her grandaunt. Her grandfather is my brother."

"That's Nathan, right."

"Yes. Nathan raised Ariel and her twin Brianna after their parents died."

"I can't believe this. I haven't known her long. I'm a transfer student from UCLA. We met on the UH tennis courts. We'd played a few impromptu doubles matches during spring semester and gone out for dinner a couple of times. When we got to talking about our educational goals and plans for the next couple of years, we found we had a lot in common and decided we'd look for an apartment to share.

"I wondered why I hadn't heard from her after she'd looked at an apartment we'd heard about. I tried her cell phone, but only got her voicemail. I've met a couple of her friends over drinks, but didn't get their full names. And when I tried looking on-line and in the phone book, I didn't find a listing under 'Nathan Harriman.'"

"That's because Nathan is a social worker. For privacy and security reasons, he's never had his home phone number listed in a phone book, and his office number is only found in professional directories."

"Well, that explains it. Please tell Mr. Harriman how sorry I am and that I did try to find out what was going on."

"TJ, I'm sorry I've had to tell you about Ariel's death. But, if you have a moment, I'd really appreciate your answering a couple of questions—since we're still trying to piece together the details of what happened to her."

"I'm glad to help, but I don't know what I could say that will be useful."

"Well, sometimes we know things without realizing it. Would you mind telling me about your last conversation with her?"

"Sure. It was on Friday, a couple of weeks ago. We were talking about the apartment we were supposed to preview. I got delayed, so she had to look at it by herself. She was going to check out the property and its amenities to see if it would work for us."

"Mmm. About what time was that?"

"It had to be around three-thirty. I felt really bad about standing her up. I'd gotten called into my professor's office, and couldn't get away. Ariel had texted me a few times, and finally tried calling me. Once I was free, I called her back."

"About how long did you talk?"

"It couldn't have been more than three minutes or so. We'd already looked at a couple of other places and agreed on what we could afford—with or without utilities. We'd also talked about the features we wanted. I was totally comfortable with her deciding whether we should take the place. I agreed to send her a check for my share of the deposit if she wanted to go ahead with a year's lease."

Not wanting to break her train of thought, I merely said, "Mmhm."

"After that, we talked about the vacation I was going on that night with my boyfriend. We were even joking about the lingerie she'd helped me buy. I remember her teasing me..."

At that point, TJ's voice broke up and I wished I was there

with her to comfort her. But TJ might have been the last person Ariel ever spoke with and I needed to push her a bit further.

"TJ, I'm sorry this is so upsetting. But, please...did Ariel say anything else? Even if you don't think it's relevant, there's no way of knowing what might help the police in their investigation."

"It was just a personal joke. She said, 'So, I can just imagine how cute you'll look prancing around in that red bustier—and what do you propose doing after that?' Oh, God, I just can't believe she's dead."

"I'm sorry to have to ask you anything else, but how did you learn about the Makiki Sunset Apartments? Do you or Ariel know someone who lives there?"

"No. But I had heard someone mention it in passing. Then one day when Ariel and I were looking at a bulletin board listing apartments for rent, we saw a business card for the complex. We just took a chance there might be an opening, and there was."

"Do you remember who you spoke to? Was it the manager, or a management company?"

"I'm sorry, but I don't know. Ariel set up the appointment."

"I see. Well, thank you so much for helping me, TJ. It means a lot to know what Ariel was planning, and that she had a new friend to share her next adventures with. I should tell you that an HPD detective will probably be calling you soon."

"Oh, sure. I'll help any way I can."

We ended our call with my promise to let her know when the memorial was scheduled. Except for a few of my close friends, this was the most emotional notification of Ariel's death I had needed to make. For the most part, it had been Nathan who had the sad duty of consoling Ariel's many friends and colleagues.

Looking down at my scribbled notes from our conversation, I realized where Al Cooper got the idea that Ariel was gay. When he was getting Mrs. Espinoza's groceries from his car, he must have overheard the girls talking. And while Ariel was joking about TJ's lingerie and getaway with her boyfriend, Al had thought he was listening to a conversation suggesting Ariel was having a romantic relationship with another girl.

Even if Al was not responsible for Ariel's death, the hatred he expressed about another human being was beyond my comprehension. I could easily envision his inner dialogue. *I heard her talking to that girlfriend of hers. Sounded real cozy, if you know what I mean. Against the Good Book it is. That's what comes of women not following their God given calling as wives and mothers.*

The details might be wrong, but that was the essence of the venom he was spewing out when Keoni and I overheard him. With all his questions about biblical scripture, I could tell his personal perspective had little to do with Mrs. Espinoza or their church. He had come up with his vile condemnation of Ariel, and all gays, on his own.

For a while, I sat without focus, feeling the emptiness that comes with the death of someone close. Picking up my phone again, I dialed John Dias to let him know I had found TJ. After thanking me, he confirmed her full name and cell number and told me that Nathan and I would be hearing from Marty Soli very soon. I had almost fallen asleep when my phone rang.

"Hi, Natalie. This is Marty Soli, at the Coroner's office. I'm glad I caught you in person.

"John Dias said you'd be calling."

"I tried Nathan, but he wasn't in and I hated to leave an impersonal message, so I said that I'd try calling you. When John and I spoke earlier, he said he's hit a wall with the one person of interest he was investigating. Since our office has completed every available test, I could see no reason to delay in releasing Ariel's death certificate, or her body."

"I see," I replied softly.

"If you or Nathan will provide authorization to your family's mortuary, we'll facilitate immediate release to them."

That made it official. "I really appreciate your calling me, Marty. I'm pretty sure Nathan's in a private consultation with a client, but he should be through shortly. I know he's made arrangements with Sandwich Island Mortuary, so you should get the paperwork almost immediately."

"I didn't realize he was still working, Natalie."

"He doesn't have a full-time practice. But some of his former colleagues occasionally need a friendly shoulder, or should I say 'couch?' He also sees a few referrals. It's a small practice, so he has an office in his home."

We concluded with a promise that Marty would hear from Nathan or the mortuary within an hour. I felt somewhat numb as I started to shut off my cell phone. Despite all the calls I had made and received that day, I had not looked at the time or date on either my phone or computer. Staring at the lit screen, I realized it was Friday...exactly two weeks since Ariel had fallen to her death. Two weeks, and we were no closer to knowing what had happened to her than when we were notified she had died.

I have always considered myself a positive person, but I could see nothing positive coming out of what Nathan, Brianna and I were experiencing. Until I make that final trek into the bright white tunnel, I doubt I will have a clear understanding of the deaths that have touched Nathan and me. As I started to dissolve into tears once again, Miss Una arrived to occupy my lap and bring me the solace of her soft fur.

At least now our family could finalize our plans and notify everyone about Ariel's memorial. As though on cue, my phone rang. I saw the incoming call was from Brianna.

"Oh Aunt Natalie, I'm so glad I got you. Grandpa Nathan didn't answer when I called earlier, and I wanted to let you know I'm coming home tomorrow!"

"Oh, honey, that's... wonderful," I said—barely pausing to think about the concerns her grandfather and I had about her safety. "I'm sorry we haven't spoken more, but I was about to call both you and your Grandpa because I've learned we can have Ariel's memorial in a few days. How did you know to come?"

She almost giggled. "Well, you're not the only one with 'the gift.' I can't say I had a vision, but two days ago I knew I had to get home as soon as possible. All I had to do was finish one project and convert my second course to independent study. I'm free until the fall. So I'm coming in tomorrow evening, on a ticket with an open-ended return."

I noted her flight information and confirmed that either Nathan or I would be at the Honolulu Airport to greet her. We signed off and I debated calling Nathan next. Not knowing how long that call might last, I opted to try Keoni's cell phone first. Since my call went directly to voicemail, he might have been on the line.

"Keoni, this is Natalie. You don't need to return this call, but I wanted to let you know we've heard from Marty Soli and we'll be able to hold Ariel's memorial soon. I'll call you back when Nathan and I have everything scheduled."

After disconnecting, I dialed Nathan's office line. If I was transferred to voicemail immediately, I would know he was still in consultation.

"Oh, Natalie. I'm glad you called. When I got out of my last session with a client, I found a message from Marty Soli, who said he'd try to reach you."

"Yes, Nathan. Marty called right after I notified Lieutenant Dias about Al Cooper." I paused to control my emotions and wipe my eyes. "Without going into all the details of the paper-work, Ariel's body is being released by the Coroner's office. You need to give the funeral home permission for transport and cremation. I told Marty that I thought you'd completed arrangements with Sandwich Island Mortuary and should be able confirm instructions with the ME's Office today."

"Thanks. You're right, dear. All I have to do is send a fax giving the mortuary permission to implement our agreement and they will forward it to the ME's office."

"That's good, Nathan. Oh, you won't believe this, but Bri just called to say she'll be arriving home tomorrow evening."

"What? How did she know to come? Well, I guess I shouldn't

be surprised," he said.

"You've got that right. She said she didn't receive any out-of-this-world message, but she knew it was time to come home."

"Well, I guess that's understandable. That's pretty much the way my 'gift' works too, Natalie. You get the visions; I get the kennings."

"Was it Mom or Grandma who had both gifts?" I asked.

"You know Mom. There was a lot she never talked about, including that," Nathan replied.

In the midst of our sorrow, it was good to laugh, even mildly for a few moments. We spoke for a while, with the most positive interaction we had had since Ariel's passing. We may not have been happy in the conventional sense, but at least we had something to focus on. With people coming from both the mainland and neighbor islands, we set the following Wednesday as the day to celebrate Ariel's life. We had already made initial notifications, so all we had to do was confirm the times and places of our two events.

The next topic Nathan and I addressed was Brianna's homecoming. I would have loved to be at the airport to greet her, but Nathan lives directly across the Ko`olau Mountains from the airport. So it seemed more logical, and sensitive, to have him pick her up alone. Besides, by the time she arrived, it would be the middle of the night for her biologically and she could turn in early. Knowing she might have plans for reconnecting with friends prior to the memorial, Nathan and I decided I would see her sometime on Sunday.

Before we hung up, we confirmed our lists of invitees. With the bulk of arrangements remaining in Nathan's hands, I said I would call John Dias and Marty Soli and let them know that Nathan was having the mortuary pick up Ariel's body. In addition, I called the learning center where I was to begin volunteering. After apologizing for having to decline working on a fixed schedule, I offered to serve as a substitute tutor for students facing exam deadlines.

Moving on to memorial invitations, I spoke to or emailed everyone on my portion of the invitation list. Several friends reminded me of other people who had known and cared for Ariel. I was delighted when they offered to invite them to the beachside service.

Another call I placed was to Margie O`Hara. Knowing the turmoil I was facing, she and Dan had left a fluid window in their schedule for our getting together. Although there would not be time for a private meeting, I was very pleased when she confirmed they could attend the beachside service before catching their plane home on Wednesday night.

With the weekend at hand, I would not be able to go to the Hawai`i State Archives until the following week. However, I could perform some research at the library. In preparation, I had emailed a couple of questions to the museum that was once the home of Queen Lili`u`okalani. Washington Place, a mansion in Greek revival style, was now the repository of many artifacts from the Queen's life. I am grateful that the curator is generous about replying to inquiries from the media and the public. Luckily, she responded almost immediately.

That evening I simplified dinner for both Miss Una and me. After pouring myself a glass of Nugan Estate Chardonnay, I decided that salmon pâté from the deli was a good starting place for both of our meals. Mine accompanied a salad of baby spinach and Maui onions, while my feline buddy consumed hers unembellished. Taking my plate to the living room, I turned on the evening news. The national headlines offered nothing of note and I concluded my supper in time to hear the opening theme music of *Wheel of Fortune*.

As I placed my dishes in the sink, my phone rang again. I disliked the thought of making lengthy explanations to people I had missed speaking with earlier, so I was relieved that the caller was Keoni.

"Hi, there. I'm so grateful it's you. It's been a marathon of phone calls today, but I wanted to speak with you before turning in for the night."

"Then I'm glad I called when I did. I didn't want to crowd you by checking back too soon. But with you sitting there without a car, I wondered if there is anything I can help you with this weekend."

"It's good of you to offer, Keoni. But I've pared my activities down and I think I'm set for a while. Let me catch you up on the schedule for the next several days. Most importantly, Ariel's memorial will be at three p.m. on Wednesday, at the Kailua Beach Park boat launch. After that, there'll be a sunset celebration of her life at Nathan's home.

"Brianna called today and said she knew it was time to come home. She's arriving tomorrow evening. I've decided to do a bit of research at the State Library tomorrow, for which I can easily catch the bus. And before you offer to take me out to the airport to welcome Brianna home, I think Nathan and she should have some time alone. So I won't see her until Sunday, when she comes over to finish our plans for Wednesday."

"Sounds good. I'm sure you and Nathan are relieved that you can move ahead with your plans for the memorial."

"You're right Keoni. Speaking of which, I'd love for you to meet Brianna prior to Wednesday. Why don't you join us for lunch on Sunday? At about one o`clock?"

"I'd be pleased to join you, Natalie. Is there anything you'd like me to bring?"

"I don't think so. I'm keeping everything as simple as possible."

"Thanks again for including me. I hope you'll be able to get some rest now that you are able to hold the memorial."

I was grateful to sleep peacefully through the night with no dreams and awake with a clear sense of purpose. In a short time, I was ready to depart for another day in downtown Honolulu. After a quick bus ride, I dropped off a portfolio of our family's pictorial history at the photo shop that specialized in unique mountings. Then I was ready to attack the library's newspaper morgue with vigor. Opening my laptop, I found a reply from the curator of Washington Place. With her answers to my questions, and lists of research topics in my files, I was ready to begin a long day of research.

Since TJ had confirmed that neither she nor Ariel knew anyone at the apartments, there was nothing else I could think of to research about the complex itself. Pearl Wong's family was the single topic that remained unchecked, but I was certain that neither she nor her sister had been involved in my grandniece's death. The only other family member I knew of was Jade's stepson. Therefore, I began by skimming through newspapers of the nineteen-sixties and seventies seeking references to the Wong-Bishop family—particularly, Richard Bishop's birth announcement. With a common surname like "Bishop," the absence of a middle name, and a vague timeline for his possible birth, I got nowhere with this line of inquiry. I did, however, find a later reference to the marriage of Méilingyù Wong and banker Richard K. Bishop II.

Moving through the decades, I occasionally found a reference to the elder Bishop's law practice. But I found nothing else about this branch of the Bishop family. Regardless of this omission, facial features seldom belie the truth. Of course, he could be of mixed ancestry. Perhaps like many of the early missionary families, he was part Hawaiian.

I had heard him referred to as Jade's "stepson," so without newspaper announcements to the contrary, he was probably the biological offspring of an earlier marriage of Richard senior. Of course, he could have been adopted or even be a *keiki hānai*. But this informal form of fostering or adopting children within Hawaiian families was beyond the scope of my expertise. Even if that was true, it was unlikely to have been mentioned in routine news reports.

With research related to the Makiki Sunset Apartments at a standstill, I shifted gears again. After considering search terms that might relate to Keoni's family home, I renewed my exploration of the Queen Lydia Lili`u`okalani Elementary School. I soon recognized that the Queen's participation in the groundbreaking and dedication of the school were newsworthy events that would have caught the attention of people at every level of society.

Too soon, I heard the public address system announce that the library was closing. Since I was not going to the airport to greet Brianna, I had plenty of time to get home and tidy the apartment for whatever guests the weekend might bring. There was no way of knowing if Brianna would arrive alone, with Nathan, or with friends of hers and Ariel's. Regardless of who else might be coming, I was glad that she would be meeting Keoni.

CHAPTER 20

The fox condemns the trap, not himself.
William Blake [1757 E-1827]

We had enjoyed beautiful weather during the last few weeks, but that Sunday a gusty storm blew in. It arrived with a bang of thunder and progressed from intermittent sprinkles to sporadic downpours. I was glad the day's activities would be indoors. The morning passed peacefully as I prepared to work with Brianna on preparations for celebrating Ariel's short life.

I was looking forward to our time together. Since her return to college after the holidays, we had communicated by phone fairly often and video conferenced when I was at Nathan's home. Despite this closeness, Nathan and I had resisted Brianna's repeated requests to return to the Islands after her twin's death.

Listening to *Sunday Brunch* on our local NPR radio station, I cleared a workspace on the dinette table. With everything prepared for the day, I sat in my recliner for a brief rest. Miss Una leapt onto my lap and I was reminded I had more than one personality to introduce to my grandniece. I looked around the apartment, thinking of my reasons for being there. I realized that although I had not determined the cause of Ariel's death, I could provide a supportive environment for Brianna to see where her twin's death had occurred.

Miss Una soon tired of having her fur rearranged and sprang onto the chair's back. I then leaned back to enjoy a relaxing cat nap. When the doorbell rang, my housemate alerted me that someone was about to enter our kingdom. I stood, fluffed my hair and trotted to the door.

"Come in, my dear," I said pulling Brianna into a desperate hug. Even though I was uncertain about the nature of her twin's death, and how it might relate to her, I felt a genuine relief to have her back home. Brushing aside a few tears, I stepped back to look at her. Aside from a darkening around her eyes, she looked good.

"I'm so glad to see you, home and safe," I affirmed.

She grabbed my hands and squeezed them. "Me, too, Aunt Natalie. I'm sorry Grandpa Nathan isn't here, but...he's not up to being where...Ariel...died."

"I understand, honey. It's been unbelievably hard for all of us."

Wiggling out of her sandals, Brianna followed me through the living room to the table where she set several slightly damp carryalls. The photo shop I used is open every day of the week, so Brianna had been able to pick up the pictures I had left for enlargement, matting and framing.

Looking around in a near daze, she struggled for words. "It looks so normal...like nothing awful had happened here."

"I really didn't want to talk about Ariel's case today, but you should know that she did not die *here*. Her death had nothing to do with the apartment...itself."

"What do you mean, Aunt Natalie?"

I took a deep breath. "Sweetheart, she did not fall from this apartment's *lānai*. I believe she fell from the beverage alcove next door."

"Oh."

"As you can imagine, the police are doing everything they can to solve the case. But there have been no results from their investigation to date," I revealed.

"So that's why you're here? To help?"

"Well, I'm not sure that's how everyone else looks at it. But, yes, that's why I came here."

Nearly in tears she said, "Oh, Aunt Natalie. I'm so sorry for everything you've been going through. You should have let me come earlier."

"Honey, there isn't anything you could have done. There's really nothing any of us can do, but take one day at a time." I said, giving her another hug.

Pointing across the room to the guest bath, I suggested she freshen up before we started our work. I was glad to have told her where the investigation stood. It meant that I didn't have to worry about keeping my recent activities a secret any longer. When she emerged from the bathroom looking a little less wan, I tried to get the day back on track.

"I know you've had breakfast, but would you like some tea, or maybe a decadent mug of coffee with brandy and chocolate sauce?"

"Well, that's an easy choice. You make the best lazy man's cappuccino." she laughed.

I made our drinks without espresso, as Brianna assembled photos and display materials.

"Aunt Natalie, they're all so awesome." Touching the corner of the centerpiece that featured Ariel's high school graduation picture, Brianna sighed. "She's so beautiful. She looks like she's going to walk out of the frame. It's so hard to believe she's gone," she said, ending with a moan.

I patted her shoulder and debated adding a second shot of brandy to her mug. I bit my lip rather than observe that except for the sun-kissed tendrils of her twin's hair, she looked exactly like Ariel.

With mugs and notebooks in hand we sat down in the living room. After discussing the furnishings in Nathan's living and dining rooms, we considered the placement of photos and mementos, and a remembrance book for guests to enter greetings. The main gathering would be in the garden facing the ocean. With all the flowers and shrubs in Nathan's yard, we had asked friends to donate to local charities in lieu of bringing floral arrangements. Aside from setting out tables and chairs, little preparation was needed. But with an event starting at sunset, we would light torches to augment the lights strung permanently around the trunks of the palm trees.

Brianna summarized the basic menu that Nathan and the Souzas had planned, knowing many guests would bring a favorite dish for the buffet. To make everyone feel part of the celebration, when we started the food line, we would ask each "chef" to tell a story of Ariel enjoying the dish they had brought to share.

Our last topic was music. A DJ who was a friend of the twins would set up his equipment under the roof of the *lānai*. In addition to playing Ariel's favorite pieces, he would take requests. There were also a few solo musicians the twins knew who would play in rotation in the large foyer. I was relieved that Brianna, as always, was as organized as my mother had been. We had barely completed our planning session when it was time to shift gears.

Promptly at one p.m., Keoni rang the bell. I opened the door and he stepped inside quickly, as the wind was blowing rather strongly. We hugged lightly and he walked over to introduce himself to Brianna and express his sorrow for the loss of her twin.

"Not knowing what Island delights you might be missing on the mainland, I brought some chili from Zippy's."

"Thanks, Keoni. It smells great. I can get chili in Oregon, but it's not the same as Zippy's. And do you know how hard it is to find steamed white rice on a mainland breakfast menu? This morning, I had a *loco moco*. Mmm, the hamburger patty was almost medium rare and the sunny-side-up egg on rice with gravy was awesome!"

We all laughed, moving toward the kitchen. I clicked on the rice cooker as Brianna put my pictures and scrapbooks in one carryall and the finished display materials into others.

"Where should I put your photos and albums, Aunt Natalie?" asked Brianna.

"Why don't you leave everything that's going home with you at the front door and drop the materials I'm keeping on my bed? In fact, Keoni can give you the grand tour of my home away from home while I set out our lunch."

"I'm delighted to serve in any way I can," Keoni replied.

As the two of them began wandering through the apartment, I turned to the kitchen. When they arrived at the table, I had set out a large spinach salad with sliced mango, fresh bread, and a pitcher of iced mango blossom tea. Next I carried in bowls of rice topped with the chili Keoni had brought. During the meal, we talked about common interests, ignoring the elephant in the room—the death which had brought us together. After lunch, I poured more tea for everyone and took a plate of Chinese almond cookies to the living room for a final chat. Keoni again took the recliner, and Brianna joined me on the sofa.

"Keoni, aside from your meeting Brianna, I wanted you to come today so I could report on the research I've conducted on your family home."

"Great. But I don't see how you've had time to do anything for *me*."

"Your project has provided welcome breaks from everything else. Twice I thought I'd found something to convince your relatives to keep the house. First, I learned that the passing of Halley's Comet in 1910 was an event that brought people from every background and social strata into the area. You see, the best viewing of the comet was at an observatory built on land donated by the Kaimukī Improvement Association and operated by the College of Hawai`i. It was up on Ocean View Drive, near Diamond Head. But despite my best efforts I found no record mentioning your family or their home.

"A second event was much more promising because it united everyday citizens with the scions of Island society. This was the construction of an elementary school named for Queen Lili`u`okalani. She even helped lay the cornerstone in April of 1912, for which she donated copies of her autobiography, her translation of the *Hawaiian Creation Chant*, and sheet music for some of her compositions. She also attended the school's opening later in the year. Beloved as she was, I knew these events were popular and that there could be some connection to your family."

"Wow, this is really interesting. And it's amazing how it fits in with what I learned from my Aunt Betty this morning," said Keoni with a smile.

"You see; yesterday several family members were sprucing up the house. As my Auntie B pulled a framed quilt square of the Hawaiian flag off the wall to clean it, she found some papers tacked onto the back. You won't believe what she found. Printed on official stationery, was a note from either Queen Lili`u`okalani or someone acting as her social secretary. It thanked my great-grandmother for the welcome glass of tea she offered her Majesty one day when the Queen's car got a flat tire during a tour of the new community in Kaimukī. It also referenced a small token of her appreciation that would be delivered shortly. It's too bad the note is water stained, and neither the date nor the signature is legible."

"Awesome," declared Brianna, while I merely nodded.

Keoni continued with his family's discovery. "Beside the royal note was a newspaper clipping from the October 15, 1912, edition of the *Hawaiian Gazette*. It was a long piece discussing the opening of the Queen Lydia Lili`u`okalani Elementary School. Penned in the margin was a comment by my great-grandmother stating that although the Queen had looked 'poorly,' it was wonderful to see her again."

"Do you think the quilt square was the *token* the Queen spoke of?" asked Brianna.

"I don't know," answered Keoni. "We'd like to think so, but I doubt there's any way of knowing for sure. What do you think, Natalie?"

"I'm with Bri—that it's an awesome find. Following annexation to the United States, depicting the Hawaiian flag in quilts was one of the few ways that Hawaiian Kingdom loyalists were allowed to visually express love for their formerly sovereign nation.

"Of course, I don't know that you could find anything to establish if the quilt square's *provenance* is really linked to the Queen. In studying some of the events in the Queen's later life, I realize how difficult it would be to prove elements of your story. One thing I do know is that after 1912, her health and *constitution* as it was then called would've made it difficult for her to take a casual tour around the island.

"So, if the Queen met anyone in your family, it would have been before the school was built, but after her trip to Washington, D.C. in 1900. That trip was remarkable. With dignity and clarity, she beseeched Congress and the president to restore the rights of her people and reverse annexation of the Kingdom of Hawai`i.

"By the way, the Queen appreciated innovation and loved to ride in her car (which she called her 'locomobile'). However, she never traveled without an entourage and there were protocols for interacting with royalty. I doubt that she would have been allowed to drink something casually offered by a commoner in public. Nevertheless, I think the mystery adds to the story's charm. I hope your family appreciates the possibility, if not the probability, of its historical significance."

"You can bet on that. I think that for the time being, they'll remove the furnishings—especially that framed quilt square—and just rent the house. Who knows, maybe someday another Hewitt will live in the home."

We all concurred that this was a great example of how a footnote in history can inspire the preservation of a family's heritage. It was then time for our gathering to break up. Brianna opened the door and turned back to hug Keoni and me. I stepped out to watch her depart. She was driving into Waikīkī to join a few friends for drinks before returning home to help Nathan begin sorting Ariel's belongings.

Ignoring the drizzle of rain, I stood watching Brianna pause at the stairs for one last look across the apartment complex. Again I was struck by how much she and Ariel resembled one another—a fact often heightened by identical elements in their wardrobes, even when purchased separately. In her white polo shirt and shorts, and long copper colored hair Brianna unknowingly looked the image of her twin on that last fateful day.

After a final wave, I turned to rejoin Keoni inside. Just then, Miss Una scooted out the door and ran toward the refreshment alcove. A moment later, she came trotting back pursued by Richard Bishop, who walked out of the alcove with a wrench in one hand and his tool bag in the other. "I thought you said this cat wouldn't be a bother," he called out to us with a frown.

At a crack of thunder, he stared past us at Brianna. "You can't be here!" he mouthed softly. With rising pitch he said, "You're not real." Then in a softer voice, "I...I'm having another nightmare." Dropping his tool bag, he walked in measured steps toward the Ariel look-alike who clearly terrified him.

Hearing the agitated voice, Brianna turned back toward the apartment.

The pupils of Richard's eyes were clearly dilated. They seemed glued to Brianna's bracelet, a near twin of the one Ariel had been wearing on the day of her death. He shook his head and spoke in a hoarse stage whisper, "It was an accident. I couldn't help what happened. I needed a fix. One minute I'm pulling out my stash, and the next you're on top of me."

With those words, he moved swiftly past me and toward Brianna. Frozen in place, I could not believe what I was hearing. Keoni pried the door from my clenched fingers. Obviously, he had heard what I did. He moved calmly to my side. We looked at each other and I could feel the controlled tension coming from his stiffened body. He nudged past me, thrusting his cell phone into my hands with a curt nod toward it.

I knew what he wanted me to do—call the police. But for a moment, I stared at the horror of the scene unfolding before me, praying it would not end the way Ariel's encounter with Richard had. Brianna looked confused. She pushed her hair back from her face and peered through the increasing rainfall to note the wrench in Richard's hand. As he quickened his pace, she knew something was wrong and began running down the stairs.

Moving like a magnet toward her, Richard pleaded in alternating tones of voice. Clearly he would do anything to eradicate the apparition that had entered his realm of daily existence.

Beginning his own descent, he said, "I...I didn't mean to do it. You scared me, standing over me like that."

Up to this point Keoni had been trying to overtake Richard with a steady stride. But as the man plunged downward after Brianna, Keoni picked up speed and began taking the stairs two at a time. Unfortunately, at the bottom he slipped in a puddle of muddy water. When he tried to regain momentum, it was clear his left ankle was hurting.

From the top of the stairs, I watched the rush of bodies onto the volleyball court as I pushed 911. Since Keoni was not close enough to be assured of stopping Richard's uncertain intentions, it was good that Brianna was well ahead of the man. "Connect me to the Police Department. I need help at the Makiki Sunset Apartments. There's a crazed addict chasing a girl he thinks is the girl he murdered a couple of weeks ago. Another murder is going to happen if you don't get here right away."

The police dispatcher knew her job and spoke in a soothing voice, but I could not calm down. Despite my heavy breathing and a background punctuated by thunder, she quickly verified the address. Then she made note that a retired police officer was in pursuit of the perpetrator, who did not seem to have a firearm but was brandishing a wrench. Following her instructions, I remained out of the fray, although I began moving toward the stairs while narrating the scene unfolding below me.

In a clearly altered state of consciousness, Richard Bishop chased Brianna around the volleyball net. "It wasn't my fault. There wasn't anything I could do," he said with a justifying whine in his voice.

Cautiously, I moved down the stairs, while continuing to relay what I was seeing and hearing to the police dispatcher. The man was wholly out of his mind.

"I was getting up and you were almost on top of me. I didn't mean to hurt you. I just grabbed you to push you out of the way. All you had to do was stay back out of my way. But you flew through my arms and went out over the wall."

When I reached the bottom of the stairs, the three players in the drama were continuing to scramble around the volley-ball net, as though inventing a new ball-less game.

I paused, almost trancelike myself. I was afraid to get any closer, but did not want to miss hearing anything that would prove relevant later.

Richard continued his diatribe. "Your...your earring. If you've come for it, I'll give it to you. It's behind the first washing machine in the laundry room in building B. And...your phone. You dropped it when ...when you fell. I put it with the earring. I'll get them both for you, if you'll come with me.

"They started it all, you know. Those old broads with their stories. How they'd brought their father's treasure from China and used it to pay for their schooling and the real estate they've bought. They don't have anyone but me to leave their treasure to. It's only fair, after everything I've done for them. My whole life wasted."

Wasted? I agreed with that. Richard's life had been flushed through his veins and down the toilet. But who did he blame for that? Everyone but himself. Just as I thought he was about to grab Brianna, she ducked under the net and dashed toward the back of the property. Richard then tried to cut her off as Keoni moved in on him.

"I wouldn't have gotten started on the stuff if it weren't for them. I was trying so hard. Taking care of my Dad when he was sick. Doing their damned errands. What have I ever gotten? An occasional cash handout, like I was their doorman. And a lousy apartment—until they need it for someone else— usually some rich bastard's kid getting' a free ride at the University."

Regardless of any boost her adrenalin was providing, I could tell Brianna was getting winded. As she looked around for a place to hide, I was amazed that despite the difference in their age and weight, the crazed man was gaining on her. Eying the seven-foot dragon fountain, she quickly disappeared behind it.

"I think I've found where the treasure is. Please come out. I'll give you anything you want," he wheedled, moving as quickly as the rain-soaked soil permitted.

Despite the soothing tone of his words, Richard was edging toward the right side of the fountain. Jumping forward, Keoni tackled him and they collapsed in a bear hug in the fountain. In their twisted crash, Keoni's left pant leg caught on a carved embellishment. Still in an adrenalin rush, Richard raised his wrench to beat back the man who was threatening him.

With great effort, Keoni shoved Richard back before the pudgy man could strike him. Suddenly, the dragon shook and its white granite eye popped out. It dropped on top of Richard's head with a thud loud enough to carry across to my vantage point. And then there was silence—except for the surge of water pouring from the dragon's mouth onto the man's head. When thick red foam splashed up, I knew that this tragic story had come to an end.

A wail of sirens broke through the haze enveloping my mind. Brianna edged back into the open and stared down at the men who had fought a modern-day duel over her. The police operator asked what was happening. I told her the action was over and that the troops had arrived. We terminated the call and I rushed forward to join my grandniece and Keoni who were seated on the edge of the fountain.

Looking at the spectacle of Richard's seated harlequin-like pose, I was relieved that the tragic cycle of murder, discovery and attempted murder was ended. My physical and emotional relief was tempered by the realization that there would be a lot of explanation and paperwork to execute before our ordeal would really end. As I looked down at the remains of the man who had caused all of this, I could almost have felt sorry for the jerk who must have been a shell of a man for decades.

Aside from the fact that someone had just died, there was one disappointing aspect to this outcome for me and for my family. Given Richard's mental state, we would probably never understand the details of how Ariel had fallen out of the cut-out in the wall. I was also sure the authorities would be frustrated in any attempts to learn whether the man had committed other offenses to support his addiction.

As I wrapped my arm around Brianna's shoulder, she sighed and squeezed my hand. I glanced across her to Keoni who signaled he was fine, in spite of the fact I knew he could not put weight on the ankle that was swelling from the trauma of being twisted severely.

I thought about how close we had all come to being victims ourselves—from the attack of a madman determined to avoid being caught. Richard had not consciously meant to hurt Ariel. In the midst of committing a drug offense, he had simply struck out of fear in a less-than-rational state of mind. But after killing her, he felt no remorse for his actions, or for the resulting pain with which her family would live without reprieve. He had just covered his tracks and pretended he had not been present at the time of her death. Regarding today, Richard had been prepared to consciously commit murder to protect himself from the terrifying image of what he thought was a ghost who had returned to haunt him.

One thing was certain. If it were not for the twin factor, we would never have learned the truth about who had perpetrated Ariel's death. The appearance of a near clone of the deceased had been the stimulus that forced this killer to publically acknowledge his actions. Thank God all three of us had heard his confession, which at least clarified the sequence of events that ended with Ariel's fall onto Al Cooper's car.

At that moment, the clouds rolled back and a hint of sun peeked out. Car doors opened and slammed shut and I watched as a procession of law enforcement and emergency service specialists gathered. Heading the pack were Lieutenant John Dias and his partner, Sergeant Nakamura. They quickly grasped the fact that none of us were moving, and that the unknown man in the fountain was clearly beyond any interaction with the authorities.

The detective had never met Brianna and the initial look on his face showed almost as much surprise as Richard's had. Quickly restoring his professional mask, he signaled to the officers flanking him. Obviously his sergeant and the others knew their tasks, as they quickly separated themselves and set about securing the crime scene.

"Aside from the obvious, is anyone hurt?" The man called out, gesturing to the emergency medical team moving behind him up the volleyball court.

"Only me, JD, and I'll survive," responded Keoni.

John Dias then raised one eyebrow while looking at Keoni's condition. "Don't give me that 'I'm just fine' routine. Be a good retired cop and go quietly with the guys with the stethoscopes. I'll take your statement after you've been checked out at the Queen's Medical Center."

He signaled for the EMTs to treat Keoni and turned to Brianna and me. "Well, Natalie. It was looking like there was no reason for you to be here, and then, *bam*, you could have been the next victim."

Brianna was still clinging to me as I stared up with a pleading look for him to change the topic.

"So you're Brianna?" He said questioningly. "From the playbook I just heard, you're quite the sprinter!"

She smiled weakly and straightened up a bit.

Maintaining eye contact with me, the detective said, "Now, don't you two worry about anything right now, except going with Keoni to Queens for a little checkup—of your blood pressure if nothing else."

That sounded okay to me. I had little feeling in my hip, but I knew that once the adrenalin drained, I would undoubtedly have a few aches of my own. All of a sudden, I thought of Nathan. Thank God, my terrifying update would conclude with a peaceful, if not happy, ending.

Looking up to apartment B406, I noticed that the cause of today's incident was sauntering back in the door without a look our way. "I won't argue. But I've got a cat to secure first."

Nodding, John Dias turned away to supervise the crime scene. After the once-over by the EMTs was complete, I walked up to the apartment to make sure Miss Una was locked in with enough food and water to sustain her for a while. She barely acknowledged my presence and strolled into the master bedroom. Obviously I did not have to worry about *her* response to all the excitement. When I returned to ground level with a hastily packed overnight bag, Keoni had been placed on a stretcher. Brianna and I followed slowly toward two ambulances waiting in the parking lot. Although we were mobile, we willingly accepted a ride to the hospital.

The police band call had attracted many vehicles. Aside from police units, the street was crowded with media vans and neighbors curious about what was occurring in their normally peaceful environs. The Lieutenant appeared in front of us as a television news reporter cried out, "Hey, Dias. What'cha you got? Isn't this where that girl took a dive a couple weeks ago?"

John pointedly turned his back on the man and gently handed us up to the medic waiting in an ambulance. As the doors closed, I saw my favorite detective turning to check on Keoni's status. Since I would probably miss the evening news, I placed a rapid call to Nathan. There was no way of knowing the details that might be included in a report of the incident and I was concerned about anything that might cause *his* blood pressure to rise.

CHAPTER 21

The happiest moments of my life
have been the few which I have passed
at home in the bosom of my family.
Thomas Jefferson [1743-1826]

Brianna and I were soon given clean bills of health at the hospital. After completing our initial statements to Lieutenant Dias, we would be chauffeured to Kāne'ohe by Nathan. I would have invited Keoni to join us some greatly deserved R and R, but I knew he would have to see an orthopedist in the morning before he could be released. Once he had been checked into a private room, I was allowed to see him for a couple of moments. Already groggy from the shot he had been given for pain, it was unlikely that he would remember my visit.

Placing my small hands on top of his large ones, I said "I don't know if you can hear me, but I'm leaving under protest. I'll be back in the morning to make sure you're getting the attention you need."

His left index finger curled up over my hand. With a lopsided grin, he whispered, "After today, I'm not going to let you out of my sight for a long time."

Looking into his pale blue eyes, I stroked his stubble-roughened cheek for a moment in silence. As his breathing slowed, his eyes closed and he started to snore softly. I gently tucked his hands beneath the sheet and left the room.

Before leaving Honolulu, we stopped at the Makiki Sunset Apartments to get Miss Una. After enjoying an evening of my twin's nurturing, I drifted to sleep listening to the lullaby of nearby waves. Again, I thought of the love my parents had poured into every aspect of this ocean-side retreat. While I did not experience a new vision of them, I dipped once more into the dream of their joyful island-wide forage for furnishings.

Viewing the Chinese woman in her vibrant emerald green *cheongsam*, I again questioned my parents' ability to converse so easily in her native language. There may be a lot of things that children do not know about their parents. But you would think that something as significant as proficiency in a complex language would have been discussed at some point over the years. The issue made me wonder where they had gone those times when I thought my mom was joining my dad for some holidays during his overseas assignments.

Early the next morning, I awoke feeling somewhat revived. Nathan greeted Brianna and me with mellow Kona coffee, a salad of his fresh papayas and bananas, plus bagels with cream cheese. It was almost life as usual, sitting on the back *lānai* and watching the water lap at the edge of the property. Listening to a classic CD of Keola and Kapono Beamer, I wished we could put our lives on rewind and emerge in a past and glorious time.

While we were enjoying our first peaceful family breakfast in a long time, Keoni called from the hospital. He said he would be released soon and that there was no reason for me to come into town. "You and your family have a lot going on and I'm fine. My neighbor Ben is being dropped off at the apartment to get my truck. Then he'll pick me up and drive me home so I can catch up on some sleep. You know how it is in a hospital. With all the monitoring, there isn't enough peace to get any solid sleep."

"As long as you're sure you're all right, I won't come. Just try to get some rest for the next couple of days. But what about food and drink, or anything else you might need?"

He assured me he was well stocked for a short period of hibernation and that Ben was next door if he required any help. We ended our call when Keoni's orthopedic surgeon arrived to evaluate his prognosis.

I turned off the phone and looked at Nathan who was idly flicking a fishing line toy at Miss Una. Awakening from what seemed to be a daydream, he looked at Brianna and me with a faint smile. "I'm so grateful you're both safe and here at home this morning. It's hard to believe it was only a few months ago that we were all here celebrating the holidays and making plans for the New Year."

"There were so many things we were looking forward to," began Brianna. "After summer school, Ariel and I were going to wander around Europe for a while. I don't know what I'll do now. The trip wouldn't be the same without her." She then looked down at the table and began folding her paper napkin into an *origami* bird.

How could I respond to that truth? With the follow-up statements we needed to make regarding Richard Bishop's death, Keoni being injured, and Ariel's upcoming memorial, each of us was taking life one breath at a time.

Finally, I remarked, "Well, your calendar is blank until fall. With all the stress we've been under, don't you think Ariel would want you to take some time to decompress?"

Nathan added, "Did you know Ariel was thinking of delaying her final year of undergraduate study? She thought that if she made the right connections this summer, she might stay overseas and teach English as a second language for a while."

"I had no idea she was considering that," I said, staring at the fourth chair at the table that seemed very empty. I sighed and looked at my companions. "I've been thinking about my own calendar. The memorial isn't for a couple of days. And since we've completed most of the preparations, I've been wondering whether I should move back to the condo."

"If you do it now, I can help you, Aunt Natalie," Brianna responded.

"Well, first, I need to call Anna about using the elevator

and then figure out the issue of transportation. Keoni's ankle needs to heal and I don't want him worrying about lugging my belongings back to Waikīkī any time soon. So if I move back to the condo now, he won't have a chance to play Sir Lancelot."

Nathan looked up with a smile. "Why don't you let me call the Jacksons next door? Their son Aidan has a big truck he uses in his landscaping business. It should do the job nicely, if you don't mind the remains of his days in the field."

"That sounds fine. I'll be glad to pay him a bonus to get it done quickly. And if you're sure you're up to the company, Nathan, I think Miss Una and I will remain in the guest suite until things have settled down. There's simply been too much going on and I don't want to take the chance of my little feline explorer getting loose again during another move."

While Nathan went inside to call his neighbor, Brianna and I quickly finished breakfast. I then checked with Anna to verify the availability of the freight elevator. A few minutes later, Brianna and I were loading the dishwasher when Nathan rejoined us.

"You have a golden touch, Natalie. Aidan is glad to help out, if you can manage it today. And since he's just installed a new liner in his truck, your furniture should arrive home in pristine condition!"

I agreed to leave in an hour and hurried to dress. When Aidan pulled up in his hard-worked dirt brown Dodge Ram, I was gathering bags and boxes from Nathan's garage. It might not be an organized move, but seeing the size of his arms, I knew there was no need for additional help. As we departed, I saw Brianna and her grandfather aligning torches along the front walkway.

Moving with Aidan was not the same as it had been with Keoni. While he was a perfect young gentleman and did everything I asked of him, the process was perfunctory and prolonged. At one point, when he was moving a stack of boxes with a hand-truck borrowed from Nathan, I went over to Mrs. Espinoza's apartment.

After letting her know my relationship to Ariel and that I would not be staying for the summer, I asked if she could use some of the food remaining in my refrigerator. She expressed shock that I was the grandaunt of the girl who had died in the parking lot and then shared some news of her own. Jade Bishop had suddenly become mobile. Immediately after Richard's death, she had demanded that Al bring her to the apartment complex. And that morning, she had joined Pearl for breakfast. Apparently, Jade was resuming her role as the elder sister.

When I closed the door of unit B406 for the last time, I told Aidan I needed to return the keys to the manager. As we walked down the stairs, he said he would check to make sure everything was tied down on the truck. I approached Pearl Wong's door with mixed emotions. I had thought of asking the Wong sisters to Ariel's memorial. But the uncertainty of sand, wind, and surf—let alone explaining their presence to people who did not know the full story—seemed too much for any of us to face.

In my last conversation with John Dias, I learned that the police had found evidence that Richard had been digging holes on the property for years. He had even torn some walls apart, evidently searching for the sisters' alleged "treasure" and periodically shifting his stash of drugs. I guess that solved the mystery of the patches in the walls of some closets.

As soon as I struck the lion knocker, Pearl opened the door and beckoned me in with expressions of deep sorrow. Understandably, she and her sister were mortified by what had occurred on their property. Although Richard was Jade's stepson and therefore no biological relation of Pearl's, his crime had affected her deeply. She seemed to have aged considerably within the short time I had known her. Still precise in her dress and speech, the younger Wong sister now stood with stooped shoulders and had a walk that spoke volumes about her fear of miss-stepping. I sought words to bring her some release from the guilt she clearly felt.

After handing her the keys to the apartment, I offered to

hire a cleaning service. She immediately refused my suggestion. "You have barely been here two weeks. And with everything you have had to endure, I would not hear of such a thing. Jade had another therapy appointment this morning. She wished me to express the shame she feels for what happened to your grandniece, and insists you accept this refund of your payment."

Knowing Asian culture, I could not refuse this sincere expression of remorse. As I accepted the envelope she extended, I felt a shaking chill in her hand. "This must be hard on you as well—for a family member to be found a criminal," I replied. "You couldn't have done anything about Richard. He was too far into his drug abuse *and* his dreams of finding hidden treasure."

Pearl nodded, gesturing for me to follow her into the living room. As we sat down, she explained how she believed Richard had come to his unbelievable conclusions.

"Unfortunately, the stories on which he based his illusions were founded on some truth. It began when the boy was fifteen. At that impressionable age, Jade married his father and Richard frequently heard tales of the magical Central Kingdom of China. It is also true that we came to Hawai`i with some of our father's antiquities. As adults, we learned that Chú Huā was the purveyor of the Pearl of the Orient's final shipment of goods out of China. That nest egg financed the purchase of our first home, paid for our schooling, and provided the means for our eventual investments in real estate—like these apartments."

Pearl paused to think for a moment. "To be honest, the passionate love that existed between our parents was not the foundation of Jade's marriage. Immediately upon her graduation from college, she obtained her goal—a teaching position at our alma mater, St. Andrew's Priory School for Girls. Elated from her first day on the job, she returned home to find the house silent and without the ever-present aroma of Chú Huā's cooking."

As she again seemed lost in the past, I observed, "It's amazing how the scent of a favorite recipe can evoke a sense of our childhood home."

"Yes, it does. On the same day, I had completed my first day as a freshman at the University. I was surprised to arrive home and find that Jade had prepared dinner, which she served on our best dishes by candlelight in the dining room. She barely spoke until we were seated. Then she fanned her hand across the center of the table which held a house key, bank book and a letter written in Chinese. Jade's words were simple and to the point: Our beloved *amah* had completed her task of caring for us until we were grown and she was now returning to her homeland.

"I found the lack of details interesting, since the night before I had heard Jade and Chú Huā speaking in Chinese for a long time. Jade never revealed what they discussed and I knew I dared not ask. During our dinner, I did learn we had free title to the little bungalow and a substantial sum of money in the bank. Sadly, we never saw or heard from Chú Huā or our father after that, and we never again had an envelope arrive from Shànghǎi, or anywhere else in China."

"That must have been quite a shock, after all your years with Chú Huā," I observed.

"Indeed. Jade and I had each other, but our lives suddenly felt empty. But I should not infer we were left wholly alone. Sometimes our relatives from Maui visited. And the "uncles" from our grandfather's *hui* frequently checked on our well-being. Time passed easily in this phase of life. Jade was immersed in her teaching career and I was busy with school and caring for our home.

"It was many years later that Jade married Richard's father. He was a widower and both Jade and I were comfortable with him, since he had been our trusted family lawyer. Today we would be considered a blended family. Even without great love between them, life seemed full, continuing largely as before. Jade and Richard the elder worked and I continued to care for our home. Richard the younger, like all boys, sought his role in life.

"Jade and I enjoyed retelling the happier moments from our childhood in China, as well as the stories woven by our *amah*. It was those tales that fed Richard's fantasies that one day he would inherit great wealth. But, like Richard the elder, Jade wanted to see him mature into a responsible adult before entrusting him with any capital. Sadly, that time never came.

"When his father died, there was little of the Bishop family wealth intact. The law practice had been taken over by partners and the family's liquid assets had been drained by the illnesses of both Richard Senior and his wife. Initially we sympathized with the young man's angst regarding his father' death. But after a while, we expected him to return to school or enter a career."

I nodded my head in acknowledgment. "Too many young people refuse to take charge of their lives."

"Jade and I were rather naïve, Natalie. Neither of us realized he had fallen into the abyss of drug abuse. It was not like an alcoholic who reeks of his addiction. He had always been quiet around us and being a young man of the Islands, showed his respect by seldom making eye contact.

"When we had the opportunity to buy these apartments, we thought Richard would find focus by helping with their maintenance...that it would give him direction and lead to a fulfilling life for him. But some time ago, we recognized that would not happen and there would be no continuation of our family. Therefore, while we would never have left Richard destitute or without a home, we decided that our estates should fund an educational trust. It will provide scholarships for worthy students at the Priory and endow a chair in International Cultural Studies at the University of Hawai`i in our parents' names."

"That's an excellent way to honor your family and to help the young people of Hawai`i. You remind me of some of the end-of-life choices I need to make," I said.

She nodded with obvious pleasure. "Well, Natalie, let me again express the sorrow that Jade and I feel about what happened to your grandniece. When you told me you were planning a memorial at Kailua Beach, we wanted to contribute something to your celebration of Ariel's life. If you will give me a moment, I picked up something for you earlier this morning."

She turned and left the room and I took a final look at my gracious surroundings. I knew that one day, the items that had been precious to Jade and Pearl would find their way to the homes of many people, who, even without the exotic stories of their origins, would treasure them for many years.

Pearl soon returned with two, large, bright pink gift bags. She set them on the dining table. Reaching within one, she brought out a cellophane-wrapped flat package.

With a small bow she offered it to me. "I hope you will not find it forward of us to offer these small tokens of our respect for your family. In China we would set lantern boats upon the waters to honor the passing of our beloved. These are something new...advertised to be 'environmentally friendly.' They are Chinese wish lanterns. They will behave like normal balloons when released into the air, but they are biodegradable. I have called to verify that these lanterns are acceptable to the park authorities. If you choose, your guests on the water, as well as those on the shore, can use them to send their blessings into the sky for Ariel."

Spontaneously, I touched her tiny hand before accepting the gift. Looking at this woman who seemed diminished in body and spirit, my eyes filled with moisture. "This is most thoughtful of you and Jade. We'll gladly add this feature to our gathering."

"We are pleased if you find this small token appropriate."

"It's more than appropriate. My brother Nathan has been concerned about the people remaining on shore when the outrigger canoes put to sea. This will allow everyone to feel they are participating fully in the ceremony. Thank you so much."

Pearl and I had become close in spirit in the last couple of weeks and we hugged gently before I walked out the door.

*   *   *   *   *

It is difficult to be positive about the death of anyone—especially a young person with the promise of a full life before her. I was glad that the next day and a half passed quickly. After dropping my furnishings off at the condo, I was eager to help Brianna and Nathan finish the arrangements for Wednesday. It was a good thing other people were coordinating food, beverages and music, because there were many phone calls to place, emails to send, and visitors to accommodate.

We were fortunate that there was little red-tape to burden us. The State of Hawai`i does not consider ashes scattered at sea to be hazardous to the life forms that abound in her waters. And since our beachside event was small, we were not required to get a use permit.

The beach has always been important to our family and I knew it would continue to be our gathering place in times of joy, as well as sorrow. Nathan and I had not had an opportunity to do our private grieving, but that time will come. Sooner than later, Brianna will return to the mainland to close up her apartment for the rest of summer. Then, I expect Nathan and I will walk the beaches of Hawai`i, as we did as children. I hope it will help us realign our lives before we have to face the impending death of our Auntie Carrie.

The other man with whom I have shared this recent crisis is Keoni. Although we had spoken each evening, I had not seen him since leaving him alone in the hospital. With his leg requiring room to stretch, I took the old Malibu coupe to pick him up on Wednesday. When I pulled into his driveway, I found my heart racing. He must have been watching for me, because the door to his bungalow flew open before my feet hit the first step to the porch.

Keoni's wardrobe for the day included a vintage Hana Company aloha shirt in faux *kapa* cloth over khaki walking shorts, a straw Panama hat, and one brown leather flip flop—since his left leg was in a walking cast. He said nothing for a moment, taking in my short white sundress and an original Beth Surdut silk *haori* coat with frolicking gold fish on a red background.

He came forward and held my hands. Looking down, he pressed his thumb against the intricate carving of Ariel's silver bracelet. Raising his eyes to mine, he said, "You look, uh, I don't know if 'festive' is the right word, but I know Ariel is pleased you've dressed especially for her today!"

I tried not to cry. "She always loved this jacket. It matches the red Chinese wish lanterns we're going to release."

We walked out to the car and I opened the passenger's door so Keoni could back into the old style bench seat. He carefully straightened his left leg, pulled in his cane, and, since there was not much head room, set his hat in his lap. When we arrived forty minutes later, parking was limited and it seemed like we might end up parking outside the park. We finally found a space, but it took a while for Keoni to maneuver across the grass and sand to the boat landing. Thank goodness we had set a time of three p.m., since outrigger canoes try not to put to sea in the dark.

For a few years, Ariel and Brianna had paddled Hawaiian outrigger canoes competitively. Their former teammates were honored to participate in the memorial and had brought a pair of prized *koa* wood canoes. An additional outrigger, constructed of fiberglass, waited to carry mourners out for the seafaring part of the service. As I am uncomfortable with boats of any kind, I was not going to accompany Ariel's ashes to sea. But since Keoni had an injured leg, I would not stand alone on the shore.

At the sound of a conch shell, members of the outrigger canoe team came forward carrying upright paddles in front of them. In a dignified manner, each *wahine* placed her paddle at her designated position in one of the canoes that swayed gently awaiting its role in the ceremony. Closing in behind them, the people who had gathered to honor Ariel formed a semi-circle. With Keoni firmly holding my waist from behind, I stood bathed in love, with Nathan and Brianna on one side and Margie and Dan O`Hara on the other.

Accompanied by a single Hawaiian gourd drum, Lani King, a non-denominational minister dressed in a robe patterned in a classic *kapa* design, chanted an opening prayer in Hawaiian as we lifted our eyes skyward. Then, several of us shared our fondest memories of Ariel.

When it was my turn, I had to breathe deeply several times before beginning. "There's so much I wish I had said to Ariel— like how much I loved her, even when I couldn't be with her as much as I would have liked. Beyond that, there is little that has relevance in a moment like this, so I'd simply like to share the words of Patricia Noble, a modern philosopher I had the pleasure of meeting a few years ago:

Like a shooting star that catches the eye so briefly as it trails the flaming brilliance of its death across the infinite vastness of the midnight sky, your love has touched my life and gone. What meaning this meeting of two souls has for me, I do not know. I only know that I am better for your heart and mine touching in the night.

We came to the end of our attempt to honor Ariel's brief life quietly. With tears in the eyes of most of us, we held hands and sang *Aloha `Oe*. Composed by Queen Lydia Lili`u`okalani, it is an Island favorite for glad times and sad. I felt sure that Ariel could feel the love of all of us even as we moved apart slowly. While some people would take a final seaward journey with Ariel, others would go to Nathan's home to prepare for our sunset gathering, or like Keoni and me, remain beachside.

At another signal from the conch shell, the canoes put to sea to cast Ariel's ashes upon the waters she had loved so much. Keoni took my hand and we moved to a log near the shoreline. While the canoes became specks on the water, we watched the panorama of the busy beach park surrounding us. Parasails, surfboards and kayaks bounced in the ocean's foreground, while walkers and sunbathers passed by or frolicked in the shallow waters. No wonder this was one of Ariel's favorite places for reflection.

After a while, Keoni calmly said, "You know I'm not an invalid, Natalie. You could have gone out with the boats."

"I've told you how I feel about getting into little objects that put to sea. And besides, every seat was assigned and I know how important it is for the people going out today. They need closure—in a tangible way that they can share with one another. It's not the same for them as it is for Nathan and me, or for Brianna. She and Ariel have had a unique bond like Nathan and I do, and I don't think it will be broken merely because Ariel has crossed to the next plane of existence."

When the canoes and other unexpected boats had reached their destination and formed a circle, we heard the distant sound of the conch signaling everyone to release their wish lanterns. I brought out one from my straw bag, with a message already folded within. Silently, Keoni helped me cast it upward into the wind. As it drifted heavenward, he put his right arm around me tightly and placed his left palm tenderly over my hands. This was a special moment between us. I had no idea where our relationship was going, but his concern and support had certainly helped me through this tragic experience.

Looking down at Ariel's bracelet, I thought about the many ways women express themselves and share their lives through jewelry. I knew that Brianna and I would always feel close to Ariel whenever we wear our silver bracelets, just as the Wong sisters remember their beloved mother when they touch the *yin* and *yang* necklaces they wear.

EPILOGUE

In the end, it's not the years in your life that count.
It's the life in your years.
Abraham Lincoln [1809-1865]

After the sunset toasting of Ariel's abbreviated life, I sat staring at the waters flowing past Nathan's home. The hypnotic rhythm of the waves at high tide lulled me to near slumber. Then for a brief moment, I glimpse a different but not too distant ocean view...

In lavender shades of twilight, the city of Honolulu edges toward nighttime. Gazing down from their watchtower view, two women in traditional long Chinese cheongsams of silk brocade watch the lengthening shadows of the Old Makiki Cemetery spread out below them.

The short woman in the ivory colored dress turns to lift a bottle of champagne from a crystal bucket filled with ice. She pours careful measures into two silver flute goblets and hands one to the woman dressed in plum who is seated in a wheel chair.

"For you, Jade."

"Thank you, Pearl," replies the woman reaching up to grasp the stemware securely in her hand.

The women look toward the flickering lights of Waikīkī and remain silent for a few moments. After a while, Jade casts a few words in the Yue dialect of Chinese into the rising wind, and Pearl nods in solemn agreement.

Pearl replenishes their glasses, and turns back to the railing of the lānai. Glancing beyond the shoreline to the dinner cruise boats dancing across the bay, she sighs.

"If you squint, elder sister, the lanterns make the boats look

like the wooden junks in the Shànghăi harbor of our youth."

"There are many things that improve when viewed through half-closed eyes," agrees Jade. "Why even an apartment building can look like a villa from this height."

"And two old women appear at the onset of a youthful adventure," laughs Pearl.

For a moment, a silver moonbeam strikes the doors of a patinaed bronze crypt below them.

"Ah, Papa. Are you joining us this evening?" Jade inquires. "Do you remember the last time you cast the I Ching for us before we departed from our homeland? I believe you would agree it prepared us well for the many shifts in the course of our journey," she nods with her glass lifted in salute.

As the shadows merge, a mynah bird calls out before settling in its perch for the night. An Island breeze rustles through the fragrant eucalyptus trees.

NOTES AND ACKNOWLEDGMENTS

Through the continuing Natalie Seachrist series, I look forward to introducing historical characters and incidents within the genre of a mystery novel. Several features of the story line were inspired by my experiences during the two decades I was a resident of Hawai`i. Some background material I have drawn upon was introduced to me during undergraduate and graduate history courses, and in my work as a graduate teaching assistant in what was called the World Civilizations Program in the History Department of the University of Hawai`i.

Wherever possible, the historical facts cited are accurate. During its 1932 winter cruise, the RMS Empress of Britain was unable to make its scheduled port call in Shànghǎi due to attacks by Imperial Japanese military forces by land, sea and air. Scheduled passengers journeyed at their peril to board the ship in Hong Kong, then a British Dependent Territory. The praline ice cream remembered by Miss Pearl Wong was listed on a ship's menu for that cruise. The ship did dock in Honolulu on March the twelfth. Descriptions I have given of the ship match those found in existing records, with one exception. While Captain R. G. Latta was the ship's commanding officer, I have embellished his crew to include officers who passed out candy.

The influence of China's culture on Hawai`i has existed since the beginning of contact between these areas of the world. While records of the arrival of the first Chinese in

Hawai`i date to late 1788, substantial numbers of contract Chinese laborers were brought to Hawai`i to work on the fledgling sugar plantations in the mid-nineteenth century. Most of these workers spoke the southern regional dialects of Hong Kong, Àomén [previously called Macao in Western nations], and Guǎngdōng [formerly known as Canton or Kwangtung in English].

Although I have included a summary of aspects of the Hawaiian language, I have not attempted to draft one for Chinese, which has over 290 dialects. Because Mandarin is the official language of the People's Republic of China, the phonetic transcription system I have used for most Chinese words is the Hanyu Pinyin Romanization of the Mandarin dialect. Occasionally I have used Wade-Giles transliteration (dating to the mid- and late-nineteenth century) because of its familiarity to English speakers. This includes words like cheongsam and the name Chiang Kai-Shek, both of which are found in Internet search engines. When a word is the same in both Wade-Giles and Pinyin transcription, I have simply labeled it as Chinese in the Glossary.

Before I leave the topic of the Chinese language, I should mention that Chinese, like Japanese and other Asian languages, places the surname (family name) before a person's given name. As the Natalie Seachrist mysteries have been written primarily for an English-speaking audience, I have followed the norms of English and placed the given names of characters prior to surnames. To help me clarify Hanyu Pinyin Romanization of Chinese vocabulary, I have had the aid of Jianmei Li, a graduate student in Chinese anthropology at the University of Arizona.

As I sat finishing this book in the heat of the high desert, I reviewed the origins of this story and the many people who contributed to its conception and completion. First, I wish to acknowledge Tim Littlejohn, a State of Hawai`i library manager (and my sometimes writing partner) for his support through several projects. His interest in extending scholastic work into publishable form for a general audience led to a compilation of my seven oral history interviews titled, Conversations with Caroline Kuliaikanu`ukapu Wilcox De Lima Farias. As the Natalie Seachrist series has developed, Tim's input has been invaluable in expanding my attention to cultural sensitivity, and helping me research facts and harmonize plotline elements.

For their specialized knowledge of unique reference holdings, I wish to express my gratitude to: Gina Vergara-Bautista, archivist at The Hawai`i State Archives and Corinne Chun Fujimoto, curator of Washington Place Museum, the former home of Queen Lili`u`okalani. Invaluable input in multiple areas of expertise has been provided by Kevin C. Horstman, PhD, who specializes in geological sciences and digital image enhancement. I also thank the intrepid librarians of Pima County Public Library for their support of local authors—especially librarian Rona Rosenberg and library associate Sue Johnson of the Kirk-Bear Canyon Branch.

Fellow anthologists of Under Sonoran Skies: Prose and Poetry from the High Desert have provided unending support for many years. They include: psychotherapist and mystery writer Kay Lesh; Larry Sakin, green energy entrepreneur and political writer; the Reverend Patricia Noble, lecturer and philosopher; Susan Cosby-Patton, poet and essayist; and, poet Bill Black, who has provided assistance in several technical areas.

Special thanks go to long-term supporters who have provided personal and professional inspiration and direction. Foremost is Viki Gillespie, bookworm and bookman, whose close review has enriched this work. Additional readers include: Cotton Burlingame, sustainability and clean energy consultant; Nelda Garza, retired entrepreneur; memoirist Margherita Gale Harris; retired publisher Al Howard and his wife Betty-Jean; Bob and Susan Shrager, supporters of community education and art; Nan Andres, and other writers of Sunset Writers of East Tucson.

The process of publication of this first book in the Natalie Seachrist mystery series has been steered by Geoff Habiger of Artemesia Publishing LLC, in Tijeras, New Mexico. In my journey to find a publisher, I sought someone who would not be put off by the amount of foreign vocabulary, historical material, and multi-cultural references I wanted to include in my work. When I saw that Geoff seeks authors who can educate, inform, and entertain the reader, I hoped I had found a home for Natalie's adventures in sleuthing. The wide-ranging offerings of this select publisher may be found at www.apbooks. net.

Direction and engineering of the audio version of this book has been provided by Jim Waters of Waterworks Recording, Tucson, Arizona. A transplant from New York City, Jim Waters has produced and engineered the music of top performers for over three decades. Listings of his past projects and equipment are available on his website, www.waterworksrecording.com.

The evocative cover art for *Prospect For Murder* is the work of Yasamine June. She is a fine and multi-media artist, typographer and designer, who creates memorable images within a rich palette of color and form. To view samples of her artwork (including posters and album covers), please visit www. yasaminejune.com.

Finally, I thank my husband, Lieutenant Commander John "H" Burrows-Johnson, USN, Retired, for his patience and support through decades of varied creative projects.

Errors, of course, are my responsibility and I regret any that you may uncover. Please contact me about egregious flaws you wish to point out, as I would dislike repeating them in future books. Also, I would like to hear your suggestions regarding historical and cultural themes that might be appropriate to this series. You can contact me directly by emailing me at JBurrows-Johnson@Earthlink.com.

For further discussion of background elements, a comprehensive glossary of foreign and specialized vocabulary, and foods and beverages mentioned in *Prospect for Murder*, please visit www.ProspectForMurder.com. You are invited to examine other writing and design projects at www.ImaginingsWordpower.com. Exploration of the writing process may be found at www.blog.ImaginingsWordpower.com. If you are wondering when you will be able to experience Natalie's next adventures in murderous challenges, *Murder on Mokulua Drive* and *Murders of Conveyance* move toward publication.

A BRIEF OVERVIEW OF THE HAWAIIAN LANGUAGE

The Hawaiian language was unwritten until 1826, when Christian missionaries transcribed the sounds of the language into a thirteen-letter alphabet. Hawaiian consonants are pronounced as in standard American English. They include **H**, **K**, **L**, **M**, **N**, **P**, **W**, and the ʻokina [`]. Often, the "W" is pronounced like an English "V." As there is no "S" in the Hawaiian language, plurals are determined by the preceding article. Each vowel is sounded in Hawaiian; they are similar in pronunciation to those in Spanish, and other Latin-based European languages:

A = *Ah*, as in above
E = *Eh*, as in let
I = *Ee*, as in eel
O = *Oh*, as in open
U = *Oo*, as in soon

Diphthongs are expressed as common English sounds. The "au" transliteration is pronounced as "ow" in "How." Diacritical marks indicate emphasis and syllable separation. Placed over vowels, a **kahakō** [-] indicates a need to hold the vowel sound slightly longer, as seen in the "a" in the word "card." The **ʻokina**, [`] is both a consonant and a diacritical mark; it dictates that the preceding vowel should be pronounced more loudly.

Please note, that in accordance with standard practices, foreign words included in this work are subject to the grammatical rules of English.

GLOSSARY OF NON-ENGLISH
& SPECIALIZED VOCABULARY

This glossary reflects the meanings used within the text of this book. Please note that many Hawaiian words have multiple spellings (with or without diacritical marks) and may have multiple meanings. Some Hawaiian words, especially names, have ambiguous, layered and sometimes hidden meanings.

A

Adobo
Dressing, sauce. [Spanish] A Filipino process of cooking, featuring protein or vegetables marinated in a vinegar and garlic-based sauce, browned in oil, simmered in the marinade. The dish is often served with steamed white rice.

Ali`i
Chief, ruler, officer, aristocrat, commander. [Hawaiian]

Aloha
Love, affection, compassion, loved one. [Hawaiian] Traditional term for greeting and farewell, expressing love, friendship and mercy.

Aloha `Oe
May you be loved. [Hawaiian] Title of the beloved song written by **Queen Lili`u`okalani**.

Auwē
Alas, Too bad, or, *Oh, dear.* [Hawaiian]

B

Boat Day
Between the 1920s and the late 1940s [except during World War II], the arrival of ocean liners at Aloha Tower was a major event in Honolulu. In addition to being a communal celebration, the ships and the people they carried contributed greatly to the local economy. Passengers were greeted with **leis**, performance by **hula** dancers and the Royal Hawaiian Band. Boys and young men often dove into the waters of the harbor for coins thrown overboard by the tourists.

C

Char siu bao
Chāshāobāo [Hanyu Pinyin Romanization of the Mandarin Dialect of Chinese]. Steamed buns stuffed with barbecued pork. Named *mea ʻono puaʻa* when introduced to Hawaiʻi [*mea ʻono*, pastry or cake plus *puaʻa*, pork]. Current usage shortened to manapua.

Cheongsam
Qípáo [Pinyin]. Tight-fitting Chinese dress with a slit skirt and mandarin collar. Originated in the Qing Dynasty [1644-1911]. A modern version emerged in Shànghǎi in the 1920s.

Chiang Kai Shek
Official name, *Chiang Chieh-shih* [Wade-Giles] or *Jiǎng Jièshí* [Pinyin]. Chinese general and political leader [1887–1975]. Chief of Staff for **Dr. Sūn Yat-Sen** [*Sūn Yìxiān*, Pinyin], first Provisional President of the Republic of China [1912-1949]. When Dr. Sūn died in 1925, Jiǎng Jièshí became Chairman of the **Guómíndǎng** and Commander-in-chief of the Army. Initially focused on fighting Chinese war lords and communists, the Generalissimo turned on the Japanese Imperial Army after their 1931 invasion of Manchuria. Following the end of World War II in 1945, civil war quickly resumed. In 1949, *Mao Zedong* [*Mao Tse-Tung*, Wade-Giles] military leader and Chairman of the Chinese Communist Party established the People's Republic of China, forcing General Jiǎng Jièshí to retreat to the island of Taiwan.

D

Dim sum
Diǎnxīn [Pinyin]. *Touch the heart.* [Chinese] Pastry, light refreshment, bite-sized foods. Often dumplings filled with vegetables, meat or seafood that is usually steamed or fried. Originating in Guǎngdōng province tea houses, it was traditionally served like appetizers, as a snack or before a larger meal; now served as a complete meal, especially as a brunch.

E

E komo mai   *Welcome; enter and be refreshed.* [Hawaiian] A traditional Hawaiian greeting.

G

Guăngdōng   *Expanse East.* [Chinese] A province of the People's Republic of China [PRC] located on the South China Sea coast. It was once known as *Canton* or *Kwangtung* in English.

Guangzhou   Capital of **Guăngdōng** province. It is the third largest city in the PRC.

Guómíndăng   [Pinyin] or *Kuomintang* [Wade-Giles]. Chinese Nationalist Party. The party was founded in 1911 by Song Jiaoren and Dr. Sūn Yìxiān [***Sūn Yat-Sen***, Wade-Giles], who, with other revolutionaries, helped end the Qing Dynasty [1644-1912]. In 1925, leadership passed to General Jiăng Jièshí [***Chiang Kai-Shek***, Wade-Giles]. Following defeat of the Japanese in World War II, civil war escalated. In 1949, Mao Zedong [***Mao Tse-Tung***, Wade-Giles], Chairman and victorious military leader of the Chinese Communist Party established the People's Republic of China. General Jiăng Jièshí was forced to retreat to Taiwan, where the Guómíndăng remained the ruling political party of the Republic of China for many decades.

H

Ha gao   [Yue dialect of Chinese]. *Har gow* [Anglicized]. *Xiā jiăo* [Pinyin]. Shrimp dumplings.

Hale   *House.* [Hawaiian]

Hānai   *Foster or adopted child.* [Hawaiian] Extended or adopted family members.

Haole   *Foreigner; of foreign origin.* [Hawaiian] Current usage, *American, Englishman, Caucasian.*

Haori   [Japanese] A kimono style jacket with open front and straight sleeves.

Hawai`i**    Fiftieth state of the United States of America; name of the largest Hawaiian island. The Kingdom of Hawai`i was established by **Kamehame-ha the Great between 1795 and 1810. The Kingdom was overthrown between 1893 and 1894, after which it was replaced by the short-lived Republic of Hawai`i. Established in 1898, the Territory of Hawai`i became a state in 1959.

Hongkou Northern district of the city of **Shànghǎi**, PRC.

Honolulu *Protected Bay.* [Hawaiian] Located on the island of **O`ahu**, it is the largest city in and capital of the state of **Hawai`i.**

Ho`olaule`a *Celebration, festival, large party.* [Hawaiian]

Huay Also known as *kongsi* [Wade-Giles] and *gōngsī* [Pinyin]. Social and economic support groups comprised of members from the same district, clan and/or language group. See also **hui**.

Hui *Club, association or society.* [Hawaiian] Similar to Chinese **huay**.

Hula Traditional dance of *Hawai`i*. [Hawaiian]

I

`Iolani, Palace**  *Royal hawk.* [Hawaiian] Palace of the Hawaiian Kingdom. Originally named *Hale Ali`i*, [House of Royalty], it was built in 1845 for King **Ka-mehameha III [1813-1854]. In 1863, it was renamed by Kamehameha V [1830-1872] to honor his brother, King Kamehameha IV [1834-1863].

Iwilei *Collar bone.* [Hawaiian] A unit of measurement. A road in west **O`ahu**.

J

Jinan *South of the Ji waters.* This city is the capital of Shandong Province in the eastern part of the PRC.

Joie de vivre *Joy of living.* [French]

K

Kahakō *Macron.* [Hawaiian] A diacritical mark [-] placed over a vowel to extend pronunciation of the vowel's sound.

Kailua	*Two seas.* [Hawaiian] Bay, beach and town on the northeast end of the windward side of **O`ahu**.
Kaimukī	*The oven of the kī.* [Hawaiian] Ti plant. [Scientific name, *Cordyline terminalis*]. A neighborhood in east **Honolulu**.
Ka`iulani, Princess	*The royal or sacred one.* [Hawaiian] Niece of Queen **Lili`u`okalani**, she was the last princess of **Hawai`i**. [1875-1899] Also the name of a **Waikīkī** hotel and upscale clothing line.
Ka Leo	*The voice.* [Hawaiian] ***Ka Leo O Hawai`i, The Voice of Hawai`i***, the student newspaper of the University of Hawai`i.
Kamehameha	*Hushed silence.* [Hawaiian] Dynasty of Hawaiian Kings, founded by King Kamehameha I [1758-1819] of the island of Hawai`i who unified the Hawaiian Kingdom by 1810. He is noted for alliances with European nations that ensured Hawai`i's independence and economic growth and codifying the legal system, which included the Māmalahoe Kānāwai [*Law of the Splintered Paddle*], providing human rights to wartime non-combatants.
Kāne`ohe	*Man of Bamboo.* [Hawaiian] Town in windward **O`ahu**, west of **Kailua**.
Kapa	Cloth made from bark of **māmaki** or **wauke**. [Hawaiian]
Kapahulu	*Worn out soil.* [Hawaiian] Subdivision in the **Kaimukī** neighborhood of **O`ahu**.
Kapi`olani	*Rainbow, arch of heaven.* [Hawaiian] Name of the last Hawaiian princess [1875-1899]. Neighborhood running through **Waikīkī**; a major boulevard and community college in urban **Honolulu**.
Keiki	*Child, offspring.* [Hawaiian]
Keiki hānai	*Foster child.* [Hawaiian]
Ken, Kenning	*Perceiving knowledge, idea or situation beyond one's normal range of sight or view.* [Chiefly Scottish; from Middle English *kennen*, Old Norse *kenna*, and Old English, *cennan*].
Keoni	Diminutive form of "John." [Hawaiian]

Koa	Acacia tree. [Hawaiian] An endangered species known for its fine grained wood. [Scientific name, *Acacia koa.*]
Ko`olau	*Windward.* [Hawaiian] One of two volcanic mountain ranges that divide the island of **O`ahu**.
Kūka`iau	*Current appearing.* [Hawaiian] A gulch, village, and ranch located on the island of **Hawai`i**.
Kuomintang	See **Guómíndǎng**.
Kumu hula	Master teacher of **hula**. [Hawaiian]

L

Lānai	*Porch, balcony.* [Hawaiian]
Lanikai	Community on the southern edge of **Kailua** in windward **O`ahu**. [Hawaiian]
Labneh	Yoghurt and yoghurt cheese traditionally strained through a cloth. Popular ingredient in Middle Eastern cuisine, varying in texture, flavor, and usages.
Lei	Garland of flowers, leaves, shells, candy, or other decorations. [Hawaiian]
Lili`u`okalani, Queen	Only reigning queen and last monarch of the Hawaiian Kingdom [1838-1917]. Birth name, Lydia Lili`u Loloku Walania Wewehi Kamaka`eha; married name, Lydia K. Dominis. Her chosen royal name, Lili`u`okalani, is sometimes translated as *scorching pain of the royal chiefess,* referring to a relative's eye pain at the time of her birth. She was the author of numerous poems, chants, and lyrics, and the book *Hawaii's Story By Hawai`i's Queen.* She was also an accomplished musician and the composer of the popular song *Aloha `Oe* [*Farewell to Thee*].
Loco moco	Popular Island breakfast entrée consisting of a hamburger patty topped with a sunny-side-up fried egg served on a bed of steamed white rice and topped with brown gravy.
Lo mein	*Lāomiàn* [Pinyin]. Chinese dish with sliced vegetables and soft noodles in seasoned sauce, often served with diced meat or shrimp.

Lū`au	*Kalo [taro] tops.* [Hawaiian] Modern name for an Hawaiian feast.

M

Mahalo	*Thank you.* [Hawaiian] Often printed on public garbage cans to encourage respect for keeping the environment clean.
Maile	Flowering tree shrub in the dogbane family. Its fragrant leaves are used for making a long, open **lei**. [Scientific name, *Alyxia oliviformis*]. [Hawaiian]
Makiki	*To peck.* [Hawaiian] Type of volcanic stone used as a fishing weight or adze. Neighborhood northeast of downtown **Honolulu**.
Malasada	[Portuguese] Deep-fried doughnut.
Māmaki	*Flowering nettle plant.* [Hawaiian] [Scientific name, *Pipturus albidus*].
Mānoa	*Thick, solid, vast, deep.* [Hawaiian] Valley and neighborhood northeast of downtown **Honolulu**. Location of the main campus of the University of **Hawai`i**.
Mao Zedong	[Pinyin] Mao Tse-tung [Wade Giles]. Chinese anti-imperialist nationalist and Marxist revolutionary [1893-1976]. In 1921 he was one of fifty founding members of the Communist Party of China. Although nominally united with the republican government of Chiang Kai Shek during World War II, he became the Chairman of the Communist Party in 1945. He then pursued the successful revolution that led to his establishment of the People's Republic of China in 1949.
Mauka	*Inland, toward the mountain.* [Hawaiian]
Mochi	Molded Japanese rice cake made from glutinous rice paste.
Mukden	*Shěnyáng* [Pinyin]. Capital of PRC *Liaoning* province. Site of the 1931 Liutiaohu [or Manchurian] Incident, in which the Japanese Imperial Army fabricated an excuse for invading **Manchuria**, which they renamed *Manchukuo* [*Mǎnzhōuguó*, Pinyin] and occupied until 1945.

Mushu *Mù xū* [Pinyin]. Chinese dish of stir-fried vegetables and egg, often with meat or fish. Served with or wrapped in thin pancakes.

Mu`umu`u *Cut short, maimed, amputated.* [Hawaiian] Dress adapted from those of nineteenth-century Protestant Christian missionary women, often featuring short sleeves and no yoke.

N

Nu`uanu *Cool heights.* [Hawaiian] Valley, stream and neighborhood north of downtown **Honolulu**.

O

O`ahu *The Gathering place.* [Hawaiian] The third largest Hawaiian island; location of **Honolulu**, the state capital.

**`Okina**  A consonant in the Hawaiian language; *glottal stop.* A diacritical mark [`] used to indicate a break in sounding consonantal sounds, like that separating an interjection's syllables, like "oh-oh."

P

Pā`ina Ancient word for Hawaiian *feast.* Now used for a *meal* or *dinner party.* [Hawaiian]

Pīkake *Peacock.* [Hawaiian] Asian evergreen shrub or vine, it is a jasmine in the olive family that produces fragrant white flowers. [Scientific name, *Jasminum sambac*]

Plate Lunch Popular Island meal with Asian style protein usually served with shredded cabbage, white steamed rice, macaroni salad, and sometimes pickled vegetables.

Plumeria Flowering and fragrant tropical tree including the frangipani, a genus of flowering tree in the dogbane family. [Scientific name, *Plumeria*]

Provenance *Point of origin.* [French] Record of ownership authenticating nature, origin, and history of art or antiques.

Pūne`e *Sofa, couch, pew.* [Hawaiian]

Pūpū   *Marine or land shell; circular motif; appetizer.* [Hawaiian]

Pu`u o Kaimukī   Hill of **Kaimukī**. [Hawaiian]

S

Shànghăi   City at the mouth of the Yangtze River in the center of the coast of the PRC. Having the largest population of any city in China, or the world, it is classified as a province.

Shinai   *Fencing stick.* [Japanese] Practice sword used in Kendo, traditionally made of bamboo, now available in carbon.

Sichuan   Also *Szechwan*. Style of Chinese cuisine originating in Sichuan Province in the southwestern part of the PRC.

Sūn Yat-Sen   Dr. Sūn Yìxiān [Pinyin], born Sūn Wen [1866-1925]. Chinese revolutionary who helped overthrow the Qing Dynasty [1644-1911] and co-founded the **Guómíndăng** political party. As first provisional president of post-imperial China, he is honored by republicans and communists as the Father of Modern China. Attended `Iolani School in Honolulu, where King David Kalākaua presented him an award for English grammar. He subsequently attended Punahou School.

T

Taijitu   Also *Tai Chi. Great pole, highest point* or *goal.* [Chinese] Symbol for duality within the universal, indivisible wholeness. Meeting of **yin** and **yang**, dark and light, female and male, moon and sun.

Tan Heong Shan   *Tánxiāng* [Pinyin]. *Fragrant Sandalwood Mountain.* Name for Hawai`i, as used by Chinese immigrants. Today the word specifies the city of Honolulu.

Tierce   Also *trifecta*. A type of horse race bet, in which the bettor selects the exact order of placement by the top three horses.

U

`Ukulele
Flea. [Hawaiian] Small Portuguese guitar made popular by a lively British army officer nicknamed `ukulele.

Una
Tortoise shell. [Hawaiian]

W

Wahine
Girl, woman, lady. [Hawaiian] Something reflecting femininity.

Waikīkī
Spouting water. [Hawaiian] Name of a chiefess; famous beach on island of **O`ahu.**

Wauke
Paper mulberry tree. [Hawaiian] [Scientific name, *Broussonetia papyrifera*]

Y

Yang
Masculine force in nature [Chinese], expressed in sun, light, white, gold, and strength. Chinese surname; clan and dynasty.

Yin
Feminine force in nature, [Chinese] expressed in moon, darkness, black, silver, and passivity. Chinese surname and dynasty.

Yue
Southern state in ancient China. Dialect of Chinese spoken in the **Guǎngdōng** Province in the southern part of the PRC.

Yum cha
Tea tasting, drinking tea or having tea time with food. [Chinese]

Z

Zhōngguó
Central State. [Chinese] The most common name for China since antiquity.

Zhū lián bì hé
Perfect strand of jade and pearl gems. [Chinese]

Zhū yù
Pearl and jade. [Chinese]

CPSIA information can be obtained at www.ICGtesting.com
Printed in the USA
LVOW10*1429150716

496457LV00001B/1/P